Women & Analysis

*Dialogues on
Psychoanalytic Views
of Femininity*

Women & Analysis

*Edited by
Jean Strouse*

Grossman Publishers
A Division of the Viking Press
New York
1974

Acknowledgments

"Some Psychical Consequences of the Anatomical Distinction Between the Sexes" (1925) is reprinted from *The Standard Edition of the Complete Psychological Works of Sigmund Freud*, Vol. 19, edited by James Strachey, by permission of The Hogarth Press Ltd., London; and *The Collected Papers of Sigmund Freud*, Vol. 5, edited by James Strachey, published by Basic Books, Inc., New York, by arrangement with The Hogarth Press Ltd. and The Institute of Psycho-Analysis, London. Copyright © Sigmund Freud Copyrights Ltd., The Institute of Psycho-Analysis, and The Hogarth Press Ltd.

"Female Sexuality" (1931) is reprinted from *The Standard Edition of the Complete Psychological Works of Sigmund Freud*, Vol. 21, edited by James Strachey, by permission of The Hogarth Press Ltd., London; and *The Collected Papers of Sigmund Freud*, Vol. 5, edited by James Strachey, published by Basic Books, Inc., New York, by arrangement with The Hogarth Press, Ltd. and The Institute of Psycho-Analysis, London. Copyright © Sigmund Freud Copyrights Ltd., The Institute of Psycho-Analysis, and The Hogarth Press Ltd.

"Femininity" (1933) is reprinted from *New Introductory Lectures on Psychoanalysis* by Sigmund Freud, newly translated from the German and edited by James Strachey; by permission of W.W. Norton & Company, Inc. Copyright 1933 by Sigmund Freud. Copyright renewed 1961 by W.J.H. Sprott. Copyright © 1964, 1965 by James Strachey; and *The Standard Edition of the Complete Psychological Works of Sigmund Freud*, Vol. 22, edited by James Strachey, by permission of The Hogarth Press Ltd., London. Copyright © Sigmund Freud Copyrights, Ltd., The Institute of Psycho-Analysis, and The Hogarth Press Ltd.

"Manifestations of the Female Castration Complex" (1920) is reprinted from *The Selected Papers of Karl Abraham*, translated by Douglas Bryan and Alix Strachey, published by Basic Books, Inc., New York; and *Selected Papers on Psycho-Analysis*, The Hogarth Press Ltd., London.

"The Psychology of Woman in Relation to the Functions of Reproduction" (1924) is reprinted from the *International Journal of Psycho-Analysis*, 6, 1924, by permission of the *International Journal of Psycho-Analysis* and Helene Deutsch, M.D.

"The Flight from Womanhood" (1926) is reprinted from *Feminine Psychology* by Karen Horney, M.D., edited and with an Introduction by Harold Kelman, M.D., by permission of W.W. Norton and Company, Inc. Copyright © 1967 by W.W. Norton and Company, Inc.

"On the Nature of the Animus" (1931) is reprinted from *Animus and Anima*, Spring Publications, Postfach 190, Zurich 8024, by permission of Walter-Verlag AG Olten and Spring Publications. Copyright © Walter-Verlag AG Olten, 1967. English language translation by Cary F. Baynes copyright © 1957, 1972 by The Analytical Psychology Club of New York.

"The Stranger" by Adrienne Rich is reprinted from *Diving Into the Wreck: Poems 1971–1973*, by permission of W.W. Norton and Company, Inc. and Adrienne Rich. Copyright © 1973 by W.W. Norton and Company, Inc.

ACKNOWLEDGMENTS

"Passivity, Masochism and Femininity" (1934) is reprinted from the *International Journal of Psycho-Analysis*, 16, 1935 by permission of the *International Journal of Psycho-Analysis*.

"The Role of Women in This Culture" (1941) is reprinted from *Psychiatry* (1941) 4:1–8, by special permission of the William Alanson White Foundation, Inc. Copyright © 1941, by the William Alanson White Psychiatric Foundation, Inc.

"Womanhood and the Inner Space" (1968) is reprinted from *Identity, Youth and Crisis* by Erik H. Erikson, by permission of W.W. Norton and Company, Inc. Copyright © 1968 by W.W. Norton and Company, Inc.

"Once More the Inner Space: Letter to a Former Student" (1973) is used by permission of W.W. Norton and Company, Inc. Copyright © 1974 by W.W. Norton and Company, Inc.

"Facts and Fancies: An Examination of Freud's Concept of Bisexuality" (1973) was originally published in *Nouvelle Revue de Psychanalyse*, Vol. 7, Spring 1973, under the title "Bisexualité et différence des sexes." It is reprinted by permission of *Nouvelle Revue de Psychanalyse* and Robert J. Stoller, M.D. Copyright © 1973 by *Nouvelle Revue de Psychanalyse*.

Contents

Women & Analysis

Introduction

Contemporary critiques of psychoanalytic theories about women often start with polite nods in the direction of Freud's genius and then proceed to dismiss the whole business as hopelessly out of date and culture-bound. Psychoanalysis, goes the argument, is nothing more than the solipsistic musings of a late-Victorian patriarch, a phallocentric Viennese bourgeois who concluded from his work with inhibited middle-class hysterics that women are by nature inferior to men.

That these polemical précis of Freudian thinking lead many feminists to dismiss psychoanalytic theory out of hand is unfortunate. For the dogma of woman's "anatomical inferiority" is only the most accessible and easily misconstrued element in a system of ideas whose significance for feminism is that it suggests so much about interactions between social organization and the deepest levels of human sexuality. These interactions, visible in individual lives, are crucial in the formation of personal, sexual, and social identity, and an understanding of them has to be the basis for any profound political or psychological understanding of women.

Freud was the first to recognize what he didn't know about women: "[The sexual life of men] alone has become accessible to research," he wrote. "That of women . . . is still veiled in an impenetrable obscurity."[1] And, "The sexual life of women is a 'dark continent' for psychology."[2] He pointed out in 1925 that the information he had about infantile sexuality was "obtained from the study of men and the theory deduced from it was concerned with male children,"[3] although many of his early ideas about infantile sexuality were derived from his work with female patients (*Studies on Hysteria*, 1895, with Josef Breuer). Freud did take the masculine as a cultural and sexual norm, and early on he "explained" the feminine in these terms as a sort of appurtenance. To think about the Oedipus conflict and the fear of castration, for instance—primary concepts in the development of psychoanalysis—is to think in terms symbolic of the sexual development of boys.

In his first full description of the Oedipus conflict (*The Interpretation of Dreams*, 1900), Freud assumed that the girl's experience was directly parallel to what he had observed and postulated for the boy: "A girl's first affection is for her father and a boy's first childish desires are for his mother."[4] And as late as 1923, in *The Ego and the Id,* he claimed that the complex processes surrounding the dissolution of the Oedipus complex are "precisely analogous" in girls and boys.

However, he became uneasy with this 'precise analogy' between the sexes as soon as he began to observe aspects of feminine psychology that did not fit in with his ideas about masculine development, and in 1919 he wrote: "The expectation of there being a complete parallel [between the two sexes] was mistaken."[5] In "Some Psychical Consequences of the Anatomical Distinction Between the Sexes" (1925, reprinted here on p. 17), Freud formulated a new thesis about feminine development that is examined in detail by Juliet Mitchell on p. 27: for both sexes, Freud observes in this paper, the child's first love object is the mother, and this relationship is the prototype for every later love relation. Boys therefore start out in life with a primary attachment to a person of the opposite sex: the mother. When, in the Oedipal phase, the attachment is sexualized and the father appears to be an insurmountable rival for the mother's love, the boy has to learn to identify with the father: he preserves his heterosexual love and establishes his masculine identity by abandoning his mother as sexual object and identifying with his father in the hope of one day becoming "father" with a woman of his own. The girl, however, follows a different path: she begins life with a primary attachment to a person of the same sex. She does not automatically desire her father: her love must change objects from mother to father in order to establish the heterosexual attachment. The girl has to accept identification with her mother and at the same time abandon the mother as love object, turning to her father instead. Her abandonment is brought about not by prohibition but by defeat: the little girl learns that she will never be able to possess the mother sexually the way father does because she is *like* the mother—she does not have a penis. She turns to her father only out of resentment

4

against her mother—for not only is the mother lost as a love object, but she has brought her daughter into the world inadequately equipped.

The negatives implicit in these ideas about feminine development are striking:

—The girl must recognize and accept her "anatomical inferiority."
—She turns to her father only in failure, angry and disappointed with her mother—and with herself.
— She must give up her active 'masculine' strivings and accept her role as passive receptor (I'll come back in a moment to the problems created by this language of *active-passive*).
— The path of female sexual development is circuitous and never fully resolved, while the male is off to a healthy, heterosexual start.

The biological determinism in these paradigms is neither flattering nor encouraging to women. But the question is not whether these views are pleasing, whether they fit in with what we want to believe about ourselves or with our notions of egalitarianism. The question is whether or not they reflect certain truths about the course of female development in patriarchal culture. And the answer, explored in the body of this book, is yes and no.

Freud was critical from the very first of the tendency to equate "masculine" with "active" and "feminine" with "passive":

> It is essential to realize that the concepts of "masculine" and "feminine", whose meaning seems so unambiguous to ordinary people, are among the most confused that occur in science. . . . Activity and its concomitant phenomena (more powerful muscular development, aggressiveness, greater intensity of libido) are as a rule linked with biological masculinity; but they are not necessarily so, for there are animal species in which these qualities are on the contrary assigned to the female. . . . [I]n human beings pure masculinity or femininity is not to be found in the psychological or biological sense. Every individual on the contrary displays a mixture of the character-traits belonging to his own and to the opposite sex; and he shows a combination of activity and passivity whether or not these last character-traits tally with his biological ones.[6]

This concept of innate bisexuality in human beings was central to Freud's thinking: he saw bisexuality as a law of nature, finding that each sex carries within it biological aspects of the other; and he carried the physical fact of bisexual potential over into psychology.

What he then made of this key concept is at times questionable, and the essays in the following pages ask some of those questions. But as an observer and clinician Freud laid out the foundations for later theoretical formulations and anticipated—sometimes in the smallest notes and asides—many of the ideas that have now superseded his own. Reading his papers and case studies now, fifty years after they were written, is still an exciting pleasure, for Freud's insights into the processes of the conscious and unconscious mind do transcend the time and place in which he worked. His observations about female sexuality document the discontinuities which our civilization forces on its female children, and they provide the most comprehensive, suggestive, and useful groundwork for the development of thinking about women that has yet been imagined.

It is the theories formulated to explain the clinical evidence that sometimes appear dated and culture-bound—that seem to mistake observable reality for natural law. For example, one can see in 1974 as Freud saw in 1925 that many little girls are openly envious of their fathers and brothers for having penises. "The psychical consequences of penis-envy," as Freud then noted, "are various and far-reaching." But the explanation of this envy need not be that women are by nature inferior to men because of their anatomical difference. Biological facts are nothing more nor less than biological facts. Their valuation reflects more about the mind of the observer and the psychosocial climate than it does about the facts themselves.

On the conscious, social level, for instance, a patriarchal culture that values achievement, competition, material success, aggression, possession, and things visible over inwardness, receptivity, peacefulness, and the intangible, will place greater value on those attributes known in the Western world as "male" than on the "female." The penis, as symbol of these attributes, represents to the girl everything she seems not to have —autonomy, independence, a freedom to move about in the world—and to the boy everything he has and doesn't want to lose, i.e., his identity. (Asked recently what he wanted to be when he grew up, a three-year-old I know answered promptly, "A big penis.")

A new view of the early bond between mother and infant held by some contemporary analysts challenges Freud's position that the male is off to a "healthier start" in life because he has a primary heterosexual relationship with his mother while the girl has to overcome both her inadequate biological endowment and her early homosexual relationship to her mother. Dr. Robert J. Stoller, in his paper on bisexuality (p. 343), sees in the pre-Oedipal "homosexual" relationship between mother and infant daughter an advantage for girls: the primary identification with the mother's femaleness in the early pre-Oedipal bond establishes the girl's sense of feminine identity with a profound strength and permanence. A boy must transfer his primary identification from mother to father—he must repudiate the feminine identification and his own "feminine" aspects. The process of differentiating his masculinity from the early mother-infant symbiosis is difficult and risky, and the threat (or promise) of a primary oneness with the mother remains throughout the normal adult life. According to Stoller, much of what we call "masculine" behavior—displays of strength, independence, cruelty, misogyny—is evidence of the constant struggle to fight off this primary feminine identification.[7]

Profound differences between male and female roles and modes of being are so effectively communicated to the infant in the first hours and weeks of life that the old "nature or nurture?" question is virtually unanswerable. On the level of "nature" or biology, though, new information in recent years has considerably altered what Freud believed to be the fundamental facts of life. Contrary to the biological premises that were medically accepted in the early part of the century, current research[8] tends to show that the human embryo in the initial stages of life is neither undifferentiated nor male: it is "female-oid." Although genetic sex is determined at fertilization, the influence of the sex genes does not begin until some weeks after conception has occurred. During these first weeks the foetus is morphologically female. Enough androgen at the appropriate time will produce in both sexes a normal penis. The absence of androgen at this time will produce in both sexes a normal clitoris. In other words, only the male embryo has to go through a differentiation process in genital development, when the hormone androgen masculinizes the genital tract. Female development proceeds normally by itself. Contrary, therefore, to Freud's assumption, the clitoris is not a smaller, undeveloped penis; instead, it is ontogenetically correct to say that the penis is an androgenized clitoris.[7, 8]

This reversal in scientific thinking from a male to a female model has been the subject of great controversy (see for example Mary Jane Sherfey's "The Evolution and Nature of Female Sexuality in Relation to Psychoanalytic Theory" in the *Journal of the American Psychoanalytic Association*, Vol. 14, No. 1, January, 1966, and the responses in Vol. 16, No. 3,

July, 1968), and is taken by some as a vindication—proof that not only are women not inferior, they are biologically stronger than and in fact superior to men.

Such shifts in valuation indicate how risky is the business of making an ideology out of what is at any moment held to be scientifically true—whether the ideology is an unconscious male supremacism or a conscious feminist tactic. The distinction between theory and ideology is sometimes blurred since the ideas that organize or explain social phenomena are never purely objective and may reflect the conscious or unconscious needs and aspirations of a particular social group or class. The problem of keeping theory separate from ideology is especially acute in both psychoanalysis and feminism, for both attempt in different ways to make a science of subjectivity—to make subjective experience the object of scientific or historical study—and both lend themselves to normative or valuational thinking at every turn.

The human foetus is "naturally" male.

The human foetus is "naturally" female.

So what? Neither statement says anything at all about life after birth, about the powerful psychological and social forces that affect the infant's sense of gender identity (see Stoller's paper on p. 343, and Person's on p. 250). Although another contemporary ideology that might be called post-industrial romanticism equates the *natural* or unmediated with the *good*—as in natural foods, organic gardening, earth shoes, homeopathy, "totally honest" personal relationships, and herbal everything—still, it is the mediation between thought and speech, between biology and social organization, between nature and culture that determines what we know of human experience. "Proof" of female inferiority by means of the assumption that maleness is the stronger, more natural state makes no more sense than "proof" of primordial female superiority through the invocation of a (natural) golden age of matriarchy in the distant anthropological past. Nothing is proved in either case, but attention is taken away from the relentless observation of feminine and masculine experience that could lead to new ideas about sexual identity.

Critical discussion of Freud's ideas about women began long before the current feminist and biological debates. As early as 1926 Karen Horney, in elaborating on Freud's observation that psychoanalysis had been one-sided in looking mainly at the minds of boys and men, very neatly showed

8

how the cultural bias of masculinity influenced the tenets of analytic theory. In her paper, "The Flight from Womanhood" (reprinted here on p. 171), Horney points out not only that psychoanalysis, as the creation of a male genius, was in many ways a masculine psychology, but that (and here she paraphrases the philosopher Georg Simmel) our whole civilization is masculine. She observes that the analytic view of feminine development is in every way identical to the ideas little boys have about little girls. Roughly: assuming that everybody has a penis, the boy notices that the girl does not and he thinks that she is a castrated or mutilated boy; he believes she has suffered the punishment he fears for himself, regards her as inferior (she has "lost" the precious organ), and cannot imagine that she will ever recover from this loss or from her envy of him.

In criticizing psychoanalysis for placing exclusive emphasis on the genital difference between the sexes, Horney suggests an alternative view that takes into account the woman's primary role in the function of reproduction. The dogma of woman's inferiority may, she writes, originate in an unconscious male tendency to depreciate women and motherhood—a tendency that is based on the male's intense envy of woman's capacity for motherhood. Horney does not deny the existence of penis envy, but she does ask that it be seen as influenced by social factors as well as by purely biological relations.

Horney's critique of the masculine bias in psychoanalysis, and the discrepancy between Freud's richly descriptive observations and the problematic theories developed to explain them, were among the several aspects of psychoanalytic thinking about women I found when, in 1971, I went to the library to see what Freud's feminist critics were talking about. I began with the three major theoretical pieces Freud wrote about women between 1925 and 1933, and then turned to his case studies of women and a number of related essays. Then I looked at the work of other analysts writing in the 1920s about the "problem" of female psychology. Some (Helene Deutsch, Marie Bonaparte, Karl Abraham, Otto Fenichel) offered detailed examples from their own clinical work to substantiate and further develop Freud's early formulations. Others, such as Ruth Mack Brunswick and Jeanne Lampl-de Groot, took other approaches, offering some new interpretations of the data while remaining within the framework of Freudian constructs. Three among the early analysts departed more radically from Freud's views on female sexuality than any of the others. These were Horney, Ernest Jones, and Melanie

Klein. Klein disagreed with Freud about the chronological placement of the Oedipus complex and therefore about all subsequent sexual development.[9]

After this first decade (ca. 1925–1935) of great interest among psychoanalysts in the psychology of women there was a falling off, and for almost thirty years relatively little was written about female sexual development. A notable exception was Clara Thompson, who, along with Harry Stack Sullivan, Erich Fromm, and Karen Horney, was part of what came to be known as "the cultural school" in psychoanalysis. Thompson wrote a great deal in the 1940s about the interpersonal factors in women's development, paying less attention than the Freudians did to biology and sexuality, and instead looking closely at the social and cultural determinants of women's experience.

There was an occasional symposium or article on feminine psychology during the 1950s, but not until the mid-1960s did the subject of women begin to appear again as an important question in the analytic literature. Among the analysts who have written about women in recent years are Alexandra Symonds, Therese Benedek, Ruth Moulton, Marjorie Barnett, Judd Marmor, Mary Jane Sherfey, and Judith Kestenberg. Erik Erikson's essay on the psychosocial development of a sense of womanhood ("Womanhood and the Inner Space") is well-known: it was presented at a *Daedalus* symposium in 1964, and appeared in Erikson's book, *Identity, Youth and Crisis* in 1968.

And both within and outside the analytic field a new body of empirical work has developed that is pertinent to any discussion of the psychology of women: contemporary studies of gender identity, notably Robert Stoller's *Sex and Gender*, the work of John Money at Johns Hopkins, and the work of Lionel Ovesey and Ethel Person in New York, examine the biological and psychosocial factors that influence the development of masculinity and femininity.

Clearly there was no monolithic "psychoanalytic view" of woman. And there was no single book that presented the large, interesting variety of views and revisions and departures. As the present volume began slowly to take shape in my mind it seemed important to take a long new look at these ideas—to try literally to see again from fresh points of view the theories that have been formulated about women, and to separate out what can be set aside as belonging to the past from what has lasting value.

The social, political, scientific, philosophical, and moral contexts in which some of these theories developed can now be seen more clearly than they could have been in 1925 or 1931. And questions as to which of these ideas actually enhance our understanding of women can now be answered with some degree of objectivity in light of new biological, developmental, and cross-cultural information.

In structure the book is a series of dialogues: I chose ten articles written about women by psychoanalysts, and invited ten people from various disciplines to write new essays in response to the analytic articles, each response to appear in "dialogue" with its subject. Freud's three theoretical pieces about women, "Some Psychical Consequences of the Anatomical Distinction Between the Sexes" (1925), "Female Sexuality" (1931), and "Femininity" (1933) open the book, with responses by Juliet Mitchell, Elizabeth Janeway, and Margaret Mead, respectively. Following the Freud section, the pairs of essays are printed in the chronological order in which the analytic articles appeared, beginning with Karl Abraham's 1920 "Manifestations of the Female Castration Complex" and Joel Kovel's response, and ending with Robert Stoller's examination of Freud's concept of bisexuality (1973). I have tried to select articles and writers that represent the development and variety of psychoanalytic views, and deal with the significant concepts involved in analytic thinking about women: biological determinism, passivity, masochism, penis envy, bisexuality, the female castration complex, childbearing, dependency, the social and cultural roles of women, and the development of sexual identity.

Most of the paired essays don't need further introduction: biographical information about all the authors appears in the *Notes on Contributors* section at the end of the book. But I'd like to make a few further comments here as background to some of the articles.

Since Erik Erikson's 1968 paper on "Womanhood and the Inner Space" had been the subject of much discussion and criticism in the women's movement, I asked Professor Erikson if he would like to respond to his own essay with a new one that would take into account some of the controversy since 1968 as well as present his current reflections on "the inner space." He replied that he would, and the result is his letter-essay, "Once More the Inner Space: Letter to a Former Student" that appears on p. 320.

Emma Jung's "On the Nature of the Animus" was brought to my attention by Barbara Gelpi, to whom I had written when I learned that she was working at Stanford on Jungian readings of Blake and the Romantic poets. I asked if she would like to write about Jung in a discussion of women and analysis, and she responded by sending me his wife's essay. Although the philosophical basis for Jung's ideas is radically different from Freud's work, which was based on the model of the natural sciences, the concept of the anima is of special interest in the present context as it presents valuable ideas about the nature of femininity.

And finally, Robert Stoller's article on Freud's concept of bisexuality is not set as a "response" to an earlier view since it functions by itself as both theory and commentary. In light of his own work with intersexuals (patients with biological bisexuality) and transsexuals (biologically intact patients who believe they are members of the opposite sex), Stoller examines Freud's theory of the development of masculinity and femininity. He finds that Freud's version of the story of gender development begins too late—not at the beginning of life, but in the Oedipal phase, *after* core gender identity is already established. Stoller's work focuses on the relationship between infant and mother, from the mother's first fantasies about her child through the early weeks and years of life, as it determines the child's sense of gender identity, and he finds that: "In brief, core gender identity results in the normal from a combination of hidden (and as yet unmeasured) only modestly effective and easily overturned, biological factors and more powerful, measurable, parental attitudes and influences playing upon the child."

The notion of profound differences between the sexes, between races, social classes, and even age groups, is not a popular one these egalitarian days. With good reason, since the descriptive "different" has so often been used to justify conditions of extreme social inequality: the conscious and unconscious valuations placed on sex and race and class undermine the concept of "separate but equal" or "different but reciprocal" that has informed so many discussions of race, sex, and poverty in the past. But if we now want to come to terms with some of the psychosocial structures that have grown out of and been imposed on biological facts of sex and race, we can't just wish away those differences.

To say that one sex is by nature superior to the other is an ideological dead-end. But so is the opposite claim—that "nature" or biology is irrelevant in the face of cultural conditioning. Anatomy all by itself is not destiny,* but it is a crucial factor in the complicated and still mysterious process that forms sexual identity. To say that nature and nurture are intricately bound up together in determining whatever it means to be feminine or masculine is not to end the discussion of psychosexual differences, but to begin it again.

Jean Strouse

NOTES

1   "Three Essays on the Theory of Sexuality" (1905), *The Standard Edition of the Complete Psychological Works of Sigmund Freud*, Vol. 7, p. 151.
2   "The Question of Lay Analysis" (1926), Ibid., 20, 212.
3   "An Autobiographical Study" (1925 [1924]), Ibid., 20, 36 (footnote, added in 1935).
4   "The Interpretation of Dreams" (1900), Ibid., 4, 257.
5   " 'A Child Is Being Beaten' " (1919), Ibid., 17, 196.
6   "Three Essays on the Theory of Sexuality" (1905), Ibid., 7, 219–220 (footnote, added in 1915).
7   Robert J. Stoller, "Facts and Fancies: An Examination of Freud's Concept of Bisexuality" (*infra*, p. 343).
8   Warren J. Gadpaille, "Research into the Physiology of Maleness and Femaleness," *Archives of General Psychiatry*, Vol. 26, 1972, pp. 193–206.
9   Melanie Klein, "Early Stages of the Oedipus Conflict," *The International Journal of Psycho-Analysis*, IX, 1928, p. 167.

*Freud never said that it was, in the sense that is commonly attributed to the phrase. He modifies Napoleon's famous "Geography is destiny" in an essay on male impotence ("The Most Prevalent Form of Degradation in Erotic Life," 1912), and his point is not that women are anatomically inferior but that the erotic and the excremental are intimately and inseparably bound up together in the genital organs of both sexes—that sexual love is not free from its animal essence.

Mitchell on Freud

Some Psychical Consequences of the Anatomical Distinction Between the Sexes (1925)

Sigmund Freud

In my own writings and in those of my followers more and more stress is laid on the necessity that the analyses of neurotics shall deal thoroughly with the remotest period of their childhood, the time of the early efflorescence of sexual life. It is only by examining the first manifestations of the patient's innate instinctual constitution and the effects of his earliest experiences that we can accurately gauge the motive forces that have led to his neurosis and can be secure against the errors into which we might be tempted by the degree to which things have become remodelled and overlaid in adult life. This requirement is not only of theoretical but also of practical importance, for it distinguishes our efforts from the work of those physicians whose interests are focused exclusively on therapeutic results and who employ analytic methods, but only up to a certain point. An analysis of early childhood such as we are considering is tedious and laborious and makes demands both upon the physician and upon the patient which cannot always be met. Moreover, it leads us into dark regions where there are as yet no signposts. Indeed, analysts may feel reassured, I think, that there is no risk of their work becoming mechanical, and so of losing its interest, during the next few decades.

In the following pages I bring forward some findings of analytic research which would be of great importance if they could be proved to apply universally. Why do I not postpone publication of them until fur-

17

ther experience has given me the necessary proof, if such proof is obtainable? Because the conditions under which I work have undergone a change, with implications which I cannot disguise. Formerly, I was not one of those who are unable to hold back what seems to be a new discovery until it has been either confirmed or corrected. My *Interpretation of Dreams* (1900) and my 'Fragment of an Analysis of a Case of Hysteria' (1905) (the case of Dora) were suppressed by me—if not for the nine years enjoined by Horace—at all events for four or five years before I allowed them to be published. But in those days I had unlimited time before me—'oceans of time'[1] as an amiable author puts it—and material poured in upon me in such quantities that fresh experiences were hardly to be escaped. Moreover, I was the only worker in a new field, so that my reticence involved no danger to myself and no loss to others.

But now everything has changed. The time before me is limited. The whole of it is no longer spent in working, so that my opportunities for making fresh observations are not so numerous. If I think I see something new, I am uncertain whether I can wait for it to be confirmed. And further, everything that is to be seen upon the surface has already been exhausted; what remains has to be slowly and laboriously dragged up from the depths. Finally, I am no longer alone. An eager crowd of fellow-workers is ready to make use of what is unfinished or doubtful, and I can leave to them that part of the work which I should otherwise have done myself. On this occasion, therefore, I feel justified in publishing something which stands in urgent need of confirmation before its value or lack of value can be decided.

In examining the earliest mental shapes assumed by the sexual life of children we have been in the habit of taking as the subject of our investigations the male child, the little boy. With little girls, so we have supposed, things must be similar, though in some way or other they must nevertheless be different. The point in development at which this difference lay could not be clearly determined.

In boys the situation of the Oedipus complex is the first stage that can be recognized with certainty. It is easy to understand, because at that stage a child retains the same object which he previously cathected with his libido—not as yet a genital one—during the preceding period while he was being suckled and nursed. The fact, too, that in this situation he regards his father as a disturbing rival and would like to get rid of him

18

and take his place is a straightforward consequence of the actual state of affairs. I have shown elsewhere[2] how the Oedipus attitude in little boys belongs to the phallic phase, and how its destruction is brought about by the fear of castration—that is, by narcissistic interest in their genitals. The matter is made more difficult to grasp by the complicating circumstance that even in boys the Oedipus complex has a double orientation, active and passive, in accordance with their bisexual constitution; a boy also wants to take his *mother's* place as the love-object of his *father*—a fact which we describe as the feminine attitude.[3]

As regards the prehistory of the Oedipus complex in boys we are far from complete clarity. We know that that period includes an identification of an affectionate sort with the boy's father, an identification which is still free from any sense of rivalry in regard to his mother. Another element of that stage is invariably, I believe, a masturbatory activity in connection with the genitals, the masturbation of early childhood, the more or less violent suppression of which by those in charge of the child sets the castration complex in action. It is to be assumed that this masturbation is attached to the Oedipus complex and serves as a discharge for the sexual excitation belonging to it. It is, however, uncertain whether the masturbation has this character from the first, or whether on the contrary it makes its first appearance spontaneously as an activity of a bodily organ and is only brought into relation with the Oedipus complex at some later date; this second possibility is by far the more probable. Another doubtful question is the part played by bedwetting and by the breaking of that habit through the intervention of training measures. We are inclined to make the simple connection that continued bed-wetting is a result of masturbation and that its suppression is regarded by boys as an inhibition of their genital activity—that is, as having the meaning of a threat of castration;[4] but whether we are always right in supposing this remains to be seen. Finally, analysis shows us in a shadowy way how the fact of a child at a very early age listening to his parents copulating may set up his first sexual excitation, and how that event may, owing to its after-effects, act as a starting-point for the child's whole sexual development. Masturbation, as well as the two attitudes in the Oedipus complex, later on becomes attached to this early experience, the child having subsequently interpreted its meaning. It is impossible, however, to suppose that these observations of coitus are of universal occurrence, so that at this point we are faced with the problem of 'primal phantasies'.[5] Thus the prehistory of the Oedipus complex, even in boys, raises all of these questions for sifting and explanation; and there is the further problem of whether we are to suppose that the process invariably follows the same course, or whether a great variety of different preliminary stages may not converge upon the same terminal situation.

In little girls the Oedipus complex raises one problem more than in boys. In both cases the mother is the original object; and there is no cause for surprise that boys retain that object in the Oedipus complex. But how does it happen that girls abandon it and instead take their father as an object? In pursuing this question I have been able to reach some conclusions which may throw light precisely on the prehistory of the Oedipus relation in girls.

Every analyst has come across certain women who cling with especial intensity and tenacity to the bond with their father and to the wish in which it culminates of having a child by him. We have good reason to suppose that the same wishful phantasy was also the motive force of their infantile masturbation, and it is easy to form an impression that at this point we have been brought up against an elementary and unanalysable fact of infantile sexual life. But a thorough analysis of these very cases brings something different to light—namely, that here the Oedipus complex has a long prehistory and is in some respects a secondary formation.

The old paediatrician Lindner [1879] once remarked that a child discovers the genital zones (the penis or the clitoris) as a source of pleasure while indulging in sensual sucking (thumb-sucking).[6] I shall leave it an open question whether it is really true that the child takes the newly found source of pleasure in exchange for the recent loss of the mother's nipple —a possibility to which later phantasies (fellatio) seem to point. Be that as it may, the genital zone is discovered at some time or other, and there seems no justification for attributing any psychical content to the first activities in connection with it. But the first step in the phallic phase which begins in this way is not the linking-up of the masturbation with the object-cathexes of the Oedipus complex, but a momentous discovery which little girls are destined to make. They notice the penis of a brother or playmate, strikingly visible and of large proportions, at once recognize it as the superior counterpart of their own small and inconspicuous organ, and from that time forward fall a victim to envy for the penis.

There is an interesting contrast between the behaviour of the two

20

sexes. In the analogous situation, when a little boy first catches sight of a girl's genital region, he begins by showing irresolution and lack of interest; he sees nothing or disavows[7] what he has seen, he softens it down or looks about for expedients for bringing it into line with his expectations. It is not until later, when some threat of castration has obtained a hold upon him, that the observation becomes important to him: if he then recollects or repeats it, it arouses a terrible storm of emotion in him and forces him to believe in the reality of the threat which he has hitherto laughed at. This combination of circumstances leads to two reactions, which may become fixed and will in that case, whether separately or together or in conjunction with other factors, permanently determine the boy's relations to women: horror of the mutilated creature or triumphant contempt for her. These developments, however, belong to the future, though not to a very remote one.

A little girl behaves differently. She makes her judgement and her decision in a flash. She has seen it and knows that she is without it and wants to have it.[8]

Here what has been named the masculinity complex of women branches off.[9] It may put great difficulties in the way of their regular development towards femininity, if it cannot be got over soon enough. The hope of some day obtaining a penis in spite of everything and so of becoming like a man may persist to an incredibly late age and may become a motive for strange and otherwise unaccountable actions. Or again, a process may set in which I should like to call a 'disavowal',[10] a process which in the mental life of children seems neither uncommon nor very dangerous but which in an adult would mean the beginning of a psychosis. Thus a girl may refuse to accept the fact of being castrated, may harden herself in the conviction that she *does* possess a penis, and may subsequently be compelled to behave as though she were a man.

The psychical consequences of envy for the penis, in so far as it does not become absorbed in the reaction-formation of the masculinity complex, are various and far-reaching. After a woman has become aware of the wound to her narcissism, she develops, like a scar, a sense of inferiority.[11] When she has passed beyond her first attempt at explaining her lack of a penis as being a punishment personal to herself and has realized that that sexual character is a universal one, she begins to share the contempt felt by men for a sex which is the lesser in so important a respect, and, at least in holding that opinion, insists on being like a man.[12]

Even after penis-envy has abandoned its true object, it continues to exist: by an easy displacement it persists in the character-trait of *jealousy*. Of course, jealousy is not limited to one sex and has a wider foundation than this, but I am of opinion that it plays a far larger part in the mental life of women than of men and that that is because it is enormously reinforced from the direction of displaced penis-envy. While I was still unaware of this source of jealousy and was considering the phantasy 'a child is being beaten', which occurs so commonly in girls, I constructed a first phase for it in which its meaning was that another child, a rival of whom the subject was jealous, was to be beaten.[13] This phantasy seems to be a relic of the phallic period in girls. The peculiar rigidity which struck me so much in the monotonous formula 'a child is being beaten' can probably be interpreted in a special way. The child which is being beaten (or caressed) may ultimately be nothing more nor less than the clitoris itself, so that at its very lowest level the statement will contain a confession of masturbation, which has remained attached to the content of the formula from its beginning in the phallic phase till later life.

A third consequence of penis-envy seems to be a loosening of the girl's relation with her mother as a love-object. The situation as a whole is not very clear, but it can be seen that in the end the girl's mother, who sent her into the world so insufficiently equipped, is almost always held responsible for her lack of a penis. The way in which this comes about historically is often that soon after the girl has discovered that her genitals are unsatisfactory she begins to show jealousy of another child on the ground that her mother is fonder of it than of her, which serves as a reason for her giving up her affectionate relation to her mother. It will fit in with this if the child which has been preferred by her mother is made into the first object of the beating-phantasy which ends in masturbation.

There is yet another surprising effect of penis-envy, or of the discovery of the inferiority of the clitoris, which is undoubtedly the most important of all. In the past I had often formed an impression that in general women tolerate masturbation worse than men, that they more frequently fight against it and that they are unable to make use of it in circumstances in which a man would seize upon it as a way of escape without any hesitation. Experience would no doubt elicit innumerable exceptions to this statement, if we attempted to turn it into a rule. The reactions of human individuals of both sexes are of course made up of masculine and feminine traits. But it appeared to me nevertheless as though masturbation

22

were further removed from the nature of women than of men, and the solution of the problem could be assisted by the reflection that masturbation, at all events of the clitoris, is a masculine activity and that the elimination of clitoridal sexuality is a necessary precondition for the development of femininity.[14] Analyses of the remote phallic period have now taught me that in girls, soon after the first signs of penis-envy, an intense current of feeling against masturbation makes its appearance, which cannot be attributed exclusively to the educational influence of those in charge of the child. This impulse is clearly a forerunner of the wave of repression which at puberty will do away with a large amount of the girl's masculine sexuality in order to make room for the development of her femininity. It may happen that this first opposition to auto-erotic activity fails to attain its end. And this was in fact the case in the instances which I analysed. The conflict continued, and both then and later the girl did everything she could to free herself from the compulsion to masturbate. Many of the later manifestations of sexual life in women remain unintelligible unless this powerful motive is recognized.

I cannot explain the opposition which is raised in this way by little girls to phallic masturbation except by supposing that there is some concurrent factor which turns her violently against that pleasurable activity. Such a factor lies close at hand. It cannot be anything else than her narcissistic sense of humiliation which is bound up with penis-envy, the reminder that after all this is a point on which she cannot compete with boys and that it would therefore be best for her to give up the idea of doing so. Thus the little girl's recognition of the anatomical distinction between the sexes forces her away from masculinity and masculine masturbation on to new lines which lead to the development of femininity.

So far there has been no question of the Oedipus complex, nor has it up to this point played any part. But now the girl's libido slips into a new position along the line—there is no other way of putting it—of the equation 'penis-child'. She gives up her wish for a penis and puts in place of it a wish for a child: and *with that purpose in view* she takes her father as a love-object.[15] Her mother becomes the object of her jealousy. The girl has turned into a little woman. If I am to credit a single analytic instance, this new situation can give rise to physical sensations which would have to be regarded as a premature awakening of the female genital apparatus. When the girl's attachment to her father comes to grief later on and has to be abandoned, it may give place to an identification with him and the girl may thus return to her masculinity complex and perhaps remain fixated in it.

I have now said the essence of what I had to say: I will stop, therefore, and cast an eye over our findings. We have gained some insight into the prehistory of the Oedipus complex in girls. The corresponding period in boys is more or less unknown. In girls the Oedipus complex is a secondary formation. The operations of the castration complex precede it and prepare for it. As regards the relation between the Oedipus and castration complexes there is a fundamental contrast between the two sexes. *Whereas in boys the Oedipus complex is destroyed by the castration complex,* [16] *in girls it is made possible and led up to by the castration complex.* This contradiction is cleared up if we reflect that the castration complex always operates in the sense implied in its subject-matter: it inhibits and limits masculinity and encourages femininity. The difference between the sexual development of males and females at the stage we have been considering is an intelligible consequence of the anatomical distinction between their genitals and of the psychical situation involved in it; it corresponds to the difference between a castration that has been carried out and one that has merely been threatened. In their essentials, therefore, our findings are self-evident and it should have been possible to foresee them.

The Oedipus complex, however, is such an important thing that the manner in which one enters and leaves it cannot be without its effects. In boys (as I have shown at length in the paper to which I have just referred [1924] and to which all of my present remarks are closely related) the complex is not simply repressed, it is literally smashed to pieces by the shock of threatened castration. Its libidinal cathexes are abandoned, desexualized and in part sublimated; its objects are incorporated into the ego, where they form the nucleus of the super-ego and give that new structure its characteristic qualities. In normal, or, it is better to say, in ideal cases, the Oedipus complex exists no longer, even in the unconscious; the super-ego has become its heir. Since the penis (to follow Ferenczi [1924]) owes its extraordinarily high narcissistic cathexis to its organic significance for the propagation of the species, the catastrophe to the Oedipus complex (the abandonment of incest and the institution of conscience and morality) may be regarded as a victory of the race over the individual. This is an interesting point of view when one considers that neurosis is based upon a struggle of the ego against the demands of

24

the sexual function. But to leave the standpoint of individual psychology is not of any immediate help in clarifying this complicated situation.

In girls the motive for the demolition of the Oedipus complex is lacking. Castration has already had its effect, which was to force the child into the situation of the Oedipus complex. Thus the Oedipus complex escapes the fate which it meets with in boys: it may be slowly abandoned or dealt with by repression, or its effects may persist far into women's normal mental life. I cannot evade the notion (though I hesitate to give it expression) that for women the level of what is ethically normal is different from what it is in men. Their super-ego is never so inexorable, so impersonal, so independent of its emotional origins as we require it to be in men. Character-traits which critics of every epoch have brought up against women—that they show less sense of justice than men, that they are less ready to submit to the great exigencies of life, that they are more often influenced in their judgements by feelings of affection or hostility—all these would be amply accounted for by the modification in the formation of their super-ego which we have inferred above. We must not allow ourselves to be deflected from such conclusions by the denials of the feminists, who are anxious to force us to regard the two sexes as completely equal in position and worth; but we shall, of course, willingly agree that the majority of men are also far behind the masculine ideal and that all human individuals, as a result of their bisexual disposition and of cross-inheritance, combine in themselves both masculine and feminine characteristics, so that pure masculinity and femininity remain theoretical constructions of uncertain content.

I am inclined to set some value on the considerations I have brought forward upon the psychical consequences of the anatomical distinction between the sexes. I am aware, however, that this opinion can only be maintained if my findings, which are based on a handful of cases, turn out to have general validity and to be typical. If not, they would remain no more than a contribution to our knowledge of the different paths along which sexual life develops.

In the valuable and comprehensive studies on the masculinity and castration complexes in women by Abraham (1921), Horney (1923) and Helene Deutsch (1925) there is much that touches closely on what I have written but nothing that coincides with it completely, so that here again I feel justified in publishing this paper.

NOTES

1 [In English in the original. It is not clear what author Freud had in mind.—The reference to Horace is to his *Ars Poetica*, 388.]

2 'The Dissolution of the Oedipus Complex' (1924). [Much of what follows is an elaboration of that paper.]

3 [Cf. ibid., p. 176.]

4 [Cf. ibid., p. 175.]

5 [Cf. the discussions in the 'Wolf Man' analysis (1918), *Standard Ed.*, 17, especially 48–60 and 95–7, and Lecture XXIII of the *Introductory Lectures* (1916–17).]

6 Cf. *Three Essays on the Theory of Sexuality* (1905) [*Standard Ed.*, 7, 179].

7 [See Editor's footnote to 'The Infantile Genital Organization', *Standard Ed.*, 19, 143.]

8 This is an opportunity for correcting a statement which I made many years ago. I believed that the sexual interest of children, unlike that of pubescents, was aroused, not by the difference between the sexes, but by the problem of where babies come from. We now see that, at all events with girls, this is certainly not the case. With boys it may no doubt happen sometimes one way and sometimes the other; or with both sexes chance experiences may determine the event.—[The statement mentioned at the beginning of this footnote appears in more than one place: e.g. in the paper on 'The Sexual Theories of Children' 1908), *Standard Ed.*, 9,212, in the case history of 'Little Hans' (1909), ibid., 10, 133, and in a passage added in 1915 to the *Three Essays* (1905), ibid., 7, 195. In a passage earlier than any of these, however, in a paper on 'The Sexual Enlightenment of Children' (1907), ibid., 9, 135, Freud in fact takes the opposite view —the one advocated here.]

9 [This term seems to have been introduced by Van Ophuijsen (1917). Freud adopted it in ' "A Child Is Being Beaten" ' (1919), *Standard Ed.*, 17, 191. Cf. also 19, 178.]

10 [For the parallel process in boys, see 'The Infantile Genital Organization' (1923), *Standard Ed.*, 19, 143–4.]

11 [Cf. *Beyond the Pleasure Principle* (1920), *Standard Ed.*, 18, 20–1.]

12 In my first critical account of the 'History of the Psycho-Analytic Movement' (1914) [*Standard Ed.*, 14, 54–5], I recognized that this fact represents the core of truth contained in Adler's theory. That theory has no hesitation in explaining the whole world by this single point ('organ-inferiority', the 'masculine protest', 'breaking away from the feminine line') and prides itself upon having in this way robbed sexuality of its importance and put the desire for power in its place! Thus the only organ which could claim to be called 'inferior' without any ambiguity would be the clitoris. On the other hand, one hears of analysts who boast that, though they have worked for dozens of years, they have never found a sign of the existence of a castration complex. We must bow our heads in recognition of the greatness of this achievement, even though it is only a negative one, a piece of virtuosity in the art of overlooking and mistaking. The two theories form an interesting pair of opposites: in the latter not a trace of a castration complex, in the former nothing else than its consequences.

13 ' "A Child Is Being Beaten" ' (1919) [*Standard Ed.*, 17, 184–5].

14 [A reference to clitoridal masturbation in girls appeared in the first edition of the *Three Essays* (1905), *Standard Ed.*, 7, 220. In the course of his 'Contributions to a Discussion on Masturbation' (1912), Freud expressed regret at the lack of knowledge about female masturbation (*Standard Ed.*, 12, 247).]

15 [Cf. 'The Dissolution of the Oedipus Complex', *Standard Ed.*, 19, 179.]

16 [Ibid., p. 177.]

26

On Freud and the Distinction Between the Sexes

Juliet Mitchell

In July 1925, Freud, from his holiday house in the Semmering outside Vienna, wrote to his friend and colleague, Karl Abraham in Berlin: "I have written a few short papers, but they are not meant very seriously. Perhaps, if I am willing to admit their parentage, I shall tell you about them later."[1] One of these "unserious" papers was the highly significant essay clumsily entitled "Some Psychical Consequences of the Anatomical Distinction Between the Sexes." Perhaps by September when he asked his daughter, Anna Freud, to present it as his contribution to that year's Psycho-Analytic Congress at Homberg Freud had changed his estimation of it. Certainly the essay contains in abbreviated form all Freud's later thoughts on the subject. In itself it marks the first published turning point in his thinking about the psychology of women. Until this point, with decreasing tenacity, he had held to his vague notions of a parallel development of girls and boys—the model being the boy. In the 1925 essay he finally discarded this equilateral theory and tentatively embarked on a new area for the exploration of female psychology and the meaning of female sexuality.

By this date Freud was chronically sick with cancer and he had for some years felt that there was little chance of his discovering anything new of substance. But multiple operations kept him alive for a further fourteen years during which, though less prolifically, he continued to work and

27

write. All his theoretical analyses of women's psychology come during this last period of work. It is perhaps interesting to reflect that Freud, with his reputation as the most honorable misogynist of them all, yet wrote very little (too little) specifically on the question of femininity. If we exclude his very early work with Josef Breuer on hysteria, in the twenty-three English volumes of his collected works there are only three brief essays devoted specifically to questions of feminine psychology and three detailed case-histories of women patients. However there are many discussions of the question scattered throughout his writings on other subjects.

It would seem valid to me to make a rough distinction between those references in the period prior to the 1920s and those that come after the first coherent statement made in "Some Psychical Consequences of the Anatomical Distinction Between the Sexes." Up to about 1920, the comments are isolated observations; after that date their repetition and re-working testifies to a preoccupation with the subject, though this may be due not so much to the specific interest in female psychology as to the type of question this forced him to ask and the new area it led him to explore. The shift in the area of interest was due to some extent to the development of his own work. But, in addition, the problem of feminine psychology was explicitly provoked by the interest of his fellow analysts. During the twenties and thirties there was considerable concentration among both men and women practitioners on producing a Freudian analysis of femininity. Karl Abraham, before his early death in December 1925, was one of the pioneers, and the one to whom Freud confessed his ignorance before he went on to make up for his negligence: "As I gladly admit, the female side of the problem is extraordinarily obscure to me. If your ideas and observations on the subject already permit communication, I should very much like to hear about them, but I can wait."[2] In fact Freud waited less than six months, not only for further correspondence with Abraham, but also for his own contribution to the subject: the 1925 essay.

"Some Psychical Consequences of the Anatomical Distinction Between the Sexes" can be said to deal with two intimately related but nevertheless distinct themes: the nature of female sexuality and the more general question of feminine psychology to be deduced from interpersonal (socio-sexual) relationships. On this first theme, except as it is influenced by the second, the essay scarcely breaks new ground upon that already

28

explored in the 1905 *Three Essays on Sexuality* (if we include the important footnotes to that treatise that Freud added periodically up until 1924). It is this question of female sexuality and, more specifically, Freud's proposition of the two zones of sensitivity—the vaginal and the clitoral —that has received most attention. If I resume Freud's arguments on this aspect here it is for reasons of their popularity—for I consider their interest not to lie in any autonomous value but in their dependence on the second, larger question of feminine psychology. And on this issue the 1925 essay inaugurates a new and crucial analysis to which I shall come later.

There are hints of most of Freud's later theories in his early letters to his one-time great friend, Wilhelm Fliess, with whom he corresponded both profusely and passionately in the late eighties and nineties. In 1897 Freud, writing to Fliess of his theory of repression, incorporated the following comments:

> . . . we can see that, with the successive waves of a child's development, he is overlaid with piety, shame, and such things. . . . These successive waves of development probably have a different chronological arrange- ment in the male and female sexes. (Disgust appears earlier in little girls than in boys.) But the main distinction between the sexes emerges at the time of puberty, when girls are seized upon by *non*-neurotic *sexual* repug- nance and males by libido. For at that period a further zone is (wholly or in part) extinguished in females which persists in males. I am thinking of the male genital zone, the region of the clitoris, in which during childhood sexual sensitivity is shown to be concentrated in girls as well as boys. Hence the flood of shame which overwhelms the female at that period, till the new, vaginal zone is awakened, whether spontaneously or by reflex action. Hence too, perhaps the anaesthesia of women . . .[3]

This position is retained in the *Three Essays* and, more carefully formu- lated, in the 1925 essay, but this persistence is not for the want of a challenge to it. The letter from Abraham that had so aroused Freud's interest precisely contested the nature of the two-stage theory of female sexuality. But Abraham was concerned with the early prevalence of vagi- nal feeling not, as recent investigations, with the continued dominance of the clitoris. Freud was skeptical of Abraham's thesis, maintaining that for the small girl the vagina would be psychically fused with the highly responsive anal area. One of Abraham's concerns was to assert that here as elsewhere there was a homology between the events of infancy and those of puberty: the adolescent girl, in transferring her orientation from

29

a desire for clitoral stimulation to a wish for vaginal penetration, was repeating in inverse direction the experience of infancy. Freud's statement that not until puberty is the vagina felt to be the main sexual organ lays greater stress on repression than does Abraham's theory. Most important, it suggests that there is no parallel development in boys and girls. Abraham's suggestion implies an original psychological "femininity," an infantile receptive vagina as the equal and opposite of the boy's penile masculinity. Freud's contention that in infancy both sexes have a masculine sexuality (the clitoris is the exact equivalent of the penis) and that it is only through a series of repressions that femininity (whose definitional sexual organ is the vagina) can be acquired, is an asymmetrical process rejecting any neat parallel between the sexes and thus by implication rejecting the notion that psychology corresponds in a one-to-one relationship with biology.

Anatomy may, at its point of hypothetical normality, give us two opposite but equal sexes (with the atrophied sex organs of the other present in each), but Freudian psychoanalytic theory does not. Freud's denial of Abraham's suggestion turned out to be neither arbitrary from a theoretical standpoint nor the random result of different empirical observation. Although, as I said earlier, the whole issue is secondary to the greater question of feminine psychology, it is necessary for the consideration of that larger question that the asymmetrical development of boys and girls should be retained in the discussion of both sexuality and psychology.

The post-Masters-and-Johnson restoration of the primacy of clitoral responsiveness claims the opposite of the theory asserted by Abraham; but it too, if applied psychologically, returns us to the dilemma of a law of even development between the sexes. Abraham's notion of an original vaginal receptivity and the opposite thesis of vaginal insensitivity and clitoral dominance may both be correct biologically or neurologically, but they make poor sense psychologically.

Let us pose the problem for the moment at its most basic level: if we live in a patriarchal society in which, from whatever your political standpoint, the sexes are treated at least differently, not to say "unequally," then is it not highly unlikely that the psychological development of the sexes should be one of parity? Psychology must reflect the social *at least* as much as the biological background—a fact which those who oppose Freud on this question, from whatever perspective, ignore completely.

In a footnote to the *Three Essays*, added in 1915, Freud wrote:

It is essential to realize that the concepts of 'masculine' and 'feminine', whose meaning seems so unambiguous to ordinary people, are among the most confused that occur in science. It is possible to distinguish at least three uses. 'Masculine' and 'feminine' are used sometimes in the sense of activity and passivity, sometimes in a biological and sometimes, again, in a sociological sense. The first of these three meanings is the essential one and the most serviceable in psycho-analysis. When . . . libido was described . . . as being 'masculine', the word was being used in this sense, for an instinct is always active even when it has a passive aim in view. . . . Activity and its concomitant phenomena (more powerful muscular development, aggressiveness, greater intensity of libido) are as a rule linked with biological masculinity; but they are not necessarily so, for there are animal species in which these qualities are on the contrary assigned to the female. . . . Such observation shows that in human beings pure masculinity or femininity is not to be found either in the psychological or biological sense. Every individual on the contrary displays a mixture of the character-traits belonging to his own and to the opposite sex; and he shows a combination of activity and passivity whether or not these last character-traits tally with his biological ones.[4]

Or as he put it fifteen years later, in 1930:

Sex is a biological fact which, although it is of extraordinary importance in mental life, is hard to grasp psychologically. We are accustomed to say that every human being displays both male and female instinctual impulses, needs and attributes; but though anatomy, it is true, can point out the characteristics of maleness and femaleness, psychology cannot. For psychology the contrast between the sexes fades away into one between activity and passivity, in which we far too readily identify activity with maleness and passivity with femaleness, a view which is by no means universally confirmed in the animal kingdom.[5]

Freud was concerned over and over again to establish that there was no one-to-one correlation between biology and psychology, that, for example, in psychological terms masculinity and femininity really reduced themselves to activity and passivity and that neither of the sexes held an absolute prerogative over either. Why then did Freud continue to use the terms with sexual connotations rather that those that were more neutral? Clearly not for reasons either of negligence or unconscious male chauvinism. Though certainly Freud was capable and guilty of both. In answering the question we get back to the asymmetry of Freud's sexual schema as opposed to the parallel paths tracked out by others working in this field.

If Freud opposed Abraham on his notion of the equilateral opposition of the vagina and the penis and if he criticised other analysts such as Ernest Jones and Karen Horney for their rejection of his crucial notion of psychic bisexuality and of a phallic stage for women, and if he continued to use a male bias in his vocabulary all this was in terms of a third assumption: the repudiation—by both men and women—of the implications of femininity. The two famous concepts of the castration complex (in men) and penis-envy (in women) are correlatives; they express an identical fear of (and necessity for) the feminine position. Hence, if Freud continued to use the terms "masculine" and "feminine" in instances where, by his own admission, activity and passivity would have done as well, it is because it was the *uneven* relationship between the two sexual possibilities, *within* a person as well as *between* persons, that he was trying to decipher. To claim that, say, the "Wolf-Man" had a "passive" attitude in this and that respect tells us nothing of the identifications and attachments to persons that he formed; to describe his desire in certain respects as a "feminine" one locates the identification with, for example, his mother (that is to say, in this particular case history). Freud's psychoanalytic theories are about sexism; that he himself propagated certain sexist views and that his work has been the bulwark of the ideological oppression of women are doubtless of great importance. But we can understand its significance only if we first realize that it was precisely the psychological formations produced within patriarchal societies that he was revealing and analysing. Opposition to Freud's asymmetrical history of the sexes, whether feminist, humanist, or counter-analytical, may well be more pleasing in the egalitarianism it assumes and sets out to demonstrate but it makes nonsense of the more profound claim that under patriarchy women are oppressed—a claim that Freud's analysis alone can help us to understand.

The 1925 essay is such a landmark precisely because here for the first time Freud gathers together his scattered observations and unpublished arguments on the *different* psycho-sexual history of boys and girls. As he himself admits, all his earlier work had taken the boy as the paradigm, automatically assuming for the girl fairly conventional variations on this male model. Because of this unargued male bias it was probably inevitable that the first efforts by other analysts to give girls a psychic history of their own should have been either the equilateral ones already mentioned or exaggerations of Freud's own phallocentrism. But in the 1925 essay (and no later writings do more than interestingly elaborate the theories propounded here) Freud establishes both a distinct development for girls and one that is formed within a male-dominated culture.

Up until about this time in Freud's work, the Oedipus complex, a shibboleth on which psychoanalysis stood or fell, had also by and large been the main starting-point of actual analyses. Without detracting from the significance of the Oedipus complex, Freud now established the importance of a new realm—the pre-Oedipal phase, in particular for girls. Hitherto he had assumed a symmetry in the Oedipal moment: boys loved their mothers and consequently wished to get rid of their unfair rivals in love, their fathers; girls desired their fathers, hence directed their jealousy against their mothers. But very early on Freud realized there was no parity here. From the outset he spoke against the desire to designate the girl's experience the "Electra complex," which would have accorded it independent and equal mythic weight. The transition that the girl must make from her love for her mother (all babies are attached to the mother) to loving her father could not be brought about by any simple chemical heterosexual attraction (or if it were, then there would be no psychology, which would be tantamount to saying that there was no person), nor could it be a simple physiological response with a homologous psychic structure superimposed—such as is supposed by Abraham's infantile vagina waiting desirously for paternal penetration. A shift of the sort from love of mother to love of father necessitates a complex psychological change. Hence before the girl can move into the positive feminine Oedipus complex (love of father) the pre-Oedipal situation must be crucial; indeed, as Freud says in the essay, the Oedipus complex for girls is only a secondary formation. (That in no way prevents its being the nuclear complex or the location of future neuroses, though that is not strictly relevant here.) This pre-Oedipal phase (for boys and girls) was at that point an unexplored region in psychoanalysis, one "where there are as yet no signposts." In fact Freud never really got far beyond an indication of the problems, which is one reason why psychoanalysis maps out the structure of neuroses but not of psychoses, and why it tells us more about the sexual development of men than of women. However, here, in pointing out the territory and the implications of the signs, Freud does the groundwork for an analysis of femininity.

Both boys and girls have feminine and masculine attitudes, both share the identifications and attachments of the pre-Oedipal phase, both have masculine and feminine Oedipus complexes, but in the latter situation

33

the key question is, which wins the day? Here the boy has to learn not to abandon his love for his mother by accepting an identification with her and the girl has to do precisely that; in other words the boy has to repudiate the possibilities of femininity and the girl has to embrace them. If we see then the Oedipus complex not as it is popularly perceived, as a symmetrical structure, but as an asymmetrical situation, we can get to the heart of the problem here. Instead of:

$$\text{Mother} \leftarrow\!\!\!\!\!\!\!\searrow\!\!\!\!\!\!\!\nearrow\!\!\!\!\!\!\!\rightarrow \text{Father}$$
$$\text{Girl} \underset{\text{loves}}{\rule{2cm}{0.4pt}}\underset{\text{loves}}{\rule{2cm}{0.4pt}} \text{Boy}$$

we have both infants loving the mother and abandoning her at the intervention of the father:

The dual relationship of mother and child is broken into by the father, who prevents the incestuous desires of both his offspring for the mother, whom he alone is allowed to possess.

The father, however, asserts his rights differently in the case of girls and boys. In the "ideal" case the boy learns to accept his inferior phallic powers (thus resolving his castration complex) but on the understanding that he will later have the same patriarchal rights and a woman of his own; the girl learns that she has no phallic powers and thus will not now or ever possess her mother or her later substitute (a wife)—indeed that she is *like* her mother, without the phallus: she recognizes her castration, envies the phallic power, and has to do her best to overcome this envy. (Freud uses the term "penis-envy" and this has produced a misleadingly biological interpretation.) When the boy accepts the possibility of castration his Oedipus complex is shattered, his sexual love for his mother is abandoned and channeled into other, ostensibly nonsexual pursuits: "the catastrophe to the Oedipus complex (the abandonment of incest and the institution of conscience and morality) may be regarded as a victory of the race over the individual."[6] Patriarchal culture prevails, and "circular" or closed (incestuous) sexuality is subdued.

The girl has another story to learn. Her love of her mother is not, like the boy's, culturally dangerous, just sexually "unrealistic" within the terms of the culture. If she persists in the belief that she has a penis (a pre-Oedipal supposition based on her phallic, clitoral activity), she will be disavowing reality and this could be the basis of a future psychosis. In the "ideal" case she will recognize her phallic inferiority, identify with the mother to whom she is to be compared, and then want to take her place with her father: "Her mother becomes the object of her jealousy. The little girl has turned into a little woman."[7] No prohibition shatters her love for her mother, but she learns that she possesses nothing with which to implement it. A sense of her inferiority, and closely connected therewith, a repression of masturbation, sets her on the path towards femininity. This repression of the clitoris that can never compete with the phallus as a thrusting and propagating power of patriarchal society foreshadows the later relinquishing of clitoral dominance at puberty and this, in its turn, is a precondition of the transference to vaginal sensitivity. The girl's positive Oedipus complex (love of the father) is entered into only by default; it is not as strong as the boy's Oedipus complex nor is there any reason fully to give it up—on the contrary, its acquisition is the first triumph of her feminine destiny under patriarchy. If we might elaborate on Freud here, we could say that where the boy's resolution and abandonment of his Oedipus complex is his entry into his cultural heritage, the girl, on the contrary, finds her cultural place in patriarchal society when she finally manages to achieve her Oedipal love for her father. This difference must have enormous implications.

I have given a schematic presentation of the central thesis of "Some Psychical Consequences of the Anatomical Distinction between the Sexes"; there are other suggestions therein that lead in other but related directions. It seems to me that in Freud's psychoanalytical schema, here as elsewhere, we have at least the beginnings of an analysis of the way in which a patriarchal society bequeaths its structures to each of us (with important variations according to the material conditions of class and race), gives us, that is, the cultural air we breathe, the ideas of the world in which we are born and which, unless patriarchy is demolished, we will pass on willy-nilly to our children and our children's children. Individual experimentation with communes and so forth can do no more than register protest. For whether or not the actual father is there does not affect the perpetuation of the patriarchal culture within the psychology of the individual; present or absent, "the father" always has his place. His actual absence may cause confusion, or, on another level, relief, but the only difference it makes is within the terms of the over-all patriarchal assumption of his presence. In our culture he is just as present in his absence. The Oedipus complex, then, expresses in miniature the power of the father or that of the name-of-the-father, but father it is. All feminist accounts that I have read or encountered misrepresent patriarchal society as one embodying the power of men in general; in fact, it is quite specifically the importance of the *father* that *patriarchy* signifies. Freud's 1925 essay is a key to the understanding of the oppression of women under patriarchy.

NOTES

1 Sigmund Freud, Letter to Karl Abraham, July 21, 1925. In *The Psychoanalytic Dialogue: The Letters of Sigmund Freud and Karl Abraham: 1907–1926*, edited by Hilda C. Abraham and Ernst L. Freud, translated (from the German) by Bernard Marsh and Hilda C. Abraham (London: the Hogarth Press; the Institute of Psycho-Analysis, 1965. New York: Basic Books, 1966), p. 391.

2 Ibid., December 3, 1924, p. 377.

3 Letter 75 to Wilhelm Fliess, November 14, 1897. *Standard Edition*, Vol. I, p. 270.

4 Freud, "Three Essays on Sexuality," 1905, *Standard Edition*, Vol. 7, pp. 219–20.

5 Freud, "Civilization and its Discontents," 1930, *Standard Edition*, Vol. 21, pp. 105–106.

6 Freud, "Some Psychical Consequences of the Anatomical Distinction Between the Sexes," 1925, *Standard Edition*, Vol. 19, p. 257.

7 Ibid., p. 256.

Janeway on Freud

Female Sexuality (1931)

Sigmund Freud

I

During the phase of the normal Oedipus complex we find the child tenderly attached to the parent of the opposite sex, while its relation to the parent of its own sex is predominantly hostile. In the case of a boy there is no difficulty in explaining this. His first love-object was his mother. She remains so; and, with the strengthening of his erotic desires and his deeper insight into the relations between his father and mother, the former is bound to become his rival. With the small girl it is different. Her first object, too, was her mother. How does she find her way to her father? How, when and why does she detach herself from her mother? We have long understood that the development of female sexuality is complicated by the fact that the girl has the task of giving up what was originally her leading genital zone—the clitoris—in favour of a new zone —the vagina.[1] But it now seems to us that there is a second change of the same sort which is no less characteristic and important for the development of the female: the exchange of her original object—her mother— for her father. The way in which the two tasks are connected with each other is not yet clear to us.

It is well known that there are many women who have a strong attachment to their father; nor need they be in any way neurotic. It is upon such women that I have made the observations which I propose to report here and which have led me to adopt a particular view of female sexuality. I was struck, above all, by two facts. The first was that where the woman's attachment to her father was particularly intense, analysis showed that it had been preceded by a phase of exclusive attachment to her mother which had been equally intense and passionate. Except for the change of her love-object, the second phase had scarcely added any new feature to her erotic life. Her primary relation to her mother had been built up in a very rich and many-sided manner. The second fact taught me that the *duration* of this attachment had also been greatly underestimated. In several cases it lasted until well into the fourth year—in one case into the fifth year—so that it covered by far the longer part of the period of early sexual efflorescence. Indeed, we had to reckon with the possibility that a number of women remain arrested in their original attachment to their mother and never achieve a true change-over towards men. This being so, the pre-Oedipus phase in women gains an importance which we have not attributed to it hitherto.

Since this phase allows room for all the fixations and repressions from which we trace the origin of the neuroses, it would seem as though we must retract the universality of the thesis that the Oedipus complex is the nucleus of the neuroses. But if anyone feels reluctant about making this correction, there is no need for him to do so. On the one hand, we can extend the content of the Oedipus complex to include all the child's relations to both parents; or, on the other, we can take due account of our new findings by saying that the female only reaches the normal positive Oedipus situation after she has surmounted a period before it that is governed by the negative complex.[2] And indeed during that phase a little girl's father is not much else for her than a troublesome rival, although her hostility towards him never reaches the pitch which is characteristic of boys. We have, after all, long given up any expectation of a neat parallelism between male and female sexual development.

Our insight into this early, pre-Oedipus, phase in girls comes to us as a surprise, like the discovery, in another field, of the Minoan-Mycenean civilization behind the civilization of Greece.

Everything in the sphere of this first attachment to the mother seemed to me so difficult to grasp in analysis—so grey with age and shadowy and almost impossible to revivify—that it was as if it had succumbed to an especially inexorable repression. But perhaps I gained this impression because the women who were in analysis with me were able to cling to the very attachment to the father in which they had taken refuge from the early phase that was in question. It does indeed appear that women analysts—as, for instance, Jeanne Lampl-de Groot and Helene Deutsch

—have been able to perceive these facts more easily and clearly because they were helped in dealing with those under their treatment by the transference to a suitable mother-substitute. Nor have I succeeded in seeing my way through any case completely, and I shall therefore confine myself to reporting the most general findings and shall give only a few examples of the new ideas which I have arrived at. Among these is a suspicion that this phase of attachment to the mother is especially intimately related to the aetiology of hysteria, which is not surprising when we reflect that both the phase and the neurosis are characteristically feminine, and further, that in this dependence on the mother we have the germ of later paranoia in women.[3] For this germ appears to be the surprising, yet regular, fear of being killed (?devoured) by the mother. It is plausible to assume that this fear corresponds to a hostility which develops in the child towards her mother in consequence of the manifold restrictions imposed by the latter in the course of training and bodily care and that the mechanism of projection is favoured by the early age of the child's psychical organization.[4]

II

I began by stating the two facts which have struck me as new: that a woman's strong dependence on her father merely takes over the heritage of an equally strong attachment to her mother, and that this earlier phase has lasted for an unexpectedly long period of time. I shall now go back a little in order to insert these new findings into the picture of female sexual development with which we are familiar. In doing this, a certain amount of repetition will be inevitable. It will help our exposition if, as we go along, we compare the state of things in women with that in men.

First of all, there can be no doubt that the bisexuality, which is present, as we believe, in the innate disposition of human beings, comes to the fore much more clearly in women than in men. A man, after all, has only one leading sexual zone, one sexual organ, whereas a woman has two: the vagina—the female organ proper—and the clitoris, which is analogous to the male organ. We believe we are justified in assuming that for many years the vagina is virtually non-existent and possibly does not produce sensations until puberty. It is true that recently an increasing number of observers report that vaginal impulses are present even in these early years. In women, therefore, the main genital occurrences of childhood

41

must take place in relation to the clitoris. Their sexual life is regularly divided into two phases, of which the first has a masculine character, while only the second is specifically feminine. Thus in female development there is a process of transition from the one phase to the other, to which there is nothing analogous in the male. A further complication arises from the fact that the clitoris, with its virile character, continues to function in later female sexual life in a manner which is very variable and which is certainly not yet satisfactorily understood. We do not, of course, know the biological basis of these peculiarities in women; and still less are we able to assign them any teleological purpose.

Parallel with this first great difference there is the other, concerned with the finding of the object. In the case of a male, his mother becomes his first love-object as a result of her feeding him and looking after him, and she remains so until she is replaced by someone who resembles her or is derived from her. A female's first object, too, must be her mother: the primary conditions for a choice of object are, of course, the same for all children. But at the end of her development, her father—a man— should have become her new love-object. In other words, to the change in her own sex there must correspond a change in the sex of her object. The new problems that now require investigating are in what way this change takes place, how radically or how incompletely it is carried out, and what the different possibilities are which present themselves in the course of this development.

We have already learned, too, that there is yet another difference between the sexes, which relates to the Oedipus complex. We have an impression here that what we have said about the Oedipus complex applies with complete strictness to the male child only and that we are right in rejecting the term 'Electra complex'[5] which seeks to emphasize the analogy between the attitude of the two sexes. It is only in the male child that we find the fateful combination of love for the one parent and simultaneous hatred for the other as a rival. In his case it is the discovery of the possibility of castration, as proved by the sight of the female genitals, which forces on him the transformation of his Oedipus complex, and which leads to the creation of his super-ego and thus initiates all the processes that are designed to make the individual find a place in the cultural community. After the paternal agency has been internalized and become a super-ego, the next task is to detach the latter from the figures of whom it was originally the psychical representative. In this remarkable

42

course of development it is precisely the boy's narcissistic interest in his genitals—his interest in preserving his penis—which is turned round into a curtailing of his infantile sexuality.[6]

One thing that is left over in men from the influence of the Oedipus complex is a certain amount of disparagement in their attitude towards women, whom they regard as being castrated. In extreme cases this gives rise to an inhibition in their choice of object, and, if it is supported by organic factors, to exclusive homosexuality.

Quite different are the effects of the castration complex in the female. She acknowledges the fact of her castration, and with it, too, the superiority of the male and her own inferiority; but she rebels against this unwelcome state of affairs. From this divided attitude three lines of development open up. The first leads to a general revulsion from sexuality. The little girl, frightened by the comparison with boys, grows dissatisfied with her clitoris, and gives up her phallic activity and with it her sexuality in general as well as a good part of her masculinity in other fields. The second line leads her to cling with defiant self-assertiveness to her threatened masculinity. To an incredibly late age she clings to the hope of getting a penis some time. That hope becomes her life's aim; and the phantasy of being a man in spite of everything often persists as a formative factor over long periods. This 'masculinity complex' in women can also result in a manifest homosexual choice of object. Only if her development follows the third, very circuitous, path does she reach the final normal female attitude, in which she takes her father as her object and so finds her way to the feminine form of the Oedipus complex. Thus in women the Oedipus complex is the end-result of a fairly lengthy development. It is not destroyed, but created, by the influence of castration; it escapes the strongly hostile influences which, in the male, have a destructive effect on it, and indeed it is all too often not surmounted by the female at all. For this reason, too, the cultural consequences of its break-up are smaller and of less importance in her. We should probably not be wrong in saying that it is this difference in the reciprocal relation between the Oedipus and the castration complex which gives its special stamp to the character of females as social beings.[7]

We see, then, that the phase of exclusive attachment to the mother, which may be called the *pre-Oedipus* phase, possesses a far greater importance in women than it can have in men. Many phenomena of female sexual life which were not properly understood before can be fully ex-

43

plained by reference to this phase. Long ago, for instance, we noticed that many women who have chosen their husband on the model of their father, or have put him in their father's place, nevertheless repeat towards him, in their married life, their bad relations with their mother.[8] The husband of such a woman was meant to be the inheritor of her relation to her father, but in reality he became the inheritor of her relation to her mother. This is easily explained as an obvious case of regression. Her relation to her mother was the original one, and her attachment to her father was built up on it, and now, in marriage, the original relation emerges from repression. For the main content of her development to womanhood lay in the carrying over of her affective object attachments from her mother to her father.

With many women we have the impression that their years of maturity are occupied by a struggle with their husband, just as their youth was spent in a struggle with their mother. In the light of the previous discussions we shall conclude that their hostile attitude to their mother is not a consequence of the rivalry implicit in the Oedipus complex, but originates from the preceding phase and has merely been reinforced and exploited in the Oedipus situation. And actual analytic examination confirms this view. Our interest must be directed to the mechanisms that are at work in her turning away from the mother who was an object so intensely and exclusively loved. We are prepared to find, not a single factor, but a whole number of them operating together towards the same end.

Among these factors are some which are determined by the circumstances of infantile sexuality in general, and so hold good equally for the erotic life of boys. First and foremost we may mention jealousy of other people—of brothers and sisters, rivals, among whom the father too has a place. Childhood love is boundless; it demands exclusive possession, it is not content with less than all. But it has a second characteristic: it has, in point of fact, no aim and is incapable of obtaining complete satisfaction; and principally for that reason it is doomed to end in disappointment[9] and to give place to a hostile attitude. Later on in life the lack of an ultimate satisfaction may favour a different result. This very factor may ensure the uninterrupted continuance of the libidinal cathexis, as happens with love-relations that are inhibited in their aim. But in the stress of the processes of development it regularly happens that the libido abandons its unsatisfying position in order to find a new one.

44

Another, much more specific motive for turning away from the mother arises from the effect of the castration complex on the creature who is without a penis. At some time or other the little girl makes the discovery of her organic inferiority—earlier and more easily, of course, if there are brothers or other boys about. We have already taken note of the three paths which diverge from this point: (a) the one which leads to a cessation of her whole sexual life, (b) the one which leads to a defiant over-emphasis of her masculinity, and (c) the first steps towards definitive femininity. It is not easy to determine the exact timing here or the typical course of events. Even the point of time when the discovery of castration is made varies, and a number of other factors seem to be inconstant and to depend on chance. The state of the girl's own phallic activity plays a part; and so too does the question whether this activity was found out or not, and how much interference with it she experienced afterwards.

Little girls usually discover for themselves their characteristic phallic activity—masturbation of the clitoris;[10] and to begin with this is no doubt unaccompanied by phantasy. The part played in starting it by nursery hygiene is reflected in the very common phantasy which makes the mother or nurse into a seducer.[11] Whether little girls masturbate less frequently and from the first less energetically than little boys is not certain; quite possibly it is so. Actual seduction, too, is common enough; it is initiated either by other children or by someone in charge of the child who wants to soothe it, or send it to sleep or make it dependent on them. Where seduction intervenes it invariably disturbs the natural course of the developmental processes, and it often leaves behind extensive and lasting consequences.

A prohibition of masturbation, as we have seen, becomes an incentive for giving it up; but it also becomes a motive for rebelling against the person who prohibits it—that is to say, the mother, or the mother-substitute who later regularly merges with her. A defiant persistence in masturbation appears to open the way to masculinity. Even where the girl has not succeeded in suppressing her masturbation, the effect of the apparently vain prohibition is seen in her later efforts to free herself at all costs from a satisfaction which has been spoilt for her. When she reaches maturity her object-choice may still be influenced by this persisting purpose. Her resentment at being prevented from free sexual activity plays a big part in her detachment from her mother. The same motive comes into operation again after puberty, when her mother takes up her duty of guarding her daughter's chastity.[12] We shall, of course, not forget that the mother is similarly opposed to a boy's masturbating and thus provides him, too, with a strong motive for rebellion.

When the little girl discovers her own deficiency, from seeing a male genital, it is only with hesitation and reluctance that she accepts the unwelcome knowledge. As we have seen, she clings obstinately to the expectation of one day having a genital of the same kind too, and her wish for it survives long after her hope has expired. The child invariably regards castration in the first instance as a misfortune peculiar to herself; only later does she realize that it extends to certain other children and lastly to certain grown-ups.[13] When she comes to understand the general nature of this characteristic, it follows that femaleness—and with it, of course, her mother—suffers a great depreciation in her eyes.

This account of how girls respond to the impression of castration and the prohibition against masturbation will very probably strike the reader as confused and contradictory. This is not entirely the author's fault. In truth, it is hardly possible to give a description which has general validity. We find the most different reactions in different individuals, and in the same individual the contrary attitudes exist side by side. With the first intervention of the prohibition, the conflict is there, and from now on it will accompany the development of the sexual function. Insight into what takes place is made particularly difficult by the fact of its being so hard to distinguish the mental processes of this first phase from later ones by which they are overlaid and are distorted in memory. Thus, for instance, a girl may later construe the fact of castration as a punishment for her masturbatory activity, and she will attribute the carrying out of this punishment to her father, but neither of these ideas can have been a primary one. Similarly, boys regularly fear castration from their father, although in their case, too, the threat most usually comes from their mother.

However this may be, at the end of this first phase of attachment to the mother, there emerges, as the girl's strongest motive for turning away from her, the reproach that her mother did not give her a proper penis —that is to say, brought her into the world as a female.[14] A second reproach, which does not reach quite so far back, is rather a surprising one. It is that her mother did not give her enough milk, did not suckle her long enough. Under the conditions of modern civilization this may be true often enough, but certainly not so often as is asserted in analyses. It would seem rather that this accusation gives expression to the general

46

dissatisfaction of children, who, in our monogamous civilization, are weaned from the breast after six or nine months, whereas the primitive mother devotes herself exclusively to her child for two or three years. It is as though our children had remained for ever unsated, as though they had never sucked long enough at their mother's breast. But I am not sure whether, if one analysed children who had been suckled as long as the children of primitive peoples, one would not come upon the same complaint. Such is the greed of a child's libido!

When we survey the whole range of motives for turning away from the mother which analysis brings to light—that she failed to provide the little girl with the only proper genital, that she did not feed her sufficiently, that she compelled her to share her mother's love with others, that she never fulfilled all the girl's expectations of love, and, finally, that she first aroused her sexual activity and then forbade it—all these motives seem nevertheless insufficient to justify the girl's final hostility. Some of them follow inevitably from the nature of infantile sexuality; others appear like rationalizations devised later to account for the uncomprehended change in feeling. Perhaps the real fact is that the attachment to the mother is bound to perish, precisely because it was the first and was so intense; just as one can often see happen in the first marriages of young women which they have entered into when they were most passionately in love. In both situations the attitude of love probably comes to grief from the disappointments that are unavoidable and from the accumulation of occasions for aggression. As a rule, second marriages turn out much better.

We cannot go so far as to assert that the ambivalence of emotional cathexes is a universally valid law, and that it is absolutely impossible to feel great love for a person without its being accompanied by a hatred that is perhaps equally great, or vice versa. Normal adults do undoubtedly succeed in separating those two attitudes from each other, and do not find themselves obliged to hate their love-objects and to love their enemy as well as hate him. But this seems to be the result of later developments. In the first phases of erotic life, ambivalence is evidently the rule. Many people retain this archaic trait all through their lives. It is characteristic of obsessional neurotics that in their object-relationships love and hate counterbalance each other. In primitive races, too, we may say that ambivalence predominates.[15] We shall conclude, then, that the little girl's intense attachment to her mother is strongly ambivalent, and that it is in consequence precisely of this ambivalence that (with the assistance of the

47

other factors we have adduced) her attachment is forced away from her mother—once again, that is to say, in consequence of a general characteristic of infantile sexuality.

The explanation I have attempted to give is at once met by a question: 'How is it, then, that boys are able to keep intact their attachment to their mother, which is certainly no less strong than that of girls?' The answer comes equally promptly: 'Because boys are able to deal with their ambivalent feelings towards their mother by directing all their hostility on to their father.' But, in the first place, we ought not to make this reply until we have made a close study of the pre-Oedipus phase in boys, and, in the second place, it is probably more prudent in general to admit that we have as yet no clear understanding of these processes, with which we have only just become acquainted.

III

A further question arises: 'What does the little girl require of her mother? What is the nature of her sexual aims during the time of exclusive attachment to her mother?' The answer we obtain from the analytic material is just what we should expect. The girl's sexual aims in regard to her mother are active as well as passive and are determined by the libidinal phases through which the child passes. Here the relation of activity to passivity is especially interesting. It can easily be observed that in every field of mental experience, not merely that of sexuality, when a child receives a passive impression it has a tendency to produce an active reaction. It tries to do itself what has just been done to it. This is part of the work imposed on it of mastering the external world and can even lead to its endeavouring to repeat an impression which it would have reason to avoid on account of its distressing content. Children's play, too, is made to serve this purpose of supplementing a passive experience with an active piece of behaviour and of thus, as it were, annulling it. When a doctor has opened a child's mouth, in spite of his resistance, to look down his throat, the same child, after the doctor has gone, will play at being the doctor himself, and will repeat the assault upon some small brother or sister who is as helpless in his hands as he was in the doctor's.[16] Here we have an unmistakable revolt against passivity and a preference for the active role. This swing-over from passivity to activity does not take place with the same regularity or vigour in all children; in some it may not occur at all. A child's behaviour in this respect may enable us to draw conclusions as to the relative strength of the masculinity and femininity that it will exhibit in its sexuality.

The first sexual and sexually coloured experiences which a child has in relation to its mother are naturally of a passive character. It is suckled, fed, cleaned, and dressed by her, and taught to perform all its functions. A part of its libido goes on clinging to those experiences and enjoys the satisfactions bound up with them; but another part strives to turn them into activity. In the first place, being suckled at the breast gives place to active sucking. As regards the other experiences the child contents itself either with becoming self-sufficient—that is, with itself successfully carrying out what had hitherto been done for it—or with repeating its passive experiences in an active form in play; or else it actually makes its mother into the object and behaves as the active subject towards her. For a long time I was unable to credit this last behaviour, which takes place in the field of real action, until my observations removed all doubts on the matter.

We seldom hear of a little girl's wanting to wash or dress her mother, or tell her to perform her excretory functions. Sometimes, it is true, she says: 'Now let's play that I'm the mother and you're the child'; but generally she fulfils these active wishes in an indirect way, in her play with her doll, in which she represents the mother and the doll the child. The fondness girls have for playing with dolls, in contrast to boys, is commonly regarded as a sign of early awakened femininity. Not unjustly so; but we must not overlook the fact that what finds expression here is the *active* side of femininity, and that the little girl's preference for dolls is probably evidence of the exclusiveness of her attachment to her mother, with complete neglect of her father-object.

The very surprising sexual activity of little girls in relation to their mother is manifested chronologically in oral, sadistic, and finally even in phallic trends directed towards her. It is difficult to give a detailed account of these because they are often obscure instinctual impulses which it was impossible for the child to grasp psychically at the time of their occurrence, which were therefore only interpreted by her later, and which then appear in the analysis in forms of expression that were certainly not the original ones. Sometimes we come across them as transferences on to the later father-object, where they do not belong and where they seriously interfere with our understanding of the situation. We find the little girl's aggressive oral and sadistic wishes in a form forced on them by early repression, as a fear of being killed by her mother—a fear which, in turn, justifies her death-wish against her mother, if that becomes conscious. It is impossible to say how often this fear of the mother is supported by an unconscious hostility on the mother's part which is sensed by the girl.[17] (Hitherto, it is only in men that I have found the fear of being eaten up. This fear is referred to the father, but it is probably the product of a transformation of oral aggressivity directed to the mother. The child wants to eat up its mother from whom it has had its nourishment; in the case of the father there is no such obvious determinant for the wish.)

The women patients showing a strong attachment to their mother in whom I have been able to study the pre-Oedipus phase have all told me that when their mother gave them enemas or rectal douches they used to offer the greatest resistance and react with fear and screams of rage. This behaviour may be very frequent or even the habitual thing in children. I only came to understand the reason for such a specially violent opposition from a remark made by Ruth Mack Brunswick, who was studying these problems at the same time as I was, to the effect that she was inclined to compare the outbreak of anger after an enema to the orgasm following genital excitation. The accompanying anxiety should, she thought, be construed as a transformation of the desire for aggression which had been stirred up. I believe that this is really so and that, at the sadistic-anal level, the intense passive stimulation of the intestinal zone is responded to by an outbreak of desire for aggression which is manifested either directly as rage, or, in consequence of its suppression, as anxiety. In later years this reaction seems to die away.

In regard to the passive impulses of the phallic phase, it is noteworthy that girls regularly accuse their mother of seducing them. This is because they necessarily received their first, or at any rate their strongest, genital sensations when they were being cleaned and having their toilet attended to by their mother (or by someone such as a nurse who took her place). Mothers have often told me, as a matter of observation, that their little daughters of two and three years old enjoy these sensations and try to get their mothers to make them more intense by repeated touching and rubbing. The fact that the mother thus unavoidably initiates the child into the phallic phase is, I think, the reason why, in phantasies of later years, the father so regularly appears as the sexual seducer. When the girl turns away from her mother, she also makes over to her father her introduction into sexual life.[18]

Lastly, intense *active* wishful impulses directed towards the mother also arise during the phallic phase. The sexual activity of this period culminates in clitoridal masturbation. This is probably accompanied by ideas of the mother, but whether the child attaches a sexual aim to the idea, and what that aim is, I have not been able to discover from my observations. It is only when all her interests have received a fresh impetus through the arrival of a baby brother or sister that we can clearly recognize such an aim. The little girl wants to believe that she has given her mother the new baby, just as the boy wants to; and her reaction to this event and her behaviour to the baby is exactly the same as his. No doubt this sounds quite absurd, but perhaps that is only because it sounds so unfamiliar.

The turning-away from her mother is an extremely important step in the course of a little girl's development. It is more than a mere change of object. We have already described what takes place in it and the many motives put forward for it; we may now add that hand in hand with it there is to be observed a marked lowering of the active sexual impulses and a rise of the passive ones. It is true that the active trends have been affected by frustration more strongly; they have proved totally unrealizable and are therefore abandoned by the libido more readily. But the passive trends have not escaped disappointment either. With the turning-away from the mother clitoridal masturbation frequently ceases as well; and often enough when the small girl represses her previous masculinity a considerable portion of her sexual trends in general is permanently injured too. The transition to the father-object is accomplished with the help of the passive trends in so far as they have escaped the catastrophe. The path to the development of femininity now lies open to the girl, to the extent to which it is not restricted by the remains of the pre-Oedipus attachment to her mother which she has surmounted.

If we now survey the stage of sexual development in the female which I have been describing, we cannot resist coming to a definite conclusion about female sexuality as a whole. We have found the same libidinal forces at work in it as in the male child and we have been able to convince ourselves that for a period of time these forces follow the same course and have the same outcome in each.

Biological factors subsequently deflect those libidinal forces [in the girl's case] from their original aims and conduct even active and in every sense masculine trends into feminine channels. Since we cannot dismiss the notion that sexual excitation is derived from the operation of certain chemical substances, it seems plausible at first to expect that biochemistry will one day disclose a substance to us whose presence produces a male sexual excitation and another substance which produces a female one. But this hope seems no less naïve than the other one—happily obsolete to-day—that it may be possible under the microscope to isolate the different exciting factors of hysteria, obsessional neurosis, melancholia, and so on.

Even in sexual chemistry things must be rather more complicated.[19] For psychology, however, it is a matter of indifference whether there is a single sexually exciting substance in the body or two or countless numbers of them. Psycho-analysis teaches us to manage with a single libido, which, it is true, has both active and passive aims (that is, modes of satisfaction). This antithesis and, above all, the existence of libidinal trends with passive aims, contains within itself the remainder of our problem.

IV

An examination of the analytic literature on the subject shows that everything that has been said by me here is already to be found in it.[20] It would have been superfluous to publish this paper if it were not that in a field of research which is so difficult of access every account of first-hand experiences or personal views may be of value. Moreover, there are a number of points which I have defined more sharply and isolated more carefully. In some of the other papers on the subject the description is obscured because they deal at the same time with the problems of the super-ego and the sense of guilt. This I have avoided doing. Also, in describing the various outcomes of this phase of development, I have refrained from discussing the complications which arise when a child, as a result of disappointment from her father, returns to the attachment to her mother which she had abandoned, or when, in the course of her life, she repeatedly changes over from one position to the other. But precisely because my paper is only one contribution among others, I may be spared an exhaustive survey of the literature, and I can confine myself to bringing out the more important points on which I agree or disagree with these other writings.

Abraham's (1921) description of the manifestations of the castration complex in the female is still unsurpassed; but one would be glad if it had included the factor of the girl's original exclusive attachment to her mother. I am in agreement with the principal points in Jeanne Lampl-de Groot's[21] (1927) important paper. In this the complete identity of the pre-Oedipus phase in boys and girls is recognized, and the girl's sexual (phallic) activity towards her mother is affirmed and substantiated by observations. The turning-away from the mother is traced to the influence of the girl's recognition of castration, which obliges her to give up her sexual object, and often masturbation along with it. The whole development is summed up in the formula that the girl goes through a phase of the 'negative' Oedipus complex before she can enter the positive one. A point on which I find the writer's account inadequate is that it represents the turning-away from the mother as being merely a change of object and does not discuss the fact that it is accompanied by the plainest manifestations of hostility. To this hostility full justice is done in Helene Deutsch's latest paper, on feminine masochism and its relation to frigidity (1930), in which she also recognizes the girl's phallic activity and the intensity of her attachment to her mother. Helene Deutsch states further that the girl's turning towards her father takes place *viâ* her passive trends (which have already been awakened in relation to her mother). In her earlier book (1925) the author had not yet set herself free from the endeavour to apply the Oedipus pattern to the pre-Oedipus phase, and she therefore interpreted the little girl's phallic activity as an identification with her father.

Fenichel (1930) rightly emphasizes the difficulty of recognizing in the material produced in analysis what parts of it represent the unchanged content of the pre-Oedipus phase and what parts have been distorted by regression (or in other ways). He does not accept Jeanne Lampl-de Groot's assertion of the little girl's active attitude in the phallic phase. He also rejects the 'displacement backwards' of the Oedipus complex proposed by Melanie Klein (1928), who places its beginnings as early as the commencement of the second year of life. This dating of it, which would also necessarily imply a modification of our view of all the rest of the child's development, does not in fact correspond to what we learn from the analyses of adults, and it is especially incompatible with my findings as to the long duration of the girl's pre-Oedipus attachment to her mother. A means of softening this contradiction is afforded by the reflection that we are not as yet able to distinguish in this field between what is rigidly fixed by biological laws and what is open to movement and change under the influence of accidental experience. The effect of seduction has long been familiar to us and in just the same way other factors —such as the date at which the child's brothers and sisters are born or the time when it discovers the difference between the sexes, or again its direct observations of sexual intercourse or its parents' behaviour in encouraging or repelling it—may hasten the child's sexual development and bring it to maturity.

Some writers are inclined to reduce the importance of the child's first and most original libidinal impulses in favour of later developmental processes, so that—to put this view in its most extreme form—the only role left to the former is merely to indicate certain paths, while the [psychical] intensities[22] which flow along those paths are supplied by later regressions and reaction-formations. Thus, for instance, Karin Horney (1926) is of the opinion that we greatly over-estimate the girl's primary penis-envy and that the strength of the masculine trend which she develops later is to be attributed to a *secondary* penis-envy which is used to fend off her feminine impulses and, in particular, her feminine attachment to her father. This does not tally with my impressions. Certain as is the occurrence of later reinforcements through regression and reaction-formation, and difficult as it is to estimate the relative strength of the confluent libidinal components, I nevertheless think that we should not overlook the fact that the first libidinal impulses have an intensity of their own which is superior to any that come later and which may indeed be termed incommensurable. It is undoubtedly true that there is an antithesis between the attachment to the father and the masculinity complex; it is the general antithesis that exists between activity and passivity, masculinity and femininity. But this gives us no right to assume that only one of them is primary and that the other owes its strength merely to the force of defence. And if the defence against femininity is so energetic, from what other source can it draw its strength than from the masculine trend which found its first expression in the child's penis-envy and therefore deserves to be named after it?

54

A similar objection applies to Ernest Jones's view (1927) that the phallic phase in girls is a secondary, protective reaction rather than a genuine developmental stage. This does not correspond either to the dynamic or the chronological position of things.

NOTES

1   [*Three Essays on the Theory of Sexuality* (1905), *Standard Ed.*, 7, 220–1. But the point had already been made in a letter to Fliess of November 14, 1897 (Freud, 1950, Letter 75).]

2   [The positive and negative Oedipus complexes were discussed by Freud in Chapter III of *The Ego and the Id* (1923), *Standard Ed.*, 19, 33.)]

3   In the well-known case of delusional jealousy reported by Ruth Mack Brunswick (1928), the direct source of the disorder was the patient's pre-Oedipus fixation (to her sister). [Cf. also Freud's own 'Case of Paranoia Running Contrary to the Psycho-Analytic Theory of the Disease' (1915).]

4   [The girl's fear of being killed by her mother is discussed further above on p. 50.]

5   [See 'The Psychogenesis of a Case of Homosexuality in a Woman' (1920), *Standard Ed.*, 18, 155n. The term had been used by Jung in his 'Versuch einer Darstellung der psychoanalytischen Theorie' (1913, 370).]

6   [For all of this see 'The Dissolution of the Oedipus Complex' (1924), *Standard Ed.*, 19, 173.]

7   It is to be anticipated that men analysts with feminist views, as well as our women analysts, will disagree with what I have said here. They will hardly fail to object that such notions spring from the 'masculinity complex' of the male and are designed to justify on theoretical grounds his innate inclination to disparage and suppress women. But this sort of psycho-analytic argumentation reminds us here, as it so often does, of Dostoevsky's famous 'knife that cuts both ways.' The opponents of those who argue in this way will on their side think it quite natural that the female sex should refuse to accept a view which appears to contradict their eagerly coveted equality with men. The use of analysis as a weapon of controversy can clearly lead to no decision.—[The Dostoevsky phrase (a simile applied to psychology) occurs in the speech for the defence in the account of Mitya's trial in Chapter X of Book XII of *The Brothers Karamazov*. Freud had quoted it already in his paper on 'Dostoevsky and Parricide' (1928). . . . The actual simile used by Freud and in the Russian original is 'a stick with two ends'.]

8   [See 'The Taboo of Virginity' (1918), *Standard Ed.*, 11, 204 ff.]

9   [Cf. ' "A Child is Being Beaten" ' (1919), *Standard Ed.*, 17, 188.]

10   [Cf. *Three Essays* (1905), *Standard Ed.*, 7, 220.]

11   [Cf. a fuller discussion of this above, p. 50.]

12   [Cf. 'A Case of Paranoia' (1915), *Standard Ed.*, 14, 267.]

13   [Cf. an instance in a footnote to Chapter III of *The Ego and the Id* (1923), *Standard Ed.*, 19, 31n.]

14   [Freud had pointed this out in the last paragraph of Section I of his paper on 'Some Character Types' (1916), *Standard Ed.*, 14, 315.]

15   [See *Totem and Taboo* (1912–13) passim, and especially the second essay.]

16   [Cf. the similar passage near the end of Chapter II of *Beyond the Pleasure Principle* (1920), *Standard Ed.*, 18, 17.]

17 [Cf. above, p. 41.]

18 [This is the last phase of a long story. When, in his early analyses, Freud's hysterical patients told him that they had been seduced by their father in childhood, he accepted these tales as the truth and regarded the traumas as the cause of their illness. It was not long before he recognized his mistake, and he admitted it in a letter to Fliess of September 21, 1897 (Freud, 1950, Letter 69). He soon grasped the important fact that these apparently false memories were wishful phantasies, which pointed the way to the existence of the Oedipus complex. An account of his contemporary reactions to these discoveries is given in Chapter III of his *Autobiographical Study* (1925), *Standard Ed.*, 20, 34–5. It was only in the present passage that Freud gave his full explanation of these ostensible memories. He discusses this whole episode at greater length in Lecture XXXIII of his *New Introductory Lectures* (1933).]

19 [Cf. the discussion of the chemistry of the sexual processes added in 1920 to the *Three Essays* (1905), *Standard Ed.*, 7, 215, where (in a footnote on the following page) the earlier version from the first edition of the book will also be found.]

20 [It should be pointed out that recent works by other writers discussed in what follows appeared *after* Freud's earlier paper on 'Some Psychical Consequences of the Anatomical Distinction between the Sexes' (1925), which covered the majority of the points in the present paper but to which he here makes no reference at all.]

21 The author's name was given when it appeared in the *Zeitschrift* as 'A. Lampl-de Groot', and I correct it here at her request.

22 [*'Intensitäten.'* Freud does not often use the word, as here, without any qualifying epithet. 'Psychische Intensität' occurs very often in *The Interpretation of Dreams* (1900), e.g. *Standard Ed.*, 4, 306–7 and 330–1. It seems, on the whole, likely that Freud is in fact using the word as an equivalent to the term 'quantity' which he preferred in the earlier 'Project' of 1895 (Freud, 1950). He seems actually to use the two terms as synonyms towards the beginning of Section (2) of his second paper on anxiety neuroses (1895), *Standard Ed.*, 3. The term 'quantity' is equated in the metapsychological paper on 'Repression' (1915) with 'instinctual energy'.]

On "Female Sexuality"

Elizabeth Janeway

Freud's ambivalence toward female sexuality has often (too often) been cited simplistically as evidence of male chauvinism. (Juliet Mitchell's comment on the 1925 paper "Some Psychical Consequences of the Anatomical Distinction Between the Sexes," which I have had the advantage of reading, is an honorable and admirable exception to this tendency as, indeed, are her remarks on Freud in her book *Woman's Estate.*) This conclusion is not only unfair to the powerful and analytic mind of Freud but, more important, it short-circuits our understanding of his work and deters us from mining it for perceptions that can be very useful in any examination of the position of women today. In my discussion of his 1931 paper "Female Sexuality," I shall call attention to some ambiguities and, indeed, some outright inaccuracies of speech; but it is for a positive purpose. I believe that these faults can reveal, as geological "faults" do for the earth, positions of strain in Freud's structure of concepts which tell us a great deal about the society in which he lived and to which we are the heirs, as we are the heirs to his thought. In raising questions of motivation and of emotive personal relationships I am not seeking to discredit Freud's enormous achievements but rather to put these in perspective, so that we can more readily call on their dynamic energy.

Let me begin by calling attention to the remarkable repetition of Freud's inaccurate reference to "the fact of castration" in the female. Little girls have not "in fact" been castrated. Not only are their bodies intact, not one of them has even suffered the penile trauma of circumcision. What, then, can Freud's consistent use of this term signify? It would be faithless to our respect for Freud's own work to pass over such a striking example of the psychopathology of everyday life. We must assume that this slip is meaningful; and indeed I believe that it leads us to the heart of Freud's dilemma about the female sex. "What do they want?" he asked and, when forced to reply, he declared that they wanted a penis.

I wish to suggest that Freud meant this symbolically, but that he did not ever (for reasons which I believe can be discerned, at least in part) find it possible to undertake an investigation of what it is that the penis symbolizes. The curious misstatement implicit in the words, "the fact of castration," seems to point this way. Was not Freud, in repeating this false phrase, calling attention (unconsciously) to a latent meaning in his theory of the castration complex which differs from its surface presentation? Indeed this meaning is so close to the surface that, time and again, it all but breaks through. No woman has been deprived of a penis; she never had one to begin with. But she *has* been deprived of something else that men enjoy: namely, autonomy, freedom, and the power to control her destiny. By insisting, falsely, on female deprivation of the male organ, Freud is pointing to an actual deprivation, and one of which he was clearly aware. In Freud's time the advantages enjoyed by the male sex over the inferior female were, of course, even greater than at present and they were also accepted, to a much larger extent, as being inevitable, inescapable. Women were evident *social* castrates, and the mutilation of their potentiality as achieving human creatures was quite analogous to the physical wound, reference to which recurs both in Freud's 1925 and 1931 papers.

The difficulties of adjusting to the feminine role are succinctly described in "Female Sexuality" in contrast to the little boy's development, which follows a straightforward path. In him, the first attachment to the mother runs head on into the fear of castration by an angry father, but the two drives then operate together in a progressive process. As the boy relinquishes his early, incestuous attachment to his mother he builds, out of respectful fear for his father, his own super-ego, which will guide him toward normal maturity. What he loses is unreal, his dream of incest. What he gains is progress on the road to the time when he will occupy his father's place in a new family, with a woman of his own.

With the girl-child things go differently. "She acknowledges the fact of castration," writes Freud, "and with it, too, the superiority of the male and her own inferiority." She does not, however, accept this in good part,

58

but rather "rebels against this unwelcome state of affairs" (p. 43).[1] Consequent on this rebellion are three possible developments; and while the normal male progression to maturity issues in a satisfactory solution, it is interesting to note that *none* of the three developments open to the girl child is really satisfactory. (As I have called attention to the significance of Freud's misstatement, "the fact of castration," I would like here to remark on the general feeling-tone of *all* Freud's writing about women: there is always a note of sadness in it, a sense that women's condition sentences them to an unfulfilled life. This is true not only of the later papers written, as Juliet Mitchell points out, at a time when Freud's natural tendency toward pessimism must have been emphasized by the pain of his cancer. As early as 1905 [in "The Case of Dora"] and 1908 [in "Civilized Sexual Morality and Modern Nervousness"] Freud describes the lives led by women as actually precarious and threatened and as abstractly painful.)

In "Female Sexuality," the first possible reaction of the girl child to her knowledge of her inferiority is given as a "general revulsion from sexuality. The little girl, frightened by the comparison with boys, grows dissatisfied with her clitoris, and gives up her phallic activity and with it her sexuality in general as well as a good part of her masculinity in other fields" (p. 43). The renunciation of the pleasure of clitoral masturbation; the lapse into passivity; these accompany the knowledge that one is inferior.

In "The Case of Dora," reporting an analysis which took place in 1900, we find these three elements occurring at the start of the girl's first neurotic illness. Freud notes "her declaration that she had been able to keep abreast with her brother up to the time of her illness, but that after that she had fallen behind him in her studies. It is as though she had been a boy up till that moment, and had then become girlish for the first time. She had in truth been a wild creature, but after the 'asthma' she became quiet and well-behaved" (*On War, Sex and Neurosis*, p. 116).[2] The "hysterical symptom" of asthma was, in Freud's view, a substitute for the masturbation which Dora gave up. (I am uncertain whether Freud himself, at the time he wrote "Female Sexuality," would have admitted Dora's experience as evidence of the onset of the positive [i.e., father-directed] Oedipus complex, for she was seven and this is rather old. However, he speaks throughout "Female Sexuality" of how late the pre-Oedipal mother-attachment can linger in girls, allowing five years as a possible "normal" age for the shift to father as love object. In any case, it is Freud himself who associates the three elements of passivity, knowledge of inferiority, and cessation of clitoral masturbation in both works.)

The second development which may overtake the girl child who discovers the physical difference which symbolizes her social difference from boys "leads her to cling with defiant self-assertiveness to her threatened masculinity. . . . The phantasy of being a man in spite of everything often persists as a formative factor over long periods" (p. 43). It can go so far as to result in "a manifest homosexual choice of object" (p. 43). I need hardly point out that to Freud and his followers such an "abnormal" choice of love object connotes a failure to reach the goal of normal maturity. The road to such maturity takes a third tack, by way of the feminine form of the Oedipus complex in which the small girl fastens her affections on her father. It is, says Freud, a "very circuitous path" (p. 43). But even when this goal is reached, the ending is not entirely happy. For, with the turning from early love for the mother to the father as object, "there is to be observed a marked lowering of the active sexual impulses and a rise of the passive ones. [And though] the active trends have been affected by frustration more strongly . . . the passive trends have not escaped disappointment either . . . and often enough when the small girl represses her previous masculinity a considerable portion of her sexual trends in general is permanently injured too" (p. 51). One is left with the depressing conclusion that the normal development to maturity in women demands not only the sacrifice of the "wrong" (active) sort of sexual impulses, but of the "right" (passive) sort as well.

There is no reason whatsoever to doubt that Freud's assessment of the disadvantages of the feminine role was entirely accurate for his time. It has been said often enough that he formed his theories, necessarily, on the basis of the clinical data that came to him, but as a general observation, this is less enlightening than it seems. What, in fact, *was* the clinical data that came to him? How did it direct his theory-formation? What did Freud take for granted as brutal and unchangeable facts of life, the ground of existence to which the Reality Principle had to adjust the overweening desires and drives of the Pleasure Principle? In "Female Sexuality," Freud is discussing the effect on the little girl of her discovery that she is not a little boy; and, in particular, how this contributes to her passage from the pre-Oedipal phase of attachment to the mother to the more adult, more realistic, positive Oedipal attachment to the father. Her

60

realization that she and her mother are alike has two effects. It convinces her that she is inferior, and it causes her to reject her formerly adored mother. Freud assumes that his readers will accept this twin assertion unquestioningly. What I am questioning is *not* Freud's assumption, for it has clearly been justified. But why did he assume it, so immediately and unreflectively?

A very simple way to reply is to look at some of the clinical data that came to Freud. Let us take the well-known case of Dora, which I cited a moment ago. I choose it for several reasons. First, it *is* well known. Second, it was an early analysis. Though not published until 1905, it was undertaken in 1900 at a time when Freud's theories had not grown toward rigidity. And third, it was of short duration, is easily followed, and turns for its problems and its solutions on just the issues under discussion: the position of women as understood by Freud in their time and context. The story of Dora is profoundly affected by the anonymity and impotence of women, beginning with her mother, and it therefore illuminates one of the axioms on which Freud founds "Female Sexuality": the catastrophic effect on the child who discovers that she is a girl.

Dora was eighteen when her father brought her to Freud and he brought her there, it appears, because Freud had earlier been able to put him on the course of a cure for a venereal disease. Dora had been suffering from depression and a series of psychosomatic illnesses, but it was the discovery of a suicide letter in her desk (though she did not in fact attempt suicide) which really alarmed her parents. She suffered a loss of consciousness after a quarrel with her father and was then induced to accept treatment. Her analysis lasted only three months, but in that time Freud uncovered much material about the girl's background. What he sets down as relevant includes not only her psychological history but a great deal of material on her social position. It is of the latter that I wish to speak, not simply because it places Dora for us, but because it placed her for Freud. It is what he took account of.

Dora was on bad terms with her mother, whom Freud never met. Nonetheless, he writes, "from the accounts given me by the girl and her father I was led to imagine her as an uncultivated woman and above all as a foolish one, who had concentrated all her interests upon domestic affairs, especially since her husband's illness and the estrangement to which it led. She presented the picture, in fact, of what might be called the 'housewife's psychosis.' She had no understanding for her children's more active interests, and was occupied all day long in cleaning the house. . . . [It is, Freud comments, a] condition, traces of which are to be found often enough in normal housewives. . . . The daughter looked down on her mother and used to criticize her mercilessly, and she had withdrawn completely from her influence" (*On War, Sex and Neurosis*, p. 40).

So much for the mother's possible therapeutic influence. Dora's older brother had served as a model when she was younger, but she had now realized that she could not follow this male pattern and her relations with him had grown distant. He tried to keep out of family disputes but, if drawn in, supported his mother. Before we come to Dora's relationship with her father, we should also note that a governess had, at one time, looked after the girl. Dora had been greatly attached to her—"until she discovered that she was being admired and fondly treated not for her own sake but for her father's [with whom the governess had fallen in love]; whereupon she obliged the governess to leave" (*On War, Sex and Neurosis*, p. 90).

We see, then, a young girl who has had no trustworthy love and support in her family except for and from her father. Her mother has betrayed her by her incapacity for real life; her beloved brother has withdrawn into the male world; the mother-substitute, the governess, has demonstrated her disloyalty. It is now her father's turn to do the same.

Dora's father was carrying on an affair with a certain Frau K. and Dora knew it. Not only did this affair disrupt her sustained Oedipal attachment to her father, but she had in earlier days been deeply fond of Frau K., serving as her confidante and sharing her bedroom when she and her father stayed with the Ks. Suddenly she finds herself caught in a repetition of the relationship with the loved and betraying governess. Frau K. does not really care about her, only about her father.

We can surmise the effect of this psychic shock. But there is another element in the situation, and that is Herr K. He has presented himself to Dora as a possible lover. She had indeed felt affection for him at one time, but under this strain she rejected him with disgust. It seems a little odd that Freud should find this reaction so unexpected for, after all, it was what a respectable young virgin should have done, and Freud understood the need for outward respectability very well. Indeed, he congratulates himself in this very study on the fact that patients have told him of how "respectable" they find his treatment (*On War, Sex and Neurosis*, p. 76).

Freud's attitude becomes even odder when we realize (and he writes himself) that Dora was being offered to Herr K. as part of a bargain, *by her own father:* "He had handed her over to this strange man in the interests of his own love affair" (*On War, Sex and Neurosis,* p. 122).

We need not deal in detail with Freud's treatment of Dora, except perhaps to note the girls's attempt to rescue herself by appealing to the conventions of the time. She demanded that her father break off his affair, and she refused to meet the Ks. I wish simply to present the situation in which a comfortably-off, marriageable girl could find herself in Freud's Vienna. Dora had indeed been attracted to Herr K., so his attentions were tempting. The one parent for whom she had had any respect and affection was tacitly urging her to yield herself to the tempter. And, of course, all her social education had informed her that if she did so, she would lose the "jewel-box" (she expressed it thus in a dream) of her virginity, the one possession of value which was hers. She had no adult protector to whom to turn. Woman after woman betrayed her, the men she loved attempted to seduce her. Under the circumstances, Dora's inner strength appears to me the most remarkable thing about her case.

This, then, is part of the clinical data on which Freud's theories were based. We can't, of course, know whether or not Dora's situation was typical, but fortunately we don't have to. Freud's theories are grounded not in what may or may not have existed in reality, but on what data came to his attention out of reality and appeared to him plausible and relevant. Clearly he did not find Dora's plight unusual. In fact, at one point he told her that her reactions were exaggerated, and he also took pains to point out her own complicitous contribution to her involvement in the K. affair as, for example, her early collaboration with her father in his efforts to visit and meet with Frau K. Before we condemn this approach as hard or cruel, we might note its realism. If Dora did in fact want to save her virtue from Herr K., she would have to do it by means of her own determination, for there was no one else to whom she could appeal. The last thing she needed was sentimental ignorance, or ambivalence, about her own purposes.

If we now come back to the 1931 paper, "Female Sexuality," with Dora's case in mind, we find that the two cast much light on one another. In 1931 Freud was emphasizing his new appreciation of the importance of the pre-Oedipal phase for the little girl, its long duration, and its possible later effects, even in the choice of a husband. A passionate father-fixation (and Dora had that; it was her father's betrayal of it which brought on her hysterical symptoms) was, Freud declared, evidence of an earlier phase of "exclusive attachment to the mother which had been equally intense and passionate" (p. 40). In addition, he remarks that the pre-Oedipal phase, and especially its long duration (and we suspect that Dora had also experienced that), were intimately related to the aetiology of hysteria; and this was his diagnosis of Dora's complaint.

More significant, however, is what Dora's story has to tell us about Freud's general theory. As we have seen, the "normal" (if necessarily unhappy) development of the girl-child involves the renunciation of her exclusive love for her mother when she understands that she is of the same sex as the mother. Freud offers a number of possible reasons for this reaction, including such physical ones as that she is bodily unfitted to play the male, complementary role with another female. But, he adds, "the strongest motive for turning away from her [is] the reproach that her mother did not give her a proper penis—that is to say, brought her into the world as a female" (p. 46).

Now if Freud were to leave it there, if the girl-child's revulsion from the mother were to be based only on her physical incapacity for sexual connection with another female, we could not argue—as long, that is as we accept the idea that Lesbianism is an unnatural, or at least a marginally satisfying, mode of sexual pleasure. But Freud does not leave it there. He speaks of this knowledge as convincing the girl-child of her *inferiority*. And here we must ask a variant of our earlier question. Why, if the mother has been so greatly loved, should the discovery that she and the girl share the same sex convince the child of being inferior? And Freud does not answer; does not tell us in so many words what his analysis of Dora makes certain he knew perfectly well: that the adored mother was, in truth, inferior all along. Instead, he puts the cart before the horse and brings forward again the old "fact of castration." "The little girl discovers her own deficiency," he writes. "When she comes to understand the general nature of this characteristic it follows that femaleness—and with it, of course, her mother—suffers a great depreciation in her eyes" (p. 46). And certainly this happens; but it could not take place unless the girl-child had already absorbed a bitter knowledge that femaleness equals inferiority. Why else should she regard the physical difference between one body and another as "a deficiency?" If she is *like* her mother, and her mother is the object of passionate attachment, how can their likeness convince the child that "this characteristic" denotes inferiority?

What I am saying is that the difference between male and female, active and passive, which Freud notes, is social as well as physical; and that the social difference, the inferiority of the female, her lack of power and freedom, slides into Freud's theorizing by the back door. The lack of a penis implies, denotes, inferiority; and when we ask why this must be, we are fobbed off with the false statement that women are castrates. That statement cannot be taken seriously *unless it is taken symbolically.* I take Freud's discoveries and illuminations very seriously indeed; and so I believe that we must admit the symbology. We must allow that women's inferiority, in Freud's mind, was somewhere understood to be the result of her lack of power; and that her lack of a penis did not simply *denote* this, but *stood* for it.

This is a statement that is either all but self-evident, or else extremely daring. Orthodox Freudians will no doubt reject it out of hand as short-sighted and reductive. They will recall Freud's rejection of the views of Alfred Adler, in whose theories the drive for superiority as an attempt to compensate for feelings of inferiority is prominent, and who was an early exponent of what Kate Millett has taught us to think of as "sexual politics." Well, like the orthodox Freudians, I find Adler too simple-minded for belief; but I think that in rejecting his overt awareness of social context, and of political urgencies (both in the psychic drama and in the world at large), Freud cut himself off from a mode of thinking that could have added a dimension to his theories. Without it (it seems to me) some of Freud's more labyrinthine formulations—and I would specifically include some of these ruminations on the female Oedipus complex—take on a pre-Copernican, epicyclical air. In addition, one must surmise that the whole post-Freudian development of analytic thought by the ego-analysts (such as Erikson) is due to Freud's hesitance to admit the reality and depth of the ego-drives toward individual and sexual power, and their use as an instrument of investigation.

One can see why he hesitated. A Jew in Hapsburg Vienna who wanted to make a psychological revolution surely had his hands full. Freud was attacking an interlinking network of shibboleths as it was. To question woman's role and her natural and proper subordination to the male, to give the weight to it which Adler did to the idea of "masculine protest" (although Adler agreed that successful protest by women was hopelessly unrealistic), would have added fuel to the fire. And indeed, we know from Freud himself that he regarded woman's proper role as that of happy wife and mother, subordinate to the male, for he told his fiancée so in no uncertain terms. And yet—

And yet Freud notes, time and again, the difficulties which the traditional role laid on women's shoulders. I have spoken of the tone of sadness that pervades his writing on women. Specifically, in " 'Civilized' Sexual Morality and Modern Nervousness," he describes the female marriage role in terms which make one's blood run cold. Here are a few excerpts:

> The 'double' code of morality conceded to the male in our society is the plainest possible admission that society itself does not believe in the possibility of adherence to those precepts [of abstinence] which it has enjoined on its members. But experience also shows that women, as the true guardians of the sexual interests of the race, are endowed with the power of sublimation only in a limited degree; [This tenet of Freud's is connected with his belief that the less powerful Oedipus complex which he posits for the girl-child necessarily provides an inadequate foundation for the development of her super-ego.] as a substitute for the sexual object the suckling child may suffice, but not the growing child, and under the disappointments of matrimony women succumb to severe, lifelong neurosis affecting the whole course of their lives. Marriage under the present cultural standard has long ceased to be a panacea for the nervous sufferings of women; even if we physicians in such cases still advise matrimony, we are nevertheless aware that a girl must be very healthy to 'stand' marriage. . . . Marital unfaithfulness would . . . be a much more probable cure for the neurosis resulting from marriage; the more strictly a wife has been brought up, the more earnestly she has submitted to the demands of civilization, the more does she fear this way of escape, and in conflict between her desires and her sense of duty she again will seek refuge in a neurosis. Nothing protects her virtue so securely as illness (*On War, Sex and Neurosis*, pp. 176–177).

Freud then goes on to discuss the effects of abstinence on men: not good. "On the whole I have not gained the impression that sexual abstinence helps to shape energetic, self-reliant men of action, nor original thinkers, bold pioneers and reformers; far more often it produces 'good weaklings' " (*On War, Sex and Neurosis*, p. 178). As for women, he continues, "The injurious results which the strict demand for abstinence before marriage produces are quite particularly apparent." The young girl has been educated to set a high premium on her chastity and kept in ignorance of what her part in marriage is to be. "The result is that when the girl is suddenly allowed by parental authority to fall in love, she cannot accomplish this mental operation. . . . Psychically she is still attached to her parents . . . and physically she shows herself frigid, which prevents her husband finding any great enjoyment in relations with her . . . so that the training that precedes marriage directly frustrates the very aim of marriage" (*On War, Sex and Neurosis*, pp. 179–180). For once, in these remarks, Freud shows himself thoroughly aware of the effect of the social context, for he declares, "I do not know whether the anaesthetic type of woman is also found outside the range of civilized education, but I consider it improbable" (*On War, Sex and Neurosis*, p. 179).

Now this is nothing less than a description of how a particular social milieu tends to produce neurosis in those most deprived, by its social ordinances, of libidinal reward. It certainly implies a recognition that woman's inferiority is socially conditioned, not simply directed by her anatomy. Indeed, it would be well to point out here that when (in his 1912 *Contribution to the Psychology of Love:* "The Most Prevalent Form of Degradation in Erotic Life") Freud made his famous statement, "Anatomy is Destiny," he was not referring to the fact that women lacked a penis or possessed a womb. Rather, he was commenting on the universal human situation that "excremental things are all too intimately and inseparably bound up with sexual things; the position of the genital organs—*inter urinas et faeces*—remains the decisive and unchangeable factor. . . . The genitals themselves have not undergone the development of the rest of the human form in the direction of beauty; they have retained their animal cast; and so even today love, too, is in essence as animal as it ever was" (*On War, Sex and Neurosis*, p. 216). This conflict between "animality" and the demands of civilization is of course a recurrent theme in Freud's writing, and the destiny which denies us complete instinctual gratification is not confined to women. In "The Case of Dora" (pp. 54–55) Freud applies it specifically to the male.

Is it possible, then, that the ambivalence of Freud's theories about female sexuality are (in part at least) the result of an effort to justify a real historical situation that existed and could not (it appeared at the time) be challenged in any useful way? It would be spurious to suggest how Freud's experience of being an inferior in his society—a Jew—related to his awareness of women's experience of being inferior in the same society. We cannot know. We do know, however, that Freud's attempts to better his position and satisfy his ambitions were never public or political. They were not ideological or collaborative, but instead contained within his professional life. In this sense they were personal and they involved his acceptance—in action, in behavior, that is; not, of course, in principle —of the restrictions placed on him. This was his cast of mind and it seems to me perfectly reasonable to find the same cast of mind at work in his behavioral acceptance of woman's traditional place. If he did not rebel against the social structure, how could he counsel them to?

His differences with Adler, I believe, reveal the same cast of mind. Freud abjured politics and direct action. Adler was a radical socialist; his wife was a friend of Trotsky's. In his theories he emphasized the influence of aggressive drives within the psyche. Freud, on the other hand, turned his ambitions from the political to the private professional area. He saw, and used, the respectability of bourgeois life as a defense behind which he could conduct and extend his own astonishing creations of thought. And yet, Ernest Jones tells us in his biography (Vol. 2, p. 131),[3] Freud took Adler's ideas very seriously. The break with Adler was bitter. It had the effect, says Jones (p. 97) of convincing Freud that he must explain and expound his technique more thoroughly. In so doing, he emphasized his differences with Adler. I shall not labor the point, but simply indicate the obvious: the break with Adler and Adler's theories of aggression and practice of politics could only reinforce Freud's disposition to ignore the existence of aggressive drives and political methods.

In addition, underlying this determination was Freud's sensitivity to his own formulation of "the reality principle" both in his own situation and in his theories of female sexuality. Freud's enormous achievements could not have been won by wish fulfillment or infantile surrender to the omnipotence of thought. And then, as a physician, his goal was therapy; and his cures had to take place in the world as it was. In that world the idea of the inevitable inferiority of women was unchallengeable.

I hope I have not developed this thesis simply as speculation. It seems clear that Freud believed that women were peculiarly disposed to neurosis. He attributes this, in "Female Sexuality," to the complicated course that their emotional attachments must follow if they are to achieve the goal of normal maturity (for Freud, normality was not something that happened, but something that was achieved, which seems to mark his idea of the starting place as one of inferiority). The very best road to maturity for a woman leaves her with diminished sexual drives and less resistance to the episodes of life which can evoke neurotic response. But I believe that we can use the earlier material I have cited to go further than this and insist on Freud's awareness of a social element molding women's lives. Certainly in his outline of Dora's position Freud was not surprised by her isolation within her own family; by her mother's incapacity to support her, or even acknowledge her daughter's danger; by Dora's expectation, based on experience, of betrayal by other women who claimed her affections—in short, by the impotence of women and the way they saw themselves, and were seen by men, as property which could be bartered about.

Not to accept this impotence (this fact of *social* castration) would have demanded a challenge to the whole social structure. Freud's appreciation of reality suggested that this was wasted effort. Even Adler, the socialist, did not imagine that the "masculine protest" felt by his female patients could change their ordained lot. "If we are to help [a girl]," he wrote (in *What Life Should Mean to You*, published here in 1931),[4] "we must find the way to reconcile her to her feminine role. . . . Girls must be educated for motherhood and educated in such a way that they like the prospect of being a mother, consider it a creative activity, and are not disappointed by their role when they face it in later life." Freud, at least, did not share Adler's optimistic view that "we" were going to accomplish this just because "we must." Rather, his sense of the world told him that "we" were not going to accomplish this very often, and that marriage-as-it-was-practiced in the world he knew was a neurosis-genetic relationship, especially for women.

Much has changed since Freud wrote. The inferiority of women, while still widely enforced, has been challenged successfully. The relationships of parents to children have also changed. For example, automatic punishment for masturbation occurs less often and less angrily; and such punishment in Freud's theories was a fundamental contribution to the child's fear of castration, and thus to the onset of the Oedipus complex. In both instances we see that the distribution of power has shifted, weakening the male figure both as husband and as father. Would not Freud have seen it too? Would he, with his strong orientation to the evidence of reality, not have assessed the changed clinical data coming to him in a different way and developed, perhaps, rather different formulations? In "Female Sexuality," Freud is telling us that a girl-child's relationship to her

69

mother is more important than he had previously thought; that the father-attachment itself is shaped on the earlier love for the mother. If, then, the mother's actual position in the world has changed—and it has —may we not suppose that the nature of her relationship with her daughter, longer-lasting than with her son, would also change? And with it, its effect on the daughter's later life? I think we are justified in doing so, and I believe that the underlying, if not quite admitted, symbology of Freud's thought, which I have attempted to investigate, actually directs us to this view.

NOTES

1 Page references not otherwise specified are to "Female Sexuality" in this volume.
2 Sander Katz, ed. *On War, Sex and Neurosis,* preface by Paul Goodman (New York: Arts and Science Press, 1947). Page references to "The Case of Dora," " 'Civilized' Sexuality and Modern Nervousness," and "The Most Prevalent Form of Degradation in Erotic Life" are taken from this collection of essays.
3 Ernest Jones, *The Life and Work of Sigmund Freud,* 3 vols. (New York: Basic Books, 1955).
4 Alfred Adler, *What Life Should Mean to You* (Boston: Little, Brown, 1931).

Mead on Freud

Femininity[1] *(1933)*

Sigmund Freud

Ladies and Gentlemen,—All the while I am preparing to talk to you I am struggling with an internal difficulty. I feel uncertain, so to speak, of the extent of my licence. It is true that in the course of fifteen years of work psycho-analysis has changed and grown richer; but, in spite of that, an introduction to psycho-analysis might have been left without alteration or supplement. It is constantly in my mind that these lectures are without a *raison d'être.* For analysts I am saying too little and nothing at all that is new; but for you I am saying too much and saying things which you are not equipped to understand and which are not in your province. I have looked around for excuses and I have tried to justify each separate lecture on different grounds. The first one, on the theory of dreams, was sup-posed to put you back again at one blow into the analytic atmosphere and to show you how durable our views have turned out to be. I was led on to the second one, which followed the paths from dreams to what is called occultism, by the opportunity of speaking my mind without constraint on a department of work in which prejudiced expectations are fighting to-day against passionate resistances, and I could hope that your judgement, educated to tolerance on the example of psycho-analysis, would not refuse to accompany me on the excursion. The third lecture, on the dissection of the personality, certainly made the hardest demands upon you with its unfamiliar subject-matter; but it was impossible for me to keep this first beginning of an ego-psychology back from you, and if we had possessed it fifteen years ago I should have had to mention it to you then. My last lecture, finally, which you were probably able to follow only by great exertions, brought forward necessary corrections—fresh attempts at solving the most important conundrums; and my introduction would have been leading you astray if I had been silent about them. As you see, when one starts making excuses it turns out in the end that it was all inevitable, all the work of destiny. I submit to it, and I beg you to do the same.

To-day's lecture, too, should have no place in an introduction; but it may serve to give you an example of a detailed piece of analytic work, and I can say two things to recommend it. It brings forward nothing but observed facts, almost without any speculative additions, and it deals with a subject which has a claim on your interest second almost to no other. Throughout history people have knocked their heads against the riddle of the nature of femininity—

> Häupter in Hieroglyphenmützen,
> Häupter in Turban und schwarzem Barett,
> Perückenhäupter und tausend andre
> Arme, schwitzende Menschenhäupter. . . .[2]

Nor will *you* have escaped worrying over this problem—those of you who are men; to those of you who are women this will not apply—you are yourselves the problem. When you meet a human being, the first distinction you make is 'male or female?' and you are accustomed to make the distinction with unhesitating certainty. Anatomical science shares your certainty at one point and not much further. The male sexual product, the spermatozoon, and its vehicle are male; the ovum and the organism that harbours it are female. In both sexes organs have been formed which serve exclusively for the sexual functions; they were probably developed from the same [innate] disposition into two different forms. Besides this, in both sexes the other organs, the bodily shapes and tissues show the influence of the individual's sex, but this is inconstant and its amount variable; these are what are known as the secondary sexual characters. Science next tells you something that runs counter to your expectations and is probably calculated to confuse your feelings. It draws your attention to the fact that portions of the male sexual apparatus also appear in women's bodies, though in an atrophied state, and, vice versa in the alternative case. It regards their occurrence as indications of *bisexuality*,[3] as though an individual is not a man or a woman but always both —merely a certain amount more the one than the other. You will then

74

be asked to make yourselves familiar with the idea that the proportion in which masculine and feminine are mixed in an individual is subject to quite considerable fluctuations. Since, however, apart from the very rarest cases, only one kind of sexual product—ova or semen—is nevertheless present in one person, you are bound to have doubts as to the decisive significance of those elements and must conclude that what constitutes masculinity or femininity is an unknown characteristic which anatomy cannot lay hold of.

Can psychology do so perhaps? We are accustomed to employ 'masculine' and 'feminine' as mental qualities as well, and have in the same way transferred the notion of bisexuality to mental life. Thus we speak of a person, whether male or female, as behaving in a masculine way in one connection and in a feminine way in another. But you will soon perceive that this is only giving way to anatomy or to convention. You cannot give the concepts of 'masculine' and 'feminine' *any* new connotation. The distinction is not a psychological one; when you say 'masculine', you usually mean 'active', and when you say 'feminine', you usually mean 'passive'. Now it is true that a relation of the kind exists. The male sex-cell is actively mobile and searches out the female one, and the latter, the ovum, is immobile and waits passively. This behaviour of the elementary sexual organisms is indeed a model for the conduct of sexual individuals during intercourse. The male pursues the female for the purpose of sexual union, seizes hold of her and penetrates into her. But by this you have precisely reduced the characteristic of masculinity to the factor of aggressiveness so far as psychology is concerned. You may well doubt whether you have gained any real advantage from this when you reflect that in some classes of animals the females are the stronger and more aggressive and the male is active only in the single act of sexual union. This is so, for instance, with the spiders. Even the functions of rearing and caring for the young, which strike us as feminine *par excellence*, are not invariably attached to the female sex in animals. In quite high species we find that the sexes share the task of caring for the young between them or even that the male alone devotes himself to it. Even in the sphere of human sexual life you soon see how inadequate it is to make masculine behaviour coincide with activity and feminine with passivity. A mother is active in every sense towards her child; the act of lactation itself may equally be described as the mother suckling the baby or as her being sucked by it. The further you go from the narrow sexual sphere the more obvious will the 'error of superimposition'[4] become. Women can display great activity in various directions, men are not able to live in company with their own kind unless they develop a large amount of passive adaptability. If you now tell me that these facts go to prove precisely that both men and women are bisexual in the psychological sense, I shall conclude that you have decided in your own minds to make 'active' coincide with 'masculine' and 'passive' with 'feminine'. But I advise you against it. It seems to me to serve no useful purpose and adds nothing to our knowledge.[5]

One might consider characterizing femininity psychologically as giving preference to passive aims. This is not, of course, the same thing as passivity; to achieve a passive aim may call for a large amount of activity. It is perhaps the case that in a woman, on the basis of her share in the sexual function, a preference for passive behaviour and passive aims is carried over into her life to a greater or lesser extent, in proportion to the limits, restricted or far-reaching, within which her sexual life thus serves as a model. But we must beware in this of underestimating the influence of social customs, which similarly force women into passive situations. All this is still far from being cleared up. There is one particularly constant relation between femininity and instinctual life which we do not want to overlook. The suppression of women's aggressiveness which is prescribed for them constitutionally and imposed on them socially favours the development of powerful masochistic impulses, which succeed, as we know, in binding erotically the destructive trends which have been diverted inwards. Thus masochism, as people say, is truly feminine. But if, as happens so often, you meet with masochism in men, what is left to you but to say that these men exhibit very plain feminine traits?

And now you are already prepared to hear that psychology too is unable to solve the riddle of femininity. The explanation must no doubt come from elsewhere, and cannot come till we have learnt how in general the differentiation of living organisms into two sexes came about. We know nothing about it, yet the existence of two sexes is a most striking characteristic of organic life which distinguishes it sharply from inanimate nature. However, we find enough to study in those human individuals who, through the possession of female genitals, are characterized as manifestly or predominantly feminine. In conformity with its peculiar nature, psycho-analysis does not try to describe what a woman is—that

76

would be a task it could scarcely perform—but sets about enquiring how she comes into being, how a woman develops out of a child with a bisexual disposition. In recent times we have begun to learn a little about this, thanks to the circumstance that several of our excellent women colleagues in analysis have begun to work at the question. The discussion of this has gained special attractiveness from the distinction between the sexes. For the ladies, whenever some comparison seemed to turn out unfavourable to their sex, were able to utter a suspicion that we, the male analysts, had been unable to overcome certain deeply-rooted prejudices against what was feminine, and that this was being paid for in the partiality of our researches. We, on the other hand, standing on the ground of bisexuality, had no difficulty in avoiding impoliteness. We had only to say: 'This doesn't apply to *you*. You're the exception; on this point you're more masculine than feminine.'

We approach the investigation of the sexual development of women with two expectations. The first is that here once more the constitution will not adapt itself to its function without a struggle. The second is that the decisive turning-points will already have been prepared for or completed before puberty. Both expectations are promptly confirmed. Furthermore, a comparison with what happens with boys tells us that the development of a little girl into a normal woman is more difficult and more complicated, since it includes two extra tasks, to which there is nothing corresponding in the development of a man. Let us follow the parallel lines from their beginning. Undoubtedly the material is different to start with in boys and girls: it did not need psycho-analysis to establish that. The difference in the structure of the genitals is accompanied by other bodily differences which are too well known to call for mention. Differences emerge too in the instinctual disposition which give a glimpse of the later nature of women. A little girl is as a rule less aggressive, defiant and self-sufficient; she seems to have a greater need for being shown affection and on that account to be more dependent and pliant. It is probably only as a result of this pliancy that she can be taught more easily and quicker to control her excretions: urine and faeces are the first gifts that children make to those who look after them, and controlling them is the first concession to which the instinctual life of children can be induced. One gets an impression, too, that little girls are more intelligent and livelier than boys of the same age; they go out more to meet the external world and at the same time form stronger object-cathexes. I cannot say whether this lead in development has been confirmed by exact observations, but in any case there is no question that girls cannot be described as intellectually backward. These sexual differences are not, however, of great consequence: they can be outweighed by individual variations. For our immediate purposes they can be disregarded.

Both sexes seem to pass through the early phases of libidinal development in the same manner. It might have been expected that in girls there would already have been some lag in aggressiveness in the sadistic-anal phase, but such is not the case. Analysis of children's play has shown our women analysts that the aggressive impulses of little girls leave nothing to be desired in the way of abundance and violence. With their entry into the phallic phase the differences between the sexes are completely eclipsed by their agreements. We are now obliged to recognize that the little girl is a little man. In boys, as we know, this phase is marked by the fact that they have learnt how to derive pleasurable sensations from their small penis and connect its excited state with their ideas of sexual intercourse. Little girls do the same thing with their still smaller clitoris. It seems that with them all their masturbatory acts are carried out on this penis-equivalent, and that the truly feminine vagina is still undiscovered by both sexes. It is true that there are a few isolated reports of early vaginal sensations as well, but it could not be easy to distinguish these from sensations in the anus or vestibulum; in any case they cannot play a great part. We are entitled to keep to our view that in the phallic phase of girls the clitoris is the leading erotogenic zone. But it is not, of course, going to remain so. With the change to femininity the clitoris should wholly or in part hand over its sensitivity, and at the same time its importance, to the vagina. This would be one of the two tasks which a woman has to perform in the course of her development, whereas the more fortunate man has only to continue at the time of his sexual maturity the activity that he has previously carried out at the period of the early efflorescence of his sexuality.

We shall return to the part played by the clitoris; let us now turn to the second task with which a girl's development is burdened. A boy's mother is the first object of his love, and she remains so too during the formation of his Oedipus complex and, in essence, all through his life. For a girl too her first object must be her mother (and the figures of wet-nurses and foster-mothers that merge into her). The first object-cathexes occur in attachment to the satisfaction of the major and simple vital needs,[6] and the circumstances of the care of children are the same for both sexes. But in the Oedipus situation the girl's father has become her love-object, and we expect that in the normal course of development she will find her way from this paternal object to her final choice of an object. In the course of time, therefore, a girl has to change her erotogenic zone and her object —both of which a boy retains. The question then arises of how this happens: in particular, how does a girl pass from her mother to an attachment to her father? or, in other words, how does she pass from her masculine phase to the feminine one to which she is biologically destined?

It would be a solution of ideal simplicity if we could suppose that from a particular age onwards the elementary influence of the mutual attraction between the sexes makes itself felt and impels the small woman towards men, while the same law allows the boy to continue with his mother. We might suppose in addition that in this the children are following the pointer given them by the sexual preference of their parents. But we are not going to find things so easy; we scarcely know whether we are to believe seriously in the power of which poets talk so much and with such enthusiasm but which cannot be further dissected analytically. We have found an answer of quite another sort by means of laborious investigations, the material for which at least was easy to arrive at. For you must know that the number of women who remain till a late age tenderly dependent on a paternal object, or indeed on their real father, is very great. We have established some surprising facts about these women with an intense attachment of long duration to their father. We knew, of course, that there had been a preliminary stage of attachment to the mother, but we did not know that it could be so rich in content and so long-lasting, and could leave behind so many opportunities for fixations and dispositions. During this time the girl's father is only a troublesome rival; in some cases the attachment to her mother lasts beyond the fourth year of life. Almost everything that we find later in her relation to her father was already present in this earlier attachment and has been transferred subsequently on to her father. In short, we get an impression that we cannot understand women unless we appreciate this phase of their pre-Oedipus attachment to their mother.

We shall be glad, then, to know the nature of the girl's libidinal relations to her mother. The answer is that they are of very many different kinds. Since they persist through all three phases of infantile sexuality, they also take on the characteristics of the different phases and express themselves by oral, sadistic-anal and phallic wishes. These wishes represent active as well as passive impulses; if we relate them to the differentiation of the sexes which is to appear later—though we should avoid doing so as far as possible—we may call them masculine and feminine. Besides this, they are completely ambivalent, both affectionate and of a hostile and aggressive nature. The latter often only come to light after being changed into anxiety ideas. It is not always easy to point to a formulation of these early sexual wishes; what is most clearly expressed is a wish to get the mother with child and the corresponding wish to bear her a child —both belonging to the phallic period and sufficiently surprising, but established beyond doubt by analytic observation. The attractiveness of these investigations lies in the surprising detailed findings which they bring us. Thus, for instance, we discover the fear of being murdered or poisoned, which may later form the core of a paranoic illness, already present in this pre-Oedipus period, in relation to the mother. Or another case: you will recall an interesting episode in the history of analytic research which caused me many distressing hours. In the period in which the main interest was directed to discovering infantile sexual traumas, almost all my women patients told me that they had been seduced by their father. I was driven to recognize in the end that these reports were untrue and so came to understand that hysterical symptoms are derived from phantasies and not from real occurrences. It was only later that I was able to recognize in this phantasy of being seduced by the father the expression of the typical Oedipus complex in women. And now we find the phantasy of seduction once more in the pre-Oedipus prehistory of girls; but the seducer is regularly the mother. Here, however, the phantasy touches the ground of reality, for it was really the mother who by her activities over the child's bodily hygiene inevitably stimulated, and perhaps even roused for the first time, pleasurable sensations in her genitals.[7]

I have no doubt you are ready to suspect that this portrayal of the abundance and strength of a little girl's sexual relations with her mother is very much overdrawn. After all, one has opportunities of seeing little girls and notices nothing of the sort. But the objection is not to the point. Enough can be seen in the children if one knows how to look. And besides, you should consider how little of its sexual wishes a child can bring to preconscious expression or communicate at all. Accordingly we are only within our rights if we study the residues and consequences of this emotional world in retrospect, in people in whom these processes of development had attained a specially clear and even excessive degree of expansion. Pathology has always done us the service of making discernible by isolation and exaggeration conditions which would remain concealed in a normal state. And since our investigations have been carried out on people who were by no means seriously abnormal, I think we should regard their outcome as deserving belief.

We will now turn our interest on to the single question of what it is that brings this powerful attachment of the girl to her mother to an end. This, as we know, is its usual fate: it is destined to make room for an attachment to her father. Here we come upon a fact which is a pointer to our further advance. This step in development does not involve only a simple change of object. The turning away from the mother is accompanied by hostility; the attachment to the mother ends in hate. A hate of that kind may become very striking and last all through life; it may be carefully overcompensated later on; as a rule one part of it is overcome while another part persists. Events of later years naturally influence this greatly. We will restrict ourselves, however, to studying it at the time at which the girl turns to her father and to enquiring into the motives for it. We are then given a long list of accusations and grievances against the mother which are supposed to justify the child's hostile feelings; they are of varying validity which we shall not fail to examine. A number of them are obvious rationalizations and the true sources of enmity remain to be found. I hope you will be interested if on this occasion I take you through all the details of a psycho-analytic investigation.

The reproach against the mother which goes back furthest is that she gave the child too little milk—which is construed against her as lack of love. Now there is some justification for this reproach in our families. Mothers often have insufficient nourishment to give their children and are content to suckle them for a few months, for half or three-quarters of a year. Among primitive peoples children are fed at their mother's breast for two or three years. The figure of the wet-nurse who suckles the child is as a rule merged into the mother; when this has not happened, the reproach is turned into another one—that the nurse, who fed the child so willingly, was sent away by the mother too early. But whatever the true state of affairs may have been, it is impossible that the child's reproach can be justified as often as it is met with. It seems, rather, that the child's avidity for its earliest nourishment is altogether insatiable, that it never gets over the pain of losing its mother's breast. I should not be surprised if the analysis of a primitive child, who could still suck at its mother's breast when it was already able to run about and talk, were to bring the same reproach to light. The fear of being poisoned is also probably connected with the withdrawal of the breast. Poison is nourishment that makes one ill. Perhaps children trace back their early illnesses too to this frustration. A fair amount of intellectual education is a prerequisite for believing in chance; primitive people and uneducated ones, and no doubt children as well, are able to assign a ground for everything that happens. Perhaps originally it was a reason on animistic lines. Even to-day in some strata of our population no one can die without having been killed by someone else—preferably by the doctor. And the regular reaction of a neurotic to the death of someone closely connected with him is to put the blame on himself for having caused the death.

The next accusation against the child's mother flares up when the next baby appears in the nursery. If possible the connection with oral frustration is preserved: the mother could not or would not give the child any more milk because she needed the nourishment for the new arrival. In cases in which the two children are so close in age that lactation is prejudiced by the second pregnancy, this reproach acquires a real basis, and it is a remarkable fact that a child, even with an age difference of only 11 months, is not too young to take notice of what is happening. But what the child grudges the unwanted intruder and rival is not only the suckling but all the other signs of maternal care. It feels that it has been dethroned, despoiled, prejudiced in its rights; it casts a jealous hatred upon the new baby and develops a grievance against the faithless mother which often finds expression in a disagreeable change in its behaviour. It becomes 'naughty', perhaps, irritable and disobedient and goes back on the advances it has made towards controlling its excretions. All of this has been very long familiar and is accepted as self-evident; but we rarely form a correct idea of the strength of these jealous impulses, of the tenacity with which they persist and of the magnitude of their influence on later development. Especially as this jealousy is constantly receiving fresh nourishment in the later years of childhood and the whole shock is repeated with the birth of each new brother or sister. Nor does it make much difference if the child happens to remain the mother's preferred favourite. A child's demands for love are immoderate, they make exclusive claims and tolerate no sharing.

An abundant source of a child's hostility to its mother is provided by its multifarious sexual wishes, which alter according to the phase of the libido and which cannot for the most part be satisfied. The strongest of these frustrations occur at the phallic period, if the mother forbids pleasurable activity with the genitals—often with severe threats and every sign of displeasure—activity to which, after all, she herself had introduced the child. One would think these were reasons enough to account for a girl's turning away from her mother. One would judge, if so, that the estrangement follows inevitably from the nature of children's sexuality, from the immoderate character of their demand for love and the impossibility of fulfilling their sexual wishes. It might be thought indeed that this first love-relation of the child's is doomed to dissolution for the very reason that it is the first, for these early object-cathexes are regularly ambivalent to a high degree. A powerful tendency to aggressiveness is always present beside a powerful love, and the more passionately a child loves its object the more sensitive does it become to disappointments and frustrations from that object; and in the end the love must succumb to the accumulated hostility. Or the idea that there is an original ambivalence such as this in erotic cathexes may be rejected, and it may be pointed out that it is the special nature of the mother-child relation that leads, with equal inevitability, to the destruction of the child's love; for even the mildest upbringing cannot avoid using compulsion and introducing restrictions, and any such intervention in the child's liberty must provoke as a reaction an inclination to rebelliousness and aggressiveness. A discussion of these possibilities might, I think, be most interesting; but an objection suddenly emerges which forces our interest in another direction. All these factors —the slights, the disappointments in love, the jealousy, the seduction followed by prohibition—are, after all, also in operation in the relation of a *boy* to his mother and are yet unable to alienate him from the maternal object. Unless we can find something that is specific for girls and is not present or not in the same way present in boys, we shall not have explained the termination of the attachment of girls to their mother.

I believe we have found this specific factor, and indeed where we expected to find it, even though in a surprising form. Where we expected to find it, I say, for it lies in the castration complex. After all, the anatomical distinction [between the sexes] must express itself in psychical consequences. It was, however, a surprise to learn from analyses that girls hold their mother responsible for their lack of a penis and do not forgive her for their being thus put at a disadvantage.

As you hear, then, we ascribe a castration complex to women as well. And for good reasons, though its content cannot be the same as with boys. In the latter the castration complex arises after they have learnt from the sight of the female genitals that the organ which they value so highly need not necessarily accompany the body. At this the boy recalls to mind the threats he brought on himself by his doings with that organ, he begins to give credence to them and falls under the influence of fear of castration, which will be the most powerful motive force in his subsequent development. The castration complex of girls is also started by the sight of the genitals of the other sex. They at once notice the difference and, it must be admitted, its significance too. They feel seriously wronged, often declare that they want to 'have something like it too', and fall a victim to 'envy for the penis', which will leave ineradicable traces on their development and the formation of their character and which will not be surmounted in even the most favourable cases without a severe expenditure of psychical energy. The girl's recognition of the fact of her being without a penis does not by any means imply that she submits to the fact easily. On the contrary, she continues to hold on for a long time to the wish to get something like it herself and she believes in that possibility for improbably long years; and analysis can show that, at a period when knowledge of reality has long since rejected the fulfilment of the wish as unattainable, it persists in the unconscious and retains a considerable cathexis of energy. The wish to get the longed-for penis eventually in spite of everything may contribute to the motives that drive a mature woman to analysis, and what she may reasonably expect from analysis—a capacity, for instance, to carry on an intellectual profession —may often be recognized as a sublimated modification of this repressed wish.

One cannot very well doubt the importance of envy for the penis. You may take it as an instance of male injustice if I assert that envy and jealousy play an even greater part in the mental life of women than of men. It is not that I think these characteristics are absent in men or that I think they have no other roots in women than envy for the penis; but I am inclined to attribute their greater amount in women to this latter influence. Some analysts, however, have shown an inclination to depreciate the importance of this first instalment of penis-envy in the phallic phase. They are of opinion that what we find of this attitude in women is in the main a secondary structure which has come about on the occasion of later conflicts by regression to this early infantile impulse. This, however, is a general problem of depth psychology. In many pathological —or even unusual—instinctual attitudes (for instance, in all sexual perversions) the question arises of how much of their strength is to be attributed to early infantile fixations and how much to the influence of later experiences and developments. In such cases it is almost always a matter of complemental series such as we put forward in our discussion of the aetiology of the neuroses.[8] Both factors play a part in varying amounts in the causation; a less on the one side is balanced by a more on the other. The infantile factor sets the pattern in all cases but does not always determine the issue, though it often does. Precisely in the case of penis-envy I should argue decidedly in favour of the preponderance of the infantile factor.

The discovery that she is castrated is a turning-point in a girl's growth. Three possible lines of development start from it: one leads to sexual inhibition or to neurosis, the second to change of character in the sense of a masculinity complex, the third, finally, to normal femininity. We have learnt a fair amount, though not everything, about all three.

The essential content of the first is as follows: the little girl has hitherto lived in a masculine way, has been able to get pleasure by the excitation of her clitoris and has brought this activity into relation with her sexual wishes directed towards her mother, which are often active ones; now, owing to the influence of her penis-envy, she loses her enjoyment in her phallic sexuality. Her self-love is mortified by the comparison with the boy's far superior equipment and in consequence she renounces her masturbatory satisfaction from her clitoris, repudiates her love for her mother and at the same time not infrequently represses a good part of her sexual trends in general. No doubt her turning away from her mother does not occur all at once, for to begin with the girl regards her castration as an individual misfortune, and only gradually extends it to other females and finally to her mother as well. Her love was directed to her *phallic* mother; with the discovery that her mother is castrated it becomes possible to drop her as an object, so that the motives for hostility, which have long been accumulating, gain the upper hand. This means, therefore, that as a result of the discovery of women's lack of a penis they are

85

debased in value for girls just as they are for boys and later perhaps for men.

You all know the immense aetiological importance attributed by our neurotic patients to their masturbation. They make it responsible for all their troubles and we have the greatest difficulty in persuading them that they are mistaken. In fact, however, we ought to admit to them that they are right, for masturbation is the executive agent of infantile sexuality, from the faulty development of which they are indeed suffering. But what neurotics mostly blame is the masturbation of the period of puberty; they have mostly forgotten that of early infancy, which is what is really in question. I wish I might have an opportunity some time of explaining to you at length how important all the factual details of early masturbation become for the individual's subsequent neurosis or character: whether or not it was discovered, how the parents struggled against it or permitted it, or whether he succeeded in suppressing it himself. All of this leaves permanent traces on his development. But I am on the whole glad that I need not do this. It would be a hard and tedious task and at the end of it you would put me in an embarrassing situation by quite certainly asking me to give you some practical advice as to how a parent or educator should deal with the masturbation of small children.[9] From the development of girls, which is what my present lecture is concerned with, I can give you the example of a child herself trying to get free from masturbating. She does not always succeed in this. If envy for the penis has provoked a powerful impulse against clitoridal masturbation but this nevertheless refuses to give way, a violent struggle for liberation ensues in which the girl, as it were, herself takes over the role of her deposed mother and gives expression to her entire dissatisfaction with her inferior clitoris in her efforts against obtaining satisfaction from it. Many years later, when her masturbatory activity has long since been suppressed, an interest still persists which we must interpret as a defence against a temptation that is still dreaded. It manifests inself in the emergence of sympathy for those to whom similar difficulties are attributed, it plays a part as a motive in contracting a marriage and, indeed, it may determine the choice of a husband or lover. Disposing of early infantile masturbation is truly no easy or indifferent business.

Along with the abandonment of clitoridal masturbation a certain amount of activity is renounced. Passivity now has the upper hand, and the girl's turning to her father is accomplished principally with the help of passive instinctual impulses. You can see that a wave of development like this, which clears the phallic activity out of the way, smooths the ground for femininity. If too much is not lost in the course of it through repression, this femininity may turn out to be normal. The wish with which the girl turns to her father is no doubt originally the wish for the penis which her mother has refused her and which she now expects from her father. The feminine situation is only established, however, if the wish for a penis is replaced by one for a baby, if, that is, a baby takes the place of a penis in accordance with an ancient symbolic equivalence. It has not escaped us that the girl has wished for a baby earlier, in the undisturbed phallic phase: that, of course, was the meaning of her playing with dolls. But that play was not in fact an expression of her femininity; it served as an identification with her mother with the intention of substituting activity for passivity. *She* was playing the part of her mother and the doll was herself: now she could do with the baby everything that her mother used to do with her. Not until the emergence of the wish for a penis does the doll-baby become a baby from the girl's father, and thereafter the aim of the most powerful feminine wish. Her happiness is great if later on this wish for a baby finds fulfilment in reality, and quite especially so if the baby is a little boy who brings the longed-for penis with him.[10] Often enough in her combined picture of 'a baby from her father' the emphasis is laid on the baby and her father left unstressed. In this way the ancient masculine wish for the possession of a penis is still faintly visible through the femininity now achieved. But perhaps we ought rather to recognize this wish for a penis as being *par excellence* a feminine one.

With the transference of the wish for a penis-baby on to her father, the girl has entered the situation of the Oedipus complex. Her hostility to her mother, which did not need to be freshly created, is now greatly intensified, for she becomes the girl's rival, who receives from her father everything that she desires from him. For a long time the girl's Oedipus complex concealed her pre-Oedipus attachment to her mother from our view, though it is nevertheless so important and leaves such lasting fixations behind it. For girls the Oedipus situation is the outcome of a long and difficult development; it is a kind of preliminary solution, a position of rest which is not soon abandoned, especially as the beginning of the latency period is not far distant. And we are now struck by a difference between the two sexes, which is probably momentous, in regard to the relation of the Oedipus complex to the castration complex. In a boy the

Oedipus complex, in which he desires his mother and would like to get rid of his father as being a rival, develops naturally from the phase of his phallic sexuality. The threat of castration compels him, however, to give up that attitude. Under the impression of the danger of losing his penis, the Oedipus complex is abandoned, repressed and, in the most normal cases, entirely destroyed, and a severe super-ego is set up as its heir. What happens with a girl is almost the opposite. The castration complex prepares for the Oedipus complex instead of destroying it; the girl is driven out of her attachment to her mother through the influence of her envy for the penis and she enters the Oedipus situation as though into a haven of refuge. In the absence of fear of castration the chief motive is lacking which leads boys to surmount the Oedipus complex. Girls remain in it for an indeterminate length of time; they demolish it late and, even so, incompletely. In these circumstances the formation of the super-ego must suffer; it cannot attain the strength and independence which give it its cultural significance, and feminists are not pleased when we point out to them the effects of this factor upon the average feminine character.

To go back a little. We mentioned [p. 85] as the second possible reaction to the discovery of female castration the development of a powerful masculinity complex. By this we mean that the girl refuses, as it were, to recognize the unwelcome fact and, defiantly rebellious, even exaggerates her previous masculinity, clings to her clitoridal activity and takes refuge in an identification with her phallic mother or her father. What can it be that decides in favour of this outcome? We can only suppose that it is a constitutional factor, a greater amount of activity, such as is ordinarily characteristic of a male. However that may be, the essence of this process is that at this point in development the wave of passivity is avoided which opens the way to the turn towards femininity. The extreme achievement of such a masculinity complex would appear to be the influencing of the choice of an object in the sense of manifest homosexuality. Analytic experience teaches us, to be sure, that female homosexuality is seldom or never a direct continuation of infantile masculinity. Even for a girl of this kind it seems necessary that she should take her father as an object for some time and enter the Oedipus situation. But afterwards, as a result of her inevitable disappointments from her father, she is driven to regress into her early masculinity complex. The significance of these disappointments must not be exaggerated; a girl who is destined to become feminine is not spared them, though they do not have the same effect. The predominance of the constitutional factor seems indisputable; but the two phases in the development of female homosexuality are well mirrored in the practices of homosexuals, who play the parts of mother and baby with each other as often and as clearly as those of husband and wife.

What I have been telling you here may be described as the prehistory of women. It is a product of the very last few years and may have been of interest to you as an example of detailed analytic work. Since its subject is woman, I will venture on this occasion to mention by name a few of the women who have made valuable contributions to this investigation. Dr. Ruth Mack Brunswick [1928] was the first to describe a case of neurosis which went back to a fixation in the pre-Oedipus stage and had never reached the Oedipus situation at all. The case took the form of jealous paranoia and proved accessible to therapy. Dr. Jeanne Lampl-de Groot [1927] has established the incredible phallic activity of girls towards their mother by some assured observations, and Dr. Helene Deutsch [1932] has shown that the erotic actions of homosexual women reproduce the relations between mother and baby.

It is not my intention to pursue the further behaviour of femininity through puberty to the period of maturity. Our knowledge, moreover, would be insufficient for the purpose. But I will bring a few features together in what follows. Taking its prehistory as a starting-point, I will only emphasize here that the development of femininity remains exposed to disturbance by the residual phenomena of the early masculine period. Regressions to the fixations of the pre-Oedipus phases very frequently occur; in the course of some women's lives there is a repeated alternation between periods in which masculinity or femininity gains the upper hand. Some portion of what we men call 'the enigma of women' may perhaps be derived from this expression of bisexuality in women's lives. But another question seems to have become ripe for judgement in the course of these researches. We have called the motive force of sexual life 'the libido'. Sexual life is dominated by the polarity of masculine–feminine; thus the notion suggests itself of considering the relation of the libido to this antithesis. It would not be surprising if it were to turn out that each sexuality had its own special libido appropriated to it, so that one sort of libido would pursue the aims of a masculine sexual life and another sort those of a feminine one. But nothing of the kind is true. There is only one libido, which serves both the masculine and the feminine sexual functions. To it itself we cannot assign any sex; if, following the conventional equation of activity and masculinity, we are inclined to describe it as masculine, we must not forget that it also covers trends with a passive aim. Nevertheless the juxtaposition 'feminine libido' is without any justification. Furthermore, it is our impression that more constraint has been applied to the libido when it is pressed into the service of the feminine function, and that—to speak teleologically—Nature takes less careful account of its [that function's] demands than in the case of masculinity. And the reason for this may lie—thinking once again teleologically—in the fact that the accomplishment of the aim of biology has been entrusted to the aggressiveness of men and has been made to some extent independent of women's consent.

The sexual frigidity of women, the frequency of which appears to confirm this disregard, is a phenomenon that is still insufficiently understood. Sometimes it is psychogenic and in that case accessible to influence; but in other cases it suggests the hypothesis of its being constitutionally determined and even of there being a contributory anatomical factor.

I have promised to tell you of a few more psychical peculiarities of mature femininity, as we come across them in analytic observation. We do not lay claim to more than an average validity for these assertions; nor is it always easy to distinguish what should be ascribed to the influence of the sexual function and what to social breeding. Thus, we attribute a larger amount of narcissism to femininity, which also affects women's choice of object, so that to be loved is a stronger need for them than to love. The effect of penis-envy has a share, further, in the physical vanity of women, since they are bound to value their charms more highly as a late compensation for their original sexual inferiority.[11] Shame, which is considered to be a feminine characteristic *par excellence* but is far more a matter of convention than might be supposed, has as its purpose, we believe, concealment of genital deficiency. We are not forgetting that at a later time shame takes on other functions. It seems that women have made few contributions to the discoveries and inventions in the history of civilization; there is, however, one technique which they may have invented—that of plaiting and weaving. If that is so, we should be tempted to guess the unconscious motive for the achievement. Nature herself would seem to have given the model which this achievement imitates by causing the growth at maturity of the pubic hair that conceals the genitals. The step that remained to be taken lay in making the threads adhere to one another, while on the body they stick into the skin and are only matted together. If you reject this idea as fantastic and regard my belief in the influence of lack of a penis on the configuration of femininity as an *idée fixe*, I am of course defenceless.

The determinants of women's choice of an object are often made unrecognizable by social conditions. Where the choice is able to show itself freely, it is often made in accordance with the narcissistic ideal of the man whom the girl had wished to become. If the girl has remained in her attachment to her father—that is, in the Oedipus complex—her choice is made according to the paternal type. Since, when she turned from her mother to her father, the hostility of her ambivalent relation remained with her mother, a choice of this kind should guarantee a happy marriage. But very often the outcome is of a kind that presents a general threat to such a settlement of the conflict due to ambivalence. The hostility that has been left behind follows in the train of the positive attachment and spreads over on to the new object. The woman's husband, who to begin with inherited from her father, becomes after a time her mother's heir as well. So it may easily happen that the second half of a woman's life may be filled by the struggle against her husband, just as the shorter first half was filled by her rebellion against her mother. When this reaction has been lived through, a second marriage may easily turn out very much more satisfying.[12] Another alteration in a woman's nature, for which lovers are unprepared, may occur in a marriage after the first child is born. Under the influence of a woman's becoming a mother herself, an identification with her own mother may be revived, against which she had striven up till the time of her marriage, and this may attract all the available libido to itself, so that the compulsion to repeat reproduces an unhappy marriage between her parents. The difference in a mother's reaction to the birth of a son or a daughter shows that the old factor of lack of a penis has even now not lost its strength. A mother is only brought unlimited satisfaction by her relation to a son; this is altogether the most perfect, the most free from ambivalence of all human relationships.[13] A mother can transfer to her son the ambition which she has been obliged to suppress in herself, and she can expect from him the satisfaction of all that has been left over in her of her masculinity complex. Even a marriage is not made secure until the wife has succeeded in making her husband her child as well and in acting as a mother to him.

A woman's identification with her mother allows us to distinguish two strata: the pre-Oedipus one which rests on her affectionate attachment to her mother and takes her as a model, and the later one from the Oedipus complex which seeks to get rid of her mother and take her place with her father. We are no doubt justified in saying that much of both of them is left over for the future and that neither of them is adequately surmounted in the course of development. But the phase of the affectionate pre-Oedipus attachment is the decisive one for a woman's future: during it preparations are made for the acquisition of the characteristics with which she will later fulfil her role in the sexual function and perform her invaluable social tasks. It is in this identification too that she acquires her attractiveness to a man, whose Oedipus attachment to his mother it kindles into passion. How often it happens, however, that it is only his son who obtains what he himself aspired to! One gets an impression that a man's love and a woman's are a phase apart psychologically.

The fact that women must be regarded as having little sense of justice is no doubt related to the predominance of envy in their mental life; for the demand for justice is a modification of envy and lays down the condition subject to which one can put envy aside. We also regard women as weaker in their social interests and as having less capacity for sublimating their instincts than men. The former is no doubt derived from the dissocial quality which unquestionably characterizes all sexual relations. Lovers find sufficiency in each other, and families too resist inclusion in more comprehensive associations.[14] The aptitude for sublimation is subject to the greatest individual variations. On the other hand I cannot help mentioning an impression that we are constantly receiving during analytic practice. A man of about thirty strikes us as a youthful, somewhat unformed individual, whom we expect to make powerful use of the possibilities for development opened up to him by analysis. A woman of the same age, however, oftens frightens us by her psychical rigidity and unchangeability. Her libido has taken up final positions and seems incapable of exchanging them for others. There are no paths open to further development; it is as though the whole process had already run its course and remains thenceforward insusceptible to influence—as though, indeed, the difficult development to femininity had exhausted the possibilities of the person concerned. As therapists we lament this state of things, even if we succeed in putting an end to our patient's ailment by doing away with her neurotic conflict.

That is all I had to say to you about femininity. It is certainly incomplete and fragmentary and does not always sound friendly. But do not forget that I have only been describing women in so far as their nature is determined by their sexual function. It is true that that influence extends very far; but we do not overlook the fact that an individual woman may be a human being in other respects as well. If you want to know more about femininity, enquire from your own experiences of life, or turn to the poets, or wait until science can give you deeper and more coherent information.

NOTES

1 [This lecture is mainly based on two earlier papers: 'Some Psychical Consequences of the Anatomical Distinction between the Sexes' (1925) and 'Female Sexuality' (1931). The last section, however, dealing with women in adult life, contains new material. Freud returned to the subject once again in Chapter VII of the posthumous *Outline of Psycho-Analysis* (1940 [1938]).]

2 Heads in hieroglyphic bonnets,
Heads in turbans and black birettas,
Heads in wigs and thousand other
Wretched, sweating heads of humans. . . .
      (Heine, *Nordsee* [Second Cycle, VII, 'Fragen'].)

3 [Bisexuality was discussed by Freud in the first edition of his *Three Essays on the Theory of Sexuality* (1905). The passage includes a long footnote to which he made additions in later issues of the work.]

4 [I.e. mistaking two different things for a single one. The term was explained in *Introductory Lectures*, XX.]

5 [The difficulty of finding a psychological meaning for 'masculine' and 'feminine' was discussed in a long footnote added in 1915 to Section 4 of the third of his *Three Essays* (1905), and again at the beginning of a still longer footnote at the end of Chapter IV of *Civilization and its Discontents* (1930).]

6 [Cf. *Introductory Lectures*, XXI.]

7 [In his early discussions of the aetiology of hysteria Freud often mentioned seduction by adults as among its commonest causes (see, for instance, Section I of the second paper on the neuro-psychoses of defence (1896), and Section II of 'The Aetiology of Hysteria' (1896). But nowhere in these early publications did he specifically inculpate the girl's father. Indeed, in some additional footnotes written in 1924 for the *Gesammelte Schriften* reprint of *Studies on Hysteria*, he admitted to having on two occasions suppressed the fact of the father's responsibility. He made this quite clear, however, in the letter to Fliess of September 21, 1897 (Freud, 1950, Letter 69), in which he first

expressed his scepticism about these stories told by his patients. His first published admission of his mistake was given several years later in a hint in the second of the *Three Essays* (1905), but a much fuller account of the position followed in his contribution on the aetiology of the neuroses to a volume by Löwenfeld (1906). Later on he gave two accounts of the effects that this discovery of his mistake had on his own mind —in his 'History of the Psycho-Analytic Movement' (1914), and in his *Autobiographical Study* (1925), (Norton, 1963). The further discovery which is described in the present paragraph of the text had already been indicated in the paper on 'Female Sexuality' (1931).]

8   [See *Introductory Lectures*, XXII and XXIII.]

9   [Freud's fullest discussion of masturbation was in his contributions to a symposium on the subject in the Vienna Psycho-Analytical Society (1912).]

10   [See p. 91.]

11   [Cf. Section II of 'On Narcissism' (1914).]

12   [This had already been remarked upon earlier, in 'The Taboo of Virginity' (1918).]

13   [This point seems to have been made by Freud first in a footnote to Chapter VI of *Group Psychology* (1921). He repeated it in the *Introductory Lectures*, XIII, and in Chapter V of *Civilization and its Discontents* (1930).]

14   [Cf. some remarks on this in Chapter XII (D) of *Group Psychology* (1921).]

On Freud's View
of Female Psychology

Margaret Mead

When I accepted the invitation to write this comment, I began composing it in my head before I reread the last of Freud's famous essays on women, an essay I had not read for perhaps thirty years. I thought I knew what he had said, and I was bored and impatient with the current attacks of some militant women writers against the inevitably limited but highly percipient insights of Freud into the importance of early periods of development and the way perception of one's own body and the bodies of the opposite sex influences character formation. I expected that I would emphasize first that pregenital phases of development are indeed important, that the Oedipus complex is a reality in all societies, since in all societies boys and girls go through a period in which their investment in their budding sexuality is both threatening to their elders and inappropriate for their stage of physical and mental maturity. The resolution of this socially inappropriate surge of sexual feeling (which is treated in psychoanalytically-based shorthand as the boy's desire to kill his father and possess his mother) can also be characterized as the point at which small boys decide to give it all up, during the latency period, and submit to the authority of the dominant elders. This world-wide phenomenon (in which small boys turn away from women, enjoy being unkempt and dirty, and show intense hostility to girls) has only a pallid complementary reflection in the lives of little girls. But here, too, we do find a period in which an active response to the opposite sex is apparently latent, if perhaps only in response to the inhibition of a stronger relationship to the father, and the recurrent unresponsiveness and hostility of boys of the same age.

I then expected to examine the special etiological series which Freud postulates: infantile sexual sensitivity in the male's penis and the girl's clitoris, followed by the shocking discovery, based on comparison between male and female children, that a boy has a penis and a girl has none, resulting in the girl's anger and the boy's fear that his penis might be lost. This series of postulated stages continues with the enhancement of the boy's fear of castration, followed by his submission and development of a superego, and the girl's reconciliation of her disappointment by blaming her mother, and transference of her early mother attachment to love for her father and her disappointment and chagrin to a desire to have a baby by her father, with the equation baby = penis. According to Freud, the girl ultimately recognizes that this also is impossible; this recognition is accompanied by her angry rejection of her clitoris and her transfer of genital sensitivity to the vagina, with a consequent capacity for a vaginal orgasm.

I expected to point out that Freud was writing when very little work had been done on children. He also worked in a specific social situation, in which women with enough initiative to come to psychoanalysis had also had to display an enormous amount of initiative to get an education reserved for men. Furthermore, his patients had been reared in a society where women's reproductive capacities were shrouded and denied recognition, and the display of male activities had reached great heights—in architecture, invention, commerce, science, and the arts—so that the male world was one of achievement and the women's world was one in which her specific type of creativity was denigrated.

I then intended to carry the discussion out of its nineteenth-century European setting into the rest of the world, and particularly into the primitive world, where I have studied the growth and development of boys and girls, the ways in which they are treated, and the ways their attitudes toward themselves and the opposite sex are expressed in myth and ritual. I expected to point out the importance of womb envy—particularly well-illustrated in Pacific island cultures, where women's reproductive role is neither hidden nor denigrated. Indeed, women's reproductivity represents an achievement that is very conspicious in comparison with the rather small exploits of men in making canoes, relatively minor building, and hunting small harmless animals. In the

96

parts of New Guinea I have studied, it is men who envy women their feminine capacities. It is men who spend their ceremonial lives pretending that it was they who had borne the children, that they can "make men." Boys are taught to bleed their penises in imitation of girls' menstruation, which was seen as a salutary bleeding, getting rid of "bad blood." Men hide their complicated noisemaking instruments—flutes, bull roarers, water drums—from the women, for these instruments impersonate the mythical monster the *tamberan,* which is the patron of the men's cult. Interestingly enough also, this monster *tamberan* is then reassigned to women as the men speak of childbirth as the "women's *tamberan,*" reassigning to the women the powers which have been ceremonially denied. It is also in this area of the world that men tell how their noisemaking impersonators of their mythical man-making powers were invented by a woman and stolen from her by men. I discussed these activities in *Male and Female* in 1949. In 1954 Bruno Bettelheim published a book called *Symbolic Wounds,* originally triggered by observation of disturbed teenagers in his special school, and, without acknowledgment, using material I had used, wrote a whole chapter speculating on why men said they had stolen their supernatural imitative feminine powers from women!

I expected also to add a few further remarks about present hypotheses concerning the origin of the kinds of precocious sexuality discovered by psychoanalysis, and to suggest that this may be a residue of a period, millions of years ago, in which early hominid creatures matured without latency. In this period, the readiness of the young male to take on his senescent elders could appear, not inappropriately, as it does now, but appropriately at the age of six, and young females may have had offspring at five or six. At present, the existence of the Oedipal phase is treated by psychoanalysis as a function of our particular kind of monogamous nuclear family, although its appearance in today's children is far from making any kind of biological or evolutionary sense. I also intended to add something about the possible origin of our present patterns of sexual behavior in a shrinking of the reproductive period, with the menopause appearing at one end of the reproductive period and latency at the other. The advantage given to a group of early prehuman beings if the lives of some of the knowledgeable old females could be preserved is patent, while the immediate functional value of a period of latency, although of immense value in the process of learning, would not be so immediately apparent in the competition among small groups of hominids.

This is what I meant to say, responding as I was to the fifty years of psychoanalytic understanding to which I have been exposed on the one hand, and to my own intensive studies of primitive people on the other. With this outline in mind, I turned to the last of Freud's three papers, and I experienced a deep shock. It is only too true that the militant feminists have a case against Freud, but not the case they thought they had: that it is only his ideas about penis envy and the normality of vaginal orgasms that have permeated and contaminated our society. Rather, Freud's ideas on women, far from expressing the early culturally limited phases of the development of one of our most important sciences, are actually an expression, and an extraordinarily naïve one, of the still contemporary attitudes about women against which the militants are battling.

Summed up, in brief, Freud asserts that girls have a hard time developing—and in fact never quite reach the heights of moral character that boys do—because they observe that they have no penises. In order that their sexual affection can be transferred to their fathers (and so to males in general) they have to suppress their previous pleasure in their clitoris, and learn to hate their mothers and accept a possible baby from their fathers as compensation for not having a penis. And this he gives as the whole story. The entire argument ignores what we have come to feel is the basis of psychoanalytic understanding: the importance of a child's experience of his or her body in *all* its manifestations.

In Freud's treatment of the subject, nowhere is any attention given to the reproductive capacities as opposed to the pleasure-giving aspects of distinctive anatomical sex differences. An active sperm and a passive ovum are mentioned once, as a sort of loose analogy, but the vagina is seen not as the entry to the womb, but simply as the appropriate displacement from the clitoris. Nor does the male fare any better. As there is no discussion of the girl's discovery of the inside of her body, facilitated by her experience of pregnancy and birth in women, so also there is no discussion of the boy's bewildered and vulnerable response to the growth, retraction, and final, painful emergence of his testicles. As babies are seen merely as substitutes for the penis, the entire creative miracle of their production is overlooked, even to the actual paternal contribution.

Karen Horney pointed out years ago that what Freud, an analyst, thought little girls thought was merely what little boys thought little girls thought. Freud's entire explanation of the differential development of super-ego, object love, and search for achievement lay simply in the high valuation of the penis—by both sexes—and the denigration of a baby, because a girl's wish for a child was treated as only a wish for a substitute penis.

With regrets for this particular socially conditioned naïveté, we may turn again to what a sophisticated cross-cultural application of Freud's great and real discoveries about pregenital behavior suggest in regard to the importance of children's early experience of anatomical sex differences. We then can explore children's behavior where middle-class Euro-American culture no longer sets the stage. In a primitive society human bodies are relatively unclothed; menstruation and defloration, pregnancy, delivery, and lactation are openly recognized. Both boys and girls learn about the males' capacities for erection, penetration, and ejaculation, and the females' capacity to produce children inside their bodies. There is no more reason for a girl to envy a boy than for a boy to envy a girl, for the contrasting and differentiated functions of each are fully apparent to children of each sex. True, in some societies the achievements of males are valued far more greatly than those of females (societies, for example, in which men herd large animals or hunt large game), but in other societies (especially those associated with horticulture) the fertility of women is highly valued. The superiority of a penis may be emphasized and reinforced by the salience of male activity over female, or, as happens in the womb-envying cultures, the little boy's desire to have a baby may be built up into compensatory ceremonial behavior among men. The fact that little boys do desire to have babies and also do experience profound disturbances in which their unpredictable testicles are identified as feminine, has now been well documented by clinical studies on little boys in our own society. So we find that a little girl—who is not, as Freud suggested, a small man without a penis, but a small female who has a womb—learns she will someday be a woman who can bear children, and that a little boy learns that he is a creature with a penis and without a womb. He, who can never bear a child, must seek achievement in other ways. In such societies, as girls accept their femininity, they accept it as positive, and as boys accept the fact that they cannot have children, they learn to place a very high valuation on achievement.

However, in all cultures, without any known exception, male activity is seen as achievement; whatever women do—gathering seeds, planting, weeding, basket-making, pot-making—is valued less than when the same activity, in some other culture, is performed by men. When men cook, cooking is viewed as an important activity; when women cook it is just a household chore. And correspondingly, if an activity once performed by women becomes more important in a society, it may be taken over by men. For example, midwifery, once a profession in which the female practitioners were both constricted and feared, has been taken over by male obstetricians.

Freud speaks of how easy it is for a boy to continue his love for his first love object, his mother, and how hard it is for a girl, who must turn against her mother. But the mother, the boy's first love object, pushes him away, out of her arms, off her lap, into activity that will demonstrate he is a male. The girl can remain near her mother, be held more warmly by both parents, cherished as she waits while her brother must go out and act, and in acting, challenge his father's superior position, and finally demonstrate to some waiting woman that he will be a fit father for her children. The more active girl may find all this discouraging; the more passive boy may find this an unbearably difficult task. But as long as both boys and girls are reared by women, the treatment of each sex has to be different, if later sex identity is to be attained.

As long as women were given the principal responsibility for the care of small children, and this responsibility included breast feeding and the need to have many children if a few were to survive, and as long as the great majority of males had to devote themselves to lifelong maintenance of households in which children were reared, an educational system which reared all females to be wives and mothers and almost all males to be husbands and fathers characterized every human society. And we find concomitants of this situation throughout history. Work that required long distances and long periods away from home—hunting, warfare, and exploration—belonged to men. Activities congruent with staying near the hearth and close to breast-feeding children belonged to women.

The first great change in the social assignment of the entire population to rearing the next generation came with the invention of agriculture, which freed some men from subsistence food-getting, and freed a few women of rank and wealth from the care and feeding of their children (but did not free even a queen from childbearing) and substituted wet nurses. Although there were periods in history when men were withdrawn from parenthood into a monastic life, and women were allowed a complementary celibacy, it was not until the Industrial Revolution that work for mere individual survival, independent of supporting households, became important. Then the lifelong support which society had always provided for child-producing, child-rearing women was withdrawn, and the working woman, often with children, was left completely on her own to fulfill the previous male task of working outside the home to support the children.

In Freud's time, a small number of women were already responding to this situation by demanding to be treated as persons independently of their roles as wives and mothers, to have a chance to have education, a chance to go to medical school, a chance to work in the world of men. The tremendous effort that it takes to break the hold of tradition when it is expressed in terms of such basic differences as sex (and of physique where different roles have been assigned to different racial groups) appeared to Freud and to many of the early analysts as associated with a tremendous drive to be masculine, and this was indeed the most obvious path to take. If a little girl was not allowed to do what her brother was allowed and encouraged to do, then obviously, all early childhood experiences of sex difference that valued his anatomical endowment would seem to devalue hers. All admonitions toward passivity (to be quiet, to be modest, to be chaste) take on invidious connotations, just as the adoption of celibacy has so often in religious history been seen as making males more feminine.

Thus the century and a half of feminism through which we have just gone has witnessed a continuing interpretation of psycho-sexual development as females suffering from the discovery that they were not born males and free.

At the same time that females were making what came to be called in psychoanalytically influenced circles a "masculine protest," periodically there appeared social movements that emphasized the importance of maternity and the need for an extension of the maternal functions into society. While the early social revolutionaries in Europe were offering women freedom from the degrading position of being treated as property by males, there were other social reformers who were glorifying childbearing, and working to abolish child labor, protect the health of working mothers, and to provide contraception to give women control over their own bodies. Just as the emphasis upon the need to share a man's world

101

focused upon a repudiation of women's primary sex characters and the role that accompanied them, so the emphasis upon women's primary sex characters underlay the emphasis on women's maternal aspects. The extreme extension of the first position presents women as handicapped by childbearing and envious of men, women who would like to reduce procreation to as brief as possible a moment in life—as it is for men—with the logical extension being artificial insemination and test-tube babies. The extreme extension of the second position, in which women are seen as handicapped because they cannot exercise their maternal functions to the full, is the emphasis on every woman's right to have a child, the right to elective abortion in which no husband or future father shares in the decision—women are pictured as capable of rearing their children alone, or with the help of other women only.

For a brief time in the period following World War II, there was an emphasis upon the father's involvement in the care of an infant, and the right of a man to be included in the delivery of his child and the enjoyment of its early infancy. These demands have lingered on, with prenatal classes for fathers as well as mothers, presence of fathers at delivery, and the demands of fathers to keep illegitimate infants whom the mothers wish to give away for adoption. In Sweden, there is an organized attempt to include men in the domestic responsibilities of the home, and to rear boys and girls with an expectation of choice between and competence in both the previously masculine roles of breadwinning outside the home and the previously feminine roles of child care and homemaking.

So over the last century we have seen a series of perturbations in the relationships between the sexes, and the interpretations placed by psychiatry and medicine in general on the compatibility or incompatibility of achievement in masculine-defined roles and women's biological functions.

One set of social changes, set in motion by a series of inventions, which began with the invention of agriculture and culminated in the Industrial Revolution, has changed the role of men in society, permitting more and more men to devote themselves to diversified activities other than the primary activities of subsistence and defense. Changes in women's roles only pallidly reflected these changes, which placed greater and greater burdens on women, who could now be turned adrift from male support and protection, but were provided little real relief from the contradiction between a sociologically defined role that placed primary importance on

102

childbearing and childrearing, and an increasing opportunity and desire by some women to be able to live as human beings, as persons, rather than subject their entire lives to caring for the next generation.

Meanwhile, another revolution (as far-reaching in effect as the successive agricultural, industrial, and electronic revolutions, which have transformed the economic life of society) was getting under way: the medical revolution. The practice of obstetrics was taken out of the hands of women, first professionalized as midwifery, and childbirth converted from a natural part of life to a quasi-surgical procedure in a hospital in which women were reduced to the passivity that men had hopefully attributed to them through the centuries. Artificial feeding was invented to replace the mother's breast, and the age-old mystery of the interior of women's bodies was now open to inspection by properly qualified male practitioners. The spread of public health measures is completing the transformation of society; the infant death rate has been markedly reduced with no comparable reduction in the infant birth rate, and the world is now faced with a population explosion that in both the industrialized and the unindustrialized countries threatens the prosperity and well-being of almost every society. The perception of this situation has produced the new climate within which societies are seeking to reduce the childbearing role of women, and simultaneously demanding that women take a part in productive activities outside the home.

The stage has thus been set for a new attempt, on the part of both men and women, to redefine their relationships to each other and to the entire social process, to redefine the role of marriage as an institution, and to examine again whether there are any biologically given ways in which anatomy is destiny, as Freud originally put it. The seriousness of this world-wide situation is reflected in the tremendous commotion going on everywhere, in renewed interest in exploring female sexuality, the female body, and in various compensatory and extreme statements, of the tit-for-tat order, like the recent one in *The New York Times* (November 14, 1972) that because "women can achieve five to six sexual climaxes to a man's one; if continuously stimulated they can reach over fifty" this means that "obviously women were not designed for monogamous or polygamous marriage." The very extremity of the present discussion signals the magnitude of the changes in store for us, and reemphasizes the importance of examining whether there are any respects in which, in spite of the inadequacy of any theory of penis envy, Freud's insistence that anatomy

103

is destiny may not, in some deeper sense, be true.

Although it is possible to demonstrate that the social definition of male and female roles throughout prehistory and history have reflected practical conditions—such as the need to breast feed and carry infants, and the need for men to work all their lives to provide for the next generation —there are many unanswered questions. We do not know whether a failure to bear a child, whatever the origin of that failure, may in some way damage a woman's capacity to realize herself as a person, hasten aging, or expose her to other risks more psychologically incapacitating than the hazards and wear and tear of many pregnancies. We do not know whether an abortion, however brief the period after conception, may not be, a least for many women, and for women of many different religious beliefs, a grievous and damaging experience. We do not know whether a bottle-fed mother can transmit to her bottle-fed baby the kind of tactile reassurance and security that infants appear to need, if they in turn, whether they be male or female, are to develop their full potentialities.

We do not know whether there may not be a value, both for women and for men, in the way that a woman's body reflects, in striking and dramatic fashion, the repetitive cycles of reproduction, and gives all of life, including aging, a different dimension from the lives of men, whose bodies register no such periodic and climactic events. We live in a period when much of human behavior has been seen as a nuisance to be eliminated—mechanically, biochemically, chemically. Menstrual cramps, defloration, pregnancy, delivery, and the menopause are all to be subjected to manipulations which limit or suppress entirely their individual and cultural significance. And we are almost completely ignorant of what the consequences of such interventions in very ancient biologically given sex differences may be. These are areas in which Freud's dictum— anatomy is destiny—must be kept very much in mind. We might easily choose a course that in its emphasis on artificial intervention in natural processes transforms human beings into beings who are incapable of the primary love and loyalty for kith and kin and country. Yet these loves and loyalties may be absolutely necessary, if we are to invoke enough devotion to the collective good to cope with the environmental crises that have resulted from Man's imposing his will, irrespective of consequences, on the natural world.

We do not know whether the fact that women's bodies are prepared to bear children may not also be a crucial determinant of certain aspects of

104

behavior traditionally regarded as feminine. Feminine intuition may only be the result of having been the girl child of a mother who was alert to her child's slightest need; but girls continue to be born from their mother's bodies, in a nine-month-long gestation, so that alertness to tiny cues may continue to be transmitted from mother to daughter, and inhibited in sons, even if both boys and girls come to be reared equally by both parents from birth.

It may be that the fact that women's bodies are prepared for a so much lengthier participation in the creation of a human being may make females—even those who bear no children—more prone to take their own bodies as the theater of action. There may be a difference, although it would be a very slight one on the very edge of genius, between the highest creative faculties of men and women, even though women can learn what men have discovered and men can learn what women have discovered. For example, men may have an edge in physics and women in psychology.

Freud opened up a whole new way of understanding ourselves, our development through history, our behavior today. It is a pity that he understood women so little, but those who have followed in his footsteps and studied children, as well as those of us who have studied human development in other societies, are nonetheless indebted to him. The path he outlined, although in his discussion of the psychology of women he was completely culture-bound, still suggests that the rhythms of human development, patterned during a million years, are ignored at our peril, and understood, give us wisdom.

BIBLIOGRAPHY

Bell, Anita I. "The Significance of Scrotal Sac and Testicles for the Prepuberty Male," *Psychoanalytic Quarterly*, 34, No. 2 (1965), 182–206.

Bettelheim, B. *Symbolic Wounds: Puberty Rites and the Envious Male*, rev. ed. New York: Macmillan, 1962.

Erikson, Erik H. *Childhood and Society*, rev. ed. New York: Norton, 1963.

Freud, Sigmund. "Some Psychological Consequences of the Anatomical Distinctions Between the Sexes." In *Collected Papers*, James Strachey, translator and ed. (The International Psycho-Analytic Library, ed. Ernest Jones, No. 37.) London: Hogarth Press, 1953, 186–197.

———. "Female Sexuality." In *The Complete Edition of the Psychological Works of Sigmund Freud*, vol. 21: *The Future of an Illusion, Civilization and Its Discontents and Other Works*, James

Strachey, translator and ed. London: Hogarth Press, 1961, 225–243.

————. "Lecture 33: Femininity," In *The Complete Edition of the Psychological Works of Sigmund Freud*, Vol. 22: *New Introductory Lectures on Psycho-Analysis and Other Works*, James Strachey, translator and editor. London: Hogarth Press, 1964, 112–135.

Hogbin, Ian. *The Island of Menstruating Men*. Scranton: Chandler Publications, 1970.

Horney, Karen. "The Flight from Womanhood: The Masculinity Complex in Women, As Viewed by Men and by Women," *International Journal of Psycho-Analysis*, 7 (1926), 324–339.

Jacobson, Edith. "Development of the Wish for a Child in Boys," *Psycho-Analytic Study of the Child*, 5 (1950), 139–152.

Kinsey, A. C., and others. *Sexual Behavior in the Human Male*. Philadelphia: Saunders, 1948.

————. *Sexual Behavior in the Human Female*. Philadelphia: Saunders, 1953.

Masters, W. H., and V. E. Johnson. *Human Sexual Response*. Boston: Little, Brown, 1966.

————. *Human Sexual Inadequacy*. Boston: Little, Brown, 1970.

Mead, Margaret. *Sex and Temperament in Three Primitive Societies*. New York: Morrow, 1963. Reprinted with new preface, Apollo editions, New York: Morrow, 1967.

————. *Male and Female*. New York: Morrow, 1949. Reprinted Apollo Editions, New York: Morrow, 1967.

————. "*Totem and Taboo* Reconsidered with Respect," *Bulletin of the Menninger Clinic*, 27, No. 4 (July 1963), 185–199.

Sherfey, Mary Jane. "The Rib Belonged to Eve: I. Formidable Jargon," *The New York Times*, November 13, 1972, p. 370.

————. "The Rib Belonged to Eve: II. Ancient Man Knew His Place," *The New York Times*, November 14, 1972, p. 47.

106

Kovel on Abraham

Manifestations of the
Female Castration Complex
(1920)

Karl Abraham

The psychological phenomena which we ascribe to the so-called castration complex of the female sex are so numerous and multiform that even a detailed description cannot do full justice to them. These questions are made still more complicated by their relations to biological and physiological processes. The following investigation, therefore, does not pretend to present the problem of the female castration complex in all its aspects, but is limited to the purely psychological consideration of material gathered from a wide field of clinical observation.

I

Many women suffer temporarily or permanently, in childhood or in adult age, from the fact that they have been born as females. Psycho-analysis further shows that a great number of women have repressed the wish to be male; we come across this wish in all products of the unconscious, especially in dreams and neurotic symptoms. The extraordinary frequency of these observations suggests that the wish is one common to and occurring in all women. If we incline to this view we place ourselves under the obligation of examining thoroughly and without prejudice the facts to which we attribute such a general significance.

Many women are often quite conscious of the fact that certain phenomena of their mental life arise from an intense dislike of being a woman; but, on the other hand, many of them are quite in the dark as regards the motives of such an aversion. Certain arguments are again and again brought forward to explain this attitude. For instance, it is said that girls even in childhood are at a disadvantage in comparison to boys because boys are allowed greater freedom; or that in later life men are permitted to choose their profession and can extend their sphere of activity in many directions, and in especial are subjected to far fewer restrictions in their sexual life. Psycho-analysis, however, shows that conscious arguments of this sort are of limited value, and are the result of rationalization—a process which veils the underlying motives. Direct observation of young girls shows unequivocally that at a certain stage of their development they feel at a disadvantage as regards the male sex on account of the inferiority of their external genitals. The results obtained from the psycho-analysis of adults fully agree with this observation. We find that a large proportion of women have not overcome this disadvantage, or, expressed psycho-analytically, that they have not successfully repressed and sublimated it. Ideas belonging to it often impinge with all the force of their strong libidinal cathexis against the barriers which oppose their entry into consciousness. This struggle of repressed material with the censorship can be demonstrated in a great variety of neurotic symptoms, dreams, etc.

This fact that the non-possession of a male organ produces such a serious and lasting effect in the woman's mental life would justify us in denoting all the mental derivatives relating to it by the collective name 'genital complex'. We prefer, however, to make use of an expression taken from the psychology of male neurotics, and to speak of the 'castration complex' in the female sex as well. And we have good reason for this.

The child's high estimation of its own body is closely connected with its narcissism. The girl has primarily no feeling of inferiority in regard to her own body, and does not recognize that it exhibits a defect in comparison with the boy's. Incapable of recognizing a *primary* defect in her body, she later forms the following idea: 'I had a penis once as boys have, but it has been taken away from me',—a theory which we repeatedly come across. She therefore endeavours to represent the painfully perceived defect as a secondary loss and one resulting from castration.

This idea is closely associated with another which we shall later treat in detail. The female genital is looked upon as a *wound*, and as such it represents an effect of castration.

110

We also come across phantasies and neurotic symptoms, and occasionally impulses and actions, which indicate a hostile tendency towards the male sex. In many women the idea that they have been damaged gives rise to the wish to revenge themselves on the privileged man. The aim of such an impulse is to castrate the man.

We find therefore in the female sex not only the tendency to represent a painfully perceived and primary defect as a secondary loss, a 'having been robbed', but also active and passive phantasies of mutilation alongside each other, just as in the male castration complex. These facts justify us in using the same designation in both sexes.

II

As was mentioned above, the girl's discovery of the male genitals acts as an injury to her narcissism. In the narcissistic period of its development the child carefully watches over its possessions and regards those of others with jealousy. It wants to keep what it has and to get what it sees. If anyone has an advantage over it two reactions occur which are closely associated with each other: a hostile feeling against the other person associated with the impulse to deprive him of what he possesses. The union of these two reactions constitutes *envy*, which represents a typical expression of the sadistic-anal developmental phase of the libido.[1]

The child's avaricious-hostile reaction to any additional possession it has noticed in another person may often be lessened in a simple manner. It may be told that it will eventually receive what it longs for. Such pacifying promises may be made to a little girl with respect to many things about her body. She can be assured that she will grow as big as her mother, that she will have long hair like her sister, etc., and she will be satisfied with those assurances; but the future possession of a male organ cannot be promised her. However, the little girl herself applies the method that has often been successful to this case, too; for some time she seems to cling to this expectation as to something self-evident, as though the idea of a lifelong defect were quite incomprehensible to her.

The following observation of a little girl of two is particularly instructive in this respect. One day, as her parents were taking coffee at table, she went to a box of cigars that stood on a low cabinet near by, opened it, and took out a cigar and brought it to her father. Then she went back and brought one for her mother. Then she took a third cigar and held

111

it in front of the lower part of her body. Her mother put the three cigars back in the box. The child waited a little while and then played the same game over again.

The fact of the repetition of this game excluded its being due to chance. Its meaning is clear: the child endowed her mother with a male organ like her father's. She represented the possession of the organ not as a privilege of men but of adults in general, and then she could expect to get one herself in the future. A cigar was not only a suitable symbol for her wish on account of its form. She had of course long noticed that only her father smoked cigars and not her mother. Her impulse to put man and woman on an equality is palpably expressed in presenting a cigar to her mother as well.

We are well acquainted with the attempts of little girls to adopt the male position in urination. Their narcissism cannot endure their not being able to do what another can, and therefore they endeavour to arouse the impression that at least their physical form does not prevent them from doing the same as boys do.

When a child sees its brother or sister receive something to eat or play with which it does not possess itself, it turns its eyes to those persons who are the givers, and these in the first instance are its parents. It does not like to be less well off than its rivals. The small girl who compares her body with her brother's, often in phantasy expects that her father will give her that part of the body she so painfully misses; for the child still has a narcissistic confidence that she could not possibly be permanently defective, and she readily ascribes to her father that creative omnipotence which can bestow on her everything she desires.

But all these dreams crumble after a time. The pleasure principle ceases to dominate psychical processes unconditionally, adaptation to reality commences, and with it the child's criticism of its own wishes. The girl has now in the course of her psychosexual development to carry out an adaptation which is not demanded of boys in a similar manner; she has to reconcile herself to the fact of her physical 'defect', and to her female sexual rôle. The undisturbed enjoyment of early genital sensations will be a considerable aid in facilitating the renunciation of masculinity, for by this means the female genitals will regain a narcissistic value.

In reality, however, the process is considerably more complicated. Freud has drawn our attention to the close association of certain ideas in the child. In its eyes a proof of love is almost the same thing as a *gift*. The first proof of love which creates a lasting impression on the child and is repeated many times is being suckled by the mother. This act brings food to the child and therefore increases its material property, and at the same time acts as a pleasurable stimulus to its erotogenic zones. It is interesting to note that in certain districts of Germany (according to my colleague Herr Koerber) the suckling of a child is called *Schenken* (to give, to pour). Within certain limits the child repays its mother's 'gift' by a 'gift' in return —it regulates its bodily evacuations according to her wishes. The motions at an early age are the child's material gift *par excellence* in return for all the proofs of love it receives.

Psycho-analysis, however, has shown that the child in this early psychosexual period of development considers its fæces as a part of its own body. The process of identification further establishes a close relation between the ideas 'fæces' and 'penis'. The boy's anxiety regarding the loss of his penis is based on this assimilation of the two ideas. He is afraid that his penis may be detached from his body in the same way as his fæces are. In girls, however, the phantasy occurs of obtaining a penis by way of defæcation—to make one themselves, therefore—or of receiving it as a gift, in which case the father as *beatus possidens* is usually the giver. The psychical process is thus dominated by the parallel, motion = gift = penis.

The little girl's narcissism undergoes a severe test of endurance in the subsequent period. Her hope that a penis will grow is just as little fulfilled as her phantasies of making one for herself or of receiving it as a gift. Thus disappointed, the child is likely to direct an intense and lasting hostility towards those from whom she has in vain expected the gift. Nevertheless, the phantasy of the child normally finds a way out of this situation. Freud has shown that besides the idea of motion and penis in the sense of a gift there is still a third idea which is identified with both of them, namely, that of a child. Infantile theories of procreation and birth adequately explain this connection.

The little girl now cherishes the hope of getting a child from her father as a substitute for the penis not granted her, and this again in the sense of a gift. Her wish for a child can be fulfilled, although not till in the future and with the help of a later love-object. It is therefore an approximation to reality. By making her father her love-object, she now enters into that stage of libido development which is characterized by the domination of the female Oedipus complex. At the same time her maternal impulses

113

develop through her identification with her mother. The hoped-for possession of a child is therefore destined to compensate the woman for her physical defect.

We regard it as normal for the libido in a woman to be narcissistically bound to a greater extent than in a man, but it is not to be inferred from this that it does not experience far-reaching alterations right up to maturity.

The girl's original so-called 'penis envy' is replaced in the first instance by envy of her mother's possession of children, in virtue of her identification with her mother. These hostile impulses need sublimation just as the libidinal tendencies directed towards her father do. A latency period now sets in, as with boys; and similarly when the age of puberty is reached the wishes which were directed to the first love-object are re-awakened. The girl's wish for the gift (child) has now to be detached from the idea of her father, and her libido, thus freed, has to find a new object. If this process of development takes a favourable course, the female libido has from now on an expectant attitude towards the man. Its expression is regulated by certain inhibitions (feelings of shame). The normal adult woman becomes reconciled to her own sexual rôle and to that of the man, and in particular to the facts of male and female genitality; she desires passive gratification and longs for a child. Her castration complex thus gives rise to no disturbing effects.

Daily observation, however, shows us how frequently this normal end of development is not attained. This fact should not astonish us, for a woman's life gives cause enough to render the overcoming of the castration complex difficult. We refer to those factors which keep recalling to her memory the 'castration' of the woman. The primary idea of the 'wound' is re-animated by the impression created by the first and each succeeding menstruation, and then once again by defloration; for both processes are connected with loss of blood and thus resemble an injury. A girl need not have experienced either of these events; as she begins to grow up, the very idea of being subjected to them in the future has the same effect on her. And we can readily understand from the standpoint of the typical infantile sexual theories that delivery (or child-birth) is also conceived of in a similar manner in the phantasies of young girls; we need only call to mind, for example, the 'Cæsarian section theory' which conceives of delivery as a bloody operation.

In these circumstances we must be prepared to find in every female person some traces of the castration complex. The individual differences are only a matter of degree. In normal women we perhaps occasionally come across dreams with male tendencies in them. From these very slight expressions of the castration complex there are transition stages leading up to those severe and complicated phenomena of a pronounced pathological kind, with which this investigation is principally concerned. In this respect also, therefore, we find a similar state of affairs to that obtaining in the male sex.

III

In his essay on 'The Taboo of Virginity' Freud contrasts the normal outcome of the castration complex, which is in accord with the prevailing demand of civilization, with the 'archaic' type. Among many primitive peoples custom forbids a man to deflorate his wife. Defloration has to be carried out by a priest as a sacramental act, or must occur in some other way outside wedlock. Freud shows in his convincing analysis that this peculiar precept has arisen from the psychological risk of an ambivalent reaction on the part of the woman towards the man who has deflorated her, so that living with the woman whom he has deflorated might be dangerous for him.

Psycho-analytical experience shows that an inhibition of the psychosexual development is manifested in phenomena which are closely related to the conduct of primitive peoples. It is by no means rare for us to come across women in our civilization of to-day who react to defloration in a way which is at all events closely related to that archaic form. I know several cases in which women after being deflorated had an outburst of affect and hit or throttled their husband. One of my patients went to sleep beside her husband after the first intercourse, then woke up, attacked him violently and only gradually came to her senses. There is no mistaking the significance of such conduct: the woman revenges herself for the injury done to her physical integrity. Psycho-analysis, however, enables us to recognize a historical element in the motivation of such an impulse of revenge. The most recent cause of the woman's desire for retaliation is undoubtedly her defloration; for this experience serves as a convincing proof of male activity, and puts an end to all attempts to obliterate the functional difference between male and female sexuality. Nevertheless every profound analysis reveals the close connection of these phantasies

115

of revenge with all the earlier events—phantasied or real—which have been equivalent to castration. The retaliation is found to refer ultimately to the injustice suffered at the hands of the father. The unconscious of the adult daughter takes a late revenge for the father's omission to bestow upon her a penis, either to begin with or subsequently; she takes it, however, not on her father in person, but on the man who in consequence of her transference of libido has assumed the father's part. The only adequate revenge for her wrong—for her castration—is the castration of the man. This can, it is true, be replaced symbolically by other aggressive measures; among these strangling is a typical substitutive action.

The contrast between such cases and the 'normal' end-stage is evident. The normal attitude of love towards the other sex is both in man and woman indissolubly bound up with the conscious or unconscious desire for genital gratification in conjunction with the love-object; whereas in the cases just described we find in the person a sadistic-hostile attitude with the aim of possession arising from anal motives, in place of an attitude of love with a genital aim. The patient's impulse to take away by force is evident from numerous accompanying psychical conditions; and closely connected with her phantasy of robbery is the idea of transferring the robbed penis to herself. We shall return to this point later.

As has already been mentioned, the woman's desires to be masculine only occasionally succeed in breaking through in this 'archaic' sense. On the other hand, a considerable number of women are unable to carry out a full psychical adaptation to the female sexual rôle. A third possibility is open to them in virtue of the bisexual disposition common to humanity —namely, to become homosexual. Such women tend to adopt the male rôle in erotic relations with other women. They love to exhibit their masculinity in their dress, in their way of doing their hair, and in their general behaviour. In some cases their homosexuality does not break through to consciousness; the repressed wish to be male is here found in a sublimated form in the shape of masculine pursuits of an intellectual and professional character and other allied interests. Such women do not, however, consciously deny their femininity, but usually proclaim that these interests are just as much feminine as masculine ones. They consider that the sex of a person has nothing to do with his or her capacities, especially in the mental field. This type of woman is well represented in the woman's movement of to-day.

It is not because I value their practical significance lightly that I have

116

described these groups so briefly. But both types of women are well known and have been discussed in psycho-analytical literature, so that I need not enlarge on the subject and can rapidly pass on to the consideration of the *neurotic transformations* of the castration complex. Of these there are a great number, and I will endeavour to describe accurately—some of them for the first time—and to render them intelligible from a psycho-analytical point of view.

IV

The neurotic transformations originating in the female castration complex may be divided into two groups. The phenomena of the one group rest on a strong, emotionally-toned, but not conscious desire to adopt the male rôle, *i.e.* on the phantasy of possessing a male organ; those of the other express an unconscious refusal of the female rôle, and a repressed desire for revenge on the privileged man. There is no sharp line of demarcation between these two groups. The phenomena of one group do not exclude those of the other in the same individual; they supplement each other. The preponderance of this or that attitude can nevertheless often be clearly recognized, so that we may speak of the preponderating reaction of a *wish-fulfilment type* or of a *revenge type.*

We have already learned that besides the normal outcome of the female castration complex there are two abnormal forms of conscious reaction, namely, the homosexual type and the archaic (revenge) type. We have only to recall the general relation between perversion and neurosis with which we are familiar from Freud's investigations in order to be able to understand the two neurotic types above described in respect of their psychogenesis. They are the 'negative' of the homosexual and sadistic types described above; for they contain the same motives and tendencies, but in repressed form.

The psychical phenomena which arise from the unconscious wishes for physical masculinity or for revenge on the man are difficult to classify on account of their multiplicity. It has also to be borne in mind that neurotic symptoms are not the sole expressions of unconscious origin which have to concern us here; we need only refer to the different forms in which the same repressed tendencies appear in dreams. As I have said at the beginning, therefore, this investigation cannot pretend to give an exhaustive account of the phenomena arising from the repressed castration complex, but rather lays stress on certain frequent and instructive forms of it, and especially some which have not hitherto been considered.

The *wish-fulfilment* which goes farthest in the sense of the female castration complex comprises those symptoms or dreams of neurotics which convert the fact of femininity into its opposite. In such a case the unconscious phantasies of the woman make the assertion: 'I am the fortunate possessor of a penis and exercise the male function'. Van Ophuijsen gives an example of this kind in his article on the 'masculine complex' of women.[2] It concerns a conscious phantasy from the youth of one of his patients, and gives us therefore at first only an insight into the patient's still unrepressed active-homosexual wishes; but at the same time therefore it clearly demonstrates the foundation of those neurotic symptoms which give expression to the same tendencies after they have become repressed. The patient used to place herself in the evening between the lamp and the wall and then hold her finger against the lower part of her body in such a manner that her shadow appeared to have a penis. She thus did something very similar to what the two-year-old child did with the cigar.

In conjunction with this instructive example I may mention the dream of a neurotic woman. She was an only child. Her parents had ardently desired a son and had in consequence cultivated the narcissism, and particularly the masculinity wishes, of their daughter. According to an expression of theirs she was to become 'quite a celebrated man'. In her youthful day-dreams she saw herself as a 'female Napoleon', in which she began a glorious career as a female officer, advanced to the highest positions, and saw all the countries of Europe lying at her feet. After having thus shown herself superior to all the men in the world, a man was to appear at last who surpassed not only all men but also herself; and she was to subject herself to him. In her marital relations in real life she had the most extreme resistance against assuming the feminine rôle; I shall mention symptoms relating to this later. I quote here one of my patient's dreams.

'My husband seizes a woman, lifts up her clothes, finds a peculiar pocket and pulls out from it a hypodermic morphia syringe. She gives him an injection with this syringe and he is carried away in a weak and wretched state.'

The woman in this dream is the patient herself, who takes over the active rôle from the man. She is able to do this by means of a concealed penis (syringe) with which she practises coitus on him. The weakened condition of the man signifies that he is killed by her assault.

Pulling out the syringe from the pocket suggests the male method of urinating, which seemed enviable to the patient in her childhood. It has, however, a further significance. At a meeting of the Berlin Psycho-Analytical Society Boehm has drawn attention to a common infantile sexual theory according to which the penis originally ascribed to both sexes is concealed in a cleft from which it can temporarily emerge.

Another patient, whose neurosis brought to expression the permanent discord between masculinity and femininity in most manifold forms, stated that during sexual excitation she often had the feeling that something on her body was swelling to an enormous size. The purpose of this sensation was obviously to give her the illusion that she possessed a penis.

In other patients the symptoms do not represent the wish to be masculine as fulfilled, but show an expectation of such an event in the near or distant future. While the unconscious in the cases just described expresses the idea, 'I am a male', it here conceives the wish in the formula, 'I shall receive the "gift" one day; I absolutely insist upon that!'

The following conscious phantasy from the youth of a neurotic girl is perfectly typical of the unconscious content of many neurotic symptoms. When the girl's elder sister menstruated for the first time she noticed that her mother and sister conversed together secretly. The thought flashed across her, 'Now my sister is certainly getting a penis', and that therefore she herself would get one in due course. This reversal of the real state of affairs is highly characteristic: the acquisition of that longed-for part of the body is precisely what is put in place of the renewed 'castration' which the first menstruation signifies.

A neurotic patient in whom psycho-analysis revealed an extraordinary degree of narcissism one day showed the greatest resistance to treatment, and manifested many signs of defiance towards me which really referred to her deceased father. She left my consulting room in a state of violent negative transference. When she stepped into the street she caught herself saying impulsively: 'I *will not* be well until I have got a penis'. She thus expected this gift from me, as a substitute for her father, and made the effect of the treatment dependent upon receiving it. Certain dreams of the patient had the same content as this idea which suddenly appeared from her unconscious. In these dreams, being presented with something occurred in the double sense of getting a child or a penis.

Compromises between impulse and repression occur in the sphere of the castration complex as elsewhere in the realm of psychopathology. In many cases the unconscious is content with a substitute-gratification in place of a complete fulfilment of the wish for a penis in the present or the future.

A condition in neurotic women which owes one of its most important determinants to the castration complex is *enuresis nocturna*. The analogy between the determination of this symptom in female and male neurotics is striking. I may refer to a dream of a male patient of fourteen who suffered from this complaint. He dreamt that he was in a closet and urinating with manifest feelings of pleasure, when he suddenly noticed that his sister was looking at him through the window. As a little boy he had actually exhibited with pride before his sister his masculine way of urinating. This dream, which ended in enuresis, shows the boy's pride in his penis; and enuresis in the female frequently rests on the wish to urinate in the male way. The dream represented this process in a disguised form and ended with a pleasurable emptying of the bladder.

Women who are prone to *enuresis nocturna* are regularly burdened with strong resistances against the female sexual functions. The infantile desire to urinate in the male position is associated with the well-known assimilation of the ideas of urine and sperma, and of micturition and ejaculation. The unconscious tendency to wet the man with urine during sexual intercourse has its origin in this.

Other substitute formations show a still greater displacement of the libido in that they are removed some distance from the genital region. When the libido for some reason or other has to turn away from the genital zone it is attracted to certain other erotogenic zones, the particular ones chosen being a result of individual determinations. In some neurotic women the nose acquires the significance of a surrogate of the male genital. The not infrequent neurotic attacks of redness and swelling of the nose in women represents in their unconscious phantasy an erection in the sense of their desire to be masculine.

In other cases the eyes take over a similar rôle. Some neurotic women get an abnormally marked congestion of the eyes with every sexual excitation. In a certain measure this congestion is a normal and common accompaniment of sexual excitation. However, in those women of whom we are speaking it is not simply a case of a quantitative increase of the condition, lasting for a short period; but they exhibit a redness of the

120

sclerotics accompanied by a burning sensation, while swelling persists for several days after each sexual excitation, so that in such cases we are justified in speaking of a *conjunctivitis neurotica.*

I have seen several women patients, troubled by many neurotic consequences of the castration complex, who thought of this condition of the eyes, which was often associated with a feeling of having a fixed stare, as an expression of their masculinity. In the unconscious the 'fixed stare' is often equivalent to an erection. I have already alluded to this symptom in an earlier article dealing with neurotic disturbances of the eyes.[3] In some cases the person has the idea that her fixed stare will terrify people. If we pursue the unconscious train of thought of these patients who identify their fixed stare with erection, we can understand the meaning of their anxiety. Just as male exhibitionists seek among other things to terrify women by the sight of the phallus, so these women unconsciously endeavour to attain the same effect by means of their fixed stare.

Some years ago a very neurotic young girl consulted me. The very first thing she did on entering my consulting-room was to ask me straight out whether she had beautiful eyes. I was startled for a moment by this very unusual way of introducing oneself to a physician. She noticed my hesitation, and then gave vent to a violent outburst of affect on my suggesting that she should first of all answer *my* questions. The general behaviour of the patient, whom I only saw a few times, made a methodical psychoanalysis impossible. I did not succeed even in coming to a clear diagnosis of the case, for certain characteristics of the clinical picture suggested a paranoid condition. Nevertheless, I was able to obtain a few facts concerning the origin of her most striking symptom, and these, in spite of their incompleteness, offered a certain insight into the structure of her condition.

The patient told me that she had experienced a great fright as a child. In the small town where she was living at that time a boa constrictor had broken out from a menagerie and could not be found; and as she was passing through a park with her governess she believed that she suddenly saw the snake in front of her. She became quite rigid with terror, and ever since was afraid that she might have a fixed stare.

It could not be decided whether this experience was a real one or whether it was wholly or partially a phantasy. The association, snake = rigidity, is familiar and comprehensible to us. We also recognize the snake as a male genital symbol. Fixity of the eye is then explicable from the identification, fixed eye = snake = phallus. The patient, however, protected herself against this wish for masculinity, and put in its place the compulsion to get every man to assure her that her eyes were beautiful, *i.e.* had feminine charms. If anyone hesitated to answer her question in the affirmative it is probable that she became exposed to the danger of being overwhelmed by her male-sadistic impulse which she repressed with difficulty, and fell into a state of anxiety at the rising force of her masculine feelings.

I should like to point out here that these various observations by no means do justice to the great multiplicity of the symptoms belonging to this group. Besides these examples which illustrate the vicarious assumption by various parts of the body of the male genital rôle, there are others which show that objects which do not belong to the body can also be made use of for the same purpose, provided their form and use permits in any way of a symbolic interpretation as a genital organ. We may call to mind the tendency of neurotic women to use a syringe and to give themselves or relatives enemas.

There are numerous points of contact here with the normal expressions of the female castration complex, especially with typical female symptomatic acts. Thrusting the end of an umbrella into the ground may be mentioned as an example. The great enjoyment many women obtain from using a hose for watering the garden is also characteristic, for here the unconscious experiences the ideal fulfilment of a childhood wish.

Other women are less able or less inclined to find a substitutive gratification of their masculinity wishes in neurotic surrogates. Their symptoms give expression to a completely different attitude. They represent the male organ as something of secondary importance and unnecessary. To this attitude belong all the symptoms and phantasies of *immaculate conception*. It is as though these women want to declare by means of their neurosis: 'I can do it by myself'. One of my patients experienced an immaculate conception of this kind while in a dream-like, hazy state of consciousness. She had had a dream once before in which she held a box with a crucifix in her hands; the identification with the Virgin Mary is here quite clear. I invariably found that neurotic women who showed these phenomena exhibited especially pronounced anal character-traits. The idea of being 'able to do it alone' expresses a high degree of obstinacy, and this is also prominent in these patients. They want, for example, to find out everything in their psycho-analysis by themselves without the

122

help of the physician. They are as a rule women who through their obstinacy, envy, and self-overestimation destroy all their relationships with their environment, and indeed their whole life.

V

The symptoms we have so far described bear the character of a positive wish-fulfilment in the sense of the infantile desire to be physically equal to the man. But the last-mentioned forms of reaction already begin to approximate to the *revenge type*. For in the refusal to acknowledge the significance of the male organ there is implied, although in a very mitigated form, an emasculation of the man. We therefore approach by easy stages to the phenomena of the second group.

We regularly meet two tendencies in repressed form in the patients of this second group: a desire to take revenge on the man, and a desire to seize by force the longed-for organ, *i.e.* to rob him of it.

One of my patients dreamed that she and other women were carrying round a gigantic penis which they had stolen from an animal. This reminds us of the neurotic impulse to steal. So-called kleptomania is often traceable to the fact that a child feels injured or neglected in respect of proofs of love—which we have equated with gifts—or in some way disturbed in the gratification of its libido. It procures a substitute pleasure for the lost pleasure, and at the same time takes revenge on those who have caused it the supposed injustice. Psycho-analysis shows that in the unconscious of our patients there exist the same impulses to take forcible possession of the 'gift' which has not been received.

Vaginismus is from a practical point of view the most important of the neurotic symptoms which subserve repressed phantasies of castrating the man. The purpose of vaginismus is not only to prevent intromission of the penis, but also, in the case of its intromission, not to let it escape again, *i.e.* to retain it and thereby to castrate the man. The phantasy therefore is to rob the man of his penis and to appropriate it.

The patient who had produced the previously-mentioned dream of the morphia syringe showed a rare and complicated form of rejection of the male at the beginning of her marriage. She suffered from an hysterical adduction of her thighs whenever her husband approached her. After this had been overcome in the course of a few weeks there developed as a fresh symptom of refusal a high degree of vaginismus which only completely disappeared under psycho-analytic treatment.

This patient, whose libido was very strongly fixated on her father, once had a short dream before her marriage, which she related to me in very remarkable words. She said that in the dream her father had been run over and had 'lost some leg or other and his money'.[4] The castration idea is here not only expressed by means of the leg but also by the money. Being run over is one of the most frequent castration symbols. One of my patients whose 'totem' was a dog dreamed that a dog was run over and lost a leg. The same symbol is found in phobias that some particular male person may be run over and lose an arm or a leg. One of my patients was the victim of this anxiety with reference to various male members of her family.

For many years, and especially during the late war, I have come across women who take particular erotic interest in men who have lost an arm or a leg by amputation or accident. These are women with particularly strong feelings of inferiority; their libido prefers a mutilated man rather than one who is physically intact. For the mutilated man has also lost a limb, like themselves. It is obvious that such women feel an affinity to the mutilated man; they consider him a companion in distress and do not need to reject him with hate like the sound man. The interest some women have in Jewish men is explicable on the same grounds; they regard circumcision as at any rate a partial castration, and so they can transfer their libido on to them. I know cases in which a mixed marriage of this kind was contracted by women chiefly as a result of an unconscious motive of this nature. They also show an interest in men who are crippled in other ways and have thereby lost their masculine 'superiority'.

It was the psycho-analysis of a girl seventeen years old that gave me the strongest impression of the power of the castration complex. In this case there was an abundance of neurotic conversions, phobias, and obsessive impulses, all of which were connected with her disappointment at being a female and with revenge phantasies against the male sex. The patient had been operated on for appendicitis some years previously.[5] The surgeon had given her the removed appendix preserved in a bottle of spirit, and this she now treasured as something sacred. Her ideas of being castrated centred round this specimen, and it also appeared in her dreams with the significance of the once possessed but now lost penis.[6] As the surgeon happened to be a relative it was easy for her to connect the 'castration' performed by him with her father.

Among the patient's symptoms which rested on the repression of active castration wishes was a phobia which can be called *dread of marriage*. This anxiety was expressed in the strongest opposition to the idea of a future marriage, because the patient was afraid 'that she would have to do something terrible to her husband'. The most difficult part of the analysis was to uncover an extremely strong rejection of genital erotism, and an intense accentuation of mouth erotism in the form of phantasies which appeared compulsively. Her idea of oral intercourse was firmly united with that of biting off the penis. This phantasy, which is frequently expressed in anxiety and phenomena of the most varied kinds, was in the present case accompanied by a number of other ideas of a terrifying nature. Psycho-analysis succeeded in stopping this abundant production of a morbid imagination.

These kinds of anxiety prevent the subject from having intimate union with the other sex, and thereby from carrying out her unconsciously intended 'crime'. The patient is then the only person who has to suffer from those impulses, in the form of permanent sexual abstinence and neurotic anxiety. The case is altered as soon as the active castration phantasy has become somewhat distorted and thereby unrecognizable to consciousness. Such a modification of the manifest content of the phantasies makes it possible for the tendencies in question actually to have stronger external effects. It can, for instance, cause the idea of robbing the man of his genital to be abolished and the hostile purpose to be displaced from the organ to its function, so that the aim is to destroy his potency. The wife's neurotic sexual aversion will now often have a repelling effect on the man's libido so that a disturbance of his potency does actually occur.

A further modification of the aggressive impulse is seen in an attitude of the woman to the man that is fairly frequent and that can be exceedingly painful to him; it is the impulse to *disappoint* him. To disappoint a person is to excite expectations in him and not fulfil them. In her relations with the man the woman can do this by responding to his advances up to a certain point and then refusing to give herself to him. Such behaviour is most frequently and significantly expressed in *frigidity* on the part of the woman. Disappointing other persons is a piece of unconscious tactics which we frequently find in the psychology of the neuroses and which is especially pronounced in obsessional neurotics. These neurotics are unconsciously impelled towards violence and revenge, but on account of the contrary play of ambivalent forces these impulses are incapable of effectually breaking through. Since their hostility cannot express itself in actions, these patients excite expectations of a pleasant nature in their environment and then do not fulfil them. In the sphere of the female castration complex the tendency to disappoint can be formulated in respect of its origin as follows:

First stage: I rob you of what you have because I lack it.

Second stage: I rob you of nothing. I even promise you what I have to give.

Third stage: I will not give you what I have promised.

In very many cases frigidity is associated with a conscious readiness on the part of the woman to assume the female rôle and to acknowledge that of the man. Her unconscious striving has in part as its object the disappointment of the man, who is inclined to infer from her conscious willingness the possibility of mutual enjoyment. Besides this, she has the desire to demonstrate to herself and her partner that his sexual ability is of no importance.

If we penetrate to the deeper psychic layers we recognize how strongly the desire of the frigid woman to be male dominates her unconscious. In a previous article I have attempted to show in accordance with Freud's well-known observations on frigidity[7] that this condition in the female sex is the exact analogue of a disturbance of potency in the man, namely, 'ejaculatio præcox'.[8] In both conditions the libido is attached to that erotogenic zone which has normally a similar significance in the opposite sex. In cases of frigidity the pleasurable sensation is as a rule situated in the clitoris and the vaginal zone has none. The clitoris, however, corresponds developmentally with the penis.

Frigidity is such an exceedingly widespread disturbance that it hardly needs to be described or exemplified. On the other hand, it is less well known that the condition has varying degrees of intensity. The highest degree, that of actual anæsthesia, is rare. In these cases the vaginal mucous membrane has lost all sensitiveness to touch, so that the male organ is not perceived in sexual intercourse. Its existence is therefore actually denied. The common condition is a relative disturbance of sensitivity, in which contact is perceived but is not pleasurable. In other cases a sensation of pleasure is felt but does not go on to orgasm, or, what is the same thing, the contractions of the female organ corresponding with the climax of pleasure are absent. It is these contractions that signify the complete and positive reaction of the woman to the male activity, the absolute affirmation of the normal relation between the sexes.

Some women do obtain gratification along normal paths but endeavour to make the act as brief and prosaic as possible. They refuse all enjoyment of any preliminary pleasure; and in especial they behave after gratification as if nothing had happened that could make any impression on them, and turn quickly to some other subject of conversation, a book or occupation. These women thus give themselves up to the full physical function of the woman for a few fleeting moments only to disown it immediately afterwards.

It is an old and well-known medical fact that many women only obtain normal sexual sensation after they have had a child. They become, so to speak, only female in the full sense by the way of maternal feelings. The deeper connection of this is only to be comprehended in the light of the castration complex. As we know, a child was at an early period the 'gift' which was to compensate the little girl for the missed penis. She receives it now in reality, and thus the 'wound' is at last healed. It is to be noted that in some women there exists a wish to get a child from a man against his will; we cannot fail to see in this the unconscious tendency to take the penis from the male and appropriate it in the form of a child. The other extreme in this group is represented by those women who wish to remain childless at all costs. They decline any kind of 'substitute', and would be constantly reminded of their femininity in the most disturbing manner if they became mothers.

A relative frigidity exists not only in the sense of the degree of capacity for sensation, but also in the sense that some women are frigid with certain men and capable of sensation with others.

It will probably be expected that a marked activity on the part of the man is the most favourable condition to call forth sexual sensations in women who are frigid in this second sense. This, however, is not always the case; on the contrary, there are many women in whom a debasement of the man is just as essential a condition of love as is the debasement of the woman to many neurotic men.[9] A single example may be given in illustration of this by no means rare attitude. I analyzed a woman whose love-life was markedly polyandrous, and who was invariably anæsthetic if she had to acknowledge that the man was superior to her in any way. If, however, she had a quarrel with the man and succeeded in forcing him to give in to her, her frigidity disappeared completely. Such cases show

127

very clearly how necessary is the acknowledgement of the male genital function as a condition of a normal love-life on the part of the woman. We also meet here with one source of the conscious and unconscious impulses of prostitution in women.

Frigidity is practically a *sine qua non* of prostitution. The experiencing of full sexual sensation binds the woman to the man, and only where this is lacking does she go from man to man, just like the continually ungratified Don Juan type of man who has constantly to change his love-object. Just as the Don Juan avenges himself on all women for the disappointment which he once received from the first woman who entered into his life, so the prostitute avenges herself on every man for the gift she had expected from her father and did not receive. Her frigidity signifies a humiliation of all men and therefore a mass castration to her unconscious; and her whole life is given up to this purpose.[10]

While the frigid woman unconsciously strives to diminish the importance of that part of the body which is denied her, there is another form of refusal of the man which achieves the same aim with opposite means. In this form of refusal the man is nothing else than a sex organ and therefore consists only of coarse sensuality. Every other mental or physical quality is denied him. The effect is that the neurotic woman imagines that the man is an inferior being on account of his possession of a penis. Her self-esteem is actually enhanced, and indeed she can rejoice at being free from such a mark of inferiority. One of my patients who showed a very marked aversion to men had the obsessing hallucination of a very big penis whenever she saw a man. This vision continually brought to her mind the fact that there was nothing else in men than their genital organ, from which she turned away in disgust, but which at the same time represented something that greatly interested her unconscious. She had certain phantasies connected with this vision which were of a complementary nature. In these she represented herself as though every opening in her body, even her body as a whole, was nothing else than a receptive female organ. The vision therefore contained a mixture of overestimation and depreciation of the male organ.

VI

We have already shown that the woman's tendency to depreciate the importance of the male genital undergoes a progressive sexual repres-

128

sion, and often appears outwardly as a general desire to humiliate men. This tendency is often shown in an instinctive avoidance of men who have pronounced masculine characteristics. The woman directs her love-choice towards the passive and effeminate man, by living with whom she can daily renew the proof that her own activity is superior to his. Just like manifest homosexual women, she likes to represent the mental and physical differences between man and woman as insignificant. When she was six years old one of my patients had begged her mother to send her to a boys' school in boy's clothes because 'then no one would know that she was a girl'.

Besides the inclination to depreciate men there is also found a marked sensitiveness of the castration complex towards any situation which can awaken a feeling of inferiority, even in the remotest way. Women with this attitude refuse to accept any kind of help from a man, and show the greatest disinclination to follow any man's lead. A young woman betrayed her claims to masculinity, repressed with difficulty, by declining to walk along a street covered in deep snow in her husband's footsteps. A further very significant characteristic of this patient may be mentioned here. As a child she had had a strong desire for independence, and in adolescence she used to be very envious of the calling of two women in particular—the cashier in her father's office, and the woman who swept the street in her native town. The cause of this attitude is obvious to the psycho-analyst. The cashier sweeps money together and the crossing-sweeper sweeps dirt, and both things have the same significance in the unconscious. There is here a marked turning away from genital sexuality in favour of the formation of anal character traits, a process which I shall mention in another connection.

How strong a person's disinclination to be reminded of her femininity in any way can be is already well shown in the behaviour of children. It not infrequently happens that little girls give up knowledge they have already obtained of procreation and birth in favour of the stork fable. They dislike the rôle bestowed upon them by Nature, and the stork tale has the advantage that in it children originate without the man's part being a more privileged one than theirs in respect of activity.

The most extreme degree of sensitiveness in regard to the castration complex is found in the rarer case of psychical depression. Here the woman's feeling of unhappiness on account of her femininity is wholly unrepressed; she does not even succeed in working it off in a modified form. One of my patients complained about the utter uselessness of her life because she had been born a girl. She considered the superiority of men in all respects as obvious, and just for this reason felt it so painfully. She refused to compete with men in any sphere, and also rejected every feminine act. In particular she declined to play the female rôle in sexual life, and equally so the male one. In consequence of this attitude all conscious eroticism was entirely foreign to her; she even said that she was unable to imagine any erotic pleasure at all. Her resistance against female sexual functions assumed grotesque forms. She transferred her rejection of them to everything that reminded her, if only remotely, of bearing fruit, propagation, birth, etc. She hated flowers and green trees, and found fruit disgusting. A mistake which she made many times was easily explicable from this attitude; she would read *furchtbar* ('frightful') instead of *fruchtbar* ('fruitful'). In the whole of Nature only the winter in the mountains could give her pleasure; there was nothing to remind her there of living things and propagation, but only rock, ice, and snow. She had the idea that in marriage the woman was of quite secondary importance, and an expression of hers clearly showed how much this idea was centred in her castration complex. She said that the ring—which was to her a hated female symbol—was not fit to be a symbol of marriage, and she suggested a nail as a substitute. Her over-emphasis of masculinity was quite clearly based on her penis envy as a little girl—an envy which appeared in a strikingly undisguised form when she was grown up.

In many women the failure to reconcile themselves to their lack of the male organ is expressed in neurotic horror at the sight of wounds. Every wound re-awakens in their unconscious the idea of the 'wound' received in childhood. Sometimes they have a definite feeling of anxiety at the sight of wounds; sometimes this sight or the mere idea of it causes a 'painful feeling in the lower part of the body'. At the commencement of her psycho-analysis the patient whom I mentioned above as having a complicated form of vaginismus spoke of her horror of wounds before there had been any mention of the castration complex. She said that she could look at large and irregular wounds without being particularly affected, but that she could not bear to see a cut in her skin or on another person, however small it was, if it gaped slightly and if the red colour of the flesh was visible in the depth of the cut. It gave her an intense pain in the genital region coupled with marked anxiety, 'as though something had been cut away there'. (Similar sensations accompanied by anxiety are found in men with a marked fear of castration.) In many women it does not need the sight of a wound to cause feelings of the kind described; they have an aversion, associated with marked affect, to the idea of surgical operations and even to knives. Some time ago a lady who was a stranger to me and who would not give her name rang me up on the telephone and asked me if I could prevent an operation that had been arranged for the next day. On my request for more information she told me she was to be operated on for a severe uterine hæmorrhage due to myomata. When I told her it was not part of my work to prevent a necessary and perhaps life-saving operation she did not reply, but explained with affective volubility that she had always been 'hostile to all operations', adding, 'whoever is once operated on is for ever afterwards a cripple for life'. The wild exaggeration of this statement becomes comprehensible if we remember that from the point of view of the unconscious an operation of this sort has made the little girl a 'cripple' in early childhood.

VII

A tendency with which we are well acquainted and which we have already mentioned leads in the sphere of the female castration complex to modifications of the woman's aversion to that which is tabooed, and even to a conditional admission of it and in especial to compromise formations between impulse and repression.

In some of our patients we come across phantasies which are concerned with the possibility of an acceptance of the man and which formulate the conditions under which the patient would be prepared to reconcile herself to her femininity. I will mention a certain proviso which I have met with many times; it is: 'I could be content with my femininity if I were absolutely the most beautiful of all women'. All men would lie at the feet of the most beautiful woman, and the woman's narcissim would consider this power not a bad compensation for the defect she is so painfully aware of. It is in fact easier for a beautiful woman to assuage her castration complex than for an ugly one. Nevertheless, this idea of being the most beautiful of all women does not have the aforesaid softening effect in all cases. I know of a woman who said: 'I should like to be the most beautiful of all women so that all men would adore me. Then I would show them the cold shoulder.' In this case the craving for revenge is clear enough; this remark was made by a woman of an extremely tyrannical nature

131

which was based on a wholly unsublimated castration complex.

Most women, however, are not so extreme. They are inclined to compromise and to satisfy themselves with relatively harmless expressions of their repressed hostility. In this connection we are able to understand a characteristic trait in the conduct of many women. We must keep in view the fact that sexual activity is essentially associated with the male organ, that the woman is only in the position to excite the man's libido or respond to it, and that otherwise she is compelled to adopt a waiting attitude. In a great number of women we find resistance against being a woman displaced to this necessity of waiting. In their married life these women take a logical revenge upon the man in that they *keep him waiting* on every occasion in daily life.

There is another proviso of a similar nature to the above mentioned 'If I were the most beautiful woman'. In some women we find a readiness to admit the activity of the male and their own passivity, provided that they are desired by the most manly (greatest, most important) man. We have no difficulty in recognizing here the infantile desire for the father. I have already related from one of my psycho-analyses an example of a phantastic form of this idea. I was able to follow the development of a similar phantasy through different stages in the psycho-analysis of other patients. The original desire ran: 'I should like to be a man'. When this was given up, the patient wished to be 'the only woman' ('the only woman belonging to my father' being originally meant). When this wish had to give way to reality, too, the idea appeared: 'As a woman I should like to be unmatchable'.

Certain compromise formations are of far greater practical importance, and though well known to psycho-analysts nevertheless merit special consideration in this connection. They concern the acknowledgement of the man, or, to be more correct, his activity and the organ serving it, under certain limiting conditions. The woman will tolerate and even desire sexual relations with the man so long as her own genital organ is avoided, or is, so to speak, considered as non-existent. She displaces her libido on to other erotogenic zones (mouth, anus) and softens her feelings of displeasure originating in the castration complex by thus turning away her sexual interest from her genital organ. The body openings which are now at the disposal of the libido are not specifically female organs. Further determinants are found in the analysis of each of this kind of cases, one only of which need be mentioned, namely, the possibility of active castration through biting by means of the mouth. Oral and anal perversions in women are thus to a considerable extent explicable as effects of the castration complex.

Among our patients we certainly have to deal more frequently with the negative counterpart of the perversions, *i.e.* with conversion symptoms which occur in relation to the specific erotogenic zones, than with the perversions themselves. Examples of this kind have already been given above. I referred among other cases to that of a young girl who had a phobia of having to do some horrible thing to her husband in the event of her marriage. The 'horrible thing' turned out to be the idea of castrating him through biting. The case showed most clearly how displacement of the libido from the genital to the mouth zone can gratify very different tendencies simultaneously. In such phantasies the mouth serves equally to represent the desired reception of the male organ and its destruction. Facts like these warn us not to be too ready to over-estimate a single determinant. Although in the preceding presentation we have estimated the castration complex as an important impelling force in the development of neurotic phenomena, we are not justified in over-valuing it in the way Adler does when he represents the 'masculine protest' as the essential *causa movens* of the neuroses. Experience that is well-founded and verified anew every day shows us that precisely those neurotics of both sexes who loudly proclaim and lay emphasis on their masculine tendencies frequently conceal—and only superficially—intense female-passive desires. Our psycho-analytic experience should constantly remind us of the over-determination of all physical structures. It has to reject as one-sided and fragmentary every psychological method of working which does not take into full account the influence of various factors on one another. In my present study I have collected material belonging to the castration complex from a great number of psycho-analyses. And I should like to say expressly that it is solely for reasons of clearness that I have only occasionally alluded to the ideas connected with female-passive instincts which none of my patients failed to express.

VIII

Women whose ideas and feelings are influenced and governed by the castration complex to any great extent—no matter whether consciously or unconsciously—transplant the effect of this complex on to their children. They influence the psychosexual development of their daughters either by speaking disparagingly of female sexuality to them, or by unconsciously showing their aversion to men. The latter method is the more permanently effective one, because it tends to undermine the heterosexuality of the growing girl. On the other hand, the method of depreciation can produce really traumatic effects, as when a mother says to her daughter who is about to marry, 'What is going to happen now is disgusting'.

It is in particular those neurotic women whose libido has been displaced from the genital to the anal zone who give expression to their disgust of the male body in this or a similar manner. These women also produce serious effects on their sons without foreseeing the result of their attitude. A mother with this kind of aversion to the male sex injures the narcissism of the boy. A boy in his early years is proud of his genital organs; he likes to exhibit them to his mother, and expects her to admire them. He soon sees that his mother ostentatiously looks the other way, even if she does not give expression to her disinclination in words. These women are especially given to prohibiting masturbation on the grounds that it is disgusting for the boy to touch his genital organ. Whereas they are most careful to avoid touching and even mentioning the penis, they tend to caress the child's buttocks and are never tired of speaking of its 'bottom', often getting the child to repeat this word. They also take an excessive interest in the child's defæcatory acts. The boy is thus forced into a new orientation of his libido. Either it is transferred from the genital to the anal zone, or the boy is impelled towards a member of his own sex—his father in the first instance—to whom he feels himself bound by a bond which is quite comprehensible to us. At the same time he becomes a woman-hater, and later will be constantly ready to criticize very severely the weaknesses of the female sex. This chronic influence of the mother's castration complex seems to me to be of greater importance as a cause of castration-fear in boys than occasionally uttered threats of castration. I can produce abundant evidence for this view from my psycho-analyses of male neurotics. The mother's anal-erotism is the earliest and most dangerous enemy of the psychosexual development of children, since she has more influence on them in the earliest years of life than the father.

To every one of us who is a practising psycho-analyst the question occurs at times whether the trifling number of individuals to whom we can give assistance justifies the great expenditure of time, labour and patience it involves. The answer to this question is contained in what has been said above. If we succeed in freeing such a person from the defects of his psychosexuality, *i.e.* from the difficulties of his castration complex, we obviate the neuroses of children to a great extent, and thus help the coming generation. Our psycho-analytic activity is a quiet and little appreciated work and the object of much attack, but its effect on and beyond the individual seems to us to make it an aim worth a great deal of labour.

NOTES

1 For a more detailed discussion of the character-trait of envy, cf. Chapter XXIII., 'Contributions to the Theory of the Anal Character', in *Selected Papers of Karl Abraham* (New York: Basic Books) or Abraham, *Selected Papers on Psycho-Analysis* (London: The Hogarth Press Ltd., 1927).

2 Beiträge zum Männlichkeitskomplex der Frau' (1917).

3 Cf. Chapter IX, Abraham, *op. cit.*

4 *Vermögen'* ('money') also means 'capacity' and 'sexual potency'.—*Trans.*]

5 The removal of the vermiform appendix often stimulates the castration complex in men as well.

6 Another patient imagined she had a brother and had to remove his appendix.

7 *Drei Abhandlungen zur Sexualtheorie,* 4. Aufl., S. 83f.

8 Cf. Chap. XIII, Abraham, *op. cit.*

9 See Freud, 'Beiträge zur Psychologie des Liebeslebens', sections I. and II.

10 The remarks of Dr. Theodor Reik in a discussion at the Berlin Psycho-Analytical Society have suggested this idea to me.

The Castration Complex Reconsidered

Joel Kovel

Freud once likened himself to a conquistador—a revealing image that suggests both the boldness of early psychoanalytic writing and its axiomatic assumption of male superiority. Karl Abraham's essay on the female castration complex is a good example: a brilliant clinical account, all the more marvelous for having been written virtually without benefit of tradition, it is yet riddled with masculine bias.

Bias clearly does not belong in a scientific work; yet its presence here does not so much invalidate Abraham's findings as put them in a broader light. We might regard the illusions to which a thinker of this caliber falls victim as something of a toll demanded of the psychoanalytic explorers out of their loyalty to the patriarchal system whose assumptions they were shattering.

Thus we have Abraham calling attention to the living psychic root of the oppression of women in terms which justify that oppression. "The normal adult woman becomes reconciled to her own sexual role. . . . she desires passive gratification and longs for a child. Her castration complex thus gives rise to no disturbing effects."

No, because the effects are then given over to the world. This is the basic meaning of that garbage pail of a word, "normal." The normal person is basically one who need not recognize his or her madness owing to its having been ceded to the surround. No less an analytic classicist than Edward Glover wrote once that "normality may be a form of mad-

136

ness which goes unrecognized because it happens to be a good adaptation to reality."

The obvious corollary is that reality—i.e., culture—contains deposits of crystallized madness, and imposes them back upon the developing person. Thus we must look well beyond the bounds of individual psychology, and certainly beyond the effects of biological givens upon behavior. There are, no doubt, such effects—most notably in the impact of biology upon body image. But these quite real biological distinctions are not the essence of the difficulty between the sexes; and the arguments that rage over the biological question, whether they assert from one side that anatomy is destiny or rebut from the other that it is irrelevant, often succeed only in indicating, through a common false premise, where the true problem resides. For both kinds of arguments, seemingly so opposed, build on the assumption that what has to be determined is whether it matters if one really has a penis or not; both meanwhile avoid the critical reality of why people are so intolerant of perceived gender and why they structure their social relations accordingly.

The biological fact—like any other fact—is of no value in itself; it is given value only by our wishes. The astoundingly common failure to recognize this simple truth reveals just how powerful are the passions which have become entrenched here, and how they force us either to eliminate great portions of our vision or to discount or otherwise distort what is seen.

Freud's insights into human nature have become so heavily larded over by several generations of culture that we easily lose sight of what he brought to our attention. We tend to think, for example, that because ideas like the castration complex can be written about, we are now conscious of them. That is, of course, tempting; one likes to have a miscreant in sight and under control, and if there ever was a disturber of the peace it is the castration complex. But to know about is not to know. Freud asserted, and we might as well take him seriously, that such knowing was perpetually resisted by powerful counterforces, that it is radically cut off from the middle-ground of consciousness where our lives are lived, that only specialized and arduous efforts would succeed in bringing it to awareness and that even then awareness would remain subject to an ever present trend towards erosion.

We are gorgeously unstructured at birth and spend the rest of our days

137

trying to synthesize the hodgepodge flung at us by life. Nothing is more compelling than the erotic, for it draws us most strongly onward and promises both completion and dissolution; it bids us give up who we are to realize an ancient yearning which is at once ecstasy and nothingness, and it signifies the yielding up of all those ramparts against infantile anxieties which themselves arose in an earlier erotic situation.

Where there is anxiety of this sort there is hatred as well, set aside in order that the world should make sense, that body integrity be maintained and that the love of those needed remain preserved. Sex threatens the tenuous order we have established: it promises the greatest pleasure and, with the return of hatred, the greatest pain; and it is no wonder therefore that special conditions should have always been set up to channel the hatred and so make possible some sexuality—although at the price of its attenuation. I am but returning here to Freud's realization of the opposition between sexuality and civilization, an insight which remains true despite many important changes in sexual patterns (developments which have themselves fostered the spirit of feminism).

The castration complex is the internal documentation of this opposition. It is the implanting of hatred into the sexual act and the differentiation of its partners into the injurer and the injured. And while both sexes are afflicted, and probably suffer equally,[1] it is the male who is inherently more vulnerable—not so much because of the real or fancied vulnerability of his precious member as the deep anxiety caused by his infantile attachment to a person of the opposite sex. At the core of the male castration complex is the fear of passively being absorbed back into the mother. Every genital sexual urge carries with it the trace of this earlier relationship and it is only, I think, by the provision of patriarchal civilization that the male can reassure himself that this deeper catastrophe will not occur. Patriarchy, however, not only fails to solve the problem but adds new and more prominent difficulties: it brings to the fore the further threat of castration by the father as punishment for envy of his prerogatives; and it institutionalizes penis-worship. These dubious boons are gladly chosen, however, for they help minimize the deeper threat. Fathers are needed to keep mothers in their place, women need to be devalued, the hatred and fear needs to be distilled out of sex—and so it is that the natural form of the female genital becomes identified with a wound and its functions with those of the cesspool. Woman becomes Circe and Medusa, and a man's task in civilization is to control her.

Civilization, built out of repression, provides a real counterweight to men's deepest fears by placing great value on male achievements, thus vindicating the craziness that went into its making. By structuring itself according to the male castration complex, civilization sets the conditions under which women are forced to define themselves as castrated. The psyche is hemmed in then, not by biology, but by the social processing of biological givens.

The castration complex is sexual madness internalized and made unconscious. It makes life a walled city, then stands unseen outside its gates. And it dictates that within this city women need be oppressed, in order to keep us from experiencing its terror. The oppression of women is thus secured by the castration complex even as the complex feeds on the very world of oppressiveness it engenders.

What a villain is the inner voice that tells a woman to hate what she is and envy what she is not! It will not be quieted by pointing to the social injustices that sustain it. Nor does it go away when the obvious truth is pointed out: that male worldly prerogatives have as much innate value as those of the four-year-old boy who amazes his sister by peeing while standing up; or that they are often no real boon at all—unless one thinks that slaughtering one another in warfare or dropping dead in hot pursuit of success are worth a few extra inches of visible flesh.

And yet people think just that. They think it consciously and they think it—with greater force—unconsciously. And while the conscious belief can be reasoned away or appealed to with the aid of moral or practical countermeasures, its demonic companion will not so readily yield. Human narcissism is simply too strong and too deeply rooted in irrational fears. If phallic pride were simply a positive trait then it could be successfully inveighed against by calling attention to the injustices it spawns. But as it is grounded in the negation of infantile fears, then it can only intensify itself under attack. And the female castration complex is built on essentially the same dread: one level of equality that no one is eager to admit. Consequently—here we see the castration complex at work again to distort our thinking—it is easily assumed that women suffer only from envy of the penis; they have no fear for their own genital, since, of course, everybody knows that women have no genital, hence nothing to lose. But if we recognize this as the nonsense it is, we will appreciate that no sex has a monopoly on fears of mutilation and that an inferior self-image is not just something drummed in from the outside, but a protection against experiencing these fears. In this regard, then, the female castration complex also shares a tendency toward reinforcing the status quo despite all protest.

There is a deeper ambiguity here, which can only be hinted at. Beneath the realization that motives for protest and submission are yoked together at the unconscious level is the further truth that the very sense of justice appealed to by liberatory movements is a male ideal, albeit purified; looking into its cultural origins, one finds its root in opposition to a submerged principle of female castration. Aeschylus made this into a parable on the origins of civilization itself. The Eumenides, principle of the castrating and castrated mother Clytaemnestra, threaten to hound Orestes into madness as punishment for his revenge on behalf of his father. Only a male-dominated culture could protect him; and the actual historical triumph of this culture is celebrated by the poet in his transformation of the mother-principle into Athene, a motherless man's woman, the original *alma mater,* and a safe house-goddess for phallic civilization. Good psychologist that he was, Aeschylus realized that the Eumenides would remain permanently rooted in the repressed, hence that the image of woman summoned up by them would ever after have to be contended with as a constant unconscious goad to the realization of ideals (e.g. the sense of justice) that embody its opposite.

Now the above poses no mean challenge for women. Not biology, not consciously manipulable attitudes, but an entire culture is stacked against feminism. Yet to claim that the problem is deep-rooted, complex, and ambiguous is not to encourage acceptance of the existing state of affairs. The values inherent in a psychoanalytic approach add up only to respect for truthfulness about the whole range of human functioning; they say nothing about the desirability of the cultural equilibrium which has been worked out, and nothing therefore about any political stance, despite the middle-of-the-road or moderately liberal posture which most analysts in fact take. Politics is a matter of values—which may have their own determinants, yet remain of necessity a matter of choice. In any case, the truth has to be contended with, and any liberatory movement which fails to take into account the full spectrum of what it opposes will stumble over the portion ignored. Those who concentrate simply on affecting conscious values or material relationships are going to be sucked back into the assumptions of the established order if they are unable to take account of the unconscious in general, or the castration complex in particular.

140

And by the same standard, any effort that fancies it can accomplish liberation by analysis, or some other primary transformation in awareness, is equally hobbled, albeit on the other foot. Abraham's essay is a good example of the limitations of this approach. By simply demonstrating an unconscious complex without any coordinated social critique, the individual is given no choice other than to go along with the cultural delusion which is civilization's classic response to its discontents.

The corrective to this delusion is not universal psychoanalysis, but a coordination of social critique with psychoanalytic understanding. The nucleus of castration fear within social institutions will otherwise go unrecognized—as will many intermediate structures such as the family. It is ironic that the women's movement should find itself so at odds with psychoanalysis, since no other body of knowledge better comprehends the roots of the injustices which feminism attacks. Yet reactionary trends in both movements have so far prevented any real cross-fertilization.

What would such conjugation be like? We know enough by now to sense its rough outline, even if most of the work lies ahead. A new synthesis would have first of all to be genuinely critical: to stand sufficiently far from established forms to expose their inner contradictions. That stance was inherent in the work of both Freud and Marx, and their ideas remain the basis of any critical and comprehensive approach.

A genuine synthesis of this sort would bid to correct Marxist thought at its weakest point—appreciation of sexuality and the irrational—even as it correspondingly amplified psychoanalytic theory. By including material contributions to the sexual problem along with sexual aspects of political economy, it would begin to recognize the fundamental unity of the repressive process in civilization. Feminism could then be seen as a response to one particular form of repression which has crystallized out of the general process. Individual women could respond according to the ways in which their own identities had been affected, yet always in the context of this more general analysis of or perspective on civilization and its functions. Without such a comprehensive framework I suspect that the women's movement may atrophy as a serious social force.

It might be helpful here to make a comparison with another particular manifestation of historical disease—racism. It has often been observed that women and blacks share a common type of oppression. That this idea is more than propaganda is shown by the intricate but powerful historical connection between sexual repressiveness, racial relations, and the for-

141

tunes of capitalism. This is not the place to detail the pattern, but sexual segregation and racial segregation seem to have gone together, and both increased with the decline of slavery and the rise of industrialization: recent research has disclosed, for example, that separate toilet facilities for men and women were introduced with the modern factory in the nineteenth century.

We cannot understand these phenomena without taking into account the psychohistorical playing out of the particular Western style of the castration complex. What is distinctively Western from a psychohistorical point of view is, as I tried to detail in another study,[2] the imposition of a special kind of anality onto culture and its transformation into the abstract, calculating mentality. Such rationality developed in part as a flight from an excrementally envisaged body which, for all its horror, was still intensely desired. Culture was then structured to provide certain manageable forms of that body for repossession by the white male mind. As is often the case, the means of control is but one step removed from the source of fear, here building upon a symbolic elaboration of the momentous proximity of the genital and excretory organs. "Female" became firmly identified with that which is castrated, dark, soft, smelly, wet (ergo: weak, unreliable, stupid, etc.)—much as "black" became associated with that which is castrated, dark, sensual, submissive (weak, unreliable, stupid . . .)—while (white) male came to stand for the opposite.

Symbols must be grounded in a material social order if they are to matter historically. And so we come to live in a world which certifies delusion as truth from many angles, imposing beyond consciousness a logic all its own. The worship of cold machines and hard facts makes woman into something to be shunned and put down—just as it does darker people. Both become the victims who have to be blamed for their oppression; and in each case the need to rationalize what is going on has spurred some of the proudest flights of the white phallic mind. (Only think how much of our industrial history encompasses this dynamic.) With the latent frights of repressed fantasies keeping us in line, we have been only too willing to go along. Thus we freely elect a President who will not be "soft" on communism and thinks he proves his masculinity by flattening unruly Asians while watching football; or we give the greatest value to those pursuits which rape and soil nature. And thus we get those millions of particular internalized variations on the chronicle of our his-

142

tory in the various male and female castration complexes which show up in the consulting room.

No doubt mounting contradictions within the patriarchal system make possible the thrust of feminism, as they have other liberatory movements. It seems important to remember that psychoanalysis was also born out of contradictions—in nineteenth-century European patriarchy—despite its having at times been used against newer ideas and movements. Freud, Abraham, and other psychoanalytic pioneers took advantage of the breakup of older forms to create a new vision. Naturally enough, they carried along past assumptions—indeed were analysing themselves, with their heritage of phallocentric attitudes, and could not but drag some of them into their theory and values. But feminism too can be covertly yoked to that which it aims to transcend. One measure of such bondage would be failure to make use of the critical truth in psychoanalysis. Insofar as feminism and psychoanalysis fail to appreciate their common source in erotic protest, they remain in thrall to the repressiveness against which that protest is lodged.

NOTES

1 As against individuals, in whom the suffering may vary greatly, according, one would think, to the degree of love and coherence in their families. The relationship between individual, family and society is too elaborate—even in our limited state of understanding—to be considered here; yet it is the crux of the entire problem.

2 *White Racism: A Psychohistory*, New York: Pantheon Books, 1970.

Cavell on Deutsch

The Psychology of Women in Relation to the Functions of Reproduction[1] (1924)

Helene Deutsch

Psycho-analytic research discovered at the very outset that the development of the infantile libido to the normal heterosexual object-choice is in women rendered difficult by certain peculiar circumstances.

In males the path of this development is straightforward, and the advance from the 'phallic' phase does not take place in consequence of a complicated 'wave of repression', but is based upon a ratification of that which already exists and is accomplished through ready and willing utilization of an already urgent force. The essence of the achievement lies in the mastery of the Oedipus attitude which it connotes, and in overcoming the feelings of guilt bound up with this.

The girl, on the other hand, has in addition to this a two-fold task to perform: (1) she has to renounce the masculinity attaching to the clitoris; (2) in her transition from the 'phallic' to the 'vaginal' phase she has to discover a new genital organ.

The man attains his final stage of development when he discovers the vagina in the world outside himself and possesses himself of it sadistically. In this his guide is his own genital organ, with which he is already familiar and which impels him to the act of possession.

The woman has to discover this new sexual organ *in her own person*, a discovery which she makes through being masochistically subjugated by

147

the penis, the latter thus becoming the guide to this fresh source of pleasure.

The final phase of attaining to a definitively feminine attitude is not gratification through the sexual act of the infantile desire for a penis, but full realization of the vagina as an organ of pleasure—an exchange of the desire for a penis for the real and equally valuable possession of a vagina. This newly-discovered organ must become for the woman 'the whole ego in miniature', a 'duplication of the ego', as Ferenczi[2] terms it when speaking of the value of the penis to the man.

In the following paper I shall try to set forth how this change in the valuation of a person's own genital organ takes place and what relation it bears to the function of reproduction in women.

We know how the different organizations of libido succeed one another and how each successive phase carries with it elements of the previous ones, so that no phase seems to have been completely surmounted but merely to have relinquished its central rôle. Along each of these communicating lines of development the libido belonging to the higher stages tends regressively to revert to its original condition, and succeeds in so doing in various ways.

The consequence of this oscillation of libido between the different forms taken by it in development is not only that the higher phases contain elements of the lower ones, but, conversely, that the libido on its path of regression carries with it constituents of the higher phases which it interweaves with the earlier ones, a process which we recognize subsequently in phantasy-formation and symptoms.

Thus the first or oral phase is auto-erotic, that is to say, it has no object either narcissistically, in the ego, or in the outside world. And yet we know that the process of weaning leaves in the Ucs[3] traces of a narcissistic wound. This is because the mother's breast is regarded as a part of the subject's own body and, like the penis later, is cathected with large quantities of narcissistic libido. Similarly, the oral gratification derived from the act of sucking leads to discovering the mother and to finding the first object in her.

The mysterious, heterosexual part of the little girl's libido finds its first explanation already in the earliest phase of development. To the tender love which she devotes to her father ('the sheltering male') as the nearest love-object side by side with the mother is added a large part of that sexual libido which, originating in the oral zone, in the first instance cathected the maternal breasts. Analysis of patients shows us that in a certain phase of development the Ucs equates the paternal penis with the maternal breast as an organ of suckling. This equation coincides with the conception of coitus (characteristic of this phase) as a relation between the mouth of the mother and the penis of the father and is extended into the theory of oral impregnation. The passive aim of this phase is achieved through the mucous membrane of the mouth zone, while the active organ of pleasure is the breast.

In the sadistic-anal phase the penis loses its significance (for phantasy-life) as an organ of suckling and becomes an organ of mastering. Coitus is conceived of as a sadistic act; in phantasies of beating, as we know, the girl either takes over the rôle of the father, or experiences the act masochistically in identification with the mother.

In this phase the passive aim is achieved through the anus, while the column of fæces becomes the active organ of pleasure, which, like the breast in the first phase, belongs at one and the same time to the outside world and to the subject's own body. By a displacement of cathexis the faeces here acquire the same narcissistic value as the breast in the oral phase. The birth-phantasy of this phase is that of the 'anal child'.

We are familiar with the biological analogy between the anus and the mouth; that between the breast and the penis as active organs arises from their analogous functions.

One would suppose it an easy task for feminine libido in its further development to pass on and take possession of the third opening of the female body—the vagina. Biologically, in the development of the embryo, the common origin of anus and vagina in the cloaca has already foreshadowed this step. The penis as an organ of stimulation and the active agent for this new erotogenic zone perhaps attains its function by means of the equation: breast—column of fæces—penis.

The difficulty lies in the fact that the bisexual character of development interposes between anus and vagina the masculine clitoris as an erotogenic zone. In the 'phallic' phase of development the clitoris attracts to itself a large measure of libido, which it relinquishes in favour of the 'feminine' vagina only after strenuous and not always decisive struggles. Obviously, this transition from the 'phallic' to the 'vaginal' phase (which later coincides with what Abraham[4] terms the 'postambivalent') must be recognized as the hardest task in the libidinal development of the woman.

The penis is already in the early infantile period discovered auto-

149

erotically. Moreover, its exposed position makes it liable to stimulation in various ways connected with the care of the baby's body, and thus it becomes an erotogenic zone before it is ready to fulfil its reproductive function. All three masturbatory phases are dominated by this organ.

The clitoris (which is in reality so inadequate a substitute for the penis) assumes the importance of the latter throughout the whole period of development. The hidden vagina plays no part. The child is unaware of its existence, possibly has mere vague premonitions of it. Every attempt to pacify the little girl's envy of the penis with the explanation that she also has 'something' is rightly doomed to complete failure; for the possession of something which one neither sees nor feels cannot give any satisfaction. Nevertheless, as a zone of active energy the clitoris lacks the abundant energy of the penis; even in the most intense masturbatory activity it cannot arrogate to itself such a measure of libido as does the latter organ. Accordingly the primal distribution of libido over the erotogenic zones is subject to far less modification than in the male, and the female, owing to the lesser tyranny of the clitoris, may all her life remain more 'polymorph-pervers', more infantile; to her more than to the male 'the whole body is a sexual organ'. In the wave of development occurring at puberty this erotogenicity of the whole body increases, for the libido which is forced away from the clitoris (presumably by way of the inner secretions) flows back to the body as a whole. This must be of importance in the later destiny of the woman, because in this way she is regressively set back into a state in which, as Ferenczi[5] shows, she 'cleaves to intrauterine existence' in sexual things.

In 'transformations which take place at puberty' (and during the subsequent period of adolescence) libido has therefore to flow towards the vagina from two sources: (1) from the whole body, especially from those erotogenic zones that have the most powerful cathexis, (2) from the clitoris, which has still to some extent retained its libidinal cathexis.

The difficulty lies in the fact that the clitoris is not at all ready to renounce its rôle, that the conflict at puberty is associated with the traumatic occurrence of menstruation; and this not only revives the castration-wound but at the same time represents, both in the biological and the psychological sense, the disappointment of a frustrated pregnancy. The periodic repetition of menstruation every time recalls the conflicts of puberty and reproduces them in a less acute form.

At the same time there is no doubt that the whole process of menstruation is calculated to exercise an eroticizing and preparatory influence upon the vagina.

The task of conducting the libido to the vagina from the two sources which I have mentioned devolves upon the activity of the penis, and that in two ways.

First, libido must be drawn from the whole body. Here we have a perfect analogy to the woman's breast, which actively takes possession of the infant's mouth and so centres the libido of the whole body in this organ. Just so does the vagina, under the stimulus of the penis and by a process of displacement 'from above downwards', take over the passive rôle of the sucking mouth in the equation: penis—breast. This oral, sucking activity of the vagina is indicated by its whole anatomical structure (with their corresponding terms).

The second operation accomplished by the penis is the carrying-over of the remaining clitoris-libido to the vagina. This part of the libido still takes a male direction, even when absorbed by the vagina; that is to say, the clitoris renounces its male function in favour of the penis that approaches the body from without.

As the clitoris formerly played its 'masculine' part by identification with the paternal penis, so the vagina takes over its rôle (that of the clitoris) by allowing one part of its functions to be dominated by an identification with the penis of the partner.

In certain respects the orgastic activity of the vagina is wholly analogous to the activity of the penis. I refer to the processes of secretion and contraction. As in the man, we have here an 'amphimixis' of urethral and anal tendencies—of course greatly diminished in degree. Both these component-instincts develop their full activity only in that 'extension' of the sexual act, pregnancy and parturition.

We see then that one of the vaginal functions arises through identification with the penis, which in this connection is regarded as a possession of the subject's own body. Here the psychic significance of the sexual act lies in the repetition and mastery of the castration-trauma.

The truly passive, feminine attitude of the vagina is based upon the oral, sucking activity discussed above.

In this function coitus signifies for the woman a restoring of that first relation of the human being with the outside world, in which the object is orally incorporated, introjected; that is to say, it restores that condition of perfect unity of being and harmony in which the distinction between

151

subject and object was annulled. Thus the attainment of the highest, genital, 'post-ambivalent' (Abraham) phase signifies a repetition of the earliest, pre-ambivalent phase.

In relation to the partner the situation of incorporating is a repetition of sucking at the mother's breast; hence incorporation amounts to a repetition and mastery of the trauma of weaning. In the equation penis —breast, and in the sucking activity of the vagina, coitus realizes the fulfilment of the phantasy of sucking at the paternal penis.

The identifications established between the two partners in the preparatory act (Ferenczi) now acquire a manifold significance, identification with the mother taking place in two ways: (1) through equating the penis with the breast, (2) through experiencing the sexual act masochistically, i.e. through repeating that identification with the mother which belongs to the phase of a sadistic conception of coitus.

Through this identification, then, the woman plays in coitus the part of mother and child simultaneously—a relation which is continued in pregnancy, when one actually is both mother and child at the same time.

As the object of maternal libido in the act of suckling, the partner therefore becomes the child, but at the same time the libido originally directed towards the father must be transferred to the partner (according to the equation: penis—organ of suckling and to the conception of coitus as a sadistic act of mastery). This shows us that ultimately coitus represents for the woman incorporation (by the mouth) of the father, who is made into the child and then retains this rôle in the pregnancy which occurs actually or in phantasy.

I arrived at this identification-series, which is complicated and may seem far-fetched, as a result of all the experience which I have had of cases of frigidity and sterility.

Ferenczi's 'maternal regression' is realized for the woman in equating coitus with the situation of sucking. The last act of this regression (return into the uterus), which the man accomplishes by the act of introjection in coitus, is realized by the woman in pregnancy in the complete identification between mother and child. In my opinion the mastery of 'the trauma of birth', which Rank[6] has shown to be so important, is accomplished by the woman above all in the actively repeated act of parturition, for to the Ucs carrying and being carried, giving birth and being born, are as identical as giving suck and sucking.

This conception of coitus reflects the whole psychological difference

152

displayed by men and women in their relation to the object-world. The man actively takes possession of some piece of the world and in this way attains to the bliss of the primal state. And this is the form taken by his tendencies to sublimation. In the act of incorporation passively experienced the women introjects into herself a piece of the object-world which she then absorbs.

In its rôle of organ of sucking and incorporation the vagina becomes the receptacle not of the penis but of the child. The energy required for this function is derived not from the clitoris, but, as I said before, from the libidinal cathexis of the whole body, this libido being conducted to the vagina by channels familiar to us. The vagina now itself represents the child, and so receives that cathexis of narcissistic libido which flows on to the child in the 'extension' of the sexual act. It becomes the 'second ego', the ego in miniature, as does the penis for the man. A woman who succeeds in establishing this maternal function of the vagina by giving up the claim of the clitoris to represent the penis has reached the goal of feminine development, *has become a woman.*

In men the function of reproduction terminates with the act of introjection, for with them that function coincides with the relief from sexual tension by ejaculation.

Women have to perform in two phases the function which men accomplish in a single act; nevertheless the first act of incorporation contains elements which indicate the tendency to get rid of the germ-plasm by expulsion, as is done by the male in coitus. Orgasm in the woman appears not only to imply identification with the man but to have yet another motive; it is the expression of the attempt to impart to coitus itself in the interest of the race the character of parturition (we might call it a 'missed labour'). In animals the process of expulsion of the products of reproduction very often takes place during the sexual act in the female as well as in the male.

In the human female this process is not carried through, though it is obviously indicated and begun in the orgastic function; it terminates only in the second act, that of parturition. The process therefore is a *single* one, which is merely divided into two phases by an interval of time. As the first act contains (in orgasm) elements of the second, so the second is permeated by the pleasure-mechanisms of the first. I even assume that the act of parturition contains the acme of sexual pleasure owing to the relief from stimulation by the germ-plasm. If this be so, parturition is a process of 'autotomy' analogous to ejaculation (Ferenczi), requiring, however, the powerful stimulus of the matured fœtus in order that it may function. This reverses the view which Groddeck first had the courage to put forward, at the Hague Congress,that parturition is associated with pleasure owing to its analogy with coitus. It would rather seem that coitus acquires the character of a pleasurable act mainly through the fact that it constitutes an attempt at and beginning of parturition. In support of my view I would cite the following considerations.

Freud[7] has told us that the sadistic instincts of destruction reach their fullest development when the erotic sexual instincts are put out of action. This happens after their tension has been relieved in the act of gratification. The death-instinct has then a free hand and can carry through its claims undisturbed. A classical instance of this is furnished by those lower animals in which the sexual act leads to death.

This applies to the fertilizing male, but repeats itself *mutatis mutandis* in the female also, when the fertilized ovum is expelled after a longer or shorter interval during which it has matured in the maternal body. There are many species of animals, e.g. certain spiders, in which the females perish when they have fulfilled the function of reproduction. If the liberation of the death-instinct is a consequence of the gratification of sexual trends, it is only logical to assume that this gratification reaches its highest point in the female only in the act of parturition.

In actual fact parturition is for the woman an orgy of masochistic pleasure, and the dread and premonition of death which precede this act are clearly due to a perception of the menace of the destructive instincts about to be liberated.

Conditions of insanity sometimes met with after delivery are characterized by a specially strong tendency to suicide and murderous impulses towards the newly-born child.

These facts in my opinion confirm my assumption that parturition constitutes for women the termination of the sexual act, which was only inaugurated by coitus, and that the ultimate gratification of the erotic instinct is analogous to that in men and takes place at the moment when soma and germ-plasm are separated.

The interval in time between the two acts is filled by complicated processes in the economy of the libido.

The object incorporated in coitus is introjected physically and psychically, finds its extension in the child, and persists in the mother as a part of her ego.

Thus we see that the mother's relation to the 'child' as a libidinal object is two-fold: on the one hand it is worked out within the ego in the interaction of its different parts; on the other hand it is the extension of all those object-relations which the child embodies in our identification-series. For even while the child is still in the uterus its relation to the mother is partly that of an object belonging to the outside world, such as it ultimately becomes.

The libido which in the act of incorporation has regressed to the earliest stage of development seeks out all the positions which it had abandoned, and the harmonious state of identity between subject and object does not always remain so harmonious in relation to the child as object.

The ambivalent tendencies of later phases of development, which have already manifested themselves in coitus, become stronger during pregnancy. The ambivalent conflict which belongs to the 'later oral phase of development' finds expression in the tendency to expel again (orally) the object which has been incorporated.

This manifests itself in vomiting during pregnancy and in the typical eructations and peculiar cravings for food, etc.

The regressive elements of the sadistic-anal phase finds expression in the hostile tendencies to expulsion manifested in the pains which appear long before delivery. If these predominate over the tendencies to retain the fœtus, the result is miscarriage. We recognize these elements again in the transitory, typically anal, changes in the character of pregnant women. The old equation, child—fæces, is in this phase revived in the Ucs, owing to the child's position in the body as something belonging to that body and yet destined to be severed from it.

In the oral incorporation a quantity of narcissistic libido has already flowed to the child as a part of the subject's own ego. Similarly the libidinal relation in the identification, child—fæces, is again a narcissistic one.

But as fæces become for children, in reaction against their original narcissistic overestimation of them, the essence of what is disgusting, so in this phase of pregnancy there arise typical feelings of disgust, which become displaced from the child to particular kinds of food, situations, etc.

It is interesting that all these sensations disappear in the fifth month of pregnancy with the quickening of the child. The mother's relation to it is now determined in two directions. In the first place that part of her own body which is moving to and fro and vigorously pulsing within her is equated with the penis; and her relation to the child, which is still rooted in the depths of her narcissism, is now raised to a higher stage of development, namely, the 'phallic'. At the same time the child gives proof through a certain developing independence that it belongs to the outside world and in this way enters more into an object-relation to the mother.

I have tried thus briefly to reveal in the state of pregnancy deposits of all the phases of development. I shall now return to the mother-child relation that I mentioned before, which begins with the process of incorporation, makes the child a part of the subject's own ego and works itself out within that ego.

In this process the libidinal relations to the child are formed as follows: in the process of introjection the quantities of libido sent out to the partner in the sexual act flow back to the subject's narcissism. This is a very considerable contribution, for, as I have shown, in effecting a cathexis of the partner libido was drawn from the old father-fixation *and* mother-fixation.

The libido thus flowing into the ego constitutes the secondary narcissism of the woman as a mother, for, though it is devoted to the object (the child), that object represents at the same time a part of her ego. The change in the ego of the pregnant woman which follows on the process of introjection is a new edition of a process which has already taken place at a previous time: the child becomes for her the incarnation of the ego-ideal which she set up in the past. It is now for the second time built up by introjecting the father.

The narcissistic libido is displaced on to this newly erected super-ego, which becomes the bearer of all those perfections once ascribed to the father. A whole quantity of object-libido is withdrawn from its relations to the outside world and conducted to the child as the super-ego. Thus the process of sublimation in the woman is effected through her relation to her child.

The man measures and controls his ego-ideal by his productions through sublimation in the outside world. To the woman, on the other hand, the ego-ideal is embodied in the child, and all those tendencies to sublimation which the man utilizes in intellectual and social activity she directs to the child, which in the psychological sense represents for the woman her sublimation product. Hence the relation, mother-child, in pregnancy has more than one determinant. Since the child in the uterus becomes a part of the ego and large quantities of libido flow to it, the libidinal cathexis in the ego is heightened, narcissism is increased, and that primal condition is realized in which there was as yet no distinction between ego-libido and object-libido.

This primal condition, however, is disturbed by two factors: (1) by a process of sublimation the child becomes the super-ego, and our experience in other directions teaches us that this may enter into vigorous opposition to the ego; (2) the child is at the same time an object belonging to the outside world, in relation to which the ambivalent conflicts of all phases of libidinal development are stirred up.

Our observations enable us to distinguish two characteristic types of women according to their mental reactions to pregnancy. There are a number of women who endure their pregnancy with visible discomfort and depression. A similar unfavourable change takes place in their bodily appearance: they become ugly and shrunken, so that as the child matures they actually change into a mere appendage to it, a condition highly uncomfortable for themselves. The other type consists of those women who attain during pregnancy their greatest physical and psychical bloom.

In the first case the woman's narcissism has been sacrificed to the child. On the one hand the super-ego has mastered the ego, and on the other the child as a love-object has attracted to itself such a large measure of ego-libido that the ego is impoverished. Possibly this explains those states of melancholia which occur during pregnancy.

In the other type of woman the distribution of libido during pregnancy is different. That part of the libido which has now been withdrawn from the outside world is directed towards the child as a part of the ego. This can happen only when the formation of the super-ego is less powerful and the child is regarded less as an object and more as a part of the ego. When this is so the result is a heightening of the secondary narcissism, which is expressed in an increased self-respect, self-satisfaction, etc.

It seems as though we might conclude from these remarks that that unity, mother—child, is not so completely untroubled as we might suppose.

The original harmony of the primal state, inaugurated in the process of introjection during the sexual act, is soon disturbed by manifestations of ambivalence towards the child in the uterus. From this point of view parturition appears as the final result of a struggle which has long been raging. The stimulus which proceeds from the fœtus becomes insupportable and presses for discharge. Every hostile impulse which has already been mobilized during pregnancy reaches its greatest intensity in this decisive battle. Finally the incorporated object is successfully expelled into the outside world.

We have seen that the introjected object takes the place of the ego-ideal in the restored unity of the ego. When projected into the outside world it retains this character, for it continues to embody the subject's own unattained ideals. This is the psychological path by which, as Freud[8] recognized, women attain from narcissism to full object-love.

The final 'maternal regression' takes place in pregnancy through identification with the child: 'the trauma of birth' is mastered through the act of parturition.

Having regard to this identity of mother and child, we may perhaps draw certain conclusions from the mother's frame of mind as to the mental condition of the child. This of course undergoes amnesia, and then is only vaguely hinted at in dreams, phantasies, etc.

In actual fact the woman feels as though the world were out of joint and coming to an end; she has a sense of chaotic uneasiness, a straining, bursting sensation displaced from the avenues of birth to her head, and with these feelings is associated an intense dread of death. Possibly here we have a complete repetition of the anxiety attaching to the trauma of birth and a discharge of it by means of actual reproduction. That which men endeavour to attain in coitus and which impels them to laborious sublimations women attain in the function of reproduction.

It is known that in the dreams of pregnant women there very often appears a swimming child. This child may always be recognized as the dreamer herself, endowed with some quality which makes her, or in childhood made her, particularly estimable in her own eyes—it is as it were an illustration of the formation of the ego-ideal in relation to the child. The birth-phantasies of women who are already mothers prove on thorough investigation to represent details of two separate births interwoven into one: the birth of the subject herself (never recalled to memory) and the delivery of a child.

158

The mental state of the woman after delivery is characterized by a feeling of heavy loss. After a short phase in which the sense of victorious termination of the battle preponderates, there arises a feeling of boundless emptiness and disappointment, certainly analogous to the feeling of a 'lost Paradise' in the child which has been expelled.

This blank is filled only when the first relation to the child as an object in the outside world is ultimately established. The supposition that this relation is already present during the act of delivery itself is borne out by the observation which Rank[9] has already made in another connection, namely, that mothers who are in a state of narcosis during delivery have a peculiar feeling of estrangement towards their children. These mothers do not go through the phase of emptiness and disappointment, but on the other hand their joy in the child is not so intense as when delivery has taken place naturally. The child which is perceived by their senses is regarded as something alien.

This factor of loss clearly contributes to the joy of finding the child again. Apart from this, it is precisely this last factor of 'severance' which completes the analogy with coitus. The vaginal passage constitutes a frontier where the child is for the last time a part of the subject's own body and at the same time is already the object which has been thrust out. Here we have a repetition of the coitus-situation, in which the object was still felt to be a piece of the outside world but, being introjected, was on the border-line between the outside world and the ego.

Although the child has been hailed after delivery as an object belonging to the outside world, the bliss of the primal state, the unity of subject and object, is nevertheless re-established in lactation. This is a repetition of coitus, rendered with photographic faithfulness, the identification being based on the oral incorporation of the object in the act of sucking. Here again we have the equation: penis = breast. As in the first instance the penis took possession of one of the openings of the woman's body (the vagina), and in the act of mastery created an erotogenic centre, so now the nipple in a state of erection takes possession of the infant's mouth. As in coitus the erotogenicity of the whole body was attracted to the vagina, so here the whole disseminated libido of the newly-born infant is concentrated in the mouth. That which the semen accomplished in the one instance is accomplished in the other by the jet of milk. The identification made in childish phantasy between the mother's breast and the father's penis is realized a second time: in coitus the penis takes on

159

the rôle of the breast, while in lactation the breast becomes the penis. In the identification-situation the dividing line between the partners vanishes, and in this relation, mother—child, the mother once more annuls the trauma of weaning.

The identification, penis—breast, threw light on a remarkable disturbance in lactation which I had the opportunity of observing analytically. A young mother with a very ambivalent attitude towards her child was obliged to give up suckling it, although she wished to continue and her breasts were functioning excellently. But what happened was that in the interval between the child's meals the milk poured out in a stream, so that the breast was empty when she wished to give it to the child. The measures she took to overcome this unfortunate condition recalled the behaviour of men suffering from ejaculatio præcox, who convulsively endeavour to hasten the sexual act but are always overtaken by their infirmity. In the same way this woman tried to hasten the feeding of the child, but with the same ill success—it was always too late. The analysis of this disturbance was traced to a urethral source in her, as in ejaculatio præcox in the man. In a disturbance of lactation more frequently met with, namely, the drying up of the secretion, the other (anal) components of the process undoubtedly predominate.

The relation between the genital processes and lactation finds very characteristic expression at the moment when the child is put to the breast. Sometimes there is even a convulsion in the uterus, as though it were terminating its activity only now when it resigns it to the breast.

So the act of reproduction, begun in oral incorporation, completes the circle by representing the same situation at the end as at the beginning.

The whole development of the libido is rapidly revived and run through once more, the effect of the primal traumata is diminished by repetitive acts, and the work of sublimation is accomplished in relation to the child. But for the bisexual disposition of the human being, which is so adverse to the woman, but for the clitoris with its masculine strivings, how simple and clear would be her way to an untroubled mastering of existence!

NOTES

1 Read before the Eighth International Psycho-Analytical Congress, Salzburg, April 1924.

2 Ferenczi, *Versuch einer Genitaltheorie* (Internationale Psychoanalytische Bibliothek, Band XV, 1924).

3 [This has been adopted as the English rendering of *Ubw*, Pcs as that of *Vbw*, Cs as that of *Bw*, and Pcpt-Cs (perception-consciousness) as that of *W-Bw*.—ED.]

4 Abraham, *Versuch einer Entwicklungsgeschichte der Libido* (Neue Arbeiten zur Aerztlichen Psychoanalyse, 1924).

5 Loc. cit.

6 Rank, *Das Trauma der Geburt* (Internationale Psychoanalytische Bibliothek, Bd. XIV, 1924).

7 Freud, *Das Ich und das Es.*

8 Freud, 'On Narcissism: an Introduction', *Collected Papers*, Vol. IV.

9 Loc. cit.

Since 1924:
Toward a New Psychology
of Women

Marcia Cavell

There is a danger in reading Deutsch's 1924 article "The Psychology of Women in Relation to the Functions of Reproduction" that one will assume her to be speaking for "Freudians" in general. In Freud's own times, no question was considered closed. And since then, even within the ranks of the orthodox, there have been revisions amounting to revolutions. This is not to deny the existence of closed-minded analysts; but rather to say that the layman's assumption that there is one official body of theory which now constitutes "the Freudian view" is mistaken.

In "The Psychology of Women . . ." Deutsch closely follows Freud on this subject. But many analysts, both "classical" and "dissident," have taken very different positions in regard to the origins of a sense of femininity, about the meaning and importance of penis envy, and about the nature of masochism in women.[1] I assume this heterogeneity will be amply demonstrated throughout this volume, so that I do not need to emphasize that my critical comments do not imply a rejection of the methods and discoveries of Freudian psychoanalysis. I will therefore restrict my attention to the following interrelated points in Deutsch's article: her use of the libido theory, her notion that the clitoris is a phallic organ, and her views on masochism.

For those who are not familiar with it, the libido theory is the attempt to explain behavior, including the workings of the psyche, on the model

162

of a thermodynamic system. Freud's youthful thinking was formed by the scientific world in which he was trained, and his early models were consequently mechanistic. Just as it was essential to the development of modern physics that the old teleological explanations of inanimate bodies be replaced by explanations whose basic terms were matter and motion, so the nineteenth-century positivists postulated that any science worthy of the name must banish teleology. Wanting to found psychology on a biological basis, Freud accordingly created a lexicon in which the vocabulary of persons disappears—of love and hate, encounter and withdrawal, value and agency—and in its place we find a vocabulary of force, drive, energy, cathexis, anti-cathexis, mental apparatus—and so on. Purpose is replaced by cause. People are envisioned as closed energy systems, driven from behind, and never as going forward toward goals posited by their own or society's values and imaginations.

Ironically, biologists themselves were coming to a fundamental change in their thinking which would bring back teleology and which would emphasize the dependence of biological processes on the environment. Evolutionary biologists no longer think of organisms in terms of a playing out of fixed, innate drives. Whatever instincts are, in human beings they are particularly malleable and express themselves only in and through a particular environment and culture. As it pertains to humans, biology is psycho-biology. Such men as Heinz Hartmann and Sandor Rado attempted to bring psychoanalytic theory into line with the new biology by viewing human behavior as a constant attempt at adaptation. But Deutsch's 1924 article preceded their work by a decade or so and reflects the earlier neglect of environmental influence on human development.

Yet despite Hartmann's emendations, psychoanalytic explanations are not simply extensions of biological ones. Where biology imputes function and purpose to behavior, psychoanalysis needs in addition the notion of meaning or intentionality. This was a critical discovery of Freud's to which he gave the name "psychic reality": the discovery that the constructions we place on events have as determining an effect on behavior as the events themselves. (Anatomy itself is not destiny; but how we feel about our anatomy gives destiny a direction.) Many of us think that this essential psychoanalytic notion is incompatible with Freud's project to reduce human behavior to a complex of mechanisms.

The defects of the libido theory are nowhere more evident than in Deutsch's article, and are in part responsible for the way in which she deals with female sexuality. She imagines zones of the body to have a life of their own, independent of the meaning given them by the whole person or by the woman's social and cultural environment. Occasionally one has the impression that it is genitalia which are being analyzed rather than people. "In the 'phallic' phase of development," Deutsch writes, "the clitoris attracts to itself a large measure of libido, which it relinquishes in favour of the 'feminine' vagina only after strenuous and not always decisive struggles." In ordinary English this becomes: In a certain phase of her development the little girl discovers her clitoris and gets pleasure from it. But unfortunately, Deutsch concludes, "as a zone of active energy the clitoris lacks the abundant energy of the penis; even in the most intense masturbatory activity it cannot arrogate to itself such a measure of libido as does the latter organ." In short, a girl receives less pleasure from playing with her clitoris than a boy does from his penis. Demystified in this way, the claim is at best questionable, and probably false.[2]

Speaking psychologically, Deutsch seems to assume that the phantasies accompanying clitoral masturbation are phallic, that is, aggressive and penetrative. This is how she arrives at the view that the woman's aggression must turn back masochistically on herself if she is to be able to receive the "sadistic" penis. Since I am not an analyst, I don't know about the emotional tone that accompanies the sexual activities of little girls at the age she has in mind. In women, however, clitoral masturbation is accompanied by phantasies of all kinds, and the sensations are not those of "mastery" but typically of being overwhelmed.

More important is Deutsch's acceptance of Freud's view that activity (libido) is masculine, and his confusion of passivity with receptivity. As always, Freud wanted to base his thinking on biology. Yet there is even no biological reason for thinking that the vagina is passive. It is a receptive organ; but unless it is unaroused, it is certainly active, and in fact its contractions are apparently at least as responsible as the motility of the sperm for the latter's reaching the ovum. There are as many ways of being active as there are of being human. To pierce and to enter are one kind of activity. To grasp and to hold are another. On the subjective level, a woman's feelings during intercourse may be such a confusion of pleasures—of surrounding someone she loves, of receiving him inside her, of entrusting herself to him and encouraging him to trust her, of giving and taking—that I wouldn't know how to characterize either man or woman

164

as the active or the passive partner. It is true that some women are frightened of vaginal penetration, of receptivity in that sense (sometimes the wish for a penis is a reaction to this more basic feeling); but what they need to overcome is this fear, and not their desire for personal efficacy.

Surely Deutsch is right in saying that the woman who consciously or unconsciously regards her clitoris as her primary sexual organ has something to hide, some reason to deny the existence or the importance of her invisible vagina and uterus, and that she may indeed think of herself as a defective male. Phantasied castration amounts to real psychological castration and is a cry for help. Deutsch's answer to such women—though it's an answer which may take years of therapy for them to hear—is that "the final phase of attaining to a definitively feminine attitude is not gratification through the sexual act of the infantile desire for a penis, but full realization of the vagina as an organ of pleasure—an exchange of the desire for a penis for the real and equally valuable possession of a vagina."

Whether or not she is also right, however, in thinking that all girl children are biologically destined to want a penis is another question. In a class on child development which I attended recently with a group of psychiatrists—mostly men—who were taking their psychoanalytic training, I raised the obvious question whether the girl child perceives herself as lacking something valuable because others around her do, or whether this is a perception at which she would inevitably arrive by herself. A few of my classmates dismissed the question as irrelevant on the ground that whatever the source of the perception, the sense of loss is internalized; and that therefore it will have to be treated in the same way in either case. To me and to many analysts that seems false. If a woman feels defective because, for example, she was treated as defective as a very young child, then her therapy will focus not only on her feelings about her body, but also on her way of relating to people and to all aspects of her feelings about herself. Her distress over not having a penis may hide, in such an instance, a much more profound sense of loss or inadequacy. If Freud and Deutsch were right, theoretically one could never question why a woman feels castrated. If Karen Horney and Ruth Moulton are right, one can and should pursue that question in a number of different directions and on a number of different levels of a woman's development. Remarks in a recent interview in *The New York Times*[3] suggest that Deutsch herself may have changed her mind: "Yes, there is penis envy," she said; but "in a society open to women, with accepting parents, the impact will be very different than it used to be."

Deutsch's ignoring of environmental factors—a part of her adherence to the libido theory—also accounts in large measure for her views on masochism. As is well known, Freud thought that aggression is instinctual, and along with it, masochism and sadism. In recent years there has been much controversy among biologists, ethologists, psychologists, and psychoanalysts about this question. I don't know how representative of practicing analysts the views are that I am going to outline here. I do know that they are at least familiar to all, and accepted by many. A number of well-known and supposedly traditional psychoanalysts[4] view masochism not as instinctive but as adaptive, which is in no way to endorse it, but rather to say that for various reasons it is the (unhealthy) means which the individual has been driven to adopt in the attempt to resolve conflicting needs. In a paper delivered before the Society of Medical Psychoanalysts in 1953, I. Bieber summarized this position as follows: "Neither masochism nor sadism is ever part of normal sexual behavior. Freud's belief that sadism was part of the normal masculine sexuality and masochism of feminine sexuality arose both from his mistaken idea that sado-masochism was instinctual and from his orientation to masculine superiority."[5] Elsewhere in the same article he defines masochism "as a state wherein acts or attitudes are oriented consciously or unconsciously toward bringing about pain, or situations that are realistically destructive to the individual and his interests. Such acts or attitudes have an adaptational function, particularly a defensive one, inasmuch as they are designed to preserve the organism from what is perceived as a great injury."[6] The problem is that the defense is badly designed or may have become part of the individual's character after the need which it once served no longer exists, and that the injury may be misperceived.

It may or may not be true that by any definition women are more masochistic than men. But the important distinction between what is the case and what could be the case, between human nature as we find it in a given situation or culture and human nature as it might be, is so often lacking in Freud's work. As Kardiner, Karish and Ovesey write in their classic "A Methodological Study of Freudian Theory":

166

The Freudian concept of a feminine character derived from the feminine component of a bisexual constitution suffers from the same defects that are to be found in his psychology of men. Here, once more, Freud attributed to genetic predisposition what, in reality, were the consequences of an interaction between women and the social institution of the male-oriented culture in which they lived.[7]

"The Psychology of Women . . ." articulates many of the positions that have made Freudianism a prime target of the Women's Movement. To some extent the animus seems to me justified: Of course women are angry when told they must renounce an important source of pleasure, and that the masochistic impulses which may have driven them into therapy in the first place are to be accepted as part of feminine nature. More fundamentally, they are angry when they feel they are not being seen as persons with the same needs for growth and for diversity of activity as men. Furthermore, Deutsch's failure to distinguish between the women she has seen as patients and women as they can be seems to lend support to just that view of woman as childish, acquiescent, the natural Yes-man, which has been fostered by so many voices and powers in this society. Though I think this last would be a misreading, it is a view which unfortunately can be used by analysts, male or female, who are not themselves free of those anxieties which can be appeased by keeping women "in their place."

In the *Times* interview Deutsch claimed to have always been a feminist. And I think she did not intend to women the disservice implicit in her early work. Perhaps the problem is that one cannot separate the sexual life from the rest of life in the way she attempted. One cannot have a theory which says that women should be passive in bed but active elsewhere. Deutsch now encourages women to be active in every possible way. In the same interview she was asked what she hopes for in a woman patient. Her answer was that, among other things, the woman have a passionate interest in something other than the possible man and children in her life. And I suspect that as a therapist rather than as a theorist, she hoped for something similar in her women patients even fifty years ago. Certainly many analysts now take passivity, dependency, masochism, and the need to be treated as a child, not as the stigmata of femininity but as neurotic symptoms to be outgrown.

NOTES

1 For different views about all of these questions, see contributions by F. Fromm-Reichmann, M. B. Cohen, P. Chodoff, R. Stoller, E. Jones, K. Horney, C. Thompson, R. Moulton in *Psychoanalysis and Women*, edited by Jean Baker Miller, M.D. (Baltimore: Penguin Books, 1973).

2 In an article entitled "Changing Patterns of Femininity: Psychoanalytic Implications," Dr. Judd Marmor argues: "Helene Deutsch's dismissal of the clitoris as an 'inferior organ' in terms of its capability to provide libidinal gratification is a remarkable example of culturally influenced amblyopia. . . . The actual fact . . . is that although the female organ is minute compared with the male organ . . . the size of its nerves . . . and nerve endings . . . compare strikingly with the same provision for the male." In Miller, *op. cit.*, p. 232.

3 February 13, 1972

4 C. Brenner, "The Masochistic Character," *Journal of the American Psychoanalytic Association*, Vol. 7: 197–226, 1969, I. Bieber, "The Meaning of Masochism," *American Journal of Psychotherapy*, Vol. 7: 433–488, 1953, and R. Lowenstein, "A Contribution to the Psychoanalytic Theory of Masochism," *Journal of the American Psychoanalytic Association*, Vol. 5: 197–234, 1957, among others.

5 "The Meaning of Masochism," *American Journal of Psychotherapy*, 7, 1953, p. 439.

6 *Ibid.*, p. 488.

7 Part III, "Narcissism, Bisexuality and the Dual Instinct Theory," *Journal of Nervous and Mental Diseases*, 129, 1959, p. 215.

Coles on Horney

The Flight from Womanhood: The Masculinity-Complex in Women as Viewed by Men and by Women (1926)

Karen Horney

In some of his latest works Freud has drawn attention with increasing urgency to a certain one-sidedness in our analytical researches. I refer to the fact that till quite recently the minds of boys and men only were taken as objects of investigation.

The reason for this is obvious. Psychoanalysis is the creation of a male genius, and almost all those who have developed his ideas have been men. It is only right and reasonable that they should evolve more easily a masculine psychology and understand more of the development of men than of women.

A momentous step toward the understanding of the specifically feminine was made by Freud himself in discovering the existence of penis envy, and soon after, the work of van Ophuijsen and Abraham showed how large a part this factor plays in the development of women and in the formation of their neuroses. The significance of penis envy has been extended quite recently by the hypothesis of the phallic phase. By this we mean that in the infantile genital organization in both sexes only one genital organ, namely the male, plays any part, and that it is just this that distinguishes the infantile organization from the final genital organization of the adult.[1] According to this theory, the clitoris is conceived of as a phallus, and we assume that little girls as well as boys attach to the

171

clitoris in the first instance exactly the same value as to the penis.[2]

The effect of this phase is partly to inhibit and partly to promote the subsequent development. Helene Deutsch has demonstrated principally the inhibiting effects. She is of the opinion that at the beginning of every new sexual function (e.g., at the beginning of puberty, of sexual intercourse, of pregnancy and childbirth), this phase is reactivated and has to be overcome every time before a feminine attitude can be attained. Freud has elaborated her exposition on the positive side, for he believes that it is only penis envy and the overcoming of it which gives rise to the desire for a child and thus forms the love bond to the father.[3]

The question now arises as to whether these hypotheses have helped to make our insight into feminine development (insight that Freud himself has stated to be unsatisfactory and incomplete) more satisfactory and clear.

Science has often found it fruitful to look at long-familiar facts from a fresh point of view. Otherwise there is a danger that we shall involuntarily continue to classify all new observations among the same clearly defined groups of ideas.

The new point of view of which I wish to speak came to me by way of philosophy, in some essays by Georg Simmel.[4] The point that Simmel makes there and that has been in many ways elaborated since, especially from the feminine side,[5] is this: Our whole civilization is a masculine civilization. The State, the laws, morality, religion, and the sciences are the creation of men. Simmel by no means deduces from these facts, as is commonly done by other writers, an inferiority in women, but he first of all gives considerable breadth and depth to this conception of a masculine civilization: "The requirements of art, patriotism, morality in general and social ideas in particular, correctness in practical judgment and objectivity in theoretical knowledge, the energy and the profundity of life —all these are categories which belong as it were in their form and their claims to humanity in general, but in their actual historical configuration they are masculine throughout. Supposing that we describe these things, viewed as absolute ideas, by the single word 'objective,' we then find that in the history of our race the equation objective = masculine is a valid one."

Now Simmel thinks that the reason why it is so difficult to recognize these historical facts is that the very standards by which mankind has estimated the values of male and female nature are "not neutral, arising out of the differences of the sexes, but in themselves essentially masculine. . . . We do not believe in a purely 'human' civilization, into which the question of sex does not enter, for the very reason that prevents any such civilization from in fact existing, namely, the (so to speak) naïve identification of the concept 'human being'[6] and the concept 'man,'[7] which in many languages even causes the same word to be used for the two concepts. For the moment I will leave it undetermined whether this masculine character of the fundamentals of our civilization has its origin in the essential nature of the sexes or only in a certain preponderance of force in men, which is not really bound up with the question of civilization. In any case this is the reason why, in the most varying fields, inadequate achievements are contemptuously called 'feminine,' while distinguished achievements on the part of women are called 'masculine' as an expression of praise."

Like all sciences and all valuations, the psychology of women has hitherto been considered only from the point of view of men. It is inevitable that the man's position of advantage should cause objective validity to be attributed to his subjective, affective relations to the woman, and according to Delius[8] the psychology of women hitherto actually represents a deposit of the desires and disappointments of men.

An additional and very important factor in the situation is that women have adapted themselves to the wishes of men and felt as if their adaptation were their true nature. That is, they see or saw themselves in the way that their men's wishes demanded of them; unconsciously they yielded to the suggestion of masculine thought.

If we are clear about the extent to which all our being, thinking, and doing conform to these masculine standards, we can see how difficult it is for the individual man and also for the individual woman really to shake off this mode of thought.

The question then is how far analytical psychology also, when its researches have women for their object, is under the spell of this way of thinking, insofar as it has not yet wholly left behind the stage in which frankly and as a matter of course masculine development only was considered. In other words, how far has the evolution of women, as depicted to us today by analysis, been measured by masculine standards and how far therefore does this picture fail to present quite accurately the real nature of women.

If we look at the matter from this point of view our first impression is a surprising one. The present analytical picture of feminine development (whether that picture be correct or not) differs in no case by a hair's breadth from the typical ideas that the boy has of the girl.

We are familiar with the ideas that the boy entertains. I will therefore only sketch them in a few succinct phrases, and for the sake of comparison will place in a parallel column our ideas of the development of women.

THE BOY'S IDEAS	OUR IDEAS OF FEMININE DEVELOPMENT
Naïve assumption that girls as well as boys possess a penis	*For both sexes it is only the male genital which plays any part*
Realization of the absence of the penis	*Sad discovery of the absence of the penis*
Idea that the girl is a castrated, mutilated boy	*Belief of the girl that she once possessed a penis and lost it by castration*
Belief that the girl has suffered punishment that also threatens him	*Castration is conceived of as the infliction of punishment*
The girl is regarded as inferior	*The girl regards herself as inferior. Penis envy*
The boy is unable to imagine how the girl can ever get over this loss or envy	*The girl never gets over the sense of deficiency and inferiority and has constantly to master afresh her desire to be a man*
The boy dreads her envy	*The girl desires throughout life to avenge herself on the man for possessing something which she lacks*

The existence of this over-exact agreement is certainly no criterion of its objective correctness. It is quite possible that the infantile genital organization of the little girl might bear as striking a resemblance to that of the boy as has up till now been assumed.

But it is surely calculated to make us think and take other possibilities into consideration. For instance, we might follow Georg Simmel's train of thought and reflect whether it is likely that female adaptation to the male structure should take place at so early a period and in so high a degree that the specific nature of a little girl is overwhelmed by it. Later

I will return for a moment to the point at which it does actually seem to me probable that this infection with a masculine point of view occurs in childhood. But it does not seem to me clear offhand how everything bestowed by nature could be thus absorbed into it and leave no trace. And so we must return to the question I have already raised—whether the remarkable parallelism I have indicated may not perhaps be the expression of a one-sidedness in our observations, due to their being made from the man's point of view.

Such a suggestion immediately encounters an inner protest, for we remind ourselves of the sure ground of experience upon which analytical research has always been founded. But at the same time our theoretical scientific knowledge tells us that this ground is not altogether trust-worthy, but that all experience by its very nature contains a subjective factor. Thus, even our analytical experience is derived from direct obser-vation of the material that our patients bring to analysis in free associa-tions, dreams, and symptoms and from the interpretations we make or the conclusions we draw from this material. Therefore, even when the technique is correctly applied, there is in theory the possibility of varia-tions in this experience.

Now, if we try to free our minds from this masculine mode of thought, nearly all the problems of feminine psychology take on a different appear-ance.

The first thing that strikes us is that it is always, or principally, the genital difference between the sexes which has been made the cardinal point in the analytical conception and that we have left out of considera-tion the other great biological difference, namely, the different parts played by men and by women in the function of reproduction.

The influence of the man's point of view in the conception of mother-hood is most clearly revealed in Ferenczi's extremely brilliant genital theory.[9] His view is that the real incitement to coitus, its true, ultimate meaning for both sexes, is to be sought in the desire to return to the mother's womb. During a period of contest man acquired the privilege of really penetrating once more, by means of his genital organ, into a uterus. The woman, who was formerly in the subordinate position, was obliged to adapt her organization to this organic situation and was prov-ided with certain compensations. She had to "content herself" with sub-stitutes in the nature of fantasy and above all with harboring the child, whose bliss she shares. At the most, it is only in the act of birth that she

175

perhaps has potentialities of pleasure denied to the man.[10]

According to this view the psychic situation of a woman would certainly not be a very pleasurable one. She lacks any real primal impulse to coitus, or at least she is debarred from all direct—even if only partial—fulfillment. If this is so, the impulse toward coitus and pleasure in it must undoubtedly be less for her than for the man. For it is only indirectly, by circuitous ways, that she attains to a certain fulfillment of the primal longing—i.e., partly by the roundabout way of masochistic conversion and partly by identification with the child she may conceive. These, however, are merely "compensatory devices." The only thing in which she ultimately has the advantage over the man is the, surely very questionable, pleasure in the act of birth.

At this point I, as a woman, ask in amazement, and what about motherhood? And the blissful consciousness of bearing a new life within oneself? And the ineffable happiness of the increasing expectation of the appearance of this new being? And the joy when it finally makes its appearance and one holds it for the first time in one's arms? And the deep pleasurable feeling of satisfaction in suckling it and the happiness of the whole period when the infant needs her care?

Ferenczi has expressed the opinion in conversation that in the primal period of conflict which ended so grievously for the female, the male as victor imposed upon her the burden of motherhood and all it involves.

Certainly, regarded from the standpoint of the social struggle, motherhood *may* be a handicap. It is certainly so at the present time, but it is much less certain that it was so in times when human beings were closer to nature.

Moreover, we explain penis envy itself by its biological relations and not by social factors; on the contrary, we are accustomed without more ado to construe the woman's sense of being at a disadvantage socially as the rationalization of her penis envy.

But from the biological point of view woman has in motherhood, or in the capacity for motherhood, a quite indisputable and by no means negligible physiological superiority. This is most clearly reflected in the unconscious of the male psyche in the boy's intense envy of motherhood. We are familiar with this envy as such, but it has hardly received due consideration as a dynamic factor. When one begins, as I did, to analyze men only after a fairly long experience of analyzing women, one receives a most surprising impression of the intensity of this envy of pregnancy, childbirth, and motherhood, as well as of the breasts and of the act of suckling.

In the light of this impression derived from analysis, one must naturally inquire whether an unconscious masculine tendency to depreciation is not expressing itself intellectually in the above-mentioned view of motherhood. This depreciation would run as follows: In reality women do simply desire the penis; when all is said and done motherhood is only a burden that makes the struggle for existence harder, and men may be glad that they have not to bear it.

When Helene Deutsch writes that the masculinity complex in women plays a much greater part than the femininity complex in man, she would seem to overlook the fact that the masculine envy is clearly capable of more successful sublimation than the penis envy of the girl, and that it certainly serves as one, if not as the essential, driving force in the setting up of cultural values.

Language itself points to this origin of cultural productivity. In the historic times that are known to us, this productivity has undoubtedly been incomparably greater in men than in women. Is not the tremendous strength in men of the impulse to creative work in every field precisely due to their feeling of playing a relatively small part in the creation of living beings, which constantly impels them to an overcompensation in achievement?

If we are right in making this connection, we are confronted with the problem of why no corresponding impulse to compensate herself for her penis envy is found in woman. There are two possibilities: Either the envy of the woman is absolutely less than that of the man; or it is less successfully worked off in some other way. We could bring forward facts in support of either supposition.

In favor of the greater intensity of the man's envy we might point out that an actual anatomical disadvantage on the side of the woman exists only from the point of view of the pregenital levels of organization.[11] From that of the genital organization of adult women there is no disadvantage, for obviously the capacity of women for coitus is not less but simply other than that of men. On the other hand, the part of the man in reproduction is ultimately less than that of the woman.

Further, we observe that men are evidently under a greater necessity to depreciate women than conversely. The realization that the dogma of the inferiority of women had its origin in an unconscious male tendency could only dawn upon us after a doubt had arisen whether in fact this view were justified in reality. But if there actually are in men tendencies to depreciate women behind this conviction of feminine inferiority, we must infer that this unconscious impulse to depreciation is a very powerful one.

Further, there is much to be said in favor of the view that women work off their penis envy less successfully than men, from a cultural point of view. We know that in the most favorable case this envy is transmuted into the desire for a husband and child, and probably by this very transmutation it forfeits the greater part of its power as an incentive to sublimation. In unfavorable cases, however, as I shall presently show in greater detail, it is burdened with a sense of guilt instead of being able to be employed fruitfully, while the man's incapacity for motherhood is probably felt simply as an inferiority and can develop its full driving power without inhibition.

In this discussion I have already touched on a problem that Freud has recently brought into the foreground of interest:[12] namely, the question of the origin and operation of the desire for a child. In the course of the last decade our attitude toward this problem has changed. I may therefore be permitted to describe briefly the beginning and the end of this historical evolution.

The original hypothesis[13] was that penis envy gave a libidinal reinforcement both to the wish for a child and the wish for the man, but that the latter wish arose independently of the former. Subsequently the accent became more and more displaced on to the penis envy, till in his most recent work on this problem, Freud expressed the conjecture that the wish for the child arose only through penis envy and the disappointment over the lack of the penis in general, and that the tender attachment to the father came into existence only by this circuitous route—by way of the desire for the penis and the desire for the child.

This latter hypothesis obviously originated in the need to explain psychologically the biological principle of heterosexual attraction. This corresponds to the problem formulated by Groddeck, who says that it is natural that the boy should retain the mother as a love object, "but how is it that the little girl becomes attached to the opposite sex?"[14]

In order to approach this problem we must first of all realize that our empirical material with regard to the masculinity complex in women is derived from two sources of very different importance. The first is the direct observation of children, in which the subjective factor plays a relatively insignificant part. Every little girl who has not been intimidated displays penis envy frankly and without embarrassment. We see that the presence of this envy is typical and understand quite well why this is so; we understand how the narcissistic mortification of possessing less than the boy is reinforced by a series of disadvantages arising out of the different pregenital cathexes: the manifest privileges of the boy in connection with urethral erotism, the scoptophilic instinct, and onanism.[15]

I should like to suggest that we should apply the term *primary* to the little girl's penis envy, which is obviously based simply on the anatomical difference.

The second source upon which our experience draws is to be found in the analytical material produced by adult women. Naturally it is more difficult to form a judgment on this, and there is therefore more scope for the subjective element. We see here in the first instance that penis envy operates as a factor of enormous dynamic power. We see patients rejecting their female functions, their unconscious motive in so doing being the desire to be male. We meet with fantasies of which the content is: "I once had a penis; I am a man who has been castrated and mutilated," from which proceed feelings of inferiority that have for after-effect all manner of obstinate hypochondriacal ideas. We see a marked attitude of hostility toward men, sometimes taking the form of depreciation and sometimes of a desire to castrate or maim them, and we see how the whole destinies of certain women are determined by this factor.

It was natural to conclude—and especially natural because of the male orientation of our thinking—that we could link these impressions on to the primary penis envy and to reason *a posteriori* that this envy must possess an enormous intensity, an enormous dynamic power, seeing that it evidently gave rise to such effects. Here we overlooked the fact, more in our general estimation of the situation than in details, that this desire to be a man, so familiar to us from the analyses of adult women, had only very little to do with that early, infantile, primary penis envy, but that it is a secondary formation embodying all that has miscarried in the development toward womanhood.

From beginning to end, my experience has proved to me with unchanging clearness that the Oedipus complex in women leads (not only in extreme cases where the subject has come to grief, but *regularly*) to a regression to penis envy, naturally in every possible degree and shade. The difference between the outcome of the male and the female Oedipus complexes seems to me in average cases to be as follows. In boys the mother as a sexual object is renounced owing to the fear of castration, but the male role itself is not only affirmed in further development but is actually overemphasized in the reaction to the fear of castration. We see this clearly in the latency and prepubertal period in boys and generally in later life as well. Girls, on the other hand, not only renounce the father as a sexual object but simultaneously recoil from the feminine role altogether.

In order to understand this flight from womanhood we must consider the facts relating to early infantile onanism, which is the physical expression of the excitations due to the Oedipus complex.

Here again the situation is much clearer in boys, or perhaps we simply know more about it. Are these facts so mysterious to us in girls only because we have always looked at them through the eyes of men? It seems rather like it when we do not even concede to little girls a specific form of onanism but without more ado describe their autoerotic activities as male; and when we conceive of the difference, which surely must exist, as being that of a negative to a positive, i.e., in the case of anxiety about onanism, that the difference is that between a castration threatened and castration that has actually taken place! My analytical experience makes it most decidedly possible that little girls have a specific feminine form of onanism (which incidentally differs in technique from that of boys), even if we assume that the little girl practices exclusively clitoral masturbation, an assumption that seems to me by no means certain. And I do not see why, in spite of its past evolution, it should not be conceded that the clitoris legitimately belongs to and forms an integral part of the female genital apparatus.

Whether in the early phase of the girl's genital development she has organic vaginal sensations is a matter remarkably difficult to determine from the analytical material produced by adult women. In a whole series of cases I have been inclined to conclude that this is so, and later I shall quote the material upon which I base this conclusion. That such sensations should occur seems to me theoretically very probable for the following reasons. Undoubtedly the familiar fantasies that an excessively large penis is effecting forcible penetration, producing pain and hemorrhage, and threatening to destroy something, go to show that the little girl bases her Oedipus fantasies most realistically (in accordance with the plastic concrete thinking of childhood) on the disproportion in size between father and child. I think too that both the Oedipus fantasies and also the logically ensuing dread of an internal—i.e., vaginal—injury go to show that the vagina as well as the clitoris must be assumed to play a part in the early infantile genital organization of women.[16] One might even infer from the later phenomena of frigidity that the vaginal zone has actually a stronger cathexis (arising out of anxiety and attempts at defence) than the clitoris, and this because the incestuous wishes are referred to the vagina with the unerring accuracy of the unconscious. From this point of view frigidity must be regarded as an attempt to ward off the fantasies so full of danger to the ego. And this would also throw a new light on the unconscious pleasurable feelings that, as various authors have maintained, occur at parturition, or alternatively, on the dread of childbirth. For (just because of the disproportion between the vagina and the baby and because of the pain to which this gives rise) parturition would be calculated to a far greater extent than subsequent sexual intercourse to stand to the unconscious for a realization of those early incest fantasies, a realization to which no guilt is attached. The female genital anxiety, like the castration dread of boys, invariably bears the impress of feelings of guilt and it is to them that it owes its lasting influence.

A further factor in the situation, and one that works in the same direction, is a certain consequence of the anatomical difference between the sexes. I mean that the boy can inspect his genital to see whether the dreaded consequences of onanism are taking place; the girl, on the other hand, is literally in the dark on this point and remains in complete uncertainty. Naturally this possibility of a reality test does not weigh with boys in cases where the castration anxiety is acute, but in the slighter cases of fear, which are practically more important because they are more frequent, I think that this difference is very important. At any rate, the analytical material that has come to light in women whom I have analyzed has led me to conclude that this factor plays a considerable part in feminine mental life and that it contributes to the peculiar inner uncertainty so often met with in women.

Under the pressure of this anxiety the girl now takes refuge in a fictitious male role.

What is the economic gain of this flight? Here I would refer to an experience that all analysts have probably had: They find that the desire to be a man is generally admitted comparatively willingly and that when once it is accepted, it is clung to tenaciously, the reason being the desire to avoid the realization of libidinal wishes and fantasies in connection with the father. Thus the wish to be a man subserves the repression of these feminine wishes or the resistance against their being brought to light. This constantly recurring, typical experience compels us, if we are true to analytical principles, to conclude that the fantasies of being a man were at an earlier period devised for the very purpose of securing the subject against libidinal wishes in connection with the father. The fiction of maleness enabled the girl to escape from the female role now burdened with guilt and anxiety. It is true that this attempt to deviate from her own line to that of the male inevitably brings about a sense of inferiority, for the girl begins to measure herself by pretensions and values that are foreign to her specific biological nature and confronted with which she cannot but feel herself inadequate.

Although this sense of inferiority is very tormenting, analytical experience emphatically shows us that the ego can tolerate it more easily than the sense of guilt associated with the feminine attitude, and hence it is undoubtedly a gain for the ego when the girl flees from the Scylla of the sense of guilt to the Charybdis of the sense of inferiority.

For the sake of completeness I will add a reference to the other gain that, as we know, accrues to women from the process of identification with the father, which takes place at the same time. I know of nothing with reference to the importance of this process itself to add to what I have already said in my earlier work.

We know that this very process of identification with the father is one answer to the question of why the flight from feminine wishes in regard to the father always leads to the adoption of a masculine attitude. Some reflections connected with what has already been said reveal another point of view that throws some light on this question.

We know that whenever the libido encounters a barrier in its development an earlier phase of organization is regressively activated. Now, according to Freud's latest work, penis envy forms the preliminary stage to the true object love for the father. And so this train of thought suggested by Freud helps us to some comprehension of the inner necessity by which the libido flows back precisely to this preliminary stage whenever and insofar as it is driven back by the incest barrier.

I agree in principle with Freud's notion that the girl develops toward object love by way of penis envy, but I think that the nature of this evolution might also be pictured differently.

182

For when we see how large a part of the strength of primary penis envy is accrued only by retrogression from the Oedipus complex, we must resist the temptation to interpret in the light of penis envy the manifestations of so elementary a principle of nature as that of the mutual attraction of the sexes.

Whereupon, being confronted with the question of how we should conceive psychologically of this primal, biological principle, we would again have to confess ignorance. Indeed, in this respect the conjecture forces itself more and more strongly upon me that perhaps the causal connection may be the exact converse and that it is just the attraction to the opposite sex, operating from a very early period, which draws the libidinal interest of the little girl to the penis. This interest, in accordance with the level of development reached, acts at first in an autoerotic and narcissistic manner, as I have described before. If we view these relations thus, fresh problems would logically present themselves with regard to the origin of the male Oedipus complex, but I wish to postpone these for a later paper. But, if penis envy were the first expression of that mysterious attraction of the sexes, there would be nothing to wonder at when analysis discloses its existence in a yet deeper layer than that in which the desire for a child and the tender attachment to the father occur. The way to this tender attitude toward the father would be prepared not simply by disappointment in regard to the penis but in another way as well. We should then instead have to conceive of the libidinal interest in the penis as a kind of "partial love," to use Abraham's term.[17] Such love, he says, always forms a preliminary stage to true object love. We might explain the process too by an analogy from later life: I refer to the fact that admiring envy is specially calculated to lead to an attitude of love.

With regard to the extraordinary ease with which this regression takes place, I must mention the analytical discovery[18] that in the associations of female patients the narcissistic desire to possess the penis and the object libidinal longing for it are often so interwoven that one hesitates as to the sense in which the words "desire for it"[19] are meant.

One word more about the castration fantasies proper, which have given their name to the whole complex because they are the most striking part of it. According to my theory of feminine development, I am obliged to regard these fantasies also as a secondary formation. I picture their origin as follows: When the woman takes refuge in the fictitious male role, her feminine genital anxiety is to some extent translated into male terms—

the fear of vaginal injury becomes a fantasy of castration. The girl gains by this conversion, for she exchanges the uncertainty of her expectation of punishment (an uncertainty conditioned by her anatomical formation) for a concrete idea. Moreover, the castration fantasy, too, is under the shadow of the old sense of guilt—and the penis is desired as a proof of guiltlessness.

Now these typical motives for flight into the male role—motives whose origin is the Oedipus complex—are reinforced and supported by the actual disadvantage under which women labor in social life. Of course we must recognize that the desire to be a man, when it springs from this last source, is a peculiarly suitable form of rationalization of those unconscious motives. But we must not forget that this disadvantage is actually a piece of reality and that it is immensely greater than most women are aware of.

Georg Simmel says in this connection that "the greater importance attaching to the male sociologically is probably due to his position of superior strength," and that historically the relation of the sexes may be crudely described as that of master and slave. Here, as always, it is "one of the privileges of the master that he has not constantly to think that he is master, while the position of the slave is such that he can never forget it."

Here we probably have the explanation also of the underestimation of this factor in analytical literature. In actual fact a girl is exposed from birth onward to the suggestion—inevitable, whether conveyed brutally or delicately—of her inferiority, an experience that constantly stimulates her masculinity complex.

There is one further consideration. Owing to the hitherto purely masculine character of our civilization, it has been much harder for women to achieve any sublimation that would really satisfy their nature, for all the ordinary professions have been filled by men. This again must have exercised an influence upon women's feelings of inferiority, for naturally they could not accomplish the same as men in these masculine professions and so it appeared that there was a basis in fact for their inferiority. It seems to me impossible to judge to how great a degree the unconscious motives for the flight from womanhood are reinforced by the actual social subordination of women. One might conceive of the connection as an interaction of psychic and social factors. But I can only indicate these

184

problems here, for they are so grave and so important that they require a separate investigation.

The same factors must have quite a different effect on the man's development. On the one hand they lead to a much stronger repression of his feminine wishes, in that these bear the stigma of inferiority; on the other hand it is far easier for him successfully to sublimate them.

In the foregoing discussion I have put a construction upon certain problems of feminine psychology, which in many points differs from current views. It is possible and even probable that the picture I have drawn is one-sided from the opposite point of view. But my primary intention in this paper was to indicate a possible source of error arising out of the sex of the observer, and by so doing to make a step forward toward the goal that we are all striving to reach: to get beyond the subjectivity of the masculine or the feminine standpoint and to obtain a picture of the mental development of woman that will be more true to the facts of her nature—with its specific qualities and its differences from that of man—than any we have hitherto achieved.

NOTES

1 Freud, "The Infantile Genital Organization of the Libido." *Collected Papers*, Vol. II, No. XX. [Horney's references to Freud are usually to editions prior to the Standard one (*The Complete Psychological Works of Sigmund Freud* and the *Collected Papers*, published by the Hogarth Press, London).]

2 H. Deutsch, *Psychoanalyse der weiblichen Sexualfunktionen* (1925).

3 Freud, "Einige psychische Folgen der anatomischen Geschlechtsunterschiede," *Intern. Zeitschr. f. Psychoanal.*, XI (1925).

4 Georg Simmel, *Philosophische Kultur.*

5 Cf. in particular Vaerting, *Männliche Eigenart im Frauenstaat und Weibliche Eigenart im Männerstaat.*

6 German *Mensch.*

7 German *Mann.*

8 Delius, *Vom Erwachen der Frau.*

9 Ferenczi, *Versuch einer Genitaltheorie* (1924).

10 Cf. also Helene Deutsch, *Psychoanalyse der Weiblichen Sexualfunktionen;* and Groddeck, *Das Buch vom Es.*

11 K. Horney, "On the Genesis of the Castration Complex in Women," *Int. J. Psycho-Anal.*, Vol. V (1924).

12 Freud, "Über einige psychische Folgen der anatomischen Geschlechtsunterschiede."

13 Freud, "On the Transformation of Instincts with Special Reference to Anal Erotism," *Collected Papers,* Vol. II, No. XVI.

14 Groddeck, *Das Buch vom Es.*

15 I have dealt with this subject in greater detail in my paper "On the Genesis of the Castration Complex in Women."

16 Since the possibility of such a connection occurred to me, I have learned to construe in this sense—i.e., as representing the dread of vaginal injury—many phenomena that I was previously content to interpret as castration fantasies in the male sense.

17 Abraham, *Versuch einer Entwicklungsgeschichte der Libido* (1924).

18 Freud referred to this in *The Taboo of Virginity.*

19 German, *Haben-Wollen.*

Karen Horney's Flight from Orthodoxy

Robert Coles

History is a fickle friend, something we all tend to forget. It is human to be self-absorbed; we have only one life, at least here on this earth, and so we become rather possessive about what is happening to us. In the 1920s and 1930s and early 1940s Karen Horney's dissent from what was becoming, increasingly, a kind of psychoanalytic orthodoxy, seemed to most psychoanalysts a minor and inconsequential "deviation." She was yet another "culturalist," intent on diluting the hard-won body of psychoanalytic knowledge. Moreover, she was dangerously "superficial," a word pinned upon all those who emphasized social and historical forces as determinants of the mind's various developments. (Rather convenient—and in the history of various ideologies not rare: one with another point of view gets dismissed as shallow or cowardly—unable intellectually or psychologically to sustain the "right" viewpoint, which is, of course, described as a "profound" or "deep" one, requiring "courage.")

Today, of course, Karen Horney's "revisionism" strikes most of us as the purest of common sense; and within the psychoanalytic community, one suspects her ideas have gradually made their way—not obtaining any momentous, outright "acceptance," but simply becoming part of the general knowledge one historical period brings to replace assumptions or fixed beliefs common to a previous time. Certainly any number of psychoanalytic theorists have had to look again, and closely, at what Freud said about women, and at what they as analysts all too willingly went along with, or modified with perhaps too much tact or restraint,

187

meaning without the independence of mind and spirit one hears—too much, sometimes—proclaimed as the essence of scientific work. (When people call themselves scientists a little too insistently they may not only be trying to cover themselves with a certain moral authority; they may also sense all too strongly the ritualistic, sacerdotal and messianic aspects of their "calling.") So, it comes about that a woman who in April of 1941 walked out of the New York Psychoanalytic Society singing "Go Down Moses," having been told her views were utterly out of keeping with psychoanalytic theory, emerges three decades later as an appealing writer and thinker indeed, to many women, and not a few psychiatrists of both sexes who have been educated by the political and social struggles of recent years. I know from my own work in the South during the early 1960s how a new historical moment changes convictions in a wide range of people—ordinary working people, their various "leaders," and yes, ideologues of all sorts, who fancy themselves impervious to the shifting sands of mere "opinion," but who are unable to maintain such a position indefinitely: quite simply, a new generation turns elsewhere for leadership.

I have to respond out of my own life to Dr. Horney's article. It so happens that I met her just before she died. I was a medical student at Columbia's College of Physicians and Surgeons, and in the autumn of 1952 she came in as a patient to Harkness Pavilion. At the time I had a job drawing blood, and so each morning went quickly from room to room, occasionally stopping for conversation with one or another patient. At the time I had no interest in or knowledge of psychiatry or psychoanalysis, and indeed Dr. Horney was the first analyst I ever met. But I had majored in English at Harvard, and when I first came into her room, she was reading Meredith's *The Egoist*. A remark of mine prompted a remark of hers, and we were on our way. She knew the professor who had taught the seminar I had taken on Victorian writers, among them Meredith. The next morning I went to her room last, and our conversation was rather leisurely. She knew she was dying, and made no effort to conceal her knowledge from me, a stranger. She smiled at me as I took her blood and told me that there was little point to the effort, but she would cooperate. She was cheerful, however; not full of "denial," but resigned to the point that she no longer felt sadness or despair. On the third morning we had our longest and last conversation. (She went downhill rather quickly, and the doctors stopped their tests on her—and kept out all but a few visitors.) It was then that she asked me how many women were in my class at medical school. When I told her there were three, out of a hundred or so, she asked me why I thought that was the case. I replied that I didn't know. Then she asked me what I thought about medicine as a profession for women. I told her that I thought it was a hard one for a woman: so many years of training, with all the obvious, personal difficulties. We talked about them: marriage and motherhood for a woman at the same time going to school or interning or taking a residency; the resentment of women so many doctors had at the time—and by no means is that a thing of the past; and most of all, the irony that a profession so dedicated to caring for people, nurturing them, when possible, back to good health, should so overwhelmingly be made up of men. (At least in this country, she reminded me; in Russia things are far different.) As I got ready to leave she was cordial and hopeful; she thanked me for our talk, told me she hoped I would stop by again, but as if already aware that it would not be possible, she spoke of the future: "You are young, and maybe when you reach my age the world will be quite different."

I never quite knew at the time exactly what she had in mind: *what* would be different, I wondered as I walked away. We were then getting ready for the Eisenhower years, and there was not much encouragement then for social change. Moreover, I was myself twenty-three, right in the middle of obtaining training in a conservative profession. Later I would join Dr. Horney's subspecialty in that profession, but find her virtually ignored, at least by the psychoanalysts who supervised me in Boston hospitals. No one assigned her books or articles to us. She had left the fold.

Now the young psychiatrists I know do indeed read her, not uncritically, but with a good deal of interest. And this article of hers, so provocative and sensible and forthright, is one of many they find valuable. Portions of it have a clarity and vigor that are evident and satisfying; other sections refresh the reader because a writer has dared think for herself, and with both candor and feeling: "At this point I, as a woman, ask in amazement, and what about motherhood?" One pays her no compliment, simply states the obvious: what she wrote in 1926 is utterly helpful today, as we in psychiatry try hard to distinguish between the biological and developmental aspects of childhood and the social or cultural pressures which exert themselves so relentlessly upon all of us. Needless to say, only the abstract-minded theorist sets up rigid categories—*this* is a function of *that*, period. Horney speaks of an "interaction of psychic and social factors," and her sense of "interaction" is subtle and knowing; it is not a matter of "deep" or "internal" forces being tangentially affected by "superficial" or "external" ones, but rather the extraordinarily complex development of each person's life—a time, a place, a particular family, a situation in a given society, all of that becomes for a given person the basis for countless assumptions, fantasies, wishes, fears, tensions, urges, and on and on.

I do not think Karen Horney's article needs further specific elucidation from me. Again, what is remarkable about it today is the aura of obviousness and common sense it projects—a measure of how, as with many of Freud's written observations, ideas can become "a whole climate of opinion." Very important, for all its obviousness, is her sense, back in the 1920s, that men, with all their particular "needs" (not to mention biases) have built the psychoanalytic edifice—indeed for the most part write what we call "history." There is a difference between what various historians see and choose to emphasize, depending upon who they are, where they come from, and so forth; by the same token, psychoanalysts have their own reasons for emphasizing various theoretical points—all of which is ironically a commonplace, as a result of Freud's life and thought, yet has to emerge in Horney's article as a forceful rebuff: let women speak, and hear *their* "interpretations," even "biases," if you will.

I read this article of Horney's after finishing two fine articles by historians: Eileen Power's "The Position of Women" in *The Legacy of the Middle Ages* (Oxford, 1926—the year Horney's article was published) and an article by D. Herlihy called "Land, Family and Women in Continental Europe, 700–1000" (*Traditio*, 1962). From these articles, from Philippe Ariès' enormously suggestive *Centuries of Childhood*, from March Bloch's masterpiece *Feudal Society*, one gets a sense of how women of countries like ours came to occupy the position in society that Karen Horney had to take for granted, but also dared scrutinize carefully, during her lifetime. It is particularly interesting to learn that during the Middle Ages, when families worked hard on the land, when villages were important and self-sustaining centers of activity, rather than increasingly inert appendages to urban centers, women were active, very much involved in the work of the community, relatively influential and independent. For example, "women performed almost every kind of agricultural labor, with the exception of the heavy business of ploughing. They often acted as thatcher's assistants, and on many manors they did the greater part of the

190

sheep-shearing, while the care of the dairy and of the small poultry was always in their hands." Or, "of the five hundred crafts scheduled in Étienne Boileau's *Livre des Métiers* in medieval Paris, at least five were their monopoly, and in a large number of others women were employed as well as men." Slowly, we are told, with the rise of mercantile capitalism, women began to lose the rights they had acquired by custom and law. Soon enough they were confined to bourgeois households, carefully guarded, both "elevated" and of course debased: their sole job was to produce children, while men alone worked out in the "world"—or so it went in the influential bourgeois sections of the West's major cities, where the actual *circumstances* women had to confront became ever so gradually consolidated into a *view* of them: what is psychologically "natural" for them, what they are "born" to do, "made" to do. Thus economic and social events become the predecessors of "facts" and "ideas," if not whole ideological systems.

In a sense, then, Karen Horney was a prophet. She saw ahead of her time, dared look with some distance and detachment at her own profession, and in so doing, anticipated in a limited way a future historical moment. Moreover, she managed to be far-sighted without self-righteousness, rancor, or brittle defensiveness. For years I have heard various psychoanalysts dismiss her ideas out of hand, or scorn them as of little value or interest. As one goes through this article and others like it, one wonders why the rejection, why the contempt or derision, why the condescension. She herself wrote tentatively, considerately; she does not at all come across as a shrill rebel or edgy critic or driven troublemaker or dissident. She merely wants her colleagues to stop and think for a while: as bourgeois men of the first half of the twentieth century, do they have blind spots about themselves as men and about women, and if so, what are they, and how do they affect their thinking? One would think that such a request is not all that out of order; indeed, is in keeping with the essential spirit of psychoanalysis. But then, Freud had all along known, in connection with his own life and its outcome, how hard it is for any of us to break out of the various confines, psychological or otherwise, that surround us. As psychoanalysts certainly realize, we need others to give us distance on ourselves—and thereby to bring us closer to ourselves. In that regard, patients need doctors—and not incidentally, doctors need patients. So do men and women—though, of course, they have other reasons than that for getting to know each other.

191

Gelpi on Jung

On the Nature
of the Animus (1931)

Emma Jung

The anima and the animus are two archetypal figures of especially great importance. They belong on the one hand to the individual consciousness and on the other hand are rooted in the collective unconscious, thus forming a connecting link or bridge between the personal and the impersonal, the conscious and the unconscious. It is because one is feminine and the other masculine that C. G. Jung has called them anima and animus respectively.[1] He understands these figures to be function complexes behaving in ways compensatory to the outer personality, that is, behaving as if they were inner personalities and exhibiting the characteristics which are lacking in the outer, and manifest, conscious personality. In a man, these are feminine characteristics, in a woman, masculine. Normally both are always present, to a certain degree, but find no place in the person's outwardly directed functioning because they disturb his outer adaptation, his established ideal image of himself.

However, the character of these figures is not determined only by the latent sexual characteristics they represent; it is conditioned by the experience each person has had in the course of his or her life with representatives of the other sex, and also by the collective image of woman carried in the psyche of the individual man, and the collective image of man carried by the woman. These three factors coalesce to form a quantity which is neither solely an image nor solely experience, but an entity not organically coordinated in its activity with the other psychic functions. It behaves as if it were a law unto itself, interfering in the life of the individual as if it were an alien element; sometimes the interference is helpful, sometimes disturbing, if not actually destructive. We have, therefore, every cause to concern ourselves with these psychic entities and arrive at an understanding of how they influence us.

If in what follows, I present the animus and its manifestations as realities, the reader must remember that I am speaking of psychic realities,[2] which are incommensurable with concrete realities but no less effective for that reason. Here I shall attempt to present certain aspects of the animus without, however, laying claim to a complete comprehension of this extraordinarily complex phenomenon. For in discussing the animus we are dealing not only with an absolute, an immutable entity, but also with a spiritual process. I intend to limit myself here to the ways in which the animus appears in its relation to the individual and to consciousness.

Conscious and Outward Manifestations of the Animus

The premise from which I start is that in the animus we are dealing with a masculine principle. But how is this masculine principle to be characterized? Goethe makes Faust, who is occupied with the translation of the Gospel of John, ask himself if the passage, "In the beginning was the Word," would not read better if it were, "In the beginning was Power," or "Meaning," and finally he has him write, "In the beginning was the Deed." With these four expressions, which are meant to reproduce the Greek *logos,* the quintessence of the masculine principle does indeed seem to be expressed. At the same time, we find in them a progressive sequence, each stage having its representative in life as well as in the development of the animus. Power corresponds very well to the first stage, the deed follows, then the word, and finally, as the last stage, meaning. One might better say instead of power, directed power; that is will, because mere power is not yet human, nor is it spiritual. This four-sidedness characterizing the logos principle presupposes, as we see, an element of consciousness, because without consciousness neither will, word, deed, nor meaning is conceivable.

Just as there are men of outstanding physical power, men of deeds, men of words, and men of wisdom, so, too, does the animus image differ in accordance with the woman's particular stage of development or her natural gifts. This image may be transferred to a real man who comes by the animus role because of his resemblance to it; alternatively, it may

196

appear as a dream or phantasy figure; but since it represents a living psychic reality, it lends a definite coloration from within the woman herself to all that she does. For the primitive woman, or the young woman, or for the primitive in every woman, a man distinguished by physical prowess becomes an animus figure. Typical examples are the heroes of legend, or present-day sports celebrities, cowboys, bull fighters, aviators, and so on. For more exacting women, the animus figure is a man who accomplishes deeds, in the sense that he directs his power toward something of great significance. The transitions here are usually not sharp, because power and deed mutually condition one another. A man who rules over the "word" or over "meaning" represents an essentially intellectual tendency, because word and meaning correspond par excellence to mental capacities. Such a man exemplifies the animus in the narrower sense, understood as being a spiritual guide and as representing the intellectual gifts of the woman. It is at this stage, too, for the most part, that the animus becomes problematical, hence, we shall have to dwell on it longest.

Animus images representing the stages of power and deed are projected upon a hero figure. But there are also women in whom this aspect of masculinity is already harmoniously coordinated with the feminine principle and lending it effective aid. These are the active, energetic, brave, and forceful women. But also there are those in whom the integration has failed, in whom masculine behavior has overrun and suppressed the feminine principle. These are the over-energetic, ruthless, brutal, men-women, the Xantippes who are not only active but aggressive. In many women, this primitive masculinity is also expressed in their erotic life, and then their approach to love has a masculine aggressive character and is not, as is usual in women, involved with and determined by feeling but functions on its own, apart from the rest of the personality, as happens predominantly with men.

On the whole, however, it can be assumed that the more primitive forms of masculinity have already been assimilated by women. Generally speaking, they have long ago found their applications in the feminine way of life, and there have long been women whose strength of will, purposefulness, activity, and energy serve as helpful forces in their otherwise quite feminine lives. The problem of the woman of today seems rather to lie in her attitude to the animus-logos, to the masculine-intellectual element in the narrower sense; because the extension of consciousness in general, greater consciousness in all fields, seems to be an inescapable demand—as well as a gift—of our time. One expression of this is the fact that along with the discoveries and inventions of the last fifty years, we have also had the beginning of the so-called woman's movement, the struggle of women for equal rights with men. Happily, we have today survived the worst product of this struggle, the "bluestocking." Woman has learned to see that she cannot become like a man because first and foremost she is a woman and must be one. However, the fact remains that a certain sum of masculine spirit has ripened in woman's consciousness and must find its place and effectiveness in her personality. To learn to know these factors, to coordinate them so that they can play their part in a meaningful way, is an important part of the animus problem.

From time to time we hear it said that there is no necessity for woman to occupy herself with spiritual or intellectual matters, that this is only an idiotic aping of man, or a competitive drive betokening megalomania. Although this is surely true in many cases, especially of the phenomena at the beginning of the woman's movement, nevertheless, as an explanation of the matter, it is not justified. Neither arrogance nor presumption drives us to the audacity of wanting to be like God—that is, like man; we are not like Eve of old, lured by the beauty of the fruit of the tree of knowledge, nor does the snake encourage us to enjoy it. No, there has come to us something like a command; we are confronted with the necessity of biting into this apple, whether we think it good to eat or not, confronted with the fact that the paradise of naturalness and unconsciousness, in which many of us would only too gladly tarry, is gone forever.

This, then, is how matters stand fundamentally, even if on the surface appearances may sometimes be otherwise. And because so significant a turning point is concerned, we must not be astonished at unsuccessful efforts, and grotesque exaggerations, nor allow ourselves to be daunted by them. If the problem is not faced, if woman does not meet adequately the demand for consciousness or intellectual activity, the animus becomes autonomous and negative, and works destructively on the individual herself and in her relations to other people. This fact can be explained as follows: if the possibility of spiritual functioning is not taken up by the conscious mind, the psychic energy intended for it falls into the unconscious, and there activates the archetype of the animus. Possessed of the energy that has flowed back into the unconscious, the animus figure becomes autonomous, so powerful, indeed, that it can overwhelm the conscious ego, and thus finally dominate the whole personality. I must add here that I start with the view that in the human being there is a certain basic idea to be fulfilled, just as, for instance, in an egg or a seed corn there is already contained the idea of the life destined to come from it. Therefore I speak of a sum of available psychic energy which is intended for spiritual functions, and ought to be applied to them. Expressed figuratively in terms of economics, the situation is like that dealt with in a household budget, or other enterprise of some sort where certain sums of money are provided for certain purposes. In addition, from time to time sums previously used in other ways will become available, either because they are no longer needed for those purposes or because they cannot otherwise be invested. In many respects, this is the case with the woman of today. In the first place, she seldom finds satisfaction in the established religion, especially if she is a Protestant. The church which once to a large extent filled her spiritual and intellectual needs no longer offers her this satisfaction. Formerly, the animus, together with its associated problems, could be transferred to the beyond (for to many women the Biblical Father-God meant a metaphysical, superhuman aspect of the animus image), and as long as spirituality could be thus convincingly expressed in the generally valid forms of religion, no conflict developed. Only now when this can no longer be achieved, does our problem arise.

A further reason for the existence of a problem regarding the disposal of psychic energy is that through the possibility of birth control a considerable sum of energy has been freed. It is doubtful whether woman herself can rightly estimate how large is this sum which was previously needed to maintain a constant state of readiness for her biological task.

A third cause lies in the achievements of technology that substitute new means for so many tasks to which woman previously applied her inventiveness and her creative spirit. Where she formerly blew up a hearth fire, and thus still accomplished the Promethean act, today she turns a gas plug or an electrical switch and has no inkling of what she sacrifices by these practical novelties, nor what consequences the loss entails. For everything not done in the traditional way will be done in a new way, and that is not altogether simple. There are many women who, when they have reached the place where they are confronted by intellectual demands, say, "I would rather have another child," in order to escape or at least to postpone the uncomfortable and disturbing demand. But sooner or later a woman must accommodate herself to meet it, for the biological demands naturally decrease progressively after the first half of life so that in any case a change of attitude is unavoidable, if she does not want to fall victim to a neurosis or some other form of illness.

Moreover, it is not only the freed psychic energy that confronts her with a new task, but equally the aforementioned law of the time-moment, the *kairos*, to which we are all subject and from which we cannot escape, obscure though its terms appear to us to be. In fact, our time seems quite generally to require a widening of consciousness. Thus, in psychology, we have discovered and are investigating the unconscious; in physics, we have become aware of phenomena and processes—rays and waves, for instance—which up till now were imperceptible and not part of our conscious knowledge. New worlds, with the laws that govern them, open up as, for example, that of the atom. Furthermore, telegraph, telephone, radio, and technically perfected instruments of every sort bring remote things near, expanding the range of our sense perceptions over the whole earth and even far beyond it. In all of this, the extension and illumination of consciousness is expressed. To discuss further the causes and aims of this phenomenon would lead us too far afield; I mention it only as a joint factor in the problem which is so acute for the woman of today, the animus problem.

The increase in consciousness implies a leading over of psychic energy into new paths. All culture, as we know, depends on such a deflection, and the capacity to bring it about is what distinguishes men from animals. But this process involves great difficulties; indeed, it affects us almost like a sin, a misdeed, as is shown in such myths as the Fall of man, or the theft of fire by Prometheus, and that is how we may experience it in our own lives. Nor is this astonishing since it concerns the interruption or reversal of the natural course of events, a very dangerous venture. For this reason, this process has always been closely connected with religious ideas and rites. Indeed, the religious mystery, with its symbolical experience of death and rebirth, always means this mysterious and miraculous process of transformation.

As is evident in the myths just mentioned concerning the Fall of man and the stealing of fire by Prometheus, it is the logos—that is, knowledge, consciousness, in a word—that lifts man above nature. But this achievement brings him into a tragic position between animal and God. Because of it, he is no longer the child of mother nature; he is driven out of paradise, but also, he is no god, because he is still tied inescapably to his body and its natural laws, just as Prometheus was fettered to the rock. Although this painful state of suspension, of being torn between spirit and nature, has long been familiar to man, it is only recently that woman has really begun to feel the conflict. And with this conflict, which goes hand in hand with an increase of consciousness, we come back to the animus problem that eventually leads to the opposites, to nature and spirit and their harmonization.

How do we experience this problem? How do we experience the spiritual principle? First of all, we become aware of it in the outside world. The child usually sees it in the father, or in a person taking the place of the father; later, perhaps, in a teacher or elder brother, husband, friend, finally, also, in the objective documents of the spirit, in church, state, and society with all their institutions, as well as in the creations of science and the arts. For the most part, direct access to these objective forms of the spirit is not possible for a woman; she finds it only through a man, who is her guide and intermediary. This guide and intermediary then becomes the bearer or representative of the animus image; in other words, the animus is projected upon him. As long as the projection succeeds, that is, as long as the image corresponds to a certain degree with the bearer, there is no real conflict. On the contrary, this state of affairs seems to be, in a certain sense, perfect, especially when the man who is the spiritual intermediary is also at the same time perceived as a human being to whom one has a positive, human relationship. If such a projection can be permanently established this might be called an ideal relationship, ideal because without conflict, but the woman remains unconscious. The fact that today it is no longer fitting to remain so unconscious seems, however, to be proved by the circumstance that many if not most women who believe themselves to be happy and content in what purports to be a perfect animus relationship are troubled with nervous or bodily symptoms. Very often anxiety states appear, sleeplessness and general nervousness, or physical ills such as headache and other pains, disturbances of vision, and, occasionally, lung affections. I know of several cases in which the lungs became affected at a time when the animus problem became acute, and were cured after the problem was recognized and understood as such.[3] (Perhaps the organs of breathing have a peculiar relationship to spirit, as is suggested by the words animus or pneuma and *Hauch*, breath, or *Geist*, spirit, and therefore react with special sensitivity to the processes of the spirit. Possibly any other organ could just as well be affected, and it is simply a question of psychic energy which, finding no suitable application and driven back upon itself, attacks any weak point.)

Such a total transference of the animus image as that described above creates, together with an apparent satisfaction and completeness, a kind of compulsive tie to the man in question and a dependence on him that often increases to the point of becoming unbearable. This state of being fascinated by another and wholly under his influence is well known under the term "transference," which is nothing else than projection. However, projection means not only the transference of an image to another person, but also of the activities that go with it, so that a man to whom the animus image has been transferred is expected to take over all the functions that have remained undeveloped in the woman in question, whether the thinking function, or the power to act, or responsibility toward the outside world. In turn, the woman upon whom a man has projected his anima must feel for him, or make relationships for him, and this symbiotic relationship is, in my opinion, the real cause for the compulsive dependence that exists in these cases.

But such a state of completely successful projection is usually not of very long duration—especially not if the woman is in a close relationship to the man in question. Then the incongruity between the image and the image-bearer often becomes all too obvious. An archetype, such as the animus represents, will never really coincide with an individual man, the less so the more individual that man is. Individuality is really the opposite of the archetype, for what is individual is not in any way typical but the unique intermixture of characteristics, possibly typical in themselves.

When this discrimination between the image and the person sets in we become aware, to our great confusion and disappointment, that the man who seemed to embody our image does not correspond to it in the least, but continually behaves quite differently from the way we think he should. At first we perhaps try to deceive ourselves about this and often succeed relatively easily, thanks to an aptitude for effacing differences, which we owe to blurred powers of discrimination. Oftentimes we try with real cunning to make the man be what we think he ought to represent. Not only do we consciously exert force or pressure; far more frequently we quite unconsciously force our partner, by our behavior, into archetypal or animus reactions. Naturally, the same holds good for the man in his

202

attitude toward the woman. He, too, would like to see in her the image that floats before him, and by this wish, which works like a suggestion, he may bring it about that she does not live her real self but becomes an anima figure. This, and the fact that the anima and animus mutually constellate each other (since an anima manifestation calls forth the animus, and vice versa, producing a vicious circle very difficult to break), forms one of the worst complications in the relations between men and women.

But by the time the incongruity between the man and the animus figure has been discovered, a woman is already in the midst of the conflict, and there remains nothing for her to do but to carry through to completion the process of discriminating between the image within and the man outside. Here we come to what is most essentially meaningful in the animus problem, namely, the masculine-intellectual component within the woman herself. It seems to me that to relate to this component, to know it, and to incorporate it into the rest of the personality, are central elements of this problem, which is perhaps the most important of all those concerning the woman of today. That the problem has to do with a natural predisposition, an organic factor belonging to the individuality and intended to function, explains why the animus is able to attract psychic energy to itself until it becomes an overwhelming and autonomous figure.

It is probable that all organs or organic tendencies attract to themselves a certain amount of energy, which means readiness for functioning, and that when a particular organ receives an insufficient amount of energy this fact is made known by the manifestation of disturbances or by the development of symptoms. Applying this idea to the psyche, I would conclude from the presence of a powerful animus figure—a so-called "possession by the animus"—that the person in question gives too little attention to her own masculine-intellectual logos tendency, and has either developed and applied it insufficiently or not in the right way. Perhaps this sounds paradoxical because, seen from the outside, it appears as if it were the feminine principle which is not taken sufficiently into account, since the behavior of such women seems on the surface to be too masculine and suggests a lack of femininity. But in the masculinity brought to view, I see more of a symptom, a sign that something masculine in the woman claims attention. It is true that what is primarily feminine is overrun and repressed by the autocratic entrance upon the scene

203

of this masculinity, but the feminine element can only get into its right place by a detour that includes coming to terms with the masculine factor, the animus.

To busy ourselves simply in an intellectual or objectively masculine way seems insufficient, as can be seen in many women who have completed a course of study and practice a heretofore masculine, intellectual calling, but who, nonetheless, have never come to terms with the animus problem. Such a masculine training and way of life may well be achieved by identification with the animus, but then the feminine side is left out in the cold. What is really necessary is that feminine intellectuality, logos in the woman, should be so fitted into the nature and life of the woman that a harmonious cooperation between the feminine and masculine factors ensues and no part is condemned to a shadowy existence.

The first stage on the right road is, therefore, the withdrawal of the projection by recognizing it as such, and thus freeing it from the object. This first act of discrimination, simple as it may seem, nonetheless means a difficult achievement and often a painful renunciation. Through this withdrawal of the projection we recognize that we are not dealing with an entity outside ourselves but a quality within; and we see before us the task of learning to know the nature and effect of this factor, this "man in us," in order to distinguish him from ourselves. If this is not done, we are identical with the animus or possessed by it, a state that creates the most unwholesome effects. For when the feminine side is so over-whelmed and pushed into the background by the animus, there easily arise depressions, general dissatisfaction, and loss of interest in life. These are all intelligible symptoms pointing to the fact that one half of the personality is partly robbed of life by the encroachment of the animus.

Besides this, the animus can interpose itself in a disturbing way be-tween oneself and other people, between oneself and life in general. It is very difficult to recognize such a possession in oneself, all the more difficult the more complete it is. Therefore it is a great help to observe the effect one has on other people, and to judge from their reactions whether these can possibly have been called forth by an unconscious animus identification. This orientation derived from other people is an invaluable aid in the laborious process—often beyond one's individual powers—of clearly distinguishing the animus and assigning it to its right-ful place. Indeed, I think that without relationship to a person with respect to whom it is possible to orient oneself again and again, it is almost impossible ever to free oneself from the demonic clutch of the animus. In a state of identification with the animus, we think, say, or do something in the full conviction that it is we who are doing it, while in reality, without our having been aware of it, the animus has been speaking through us.

Often it is very difficult to realize that a thought or opinion has been dictated by the animus and is not one's own most particular conviction, because the animus has at its command a sort of aggressive authority and power of suggestion. It derives this authority from its connection with the universal mind, but the force of suggestion it exercises is due to woman's own passivity in thinking and her corresponding lack of critical ability. Such opinions or concepts, usually brought out with great aplomb, are especially characteristic of the animus. They are characteristic in that, corresponding to the principle of the logos, they are generally valid concepts or truths which, though they may be quite true in themselves, do not fit in the given instance because they fail to consider what is individual and specific in a situation. Ready-made, incontrovertibly valid judgments of this kind are really only applicable in mathematics, where two times two is always four. But in life they do not apply for there they do violence, either to the subject under discussion or to the person being addressed, or even to the woman herself who delivers a final judgment without having taken all of her own reactions into account.

The same sort of unrelated thinking also appears in a man when he is identified with reason or the logos principle and does not himself think, but lets "it" think. Such men are naturally especially well-suited to embody the animus of a woman. But I cannot go into this further because I am concerned here exclusively with feminine psychology.

One of the most important ways that the animus expresses itself, then, is in making judgments, and as it happens with judgments, so it is with thoughts in general. From within, they crowd upon the woman in already complete, irrefutable forms. Or, if they come from without, she adopts them because they seem to her somehow convincing or attractive. But usually she feels no urge to think through and thus really to understand the ideas which she adopts and, perhaps, even propagates further. Her undeveloped power of discrimination results in her meeting valuable and worthless ideas with the same enthusiasm or with the same respect, because anything suggestive of mind impresses her enormously and exerts an uncanny fascination upon her. This accounts for the success of so many swindlers who often achieve incomprehensible effects with a sort of pseudo-spirituality. On the other hand, her lack of discrimination has a good side; it makes the woman unprejudiced and therefore she frequently discovers and appraises spiritual values more quickly than a man, whose developed critical power tends to make him so distrustful and prejudiced that it often takes him considerable time to see a value which less prejudiced persons have long since recognized.

The real thinking of women (I refer here to women in general, knowing well that there are many far above this level who have already differentiated their thinking and their spiritual natures to a high degree) is preeminently practical and applied. It is something we describe as sound common sense, and is usually directed to what is close at hand and personal. To this extent it functions adequately in its own place and does not actually belong to what we mean by animus in the stricter sense. Only when woman's mental power is no longer applied to the mastering of daily tasks but goes beyond, seeking a new field of activity, does the animus come into play.

In general, it can be said that feminine mentality manifests an undeveloped, childlike, or primitive character; instead of the thirst for knowledge, curiosity; instead of judgment, prejudice; instead of thinking, imagination or dreaming; instead of will, wishing.

Where a man takes up objective problems, a woman contents herself with solving riddles; where he battles for knowledge and understanding, she contents herself with faith or superstition, or else she makes assumptions. Clearly, these are well-marked pre-stages that can be shown to exist in the minds of children as well as in those of primitives. Thus, the curiosity of children and primitives is familiar to us, as are also the roles played by belief and superstition. In the *Edda* there is a riddle-contest between the wandering Odin and his host, a memorial of the time when the masculine mind was occupied with riddle-guessing as woman's mind is still today. Similar stories have come down to us from antiquity and the Middle Ages. We have the riddle of the Sphinx, or of Oedipus, the hair-splitting of the sophists and scholastics.

So-called wishful thinking also corresponds to a definite stage in the development of the mind. It appears as a motif in fairy tales, often characterizing something in the past, as when the stories refer to "the time when wishing was still helpful." The magic practice of wishing that something would befall a person is founded on the same idea. Grimm, in his German mythology, points to the connection between wishing, imagining, and thinking. According to him,

> "An ancient Norse name for Wotan or Odin seems to be Oski or Wish, and the Valkyries were also called Wish Maidens. Odin, the wind-god and wanderer, the lord of the army of spirits, the inventor of runes, is a typical spirit god, but of a primitive form still near to nature."

As such, he is lord of wishes. He is not only the giver of all that is good and perfect as comprehended under wishing, but also it is he who, when evoked, can create by a wish. Grimm says, "Wishing is the measuring, outpouring, giving, creating power. It is the power that shapes, imagines, thinks, and is therefore imagination, idea, form." And in another place he writes: "In Sanskrit 'wish' is significantly called *manoratha,* the wheel of the mind—it is the wish that turns the wheel of thought."

The woman's animus in its superhuman, divine aspect is comparable to such a spirit and wind-god. We find the animus in a similar form in dreams and phantasies, and this wish-character is peculiar to feminine thinking. If we bear in mind that power to imagine means to man nothing less than the power to make at will a mental image of anything he chooses, and that this image, though immaterial, cannot be denied reality, then we can understand how it is that imagining, thinking, wishing, and creating have been rated as equivalents. Especially in a relatively unconscious condition, where outer and inner reality are not sharply distinguished but flow into one another, it is easily possible that a spiritual reality, that is, a thought or an image, can be taken as concretely real. In primitives, too, there is to be found this equivalence between outer concrete and inner spiritual reality. (Lévy-Bruhl[4] gives many examples of this, but it would take us too far afield to say more about it here.) The same phenomenon is found very clearly expressed in feminine mentality.

We are astonished to discover, on closer inspection, how often the thought comes to us that things must happen in a certain way, or that a person who interests us is doing this or that, or has done it, or will do it. We do not pause to compare these intuitions with reality. We are already convinced of their truth, or at least are inclined to assume that the mere idea is true and that it corresponds to reality. Other phantasy structures also are readily taken as real and can at times even appear in concrete form.

One of the animus activities most difficult to see through lies in this field, namely, the building up of a wish-image of oneself. The animus is expert at sketching in and making plausible a picture that represents us as we would like to be seen, for example, as the "ideal lover," the "appealing, helpless child," the "selfless handmaiden," the "extraordinarily original person," the "one who is really born to something better," and so on. This activity naturally lends the animus power over us until we voluntarily, or perforce, make up our minds to sacrifice the highly colored picture and see ourselves as we really are.

Very frequently, feminine activity also expresses itself in what is largely a retrospectively oriented pondering over what we ought to have done differently in life, and how we ought to have done it; or, as if under compulsion, we make up strings of causal connections. We like to call this thinking; though, on the contrary, it is a form of mental activity that is strangely pointless and unproductive, a form that really leads only to self-torture. Here, too, there is again a characteristic failure to discriminate between what is real and what has been thought or imagined.

We could say, then, that feminine thinking, in so far as it is not occupied practically as sound common sense, is really not thinking, but, rather, dreaming, imagining, wishing, and fearing (i.e., negative wishing). The power and authority of the animus phenomenon can be partly explained by the primitive mental lack of differentiation between imagination and reality. Since what belongs to mind—that is, thought—possesses at the same time the character of indisputable reality, what the animus says seems also to be indisputably true.

And now we come to the magic of words. A word, also, just like an idea, a thought, has the effect of reality upon undifferentiated minds. Our Biblical myth of creation, for instance, where the world grows out of the spoken word of the Creator, is an expression of this. The animus, too, possesses the magic power of words, and therefore men who have the gift of oratory can exert a compulsive power on women in both a good and an evil sense. Am I going too far when I say that the magic of the word, the art of speaking, is the thing in a man through which a woman is most unfailingly caught and most frequently deluded? But it is not woman alone who is under the spell of word-magic, the phenomenon is prevalent everywhere. The holy runes of ancient times, Indian *mantras*, prayers, and magic formulas of all sorts down to the technical expressions and slogans of our own times, all bear witness to the magic power of spirit that has become word.

208

However, it can be said in general that a woman is more susceptible to such magic spells than a man of a corresponding cultural level. A man has by nature the urge to understand the things he has to deal with; small boys show a predilection for pulling their toys to pieces to find out what they look like inside or how they work. In a woman, this urge is much less pronounced. She can easily work with instruments or machines without its ever occurring to her to want to study or understand their construction. Similarly, she can be impressed by a significant-sounding word without having grasped its exact meaning. A man is much more inclined to track down the meaning.

The most characteristic manifestation of the animus is not in a configured image *(Gestalt)* but rather in words *(logos* also means word). It comes to us as a voice commenting on every situation in which we find ourselves, or imparting generally applicable rules of behavior. Often this is how we first perceive the animus to be different from the ego, long before it has crystallized into a personal figure. As far as I have observed, this voice expresses itself chiefly in two ways. First, we hear from it a critical, usually negative comment on every movement, an exact examination of all motives and intentions, which naturally always causes feelings of inferiority, and tends to nip in the bud all initiative and every wish for self-expression. From time to time, this same voice may also dispense exaggerated praise, and the result of these extremes of judgment is that one oscillates to and fro between the consciousness of complete futility and a blown-up sense of one's own value and importance. The animus' second way of speaking is confined more or less exclusively to issuing commands or prohibitions, and to pronouncing generally accepted viewpoints.

It seems to me that two important sides of the logos function are expressed here. On the one hand, we have discriminating, judging, and understanding; on the other, the abstracting and setting up of general laws. We could say, perhaps, that where the first sort of functioning prevails the animus figure appears as a single person, while if the second prevails, it appears as a plurality, a kind of council. Discrimination and judgment are mainly individual, while the setting up and abstracting of laws presupposes an agreement on the part of many, and is therefore more appropriately expressed by a group.

It is well known that a really creative faculty of mind is a rare thing in woman. There are many women who have developed their powers of thinking, discrimination, and criticism to a high degree, but there are very few who are mentally creative in the way a man is. It is maliciously said that woman is so lacking in the gift of invention, that if the kitchen spoon had not been invented by a man, we would today still be stirring the soup with a stick!

The creativity of woman finds its expression in the sphere of living, not only in her biological functions as mother but in the shaping of life generally, be it in her activity as educator, in her role as companion to man, as mother in the home, or in some other form. The development of relationships is of primary importance in the shaping of life, and this is the real field of feminine creative power. Among the arts, the drama is outstandingly the one in which woman can achieve equality with man. In acting, people, relationships, and life are given form, and so woman is there just as creative as man. We come upon creative elements also in the products of the unconscious, in the dreams, phantasies, or phrases that come spontaneously to women. These products often contain thoughts, views, truths, of a purely objective, absolutely impersonal nature. The mediation of such knowledge and such contents is essentially the function of the higher animus.

In dreams we often find quite abstract scientific symbols which are hardly to be interpreted personally but represent objective findings or ideas at which no one is more astonished, perhaps, than the dreamer herself. This is especially striking in women who have a poorly developed thinking function or a limited amount of culture. I know a woman in whom thinking is the "inferior function,"[5] whose dreams often mention problems of astronomy and physics, and also refer to technical instruments of all sorts. Another woman, quite nonrational in type, when reproducing unconscious contents, drew strictly geometric figures, crystal-like structures, such as are found in text books on geometry or mineralogy. To others still, the animus brings views of the world and of life that go far beyond their conscious thinking and show a creative quality that cannot be denied.

However, in the field where the creative activity of woman flowers most characteristically, that is, in human relationships, the creative factor springs from feeling coupled with intuition or sensation, more than from mind in the sense of logos. Here, the animus can be actually dangerous, because it injects itself into the relationship in place of feeling, thus making relatedness difficult or impossible. It happens only too frequently

210

that instead of understanding a situation—or another person—through feeling and acting accordingly, we think something about the situation or the person and offer an opinion in place of a human reaction. This may be quite correct, well-intentioned, and clever, but it has no effect, or the wrong effect, because it is right only in an objective, factual way. Subjectively, humanly speaking, it is wrong because in that moment the partner, or the relationship, is best served not by discernment or objectivity but by sympathetic feeling. It very often happens that such an objective attitude is assumed by a woman in the belief that she is behaving admirably, but the effect is to ruin the situation completely. The inability to realize that discernment, reasonableness, and objectivity are inappropriate in certain places is often astonishing. I can only explain this by the fact that women are accustomed to think of the masculine way as something in itself more valuable than the feminine way and superior to it. We believe a masculine objective attitude to be better in every case than a feminine and personal one. This is especially true of women who have already attained a certain level of consciousness and an appreciation of rational values.

Here I come to a very important difference between the animus problem of the woman and the anima problem of the man, a difference which seems to me to have met with too little attention. When a man discovers his anima and has come to terms with it, he has to take up something which previously seemed inferior to him. It counts for little that naturally the anima figure, be it image or human, is fascinatingly attractive and hence appears valuable. Up to now in our world, the feminine principle, as compared to the masculine, has always stood for something inferior. We only begin at present to render it justice. Revealing expressions are, "only a girl," or, "a boy doesn't do that," as is often said to boys to suggest that their behavior is contemptible. Then, too, our laws show clearly how widely the concept of woman's inferiority has prevailed. Even now in many places the law frankly sets the man above the woman, gives him greater privileges, makes him her guardian, and so on. As a result, when a man enters into relationship with his anima he has to descend from a height, to overcome a resistance—that is, his pride—by acknowledging that she is the "Sovereign Lady" (Herrin) as Spitteler called her, or, in Rider Haggard's words, "She-who-must-be-obeyed."

With a woman the case is different. We do not refer to the animus as "He-who-must-be-obeyed," but rather as the opposite, because it is far

211

too easy for the woman to obey the authority of the animus—or the man —in slavish servility. Even though she may think otherwise consciously, the idea that what is masculine is in itself more valuable than what is feminine is born in her blood. This does much to enhance the power of the animus. What we women have to overcome in our relation to the animus is not pride but lack of self-confidence and the resistance of inertia. For us, it is not as though we had to demean ourselves (unless we have been identified with the animus), but as if we had to lift ourselves. In this, we often fail for lack of courage and strength of will. It seems to us a presumption to oppose our own unauthoritative conviction to those judgments of the animus, or the man, which claim a general validity. For a woman to work herself up to a point of such apparently presumptuous spiritual independence often costs a great deal, especially because it can so easily be misunderstood or misjudged. But without this sort of revolt, no matter what she has to suffer as a consequence, she will never be free from the power of the tyrant, never come to find herself. Viewed from the outside, it often seems to be just the other way round; because all too frequently one is aware only of an overweening assurance and aplomb, and very little modesty or lack of confidence is evident. In reality, this defiant and self-assured, or even contentious attitude, should be directed against the animus, and is so intended at times, but generally it is the sign of a more or less complete identification with it.

Not only in Europe do we suffer from this now superannuated veneration of men, this overvaluation of the masculine. In America, too, where it is customary to speak of a cult of woman, the attitude does not seem to be fundamentally different. An American woman physician of wide experience has told me that all her women patients suffer from a depreciation of their own sex, and that with all of them she has to drive home the necessity of giving the feminine its due value. On the other hand, there are extremely few men who undervalue their own sex; they are, on the contrary, for the most part extremely proud of it. There are many girls who would gladly be men, but a youth or man who would like to be a girl would be looked upon as almost perverse.

The natural result of this situation is that a woman's position with respect to her animus is quite different from a man's relation to his anima. And because of this difference in attitude, many phenomena which the man cannot understand as parallel to his anima experience, and vice

212

versa, are to be ascribed to the fact that in these problems the tasks of the man and the woman are different.

To be sure, the woman does not escape sacrifice. Indeed, for her to become conscious means the giving up of her specifically feminine power. For by her unconsciousness, woman exerts a magical influence on man, a charm that lends her power over him. Because she feels this power instinctively and does not wish to lose it, she often resists to the utmost the process of becoming conscious, even though what belongs to the spirit may seem to her extremely worth striving for. Many women even keep themselves artificially unconscious solely to avoid making this sacrifice. It must be admitted that the woman is very often backed up in this by the man. Many men take pleasure in woman's unconsciousness. They are bent on opposing her development of greater consciousness in every possible way, because it seems to them uncomfortable and unnecessary.

Another point which is often overlooked and which I would like to mention lies in the function of the animus in contrast to that of the anima. We usually say offhand that animus and anima are the mediators between the unconscious contents and consciousness, meaning by this that both do exactly the same thing. This is indeed true in a general way, but it seems important to me to point out the difference in the roles played by the animus and the anima. The transmission of the unconscious contents in the sense of making them visible is the special role of the anima. It helps the man to perceive these otherwise obscure things. A necessary condition for this is a sort of dimming of consciousness; that is, the establishment of a more feminine consciousness, less sharp and clear than man's, but one which is thus able to perceive in a wider field things that are still shadowy. Woman's gift as seer, her intuitive faculty, has always been recognized. Not having her vision brought to a focus gives her an awareness of what is obscure and the power to see what is hidden from a keener eye. This vision, this perception of what is otherwise invisible, is made possible for the man by the anima.

With the animus, the emphasis does not lie on mere perception—which as was said has always been woman's gift—but true to the nature of the logos, the stress is on knowledge, and especially on understanding. It is the function of the animus to give the meaning rather than the image.

It would be a mistake to think that we are making use of the animus if we turn ourselves over to passive phantasies. We must not forget that as a rule it is no achievement for a woman to give rein to her powers of phantasy; non-rational happenings or images whose meaning is not understood seem something quite natural to her; while to the man, occupation with these things is an achievement, a sort of sacrifice of reason, a descent from the light into darkness, from the clear into the turbid. Only with difficulty does he say to himself that all the incomprehensible or even apparently senseless contents of the unconscious may, nonetheless, have a value. Moreover, the passive attitude which visions demand accords little with the active nature of a man. To a woman, this does not seem difficult; she has no reservations against the non-rational, no need to find at once a meaning in everything, no disinclination to remaining passive while things sweep over her. For women to whom the unconscious is not easily accessible, who only find entrance to its contents with difficulty, the animus can become more of a hindrance than a help if it tries to understand and analyze every image that comes up before it can be properly perceived. Only after these contents have entered consciousness and perhaps already taken form ought the animus to exert its special influence. Then, indeed, its aid is invaluable, because it helps us to understand and to find a meaning.

Yet sometimes a meaning is communicated to us directly from the unconscious, not through images or symbols, but through flashes of knowledge already formulated in words. This, indeed, is a very characteristic form of expression of the animus. Yet it is often difficult to discover whether we are dealing with a familiar, generally valid, and hence collective opinion, or with the result of individual insight. In order to be clear about this, conscious judgment is again needed, as well as exact discrimination between oneself and the animus.

The Animus as it Appears in the Images of the Unconscious

Having tried to show in the foregoing how the animus manifests itself outwardly and in consciousness, I would like now to discuss how the images of the unconscious represent it, and how it appears in dreams and phantasies. Learning to recognize this figure and holding occasional conversations and debates with it are further important steps on our way to discriminating between ourselves and the animus. The recognition of the animus as an image or figure within the psyche marks the beginning of a new difficulty. This is due to its manifoldness. We hear from men that the anima almost always appears in quite definite forms which are more or less the same in all men; it is mother or loved one, sister or daughter, mistress or slave, priestess or witch; upon occasion it appears with contrasting characteristics, light and dark, helpful and destructive, now as a noble, and now as an ignoble being.

On the contrary, for women the animus appears either as a plurality of men, as a group of fathers, a council, a court, or some other gathering of wise men, or else as a lightning-change artist who can assume any form and makes extensive use of this ability.

I explain this difference in the following way: Man has really experienced woman only as mother, loved one, and so on, that is, always in ways related to himself. These are the forms in which woman has presented herself, the forms in which her fate has always been carried out. The life of man, on the contrary, has taken on more manifold forms, because his biological task has allowed him time for many other activities. Corresponding to the more diversified field of man's activity, the animus can appear as a representative or master of any sort of ability or knowledge. The anima figure, however, is characterized by the fact that all of its forms are at the same time forms of relationship. Even if the anima appears as priestess or witch, the figure is always in a special relationship to the man whose anima it embodies, so that it either initiates or bewitches him. We are again reminded of Rider Haggard's *She*, where the special relationship is even represented as being centuries old.

But as has been said, the animus figure does not necessarily express a relationship. Corresponding to the factual orientation of man and characteristic of the logos principle, this figure can come on the scene in a purely objective, unrelated way, as sage, judge, artist, aviator, mechanic, and so on. Not infrequently it appears as a "stranger." Perhaps this form in particular is the most characteristic, because, to the purely feminine mind, the spirit stands for what is strange and unknown.

The ability to assume different forms seems to be a characteristic quality of spirit; like mobility, the power to traverse great distances in a short time, it is expressive of a quality which thought shares with light. This is connected with the wish-form of thinking already mentioned. Therefore, the animus often appears as an aviator, chauffeur, skier, or dancer, when lightness and swiftness are to be emphasized. Both of these characteristics, transmutability and speed, are found in many myths and fairy tales as attributes of gods or magicians. Wotan, the wind-god and leader of the

215

army of spirits, has already been mentioned; Loki, the flaming one, and Mercury, with the winged heels, also represent this aspect of the logos, its living, moving, immaterial quality which, without fixed qualities, is to a certain extent only a dynamism expressing the possibility of form, the spirit, as it were, that "bloweth where it listeth."

In dreams or phantasies, the animus appears chiefly in the figure of a real man: as father, lover, brother, teacher, judge, sage; as sorcerer, artist, philosopher, scholar, builder, monk (especially as a Jesuit); or as a trader, aviator, chauffeur, and so forth; in short, as a man distinguished in some way by mental capacities or other masculine qualities. In a positive sense, he can be a benevolent father, a fascinating lover, an understanding friend, a superior guide; or, on the other hand, he can be a violent and ruthless tyrant, a cruel task-master, moralist and censor, a seducer and exploiter, and often, also, a pseudo-hero who fascinates by a mixture of intellectual brilliance and moral irresponsibility. Sometimes he is represented by a boy, a son or a young friend, especially when the woman's own masculine component is thus indicated as being in a state of becoming. In many women, as I have said, the animus has a predilection for appearing in a plural form as a council which passes judgment on everything that is happening, issues precepts or prohibitions, or announces generally accepted ideas.[6] Whether it appears most often as one person with a changing mask or as many persons at the same time may depend on the natural gifts of the woman in question, or on the phase of her development at the moment.

I cannot enter here into all the manifold, personal, phenomenal forms of the animus, and therefore content myself with a series of dreams and phantasies which show how it presents itself to the inner eye, how it appears in the light of the dream-world. These are examples in which the archetypal character of the animus figures is especially clear, and which at the same time point to a development. The figures in this series of dreams appeared to the woman concerned at a time when independent mental activity had become a problem, and the animus image had begun to detach itself from the person upon whom it had been projected.

> There appeared then in a dream a bird-headed monster whose body was just a distended sac or bladder able to take on any and every form. This monster was said to have been formerly in possession of the man upon whom the animus was projected, and the woman was warned to protect herself against it because it liked to devour people, and if this happened,

216

the person was not killed outright but had to continue living inside the monster.

The bladder form pointed to something still in an initial stage—only the head, the characteristic organ for an animus, was differentiated. It was the head of a creature of the air; for the rest, any shape could arise. The voracity indicated that a need for extension and development existed in this still undifferentiated entity. The attribute of greediness is illuminated by a passage from the *Khandogya Upanishad,*[7] which deals with the nature of Brahma. It is said there:

> "The wind is in truth the All-Devourer, for when the fire dies out it goes into the wind, when the sun sets, it goes into the wind, when the moon sets, it goes into the wind, when the waters dry up, they go into the wind, for the wind consumes them all. Thus it is with respect to the divinity. And now with respect to the self. The breath is in truth the All-Devourer, for when a man sleeps, speech goes into breath, the eye goes into breath, the ear too, and the *manas,* for the breath consumes them all. These then are the two All-Devourers; wind among the gods, and breath among living men."

Together with this bird-headed creature of the air there appeared to the woman a sort of fire spirit, an elementary being consisting only of flame and in perpetual motion, calling himself the son of the "lower mother." Such a mother figure, in contrast to a heavenly, light mother, embodies the primordial feminine as a power that is heavy, dark, earthbound, a power versed in magic, now helpful, now witch-like and uncanny, and often actually destructive. Her son, then, would be a chthonic fire-spirit, recalling Logi or Loki of northern mythology, who is represented as a giant endowed with creative power and at the same time as a sly, seductive rascal, later on the prototype of our familiar devil. In Greek mythology, Hephaestus, god of the fire of the earth, corresponds to him, but Hephaestus in his activity as smith points to a controlled fire, while the northern Loki incorporates a more elementary, undirected force of nature. This earth fire-spirit, the son of the lower mother, is close to woman and familiar to her. He expresses himself positively in practical activity, particularly in the handling of material and in its artistic treatment. He is expressed negatively in states of tension or explosions of affect, and often, in a dubious and calamitous way, he acts as confederate to the primordial feminine in us, becoming the instigator or auxiliary force in what are generally termed "feminine devils' or witches' arts." He

217

could be characterized as a lower or inferior logos, in contrast to a higher form which appeared as the bird-headed air creature and which corresponds to the wind-and-spirit-god, Wotan, or to the Hermes who leads souls to Hades. Neither of these, however, is born of the lower mother, both belong only to a faraway, heavenly father.

The motif of the variable form returned again in the following dream where a picture was shown bearing the title, "Urgo, the Magic Dragon."

> A snake or dragon-like creature was represented in the picture together with a girl who was under his power. The dragon had the ability to stretch out in all directions so that there was no possibility for the girl to evade his reach; at any movement of hers he could extend himself on that side and make escape impossible.

The girl, who can be taken as the soul, somewhat in the sense of the unconscious individuality, is a constantly recurring figure in all these dreams and phantasies. In our dream-picture she had only a shadowy outline, with blurred features. Still entirely in the power of the dragon, each of her movements was observed and measured by him, so that her escape seemed impossible.

However, development is shown in the following phantasy, placed in India:

> A magician is having one of his dancers perform before the king. Hypnotized by magic, the girl dances a dance of transformations, in which, throwing off one veil after another, she impersonates a motley succession of figures, both animals and men. But now, despite the fact that she has been hypnotized by the magician, a mysterious influence is exerted upon her by the king. She goes more and more into ecstasy. Disregarding the order of the magician to stop, she dances on and on, till finally, as though throwing off her body like a last veil, she falls to the earth, a skeleton. The remains are buried; out of the grave a flower grows, out of the flower, in turn, a white woman.

Here we have the same motif, a young girl in the power of a magician whose commands have to be obeyed without choice. But in the figure of the king, the magician has an opponent who sets a limit to the magician's power over the girl and brings it about that she no longer dances at command but of her own volition. The transformation, previously only indicated, now becomes a reality, because the dancer dies and then comes up from the earth in a changed and purified form.

The doubling of the animus figure here is especially important; on the one hand, he appears as the magician, on the other, as the king. In the magician, the lower form of the animus representing magic power is represented; it makes the girl take on or imitate various roles, while the king, as already said, embodies the higher principle which brings about a real transformation, not just a representation of one. An important function of the higher, that is, the personal animus, is that as a true psychopompos it initiates and accompanies the soul's transformation.

A further variation of this theme is given in the same dream: the girl has a ghostly lover who lives in the moon, and who comes regularly in the shallop of the new moon to receive a blood sacrifice which she has to make to him. In the interval, the girl lives in freedom among people as a human being. But at the approach of the new moon, the spirit turns her into a rapacious beast and, obeying an irresistible force, she has to climb a lonely height, and bring her lover the sacrifice. This sacrifice, however, transforms the moon-spirit, so that he himself becomes a sacrificial vessel, which consumes itself but is again renewed, and the smoking blood is turned into a plant-like form out of which spring many-colored leaves and flowers.

In other words, by the blood received, that is, by the psychic energy given to it, the spiritual principle loses its dangerously compulsive and destructive character and receives an independent life, an activity of its own.

The same principle appears as Bluebeard, a well-known form of animus handed down to us in story form. Bluebeard seduces women and destroys them in a secret way and for equally secret purposes.

> In our case, he bears the appropriate name of Amandus. He lures the girl into his house, gives her wine to drink, and afterwards takes her into an underground chamber to kill her. As he prepares himself for this, a sort of intoxication overcomes the girl. In a sudden impulse of love, she embraces the murderer, who is immediately robbed of his power and dissolves in air, after promising to stand by her side in the future as a helpful spirit.

Just as the ghostly spell of the moon-bridegroom was broken by the blood sacrifice—by the giving of psychic energy—so here, by embracing the terrifying monster, the girl destroys his power through love.

In these phantasies I see indications of an important archetypal form of the animus for which there are also mythological parallels, as, for example, in the myth and cult of Dionysus. The ecstatic inspiration which

219

seized the dancer in our first phantasy and which overcame the girl in the story of Bluebeard-Amandus is a phenomenon characteristic of the Dionysian cult. There also it is chiefly women who serve the god and become filled with his spirit. Roscher[8] emphasizes the fact that this service of Dionysus by women is contrary to the otherwise general custom of having the gods attended by persons of their own sex.

In the story of the moon-spirit, the blood sacrifice and transformation of the girl into an animal are themes for which parallels can also be found in the cult of Dionysus. There, living animals were sacrificed or torn to pieces by the raving maenads in their wild and god-inflicted madness. The Dionysian celebrations also differed from the cults of the Olympic gods in that they took place at night on the mountains and in the forests, just as in our phantasy the blood-offering to the moon-spirit took place at night on a mountain top. Some familiar figures from literature come to mind in this connection, as, for instance, the Flying Dutchman, the Pied Piper or Rat Catcher of Hamelin, and the Water Man or Elfin King of folk songs, all of whom employ music to lure maidens into their water- or forest-kingdoms. The "Stranger" in Ibsen's *Lady from the Sea* is another such figure in a modern setting.

Let us consider more closely the Rat Catcher as a characteristic form of the animus. The tale of the Rat Catcher is familiar: he lured the rats from every crack and corner with his piping; they had to follow him, and not only the rats, but also the children of the city—which had refused to reward his services—were irresistibly drawn after him and made to disappear into his mountain. One is reminded of Orpheus who could elicit such magic sounds from his lyre that men and beasts were forced to follow him. This feeling of being irresistibly lured and led away into unknown distances of waters, forests, and mountains, or even into the underworld, is a typical animus phenomenon, it seems to me, and difficult to explain because, contrary to the other activities of the animus, it does not lead to consciousness but to unconsciousness, as these disappearances into nature or the underworld show. Odin's Thorn of Sleep, which sent any person it touched into a deep slumber, is a similar phenomenon.

The same theme is very tellingly formulated in Sir James M. Barrie's play, *Mary Rose*. Mary Rose, who has accompanied her husband on a fishing expedition, is supposed to be waiting for him on a small island called "The Island-That-Wants-To-Be-Visited." But while she waits, she hears her name called; she follows the voice and vanishes completely.

Only after a lapse of many years does she reappear, still exactly as she was at the time of her disappearance, and she is convinced that she has been on the island only a few hours, in spite of all the years that have intervened.

What is depicted here as vanishing into nature or the underworld, or as a prick from the Thorn of Sleep, is experienced by us in ordinary living when our psychic energy withdraws from consciousness and from all application to life, disappearing into some other world, we know not where. When this happens, the world into which we go is a more or less conscious phantasy or fairy land, where everything is either as we wish it to be or else fitted out in some other way to compensate the outer world. Often these worlds are so distant and lie at such depths that no recollection of them ever penetrates our waking consciousness. We notice, perhaps, that we have been drawn away somewhere but we do not know where, and even when we return to ourselves we cannot say what took place in the interval.

To characterize more closely the form of the spirit which is acting in these phenomena, we might compare its effects to those of music. The attraction and abduction is often, as in the tale of the Rat Catcher, effected by music. For music can be understood as an objectification of the spirit; it does not express knowledge in the usual logical, intellectual sense, nor does it shape matter; instead, it gives sensuous representation to our deepest associations and most immutable laws. In this sense, music is spirit, spirit leading into obscure distances beyond the reach of consciousness; its content can hardly be grasped with words—but strange to say, more easily with numbers—although simultaneously, and before all else, with feeling and sensation. Apparently paradoxical facts like these show that music admits us to the depths where spirit and nature are still one—or have again become one. For this reason, music constitutes one of the most important and primordial forms in which woman ever experiences spirit. Hence also the important part which music and the dance play as means of expression for women. The ritual dance is clearly based on spiritual contents.

This abduction by the spirit to cosmic-musical regions, remote from the world of consciousness, forms a counterpart to the conscious mentality of women, which is usually directed only toward very immediate and personal things. Such an experience of abduction, however, is by no means harmless or unambiguous. On the one hand, it may be no more than a lapse into unconsciousness, a sinking away into a sort of sleeping twilight state, a slipping back into nature, equivalent to regressing to a former level of consciousness, and therefore useless, even dangerous. On the other hand it may mean a genuine religious experience and then, of course, it is of the highest value.

Along with the figures already mentioned, which show the animus in a mysterious, dangerous aspect, there stands another figure of a different sort. In the case we are discussing, it is a star-headed god, guarding in his hand a blue bird, the bird of the soul. This function of guarding the soul belongs, like that of guiding it, to the higher supra-personal form of the animus. This higher animus does not allow itself to change into a function subordinate to consciousness, but remains a superior entity and wishes to be recognized and respected as such. In the Indian phantasy about the dancer, this higher, masculine spiritual principle is embodied in the figure of the king; thus, he is a commander, not in the sense of a magician but in the sense of a superior spirit having nothing of the earth or the night about him. He is not a son of the lower mother, but an ambassador of a distant, unknown father, a supra-personal power of light.

All these figures have the character of archetypes[9]—hence the mythological parallels—as such they are correspondingly impersonal, or supra-personal, even though on one side they are turned toward the individual and related to her. Appearing with them is the personal animus that belongs to her as an individual; that is, the masculine or spiritual element which corresponds to her natural gifts and can be developed into a conscious function or attitude, coordinated with the totality of her personality. It appears in dreams as a man with whom the dreamer is united, either by ties of feeling or blood, or by a common activity. Here are to be found again the forms of the upper and lower animus, sometimes recognizable by positive and negative signs. Sometimes it is a long-sought friend or brother, sometimes a teacher who instructs her, a priest who practices a ritual dance with her, or a painter who will paint her portrait. Then again, a workman named "Ernest" comes to live in her house, and an elevator boy, "Constantin," takes service with her. Upon other occasions, she has to struggle with an impudent rebellious youth, or she must be careful of a sinister Jesuit, or she is offered all sorts of wonderful things by Mephistophelian tradesmen. A distinctive figure, though appearing only rarely, is that of the "stranger." Usually this unknown being, familiar to her in spite of his strangeness, brings, as an ambassador, some message or command from the distant Prince of Light.

With the passage of time, figures such as these described here become familiar shapes, as is the case in the outer world with people to whom one is close or whom one meets often. One learns to understand why now this figure, now that appears. One can talk to them, and ask them for advice or help, yet often there is occasion to guard oneself against their insistence, or to be irritated at their insubordination. And the attention must always be alert to prevent one or another of these forms of the animus from arrogating supremacy to itself and dominating the personality. To discriminate between oneself and the animus, and sharply to limit its sphere of power, is extraordinarily important; only by doing so is it possible to free oneself from the fateful consequences of identifying with the animus and being possessed by it. Hand in hand with this discrimination goes the growth of consciousness and the realization of the true Self, which now becomes the decisive factor.

In so far as the animus is a supra-personal entity, that is, a spirit common to all women, it can be related to the individual woman as a soul guide and helpful genius, but it cannot be subordinated to her conscious mind. The situation is different with the personal entity which wishes to be assimilated, with the animus as brother, friend, son, or servant. Confronted with one of these aspects of the animus, the woman's task is to create a place for it in her life and personality, and to initiate some undertaking with the energy belonging to it. Usually our talents, hobbies and so on, have already given us hints as to the direction in which this energy can become active. Often, too, dreams point the way, and in keeping with the individual's natural bent, mention will be made in them of studies, books, and definite lines of work, or of artistic or executive activities. But the undertakings suggested will always be of an objective practical sort corresponding to the masculine entity which the animus represents. The attitude demanded here—which is, to do something for its own sake and not for the sake of another human being—runs counter to feminine nature and often can be achieved only with effort. But this attitude is just what is important, because otherwise the demand that is part of the nature of the animus, and therefore justified, will obtrude itself in other ways, making claims which are not only inappropriate, as has already been said, but which produce precisely the wrong effects.

Apart from these specific activities, the animus can and should help us to gain knowledge and a more impersonal and reasonable way of looking at things. For the woman, with her automatic and oftentimes altogether too subjective sympathy, such an achievement is valuable; it can even be an aid in the field most peculiarly her own, that of relationship. For example, her own masculine component can help her to understand a man—and this should be emphasized—for even though the automatically functioning animus, with its inappropriate "objectivity," does have a disturbing effect on human relationships, nonetheless, it is also important for the development and good of the relationship that the woman should be able to take an objective, impersonal attitude.

Thus we see that there are not only intellectual activities in which animus power can work itself out, but that above all it makes possible the development of a spiritual attitude which sets us free from the limitation and imprisonment of a narrowly personal standpoint. And what comfort and help it gives us to be able to raise ourselves out of our personal troubles to supra-personal thoughts and feelings, which, by comparison, make our misfortunes seem trivial and unimportant!

To attain such an attitude and to be able to fulfil the appointed task, requires, above everything else, discipline, and this bears harder on woman, who is still nearer to nature, than on man. Unquestionably, the animus is a spirit which does not allow itself to be hitched to a wagon like a tame horse. Its character is far too much that of the elemental being; for our animus may lag leadenly behind us in a lethargy, or confuse us with unruly, flickering inspirations, or even soar entirely away with us into thin air. Strict and unfailing guidance is needed to control this unstable directionless spirit, to force it to obey and to work toward a goal.

For a large number of women today, however, the way is different. I refer to those who through study or some other artistic, executive, or professional activity, have accustomed themselves to discipline before they became aware of the animus problem as such. For these, if they have sufficient talent, identification with the animus is entirely possible. However, as far as I have been able to observe, the problem of how to be a woman frequently arises in the midst of the most successful professional activity. Usually it appears in the form of dissatisfaction, as a need of personal, not merely objective values, a need for nature, and femininity in general. Very often, too, the problem arises because these women, without wanting to, become entangled in difficult relationships; or, by accident or fate, they stumble into typically feminine situations toward

224

which they do not know what attitude to take. Then their dilemma is similar to that of the man with respect to the anima; that is, these women, too, are confronted with the difficulty of sacrificing what, to a certain degree, is a higher human development, or at least a superiority. They have to accept what is regarded as less valuable, what is weak, passive, subjective, illogical, bound to nature—in a word, femininity.

But in the long run both these different ways presuppose the same goal, and whichever way we go, the dangers and difficulties are the same. Those women for whom intellectual development and objective activity are only of secondary importance are also in danger of being devoured by the animus, that is, of becoming identical with it. Therefore it is of the greatest importance that we have a counterpoise which can hold the forces of the unconscious in check and keep the ego connected with the earth and with life.

First and foremost, we find such a check in increasing consciousness and the ever firmer feeling of our own individuality; secondly, in work in which the mental powers can be applied; and last but not least, in relationships to other people which establish a human bulwark and orientation point, over against the supra- or non-human character of the animus. The relationship of a woman to other women has great meaning in this connection. I have had occasion to observe that as the animus problem became acute, many women began to show an increased interest in other women, the relationship to women being felt as an ever-growing need, even a necessity. Perhaps this may be the beginning of a feminine solidarity, heretofore wanting, which becomes possible now only through our growing awareness of a danger threatening us all. Learning to cherish and emphasize feminine values is the primary condition of our holding our own against the masculine principle which is mighty in a double sense —both within the psyche and without. If it attains sole mastery, it threatens that field of woman which is most peculiarly her own, the field in which she can achieve what is most real to her and what she does best —indeed, it endangers her very life.

But when women succeed in maintaining themselves against the animus, instead of allowing themselves to be devoured by it, then it ceases to be only a danger and becomes a creative power. We women need this power, for, strange as it seems, only when this masculine entity becomes an integrated part of the soul and carries on its proper function

225

there is it possible for a woman to be truly a woman in the higher sense, and, at the same time, also being herself, to fulfil her individual human destiny.

NOTES

1   C. G. Jung. *Psychological Types.* New York: Harcourt, Brace & Co., Inc., 1926. Chap. XI, sects. 48, 49; also "The Relations Between the Ego and the Unconscious" in *Two Essays on Analytical Psychology.* Bollingen Series XX. New York: Pantheon Press, 1953. Pt. II, Chap. II.

2   Concerning the concept of psychic reality, see the works of C. G. Jung, especially *Psychological Types, l.c.,* Chap. I.

3   See M. Esther Harding. *The Way of All Women.* New York: Longmans, Green & Co., 1933.

4   Lucien Lévy-Bruhl. *Primitive Mentality.* London: G. Allen & Unwin Ltd., 1923, and *The Soul of the Primitive.* New York: The Macmillan Co., 1928.

5   C. G. Jung. *Psychological Types. l.c.,* Chap. XI, sect. 30.

6   Excellent examples of animus figures are to be found in fiction, see Ronald Fraser. *The Flying Draper.* London: Jonathan Cape, 1924; also *Rose Anstey.* London: Jonathan Cape, 1930; Marie Hay. *The Evil Vineyard.* Leipzig: Tauchnitz, 1924; Théodore Flournoy. *From India to the Planet Mars.* Translated by D. B. Vermilye. New York: Harper Bros., 1900.

7   "Khandogya" in *The Upanishads.* Translated by F. Max Mueller. Oxford: Clarendon Press, 1900, p. 58.

8   See W. J. Roscher. *Lexikon der griechischen und römischen Mythologie,* under *"Dionysus."*

9   C. G. Jung. *Psychological Types. l.c.,* Chap. XI, sect. 26; also *Two Essays. l.c.,* p. 135.

The Androgyne

Barbara Charlesworth Gelpi

She now realizes, Adrienne Rich said recently at a reading of her poetry, that she wrote all her early poems for men. She wrote them, that is, desiring men's approval and conscious of men's poetic theories. Reading Emma Jung's essay on the animus brings that observation back to me, because although she is writing specifically to women about a psychic phenomenon only to be found—at least in that form—in women, one senses that she is ever aware of being overheard by men. The fact is understandable, even natural; nevertheless, it tinges the essay with the very attitude that Emma Jung is trying to overcome, the universal denigration of the feminine. One sign of this is her slightly apologetic tone mixed with a deeply feminine irony when she writes: "Neither arrogance nor presumption drives us to the audacity of wanting to be like God— that is, like man. . . . No, there has come to us something like a command. . . ." That note appears as well in many suggestions through the essay that the masculine principle, because it is spiritual and intellectual, is "higher" (and we cannot but get the connotation "better") than the feminine, which is "lower" and closer to "nature" and to the unconscious. The difficulty, then, is that the terms of the discussion as well as the attitudes implicit in those terms further confuse the attempt to describe the already confusing psychological state of modern women.

It has been suggested that a wise idea, then, would be to change the terms, not to polarize the universal process, the yang and the yin, into principles called masculine and feminine but to use other, less loaded symbolic terms such as "diamond," say, and "lotus." By doing so, however, one flies in the face of a tradition so strong and so ancient that I, with the Jungians, feel that there must be truth in it. That is, the masculine and feminine principles are not simply arbitrary manila folders for filing certain qualities; they are transcendent functions, spiritual realities which must be taken into account in the psychological makeup of every human being. This is not to say that women are a different order of creatures from men, nor to say that they are the same in everything but the reproductive organs. The nature and extent of sexual difference are still mysteries; the vocabulary even for discussion, much less analysis, of the problem is inadequate. But although the terms may often "Strain/ Crack and sometimes break under the burden" they are at the same time our given and it is with them that I would like further to consider Emma Jung's argument.

Emma Jung is describing two different animus reactions in women: the first, which she takes to be the more general, is repression of the animus into the unconscious and a conscious glorification of what is understood to be one's feminine role and function. The second is identification with the animus, which makes fulfillment of the feminine role impossible or at least difficult. Her analysis needs added to it the later and more extensive discriminations of Erich Neumann. In his essay "The Psychological Stages of Feminine Development"[1] Neumann describes the original psychic state of girls as identical with that of boys: psychic unity. The ego in process of formation is still a "germ" within the unconscious, a state projected in the child's relationship to its mother. The symbiotic relationship between mother and child when the child was in the womb is but the more physical symbol of the child's identification with the mother after birth.[2]

Now for boys the continued development of the ego brings the realization of the maternal figure as "other"; there is bitterness, a sense of betrayal, in that new knowledge, but there is also great strengthening of the ego and a tendency from then on to treat relationships as a meeting of "I" and "thou." The forming ego of the girl, on the other hand, meets not difference but sameness, and so the identification with the mother may continue for a much longer time, even for life, without causing what might be diagnosed as neurosis. "In so far as she stays within this enclosure [of identification with the mother figure]" writes Neumann, "she is to be sure childish and immature from the point of view of conscious development, but she is not estranged from herself."[3] For such a woman, relationship is not a matter of "I" and "thou" but of unconscious blood identification: with the mother who bore her, with the child of her womb. And the father of the child is primarily just that; he has a function for but not finally a relation with her. She lives for and through her children, unconscious of any masculine element in herself and easily, though unconsciously, resentful of the masculine if it tries to impinge upon her.

The women of this "first phase" may not be as numerous in our society as they are in more primitive cultures, where indeed they may be the majority, but without much searching among friends and family, one can find many examples. Their presence in fairly large numbers may help to explain the resistance to feminism that leaders of the movement so often find bewildering. It is not always, as John Stuart Mill thought, that women are conditioned by men to depend upon them and live subservient to them.[4] This conditioning and its effects are important, as we shall see in the description of "third phase" women, but to women of the first phase, joining the feminist cause demands a movement out of the "primary identification" and so, though again unconsciously and therefore all the more deeply, seems a betrayal not of one's husband but of one's mother, of one's child.

The woman destined to become more conscious of herself experiences, according to Neumann, a movement into a second stage in which she is "seized by an unknown, overwhelming power which she experiences as a formless 'numinosum';[5] she becomes obsessed, that is, not by love for another person but by a worship of the masculine principle projected upon—ah, who shall say?—a singer or singing group, a horse, a fantasy lover, a religious leader, a star athlete. That worship of the masculine may bring her out of the original and more primitive phase of the feminine round of life, but it has its own dangers. First of all, it cuts her off from that life and from the strength of her own femininity, and then the power of her fantasies about the masculine may cut her off as well from relationship with a person who is a man."

Nevertheless, in what we might take to be the ordinary course of things, the latter danger is outgrown, and the woman is "freed" by her love of a particular man into the third phase: patriarchal marriage. She becomes then helpmate to a man in a society which takes only masculine, rational activity seriously and which considers her as a woman to be incapable of such activity. The society demands of her that she be the nurturing "phase-one" woman but offers none of the feminine support and society that (even if as a phase-three woman she could enjoy it) a phase-one society might give. In this symbiotic marital relation man is the intellectual, spiritual director, woman the emotional, material nourisher. Such an organization obviously is workable. It has worked through most of Western history, often, according to Neumann, because women in it regress to earlier phases and occasionally because in it the partners themselves through their love for each other transcend society's image of their roles.

But patriarchal marriage becomes steadily less viable as women become more conscious of their own potential. At the same time, the attitudes behind that marriage and behind the whole social-psychological-economic-political system in which those attitudes predominate cannot be changed unless the worth of the feminine is established.

Emma Jung describes the difficulties in modern woman's development with admirable clarity but offers very little in the way of a solution save that "unconscious" women should become conscious of their masculine qualities, and "conscious" women should keep in touch with the feminine principle by making women friends. But one of her seemingly—perhaps really—denigrating statements about women offers a wider vision. "It is well known that a really creative faculty of mind is a rare thing in woman," she writes. This is one of the places in which the presuppositions out of which she is writing become most painfully evident, for by "creative faculty of mind" she means, as her next sentence shows, rationalist, discriminatory, and critical faculties. These are the faculties which Blake called "Urizen," and though they may have a place in the "creative," they are by no means the whole of it. Indeed, taking to themselves the whole makes for the death of creativity. In her next paragraph Emma Jung offers an idea potentially similar when she says that the creativity of woman, "the real field of feminine creative power" lies in "the development of relationships." In its context the phrase seems to suggest that women should fulfill themselves primarily as homemakers; that is, they do fulfill themselves so (The patriarchy assures them that they *are* fulfilled), and the present fact becomes the future ideal. Whatever is, is right.

Yet the phrase which Emma Jung uses, "the development of relationships," suggests finally much more than that: it is the power to "see" wholes rather than discriminate parts, to make symbolic as well as actual connections between ideas, feelings, attitudes, and people. It is the Gestalt consciousness, another form of consciousness but one which poets have always known to be as powerful, as "creative," as the rational, discriminatory functions.

Erich Neumann, in *The Great Mother*, offers an interpretation or description of the feminine principle which might help to explain what I mean by "Gestalt consciousness." It is his contention, based on beautifully detailed and organized archaeological studies, that the feminine principle is not only "elementary," i.e., life-bearing and enfolding and sustaining, but also "transformative," i.e., consciousness-bearing and uplifting. If in its elementary character the feminine principle bases itself in an unconscious fulfillment of the great round of birth, copulation, and death, the transformative quality in the feminine seeks to unite that round with consciousness. In other words, the masculine principle, the "animus" in a woman, need not be thought of as acting in opposition to the feminine. Rather, the animus, like Hermes the psychopomp, may lead woman from one aspect of the feminine, the elementary, to the transformative. Nor need the "anima" in a man be thought of only as his link with unconsciousness; it also serves to bring him to greater consciousness. How this consciousness may be described or even adumbrated we shall consider later, but first we should look at what the nature of human consciousness now is taken to be.

While traveling in Africa, C. G. Jung had an unforgettable insight into what the dawn of consciousness may have been. On the Athi Plains he saw gigantic herds of grazing animals, slowly and almost soundlessly moving forward "like slow rivers":

> This was the stillness of the eternal beginning, the world as it had always been, in the state of non-being; for until then no one had been present to know that it was this world. I walked away from my companions until I had put them out of sight, and savored the feeling of being entirely alone. There I was now, the first human being to recognize that this was the world, but who did not know that in this moment he had first really created it.
>
> There the cosmic meaning of consciousness became overwhelmingly clear to me. . . . Man, I, in an invisible act of creation put the stamp of perfection on the world by giving it objective existence.[6]

Jung's experience made real to him for a moment the central human fact, that of consciousness. I say central because whether one calls consciousness a freakish and anomalous occurrence in the chemical combination that produced life or whether one calls it mystery, "a repetition in the finite mind of the eternal act of creation in the infinite I AM,"[7] it is that which makes for all the experience that we call human. Now it is interesting that as he describes that moment, Jung refers to the first human who had it as "man," not, I think, simply in the impersonal sense of "one" but with the idea that the first human to see and to see himself seeing was a man, not a woman. The event itself is totally shrouded in mystery, but the tradition is so strong in all Western culture that whether or not it happened in literal fact that a man, not a woman, first reached consciousness, it happened so according to the facts, that is the myths, by which we live.[8]

Consciousness, as we tend to conceive of it, brings humanity into being —and that is good—but has certain negative consequences as well. Though it is man's triumph, it is divisive, separating him from the natural rhythms of life by virtue of the fact that he can observe those rhythms, looking forward and backward. He becomes then subject to the peculiarly human fear of death and the human affliction of boredom. He becomes also aware of his separateness, his individuality—and that is an achievement—but at the same time becomes competitive, suffering all the endless human misery which competition involves.

So far in history, women as well as men (and not just Jungians) have associated consciousness—intellection, abstract thought—with the masculine principle. A woman may well be capable of it but if so she is thought to possess a strong "masculine" streak. But if something as bewilderingly mysterious as the appearance of consciousness was once possible, is the transmutation of that consciousness not also possible? As women grow in awareness, as, then, to use Neumann's vocabulary, the transformative aspect of the feminine principle becomes more pronounced, might we not be moving (how quickly or slowly one cannot tell) to the point where someone—perhaps a man, perhaps a woman, perhaps a pair, or a group—breaks through and "sees," thereby creating a consciousness as different from ours as ours is different from that of the grazing warthogs on the Plain of Athi?

If this new consciousness is so totally different from what we now think of as consciousness, it may be useless to speculate on its nature, but one can in a negative way see the evils identified with "masculine" consciousness which it might help to overcome. Masculine consciousness separates its possessor from "mother nature," thereby setting him free on the one hand and binding him with guilt on the other. If Emma Jung is right when she says that "the creativity of woman finds its expression in the sphere of living," in "the development of relationships," then this new consciousness might not be divisive. It might "see" the realm of intellection and the realm of matter as one in a way in which we cannot really see them now. It might also see the development of intellection and of personality as possible without the necessity of competition and so create a society based on relation, a community of knowledge and action, vision and pleasure.

James Hillman, in his speculations on the new consciousness and what it might be, begins with C. G. Jung's comments on the promulgation of Mary's assumption into Heaven as a dogma of the Catholic faith. "Understood symbolically," writes Jung, ". . . the Assumption of the body is a recognition and acknowledgment of matter, which in the last resort was identified with evil only because of an overwhelmingly 'pneumatic' tendency in man."[9] Hillman widens the scope of that insight to say:

> It is all very well to talk of new theories of matter, of the relativity of matter and spirit, of the end of materialism, of synchronicity and *unus mundus*, and of the possibility of a new, universal science where matter and spirit lose their hostile polarity, but these are all projections of the intellect unless there is a corresponding change of attitude in regard to the material part of man himself, which has, as Jung says, always been associated in our tradition with the feminine. The transformation of our world view necessitates the transformation of the view of the feminine.[10]

Much of Hillman's essay is description of the forms in which masculine self-hatred has been projected upon women;[11] the solution he comes to, however, is significantly different from the answers of Jung and of Neumann in that he sees the integration, the reacceptance of the feminine not as a goal but as a given. For, he says, if masculine and feminine are taken as really separate, then the terms in which the problem is stated makes its solution impossible: "In fact the *seeking* of the *coniunctio*, as Apollo pursuing Daphne, is self-defeating because it hyperactivates the male, driving the psyche into vegetative regression."[12]

And so in place of the traditional myth which identifies masculine consciousness with Apollo, Hillman would like to substitute the androgynous figure of Dionysus, and for the older hierarchical structure, with masculine consciousness "above" and feminine unconscious "below," he

233

suggests a new model of the psyche: ". . . rather than superimposed levels, we might speak of polycentricity, of circulation and rotation, of the comings and goings of flow."[13]

Hillman uses the earlier theories of Jung and Neumann to interpret past attitudes toward masculine and feminine, but I think that he offers a better answer than they on how in the future it might be possible to symbolize the psyche and how society might thereby be transformed. Consider for a moment Neumann's *The Origin and History of Consciousness*, at once a vision of history and a description of the psyche. In it Neumann describes the process whereby the masculine consciousness frees itself from the grip of the great mother, the negative unconscious aspect of the feminine principle. Neumann uses as the central symbol of that struggle the hero's fight with the dragon and freeing of the maiden. The dragon, symbol of "the Mothers," that is of the power of the unconscious to overwhelm him, must be overcome in order that the anima, the feminine principle in its transformative aspect, may open for him his own soul's treasure. The struggle with a matriarchal figure Neumann makes central to each life, but that struggle re-enacts one which took place in prehistory: Neumann posits an original matriarchy, powerful and given over to an unconscious round of existence for its own sake, which men threw off. All art, religion, science, and technology have come about as a result of that revolt.

Neumann's book is fascinating, but in reading it, a woman feels more than a little left out. The feminine principle functions there as that which must be overcome, "the Mothers," and as that which inspires "the Muse," but the development of consciousness in history and in individuals is described as a specifically masculine experience. "But one thing, paradoxical though it may seem, can be established as a basic law: even in woman, consciousness has a masculine character," writes Neumann.[14]

Of course, since each individual woman "contains" aspects of both the masculine and the feminine principles, Neumann's statement does not, obviously, deny the possibility of consciousness to women. Nevertheless, the suggestion seems to me to be there that such consciousness as a woman attains is in despite of the feminine.

Nevertheless Neumann would agree completely with Hillman that masculine "Apollonic" consciousness—analytic, aggressive, rationalistic—has ceased to be a means of enlightenment and has become a danger. And one need only look for oneself: at the television screen, the newspapers, the weekly magazines to see the faces of "the Fathers"—the political, religious, educational, business, military and labor leaders—so many of them men with hard mouths and soft jowls. That is, their faces show their strong "Urizenic" purpose, but they show as well how totally out of touch these men are with the feminine principle within themselves. It is repressed and unconscious, and so—as Jung often points out[15]—these men are at the mercy of unconscious emotions: hate, fear, sexual passion. Surely a society in the grip of this active but destructive masculine principle is in just as bad a situation as that earlier, hypothetical matriarchal society caught in the endless dark passivity of the "uroboric" round. Though the sun of masculine consciousness may once have illumined that dark, primeval world, now "we live in an old chaos of the sun" which, through one of Jung's favorite principles, *enantiadromia*,[16] has itself become a darkness.

If women could help society to throw off the heavy yoke of the Fathers they might eventually move humanity forward as much as did those heroes who revolted against the Great Mother. It is, however, just as difficult a battle because when a woman attacks the Fathers directly, she is in danger of mirroring the screaming virago which is the projection of their repressed and unconscious anima. That is one side of the problem. At the same time, if Neumann were to be right when he describes consciousness itself as an aspect of the universal masculine principle, then women must use the animus in its beneficent aspect to fight against the animus in its repressive aspect. She must use her masculine attributes, that is, to come to what Neumann calls "matriarchal consciousness." To all these dilemmas and paradoxes Hillman's good sense offers an answer. The definition itself of where the difficulty lies, he says, has vitiated any possible solution. Redefine the problem.

Hillman is writing as a man to and for a man's world in which men have "lost their souls." The situation is different for women; they must regain possession of their minds. As Hillman wants the presence of feminine soul in man to be taken as a given, so let the presence of mind in woman be given; let the fulfillment of that mind be considered as serious a matter as the fulfillment of man's mind, and then see how the world might change.

Such a hypothesis, such a given, might help to create the new society we need. At least, it seems useful to act *as if* this new consciousness were a reality, always taking it that by so doing we may help to create it, and

235

we cannot in any event but alleviate the evils under which we now live, dominated and domineered over as we are by "the Fathers."

We need women who are poets, who bring together the fact and the word. Those, fortunately, we have. But we need women as well, more women, in the divinity schools. We need women who are priests and preachers. We need women in the universities, not as faculty wives and in the lower levels of faculty and administration, but as presidents and trustees and full professors of universities. We need women as deans of education schools, as creators of educational theory. We need women in political life as presidential candidates, as mayors of cities, as senators and representatives. (John Stuart Mill said over a hundred years ago that women's finest genius may well lie in the area of government.)[17] All these are areas in which the creation of relationships is particularly important, and all of them now suffer from divisive, overabstract, overlegalistic, Urizenic thought.

But, it may be objected, if women become conscious of their minds while men recover their souls will men not become passive, interior, effeminate, while women become driving and reductively analytical? Our future state would then be no improvement on the present. (Indeed most men, given the possibility of that uncomfortable change in roles, would opt for present evils.) The objection is a powerful one, grounded as it is in all our notions of the "natural," but it is not a proper question in that it assumes the old dichotomies, assumes that in gaining soul one loses mind, in analyzing with the mind one loses qualities of soul. Redefine the problem. With myths, dreams, visions, poems, stories, conversations we must imagine a race in which both mind and soul are of equal importance and may be equally fulfilled for both sexes.[18]

Such is the vision of Adrienne Rich's "The Stranger".[19] In it she writes:

> Looking as I've looked before, straight down the heart
> of the street to the river
> walking the rivers of the avenues
> feeling the shudder of the caves beneath the asphalt
> watching the lights turn on in the towers
> walking as I've walked before
> like a man, like a woman, in the city
> my visionary anger cleansing my sight

236

and the detailed perceptions of mercy
flowering from that anger

if I come into a room out of the sharp misty light
and hear them talking a dead language
and if they ask me my identity
what can I say but
I am the androgyne
I am the living mind you fail to describe
in your dead language
the lost noun, the verb surviving
only in the infinitive
the letters of my name are written under the lids
of the newborn child

Adrienne Rich wrote that poem for women.

NOTES

1 Erich Neumann, "The Psychological Stages of Feminine Development," *Spring*, trans. and rev. Hildegard Nagel and Jane Pratt (New York: The Analytical Psychology Club, 1959). The article is the first section of Neumann's book, *Zur Psychologie des Weiblichen;* it was translated in one of the old, mimeographed issues of *Spring* and is not readily available but for an extensive summary of it and commentary upon it, see Anne Belford Ulanov's *The Feminine in Jungian Psychology and in Christian Theology* (Evanston: Northwestern University Press, 1971), pp. 241–284.

2 The symbol Neumann uses for this immersion of consciousness within the unconscious, of child within the mother, is the "uroboros," the serpent swallowing its tail. The meaning of the symbol is discussed in detail in his *The Origins and History of Consciousness* (New York: Bollingen Series 1954), pp. 5–38.

3 Neumann, "Psychological Stages," p. 67.

4 "Men do not want solely the obedience of women, they want their sentiments. All men, except the most brutish, desire to have, in the woman most nearly connected with them, not a forced slave but a willing one, not a slave merely, but a favourite. They have therefore put everything in practice to enslave their minds."—John Stuart Mill, *The Subjection of Women*, Everyman's Library Edition (London: Dutton, 1965), p. 232.

5 Neumann, *The Great Mother: An Analysis of the Archetype* (Princeton: Princeton University Press, 1963). In another essay, Neumann gives what I have called "Gestalt consciousness" the name "matriarchal consciousness." "On the Moon and Matriarchal Consciousness," trans. Hildegard Nagel, *Spring* (The Analytical Psychology Club, New York), 1954.

6 C. G. Jung, *Memories, Dreams, Reflections,* ed. by Aniela Jaffé (New York: Pantheon Books, 1961), pp. 255–256.

7 This description by Coleridge of the Primary Imagination, given in the *Biographia*

Literaria, is surprisingly close to Jung's description of consciousness.

8   Cf. James Hillman, "First Adam, Then Eve: On Psychological Femininity," *The Myth of Analysis* (Evanston: Northwestern University Press, 1972), pp. 217–225.

9   C. .G. Jung, "Psychological Aspects of the Mother Archetype," *The Archetypes and the Collective Unconscious*, from *The Collected Works of C. G. Jung*, XI, i, (Princeton: Princeton University Press, Bollingen Series XX, 1969), par. 197, p. 109.

10   Hillman, "On Psychological Femininity," p. 216.

11   Hillman never puts his thought as dramatically as Neumann does, but his essay suggests, as Neumann's states, that, "Only the fact that man cannot exist without woman has prevented the extirpation (otherwise so favored a procedure) of this group of 'evil' humans, upon whom the dangerousness of the unconscious has been projected."— Neumann, "Psychological Stages of Feminine Development," p. 83.

12   Hillman, "On Psychological Femininity," p. 259.

13   Ibid., p. 287.

14   *The Origins and History of Consciousness*, p. 42. Hillman calls this sentence one of "the absurdities of Neumann," an absurdity resulting from Neumann's equation of consciousness with masculinity, unconsciousness with femininity.—"On Psychological Femininity," p. 289.

15   See, for instance, *Two Essays in Analytical Psychology* (Princeton: Princeton University Press, Bollingen Series XX, 1966), pp. 197–198 and *Archetypes and the Collective Unconscious*, p. 71.

16   "Old Heraclitus," writes Jung, ". . . discovered the most marvellous of all psychological laws: the regulative function of opposites. He called it *enantiadromia*, a running contrariwise, by which he meant that sooner or later everything runs into its opposite."—*Two Essays*, p. 72.

17   Mill, after giving many examples, concludes, "Exactly where and in proportion as women's capacities for government have been tried in that proportion have they been found adequate."—*The Subjection of Women*, p. 273.

18   Emma Jung says in her book on the Grail legend: "When a myth is enacted in a ritual performance or, in more general, simpler, and profaner fashion, when a fairy-tale is told, the healing factor within it acts on whoever has taken an interest in it and allowed himself to be moved by it in such a way that through his participation he will be brought into connection with an archetypal form of the situation, and by this means enabled to put himself 'into order.'—*The Grail Legend* (London: Hodder and Stoughton, 1971), p. 37.

19   Adrienne Rich, "The Stranger," *Diving Into the Wreck: Poems 1971–73* (New York: W. W. Norton and Company, Inc., 1973).

Person on Bonaparte

❧

Passivity, Masochism and Femininity (1934)

Marie Bonaparte

1. The Pain Inherent in the Female Reproductive Functions

The most superficial observer cannot help noting that in the sphere of reproduction the lot of men and of women, in respect of pain suffered, is an unequal one. The man's share in the the reproductive functions is confined to a single act—that of coitus—which he necessarily experiences as pleasurable, since, for him, the function of reproduction coincides with the erotic function. The woman, on the other hand, periodically undergoes the suffering of menstruation, the severity of which varies with the individual; for her, sexual intercourse itself is initiated by a process which involves in some degree the shedding of her blood, namely, the act of defloration; finally, gestation is accompanied by discomfort and parturition by pain, while even lactation is frequently subject to painful disturbances.

Already in the Bible[1] woman is marked out for the pain of childbearing, the punishment for original sin. Michelet[2] describes her as *"l'éternelle blessée"* ("the everlastingly wounded one"). And, in psychoanalytic literature, Freud,[3] discussing the problem of masochism, that bewildering product of human psychosexuality, characterizes it, in its erotogenic form, as "feminine," while Helene Deutsch[4] regards it as a constant factor in female development and as an indispensable constituent in woman's acceptance of the whole of her sexuality, intermingled, as it is, with so much pain.

241

2. Erotic Pleasure in Women

There is, however, another fact no less striking even to a superficial observer. In sexual relations women are often capable of a high degree of erotic pleasure; they crave for caresses, it may be of the whole body or of some particular zone, and in these caresses the element of suffering, of masochism, is entirely and essentially absent. Moreover, in actual copulation the woman can experience pleasurable orgasm analogous to that of the man.

Of course, in this connection we must bear in mind that biological fact which, for that matter, many biologists seem not to know, although Freud has accurately appraised its importance; namely, that in women, as contrasted with men, there are two adjacent erotogenic zones—the clitoris and the vagina—which reflect and confirm the bisexuality inherent in every woman. In some instances there is an open antagonism between the two zones, with the result that the woman's genital erotism becomes centered exclusively either in the vagina or in the clitoris, with, in the latter case, vaginal anesthesia. In other instances, and I think these are the more common, the two zones settle into harmonious collaboration, enabling her to perform her erotic function in the normal act of copulation.

Nevertheless, woman's share in sexual pleasure seems to be derived from whatever virility the female organism contains. The Spanish biologist, Marañon, was in the right when he compared woman to a male organism arrested in its development, half-way between the child and the man—arrested, that is to say, precisely by the inhibitory influence exercised by the apparatus of maternity, which is subjoined to and exists in a kind of symbiosis side by side with the rest of her delicate organism.

The residue of virility in the woman's organism is utilized by nature in order to eroticize her: otherwise the functioning of the maternal apparatus would wholly submerge her in the painful tasks of reproduction and motherhood.

On the one hand, then, in the reproductive functions proper—menstruation, defloration, pregnancy and parturition—woman is biologically doomed to suffer. Nature seems to have no hesitation in administering to her strong doses of pain, and she can do nothing but submit passively to the regimen prescribed. On the other hand, as regards sexual attraction, which is necessary for the act of impregnation, and as regards the

242

erotic pleasure experienced during the act itself, the woman may be on equal footing with the man. It must be added, however, that the feminine erotic function is often imperfectly and tardily established and that, owing to the woman's passive role in copulation, it always depends—and this is a point which we must not forget—upon the potency of her partner and especially upon the time which he allows for her gratification, which is usually achieved more slowly than his own.

3. The Infantile Sadistic Conception of Coitus

Let us now go back to the childhood situation.

Psychoanalytic observations have proved beyond any doubt that when, as often happens, a child observes the coitus of adults, he invariably perceives the sexual act as an act of sadistic aggression perpetrated by the male upon the female—an act primarily of an oral character, as little children so conceive it, because the only relations between one human being and another of which they have at first any knowledge are of an oral nature. But, seeing how early the cannibalistic phase occurs, it seems certain that this *oral* relation is itself conceived of as aggressive. Nevertheless, it so frequently happens that the child is in the anal-sadistic phase when he makes these observations that his predominating impression is that of an attack made by the male upon the female, in which she is wounded and her body penetrated. Having regard to the primitive fusion of instincts we may perhaps say that the earlier these observations occur the more marked is the sadistic tinge which they assume in the child's mind. In his perception of the acts of adults the degree of his own aggressiveness, which varies with the individual child, must also play a decisive part, being projected on to what he sees.

In the mind of a child who has witnessed the sexual act the impressions received form, as it were, a stereotyped picture which persists in the infantile unconscious. As he develops and his ego becomes more firmly established, this picture is modified and worked over, and doubtless there are added to it all the sadomasochistic fantasies[5] which analysis has brought to light in children of both sexes.

The very early observations of coitus, made when the child was still in the midst of the sadistic-cloacal and sadistic-phallic phases (which, indeed, often overlap), were effected in the first instance with partial object-cathexes relating to the *organs* which children covet to gratify their libidinal and sadistic impulses. Little by little, however, the whole being of the man and of the woman becomes more clearly defined as male or female, and the difference between the sexes is at last recognized.

Thereafter, the destiny and influence of the infantile sadistic fantasies will differ with the sex of the child. The sadistic conception of coitus in boys, the actual possessors of the penetrating penis, will evade the centripetal cloacal danger and tend to take a form which is centrifugal and vital and which involves no immediate danger to their own organism. Of course it will subsequently come into collision with the *moral* barriers erected by civilization against human aggressiveness, with the castration complex especially; but the Oedipal defusion of instincts through which the boy's aggression is diverted to his father, while the greater part of his love goes to his mother, is of considerable assistance to him in distinguishing sadism from activity and subsequently orientating his penis—active but no longer sadistic—in the direction of women.

In girls, the sadistic conception of coitus, when strongly emphasized, is much more likely to disturb ideal erotic development. The time comes when the little girl compares her own genitals with the large penis of the adult male, and inevitably she draws the conclusion that she has been castrated. The consequence is that not only is her narcissism mortified by her castration but also, in her sexual relations with men, the possessors of the penis which henceforth her eroticism covets, she is haunted by the dread that her body will undergo some fearful penetration.

Now every living organism dreads invasion from without, and this is a dread bound up with life itself and governed by the biological law of self-preservation.

Moreover, not only do little girls hear talk or whispers about the sufferings of childbirth and catch sight, somehow or other, of menstrual blood; they also bear imprinted on their minds from earliest childhood the terrifying vision of a sexual attack by a man upon a woman, which they believe to be the cause of the bleeding. It follows therefore that, in spite of the instinct, which urges them forward, they draw back from the feminine erotic function itself, although of all the reproductive functions of woman this is the only one which should really be free from suffering and purely pleasurable.[6]

244

4. The Necessary Fundamental Distinction
Between Masochism and Passivity

As the little girl grows up, her reactions to the primal scene becomes more pronounced in one direction or another, according to the individual case, the determining factors being, on the one hand, her childhood experiences and, on the other, her constitutional disposition.

In the first place, there is bound to be a distinct difference between the reactions of a little girl who has actually witnessed the coitus of adults and those of a little girl who has fallen back upon phylogenetic fantasies, based on her inevitable observations of the copulation of animals. It seems that the severity of the traumatic shock is in proportion to the earliness of the period in which the child observes human coitus and to the actuality of what she observes.

Above all, however, the violence of the little girl's recoil from the sexual aggression of the male will depend on the degree of her constitutional bisexuality and the extent of the biological bases of her masculinity complex. Where both these factors are marked, she will react in very much the same way as a little boy, whose reaction, since he also is bisexual, will be likewise of the cloacal type, though very soon his vital phallic rejection of the passive, cloacal attitude will turn his libido into the convex, centrifugal track of masculinity.

For there are only two main modes of reaction to the sadistic conception of coitus harbored by the little girl's unconscious mind throughout childhood and right up to adult life. Either she must accept it and, in this case, in order to bind masochistically her passive aggression there must be an admixture of eros equivalent to the danger which, she feels, threatens her very existence. Or else, as the years pass and her knowledge of reality increases, she must recognize that the penetrating penis is neither a whip nor an awl nor a knife nor a cartridge (as in her sadistic, infantile fantasies) and must dissociate passive coitus from the other feminine reproductive functions (menstruation, pregnancy, parturition); she must accept it as the only act which is really purely pleasurable, in sharp contrast to the dark background of feminine suffering, an act in which libido—that biological force of masculine extraction—is deflected to feminine aims, always passive but here not normally masochistic.

It is true that in woman's acceptance of her role there may be a slight tincture—a homeopathic dose, so to speak—of masochism, and this, combining with her passivity in coitus, impels her to welcome and to value some measure of brutality on the man's part. Martine declared that she wished "to be beaten." But a real distinction between masochism and passivity must be established in the feminine psyche if her passive erotic function is to be normally accepted upon a firm basis. Actually, normal vaginal coitus does not hurt a woman; quite the contrary.

If, however, in childhood, when she is brought up against the sadistic conception of coitus, she has, if I may so put it, voted for the first solution, namely, a masochism which includes within its scope passivity in copulation, it by no means follows that she will accept the masochistic erotization of the vagina in coitus. Often the dose of masochism is in that case too strong for the vital ego, and it is a fact that even those women in whom the masochistic perversion is very pronounced often shun penetration and content themselves with being beaten on the buttocks, regarding this as a more harmless mode of aggression since only the outer surface of the body is concerned.

The vital, biological ego protests against and takes flight from masochism in general and may establish very powerful hypercathexes of the libido's defensive positions.

5. The Cloaca and the Phallus in Women

At this point we must remind ourselves that in females there are two erotogenic zones and that woman is bisexual in a far higher degree than man.

Earlier in this paper I quoted the views of the Spanish biologist, Marañon, who holds that a woman is a man whose development has been arrested, a sort of adolescent to whose organism is subjoined, in a kind of symbiosis, the apparatus of maternity, which is responsible for the check in development.

In woman the external sexual organs, or, more correctly, the erotogenic organs, appear to reflect her twofold nature. A woman, in fact, possesses a cloaca, divided by the rectovaginal septum into the anus and the specifically feminine vagina, the gateway to the additional structure of the maternal apparatus, and a phallus, atrophied in comparison with the male penis—the little clitoris.

How do these two zones react, on the one hand to the little girl's

constitution and, on the other, to the experiences which exercise a formative influence upon her psychosexuality?

There are various stages and phases[7] in libidinal development. The
oral phase is succeeded by the sadistic-anal phase which, in view of the
anatomical fact of the existence of the vagina in little girls, I should prefer
to call the sadistic-cloacal phase.

There is, therefore, a cavity (as yet, no doubt, imperfectly differentiated
in the child's mind) which in the little girl's sadistic conception of coitus
is penentrated in a manner highly dangerous. (The little boy, for his part,
arguing from his own physical structure, often recognizes the existence
of the anus only.) Consequently, when coitus is observed at this early age,
the result is the mobilization, first, of the erotic wish for the penis, coveted by the oral and cloacal libidinal components, and, secondly, of the
dread of penetration which wounds and is to be feared.

Before long, however, the phallic phase, which is a regular stage in the
biological development of both sexes, is reached by little girls, as by little
boys, being accompanied in the former by clitoridal masturbation.
Doubtless, at this period, masturbation is not confined exclusively to the
clitoris but is extended in a greater or lesser degree to the vulva and the
entrance to the adjacent vagina. How far this is so depends on the individual and on the amount of her constitutional femininity (her prefeminine,
erotogenic cloacality).

At this point, however, through a confusion of passivity with masochism, the little girl may take fright and reject her passive role. The dread
of male aggression may be too strong, the admixture of masochism already present too great, or too potent a dose of it may be required to bind
and accept the dread. When this is the case, her ego draws back and her
eroticism will cling, so to speak, to the clitoris. The process is something
like that of fixing a lightning conductor to a house in order to prevent
its being struck; the electricity (in this case, the child's eroticism) is diverted into a channel in which it does not endanger life.

Thus a sort of *convex erotic engram,* upon which her erotic function as a
woman will be modelled, is set up in opposition to the *concave erotic engram*
which is properly that of the female in coitus.

Now the convex orientation of libido is the very direction taken by the
eroticism of the male, as he develops anatomically, and, further, the
erotogenic, centrifugal orientation of the penis. Consequently, such an
orientation of libido in a woman is highly suggestive of a considerable

degree of constitutional masculinity. Here, passivity being more or less inextricably confused with erotogenic masochism, its *vital* (self-preservative) rejection and its *masculine* rejection coincide. *Moral* repression, on the other hand, which has its source in educational influences and is maintained by the superego, tends to attack feminine sexuality as a whole, without discrimination of its specifically vaginal or clitoridal character, and, when carried to its extreme, tends to result in total frigidity.

Nevertheless the phallus itself, an organ essentially male even when it goes by the name of the clitoris, can be used for ends which are, at bottom, feminine.

It is true that the clitoris, the rudimentary phallus, is never destined to achieve, even in its owner's imagination, the degree of activity to which the penis can lay claim, for in this respect the male organ is far better endowed by nature. The clitoris, like the little boy's penis, is first aroused when the mother is attending to the child's toilet, the experience being a passive one. Normally the clitoris, after passing through an active phase, should have a stronger tendency than the penis to revert to passivity; the little girl's biological castration complex paves the way for her regression. Next, when her positive Oedipus complex is established, with its orientation to the father, the clitoris readily becomes the instrument of those libidinal desires whose aim is passive. And this prepares the way for the clitoridal-vaginal erotic function by means of which, in so many women, the two zones fulfill harmoniously their passive role in coitus and which is opposed to the functional maladjustment of women of the clitoridal type, in whom the phallus is too highly charged with active impulses.

From the biological standpoint, nevertheless, the ideal adaptation of woman to her erotic function involves the functional suppression of the active, and even of the passive, clitoris in favor of the vagina, whose role is that of purely passive reception. But in order that the vital ego may accept this erotic passivity, which is specifically and essentially feminine, a woman, when she reaches full maturity, must as far as possible have rid herself of the infantile fear which has its origin in the sadistic conception of coitus and from the defensive reactions against the possibility of masochism which are to be traced to the same source.

NOTES

1 Genesis iii. 16.

2 *L'Amour* (1858).

3 "The Economic Problem in Masochism" (1924).

4 "The Significance of Masochism in the Mental Life of Women" (1930).

5 Cf. especially Melanie Klein, *The Psycho-Analysis of Children*, (1932).

6 In my opinion this primitive drawing back is a motion of the *vital ego* and not primarily, as Melanie Klein holds, that of a precocious *moral superego*. In this connection my view agrees more nearly with that of Karen Horney, though I differ from her on another point, namely, the constitutional phallic element—what I should term the bisexuality —in the nature of women. Cf. Melanie Klein, *The Psycho-Analysis of Children*, quoted earlier in this paper, and Karen Horney, "The Flight from Womanhood" (1926), and "The Denial of the Vagina" (1933). The outbreak of rage to be observed in so many children, when an attempt is made to give them an enema, is, I believe, to be explained as the defence set up by this same instinct of self-preservation against penetration of their bodies. This seems to me much more probable than that it is the expression of a kind of orgasm, as Freud holds (no doubt with some justice in certain cases), following Ruth Mack Brunswick (Freud, "Female Sexuality" [1931].)

7 Freud, *Three Essays on the Theory of Sexuality* (1905); Abraham, "A Short Study of the Development of the Libido" (1924).

Some New Observations on the Origins of Femininity

Ethel Person

Psychoanalysis was the first comprehensive personality theory which attempted to explain the psychological origins of the "polarities" of masculinity and femininity. That such polarities exist is not a matter for debate; the observation of distinctions between masculinity and femininity is universal. Nonetheless, the notion that the origins of these personality differences required scientific exploration in psychological terms was a major intellectual leap, and it is Freud who must be credited with this insight.

Marie Bonaparte was one of the analysts who contributed to the development of the early psychoanalytic formulations on woman; formulations not only about sexual development but also about the character traits associated with femaleness. Her article "Passivity, Masochism, and Femininity," published in the *International Journal of Psychoanalysis* in 1935, is reprinted as a section in her 1953 book, *Female Sexuality*. The article summarizes some concepts which are more fully elaborated in the longer text. It is my purpose, in this discussion, to focus primarily on Bonaparte's formulations of the origins of female character traits, particularly feminine masochism, to comment on those aspects of her theory which are still viable and those which need to be modified in the light of contemporary research, and to summarize some of the current ways in which the origins of femininity are viewed.

Bonaparte, like Freud, believed that prephallic development is essentially congruent for both sexes. Development diverges only with the child's discovery of the anatomic distinction between the sexes: the observation that boys have penises while girls do not. According to Bonaparte, the girl responds to this discovery with an assumption that she has been castrated, whereupon she accepts the notion of clitoral inferiority and renounces "phallic" auto-eroticism.

> The girl must, in effect, attribute her mutilation to the mother, for it is only secondarily, when she has accepted her own castration and sadistic coitus, she can masochistically imagine herself castrated by the father. It is a result of the primary effects of her disappointment, her castration, and of still deeper biological causes, doubtless emanating from the gonads, that the girl finally passes over to predominant father-love and, to quote Helene Deutsch, to the masochistic wish to be subjected to the triad, castration-violation-childbirth.

Thus the discovery of the anatomic distinction ushers in the girl's positive Oedipal phase. The adult woman's sexuality may be problematic for four reasons relating to development as described in this scheme: (1) penis envy, (2) the necessity of transferring genital interest from the clitoris to the vagina, (3) the necessity for switching the love object in the Oedipal phase, and (4) the vital need to defend against the masochism implicit for the woman in "sadistic coitus."

Bonaparte agreed with Freud that the discovery of the anatomic distinction is decisive not only for female sexual development, but also for the development of those personality traits associated with femaleness; passivity, masochism, and narcissism. For example, masochism is viewed as the girl's response to the assumption of her castration coupled with the infantile conception of coitus as a sadistic act in which the male is the aggressor. Bonaparte believed that there might be some pre-Oedipal precursors of masculinity or femininity (for example, a constitutional predisposition to passivity), but that, by and large, the personality traits referable to femininity are born in the phallic oedipal phase of development.

In this view, femininity primarily derives from the psychological ramifications of a single momentous and traumatic perception, the girl's discovery of her anatomic difference from boys, a difference viewed as an inadequacy. It is the child's symbolic elaboration of the perception of the distinction, not the anatomic difference *per se*, which ushers in the divergence in personality development. Whether or not one agrees with Bonaparte, it is important to note that this theory of the relationship between

251

biologic sex and psychological sex (femininity) is weighted in the direction of a psychological causality, though an inevitable one, not in the direction of a purely biological explanation.

Bonaparte was an astute observer and most of the sequences she described in psychosexual development are still observable in women's analyses. Feelings of mutilation, penis envy, and the ramifications of the Oedipus complex are almost invariably prominent. In effect, analytic observations of patients have not changed. Nonetheless, new observations on children, as well as a shift in psychoanalytic theory, have prompted a re-evaluation of the early psychoanalytic formulations about femininity. I will discuss this re-evaluation of the data in terms of two questions. First, is it possible to conceptualize certain character traits, such as masochism, in a different framework, and second, what are the current theories about the origins of femininity?

A Re-evaluation of Feminine Masochism

Masochism "may perhaps best be defined as the seeking of unpleasure, by which is meant physical or mental pain, discomfort or wretchedness, for the sake of sexual pleasure, with the qualification that either the seeking or the pleasure, or both may often be unconscious rather than conscious" (Brenner, 1959). Despite the fact that the actual masochistic sexual perversion is reported predominantly in men (Reik, 1941), most analysts assume that masochism is more prominent in the mental life of women than of men. The data base to which the label "feminine masochism" applies has never been fully elucidated, but loosely applies to the frequency of slave, prostitute, beating, and humiliation fantasies elicited during the analyses of women. Although no one has done a statistical analysis of women's fantasy life as it emerges in analysis, it might also be noted that women are given to many other sorts of fantasies as well, for example *femme fatale*, achievement, stardom, love, mothering, and marital fantasies. Masochism in women may also present itself as moral masochism, as a certain "stickiness" in relationships or in a tendency to suffer in love relationships.

Bonaparte, who, along with Deutsch, was a chief architect of the theory of feminine masochism, saw it as an inevitable concomitant of female sexual development. She described beating fantasies as a normal sequence in the psychosexual development of girls. The child first entertains fantasies of being beaten in the anal-sadistic stage. These beating fantasies are originally aggressive, not sexual, and are sexualized only in the phallic phase when a child develops the sadistic theory of intercourse. With the discovery of the sexual difference, the girl sexualizes the fantasy of being beaten.

> Vaginal sensitivity in coitus, for the adult female, in my opinion, is thus largely based on the existence, and the more or less conscious acceptance, of the child's immense masochistic beating fantasies. In coitus, the woman, in effect, is subjugated to a sort of beating by the man's penis. She receives its blows and often, even, loves their violence.

According to Bonaparte, although the girl covets the father (and his penis), she views coitus as aggressive and is therefore frightened by the thought of penetration and by the fear of a baby who will rend her apart. These fears may be masochistically bound or there may be a masculine protest with vaginal anesthesia and a fixation on clitoral eroticism or, most ideally, the girl may eventually correct this childish misperception of coitus. Nonetheless, Bonaparte believes that

> In woman's acceptance of her role there may be a slight tincture—a homeopathic dose, so to speak—of masochism, and this, combining with her passivity in coitus, impels her to welcome and to value some measure of brutality on the man's part.

Although Bonaparte is more careful than her colleagues to distinguish masochism and passivity as developmental issues, which may not, in fact, appear in the analyses of some adult women as personality trends, her conclusions parallel those of the other analysts:

> Masochism in woman is far stronger than in man. The aggression against the mother, in the girl's passive Oedipus complex, can never result in a superego equal to that produced by the boy's active Oedipus complex ... she remains, throughout life, more subject to her infantile libidinal urges than is man.

Novick and Novick (1971) have observed children in a variety of settings and conclude that the sequential stages of the beating fantasy described by Bonaparte may be a part of the developmental life of girls. Nonetheless, in the same article, they note that beating fantasies appear as a prominent theme in only six of 111 indexed cases of children's analyses at the Hempstead Clinic.

Even if one concurs that masochism is, in fact, more prominent in the mental life of women than in the mental life of men, one can still ask whether it is inevitable because of female sexual development or whether it derives from other sources, and serves certain adaptive ends. (I should emphasize that it is not self-evident to me that women are more masochistic, that is, self-defeating or self-punishing, than men, but rather it may be that women and men are equally masochistic but in different areas of life.)

There is in contemporary psychoanalytic theory a trend to view masochism as an adaptive (though neurotic) technique born in an early interpersonal drama (Kardiner *et al*, 1959), rather than as a derivative of instinct, this latter view being both implicit and explicit in Bonaparte's work. Thus, masochism can be viewed as part and parcel of an interpersonal constellation of dependency (Bieber, 1953): insofar as a person relies neurotically on someone else for magical support, the object of dependency gratification needs to be raised to superhuman status. "So long as the need exists to perceive humans with superhuman power so long will there co-exist the need for self-depreciatory and self-destructive masochistic attitudes and behavior." (Bieber, 1953). Insofar as the gender role model for women is dependent, passive, and childlike, masochism will be promoted as a character trait. Or, to quote from another analyst, ". . . masochism seems to be the weapon of the weak—i.e., of every child faced with the danger of human aggression" (Loewenstein, 1957). Lowenstein (1957) postulates "seduction of the aggressor," a forerunner of masochism, as a mechanism of childhood, which allows the child actively to preserve parental love. In this sense, as long as woman's status is dependent, masochistic tendencies will be promoted as interpersonal coping devices.

In some instances, "masochistic" fantasies permit of some other interpretation. Let us say that a woman fantasizes herself as a slave, selected for her beauty to be mistress to a potentate; on occasion, sometimes with very little prompting, the woman reveals that the fantasy does not end with a sexual connection, that, in fact, the sequel reveals her exerting her own power through influence over the potentate. Again, in this instance, what appears to be pain-dependent behavior turns out to be a vehicle of power for the weak.

There is an additional factor which promotes masochism in women. Masochistic defenses protect the individual from some imagined punishment for wrongdoing; in other words, the individual punishes himself for some transgression to ward off a symbolic danger of greater proportion. Any propensity to guilt increases the likelihood of a masochistic defense. Insofar as sexuality is more forbidden to women than to men, an increased sexual guilt will strengthen masochistic tendencies.

There is, of course, one enormous irony in the history of analytic concepts of feminine masochism. Freud (1924) described masochism as presenting itself in three shapes: (1) erotogenic, (2) feminine, and (3) moral; he was the first to describe feminine masochism *but he described it as it occurred in men.*

> Feminine masochism, on the other hand, is the form most accessible to observation, least mysterious, and is comprehensible in all its relations. We may begin our discussion with it.
>
> In men (to whom for reasons connected with the material I shall limit my remarks). . . . if one has an opportunity of studying cases in which the masochistic phantasies have undergone specially rich elaboration, one easily discovers that in them the subject is placed in a situation characteristic of womanhood, i.e. they mean that he is being castrated, is playing the passive part in coitus, or is giving birth. For this reason I have called this form of masochism *a potiori* feminine although so many of its features point to childish life.

In essence, men perceive the female lot as one of suffering and thus equate it with a masochistic position in life. It is less clear that women perceive it in this light.

From our current vantage point, it seems possible to say that insofar as masochism is predominant in women, it derives from the social role of women *vis à vis* men, not from intrinsic libidinal endowment or from the perception of the anatomic distinction or from the conception of coitus as aggressive. If coitus is perceived by children as aggressive, with the male as aggressor, that very perception may reflect the child's awareness of social roles in which the male is perceived as strong and aggressive even before the child knows what the anatomic sex difference is.

I have attempted to re-evaluate feminine masochism in terms of its psychological origins. In a larger sense, it is possible to re-evaluate the whole development of femininity and to state categorically that femininity is not simply a derivative of the girl's perception of the anatomic distinction.

Toward a Theory of Gender Differentiation

Even in the twenties and thirties not all analysts agreed with Freud's formulations on women and a lively debate on femininity appeared in the psychoanalytic literature. The essence of the argument was how penis envy ought to be regarded. In the view of Freud and his supporters, including Bonaparte, penis envy was the pivotal feature in the mental life of women. The little girl retreated into femininity because her masculinity was blocked by virtue of inadequate equipment. In the opposition view (Karen Horney, 1933, Ernest Jones, 1935), femininity was seen as primary and was thought to antedate the phallic-oedipal phase. From the beginning, in this view, the little girl is concerned with her vagina and the inside of her body; penis envy is a secondary and defensive structure and results from a dread of femininity—for example, fear of penetration. Freud's original analytic question was, "What is the effect on the girl's mental life of the discovery that the clitoris is an inferior penis?" The opposition analysts replaced this question with two others: "Is the small girl aware of her vagina?" and if so, "What are the consequences for mental life of the awareness of the vagina?" Bonaparte referred to the opposition as "those feminine apologists of the vagina." Despite the sometimes heated nature of the debate, in both these views personality follows genital awareness. The theoretical debate was never really resolved, although recently certain analysts have mediated the two positions (Barnett, 1966; Kesterberg, 1956).

Most observers have confirmed Horney's contention that male and female behavior is discrepant at a very early age, prior to the child's awareness of the anatomic sexual difference, but have felt her explanation of the discrepancy to be narrowly derived. Blind children, boys with congenital absence of the penis, and girls with congenital absence of the vagina have all been observed to differentiate along gender lines appropriate to their sex. These observations indicate that gender differentiation is not totally dependent on either an inner space (awareness of the vagina) or on the discovery of the sexual distinction.

In recent years, the introduction of the concept of gender role identity, which is the generic name for psychological maleness and femaleness (masculinity and femininity), has allowed some more objective description of the psychological differences between the sexes than Freud's original description. Gender role identity is characterized not only by sexual behavior and fantasies but also by nonsexual attributes and behavior—for example, dress, speech, mannerisms, interests, emotional responsiveness, and aggressiveness. In addition, research psychologists have noted differences in cognitive style which are linked to differences in personality, so that males are described as more aggressive, field independent, and achievement oriented while females are described as more field dependent, conformist, and suggestible. The origin of gender role identity is once more the focus of attention in psychology and psychoanalysis.

Pioneer studies by Money (Money *et al*, 1955, 1957) and Stoller (1968) indicate that the first and crucial step in psychosexual development and gender differentiation is the self-designation by the child as male or as female. Such a self-designation arises in the early years of life in agreement with the parental designation of the child's sex, that is, according to whether the child is "diagnosed" as male or female (sex of assignment). This self-designation, defined by the term *core gender*, may have unconscious as well as conscious components. The evidence for this contention comes from a study of so-called intersexed children. In children whose sex is misdiagnosed at birth (for example, girls with an adrenogenital syndrome in which the clitoris is hypertrophied and resembles a phallus and who are mistakenly diagnosed as male at birth) core gender develops in accordance with sex of assignment, not with genetic sex. In a study of seventy-six pseudo-hermaphrodites, Money (1955, 1957) found that core gender almost invariably followed the sex of assignment. He concludes that children are born with psychosexual neutrality and that the process of gender differentiation is set in motion by the development in the child of core gender (the sense, I am male or I am female). In other words, genetic girls misdiagnosed as boys and raised as boys follow masculine lines of development, whereas genetic males misdiagnosed as girls and raised as girls follow feminine lines of development. This pattern of development is essentially reversible until the age of eighteen months (some authors say eighteen months to three years). If the misdiagnosis of sex is discovered after the age of three, medical advice dictates that the child continue to be raised in the incorrect genetic sex since profound psychological upheavals accompany reversal after that age.

Why core gender is of such crucial importance in organizing personality is still a matter for theoretical elucidation. A cognitive theory offered by developmental psychologists (Kohlberg, 1966) suggests that gender is an aspect of self-identification, as well as a means for categorizing others, which aids the child in orienting to his world. As such, gender plays an organizing role in psychic structure, similar to other modalities of cognition, space, time, causation, and self-object discrimination.

In effect, then, there is contemporary agreement that gender differentiation is prephallic, observable by the end of the first year of life and immutable by the third year. It is obvious that core gender identity is laid down via some communication in the parent-infant relationship but the mechanism of this communication is unclear. Core gender identity, once established, locates the appropriate object for imitation and identification. Girls and boys develop self-esteem by engaging in behavior "appropriate" to their sex. Thus the child begins to develop along either feminine or masculine lines.

This description of gender differentiation explains how boys and girls differentiate, but it does not account for the specific attributes of the two gender roles. It is at this juncture that we must invoke a theory of social roles supplemented by psychoanalytic speculation on the psychological ramifications of genital awareness and anatomic difference. Insofar as girls identify with mature women, they may incorporate attitudes referrable to the sexual and reproductive cycle of women prior to having experienced these events in their own lives. In this way the mature sexuality of a mother influences the mind of her girl child; Bonaparte alludes to this fact in stressing the impact of the sight of menstrual blood or childbirth on a girl's conceptions of sex.

The original analytic emphasis on genital sensations, genital self-stimulation, castration anxiety, penis envy and the Oedipus complex as formative elements in the life of women has not been abolished, but is now viewed as superimposed upon earlier influences in gender differentiation. One could argue that the girl's reaction to the discovery of the sexual difference is not intrinsic to the discovery *per se*, but derives partly from characterological attributes which have already been established. Many authors (e.g., Ovesey, 1956) have noted that penis envy may not be a literal desire for the phallus, but a symbolic statement about desired male perogatives, that is, that the girl envies the masculine gender role or is fearful of the feminine one.

Given the variegated factors in gender consolidation, it is not surprising to discover that many patients present gender problems. Although some confusion of sexual identity is a theme in many analyses, there are three major syndromes in which gender pathology is prominent. In two of these, transsexualism and homosexuality, there is a large predominance of male patients; in the third category, transvestism, almost all reported cases are male (Money and Erhardt, 1973). One is struck with this finding in view of the insistent belief in the early psychoanalytic literature that female development is more problematic than male development. With the more recent emphasis on the early years of life, female development is regarded as less problematic and male development as less straightforward than was originally thought. Since the first object of identification for both sexes is the mother, the boy must switch his object of identification from mother to father. This developmental step, which the girl is spared, is vulnerable to interference from early separation anxiety or other infantile trauma. This vulnerability predisposes to the high incidence of gender pathology in men (Ovesey and Person, 1973; Greenson, 1968).

There are different implications for personality development when, as is usual in our culture, males are reared by females and females are reared by females. The girl must switch her love object but the boy must switch his object of identification. Both of these developmental issues have received attention in the psychoanalytic literature, but I believe the difference in the two childhood situations has ramifications in many other ways as well. A moderately high degree of cross-gender identification is promoted by the typical boyhood experience; cross-gender identification is correlated with field-independence. Men fear entrapment in marriage more than women; is this because the wife is of the same sex as the primary caretaker of childhood? What are the differences in empathy, intuitive understanding, rivalries, sexuality, and mutuality that the mother feels for her own sex compared with the other sex and what consequences do these differences have in the mental life of the child?

I have tried to indicate that the origins of gender differentiation are more variegated and more complicated than those proposed in the original psychoanalytic formulations of Freud, Bonaparte, and others. (I have omitted any reference to a biological component in neonatal sex differences—the male-brain, female-brain theory. This work is still controversial and I have chosen to focus on psychological components in gender differentiation. For an excellent review of the literature on gender differentiation which discusses biological, as well as psychological, factors, see

Kleeman [1971]; for a complete elaboration of the biological component, see Money and Ehrhardt [1973].) Some of the aspects of femininity which they describe are discernible in women, but may be seen as springing from different roots and, therefore, as less inevitable than was originally posited. Femininity does not derive exclusively from the child's discovery of the anatomic distinction, but has a long prephallic history. The new theoretical emphasis on prephallic factors in gender differentiation dovetails with the recent interest in psychoanalytic circles in the first several years of life, with emphasis on the emergence of self-object representations and the process of identity formation.

Conclusion

No one ever believed that the pioneer analytic work on women constituted a final understanding of femininity. Freud himself stated explicitly, "If you want to know more about femininity, enquire from your own experiences of life, or turn to the poets, or wait until science can give you deeper and more coherent information" (Freud, 1932). Some forty years have elapsed since the original psychoanalytic formulations about women were published. In those forty years, particularly in the last few decades, direct child observation, studies on pseudo-hermaphrodites, and new concepts in both psychology and psychoanalysis offer some "deeper and more coherent information" which has allowed for a critical reappraisal of the early psychoanalytic formulations.

Bonaparte's insights are clinically useful today. Her error was in confusing the *meaning* of certain themes which emerge in analysis with *causality*. There is currently substantial evidence to indicate that specific female character traits, such as masochism, and femininity in general, have a much more complicated derivation than was originally believed. Specifically, one cannot derive all aspects of femininity from the girl's discovery of the anatomic distinction between the sexes. In my view, the specific attributes of femininity are not inevitable concomitants of femaleness, but are to a large degree subject to modification in response to changes in child-rearing practices and social roles.

BIBLIOGRAPHY

Barnett, M. C. (1966), "Vaginal Awareness in the Infancy and Childhood of Girls," *Journal of the American Psychoanalytic Association* 14: 129–141.

Bieber, I. (1953), "The Meaning of Masochism," *American Journal of Psychotherapy* 7: 433–488.

Bonaparte, M. (1953), *Female Sexuality*, New York, International Universities Press, Inc.

Brenner, C. (1959), "The Masochistic Character," *Journal of the American Psychoanalytic Association*, 7: 197–226.

Freud, S. (1932), "Femininity," *Standard Edition*, 22.

———. (1924), "The Economic Problem in Masochism," *Collected Papers*, Vol. II, 255–268.

Greenson, R.R. (1968), "Dis-identifying from Mother: Its Special Importance for the Boy," *International Journal of Psycho-Analysis* 49: 370–374.

Horney, K. (1933), "The Denial of the Vagina," *Journal of the American Psychoanalytic Association*, 14: 57–70.

Jones, E. (1935), "Early Female Sexuality," *International Journal of Psycho-Analysis*, 16: 263–273.

Kardiner, A.; Karush, A., and Ovesey, L., (1959), "A Methodological Study of Freudian Theory," Part III—Narcissism, Bisexuality and the Dual Instinct Theory; *Journal of Nervous and Mental Diseases*, 129: 215–220.

Kestenberg, J. (1956), "Vicissitudes of Female Sexuality," *Journal of the American Psychoanalytic Association*, 4: 453–476.

Kleeman, J. A. (1971), "The Establishment of Core Gender Identity in Normal Girls. I. (a) Introduction; (b) Development of the Ego Capacity to Differentiate," *Archives of Sexual Behavior* 1: 103–116.

Kohlberg, L. (1966), "A Cognitive-Developmental Analysis of Children's Sex Role Concepts and Attitudes," pp 82–173 in *The Development of Sex Differences*, ed. E. E. Maccoby, Stanford University Press.

Loewenstein, R. (1957), "A Contribution to the Psychoanalytic Theory of Masochism," *Journal of the American Psychoanalytic Association*, 5: 197–234.

Money, J., and Ehrhardt, A. (1973), *Man and Woman, Boy and Girl*, Johns Hopkins University Press, Baltimore.

Money, J., Hampson, J. G., and Hampson, J. L. (1955), "Hermaphroditism: Recommendations Concerning Assignment, Change of Sex, and Psychological Management," *Bulletin of the Johns Hopkins Hospital*, 97: 284–330.

Money, J.; Hampson, J. G., and Hampson, J. L. (1957), "Imprinting, and the Establishment of Gender Roles," *Archives of Neurology and Psychiatry*, 77: 333–336.

Novick, J., and Novick, K. K. (1972), "Beating Fantasies in Children," *International Journal of Psycho-Analysis*, 53: 237–242.

Ovesey, L. (1956), "Masculine Aspirations in Women: An Adaptational Analysis," *Psychiatry*, 19: 341–351.

Ovesey, L., and Person, E. (1973), "Gender Identity and Sexual Pathology in Men: A Psychodynamic Analysis of Homosexuality, Transsexualism and Transvestism," *Journal of the American Academy of Psychoanalysis*, 1: 53–72.

Reik, T. (1941) *Masochism in Modern Man*, Farrar and Rinehart, New York.

Stoller, R. J. (1968), *Sex and Gender*, Science House, New York.

Moulton on Thompson

The Role of Women
in This Culture (1941)
Clara M. Thompson

A comprehensive presentation of the situation of women in this culture
is far beyond the scope of this paper. It is a task for careful research. The
aim here is merely to present observations and speculations on the cultural problems seen through the eyes of psychoanalytic patients. This
offers a limited but very significant view of the situation.

These observations are limited, in the first place, because for economic
reasons psychoanalysis is not yet available to any extent to the lower
classes. Second, for emotional reasons, groups with strong reactionary
cultural attitudes are seldom interested in psychoanalysis. Finally, individuals leading fairly contented lives lack the impulse to be analyzed.
This means that we are dealing in this paper chiefly with the ideas and
points of view of the discontented, and they happen to be for the most
part from the upper classes. Although this is a special group within the
culture, it is an important group because, on the whole, it is a thinking
group, nonconformist, and seeking to bring about changes in the cultural
situation. The study of the types of cultural problems presented by
women in analysis thus gives important information about the problems
of women in the culture.

There will be no attempt in this paper to make an extensive study of
early conditioning and traumatic factors in the lives of women but rather
to show how women have found means of expressing their strivings,
neurotic and otherwise, in the present culture of the United States.

When Freud first wrote his *Studies in Hysteria*[1] in the 1890's, he described a type of woman with ambitions and prospects very different from those found in the average psychoanalytic patient of today. That a radical change has occurred is partly due to Freud's own efforts in clarifying the whole question of the sexual life, but largely due to changes in the economic and social status of women. These changes were already occurring before the time of Freud.

In this country today women occupy a unique position. They are probably freer to live their own lives than in any patriarchal country in the world.[2] This does not mean that they have ceased to be an underprivileged group. They are discriminated against in many situations without regard for their needs or ability. One would expect, therefore, to find the reality situation bringing out inferiority feelings not only because of a reaction to the immediate situation but because of family teaching in childhood based on the same cultural attitude. One would expect to find, also very frequently, resentment toward men because of their privileged position, as if the men themselves were to blame for this. These are some of the more important factors that contribute to a woman's feeling of inferiority.

As we know, the culture of Europe and America has been based for centuries on a patriarchal system. In this system, exclusive ownership of the female by a given male is important. One of the results has been the relegating of women to the status of property without a voice in their own fate. To be sure, there have always been women who, by their cleverness or special circumstances, have been able to circumvent this position, but in general, the girl child has been trained from childhood to fit herself for her inferior role; and, as long as compensations were adequate, women have been relatively content. For example, if in return for being a man's property a woman receives economic security, a full emotional life centering around husband and children, and an opportunity to express her capacities in the management of her home, she has little cause for discontent. The question of her inferiority scarcely troubles her when her life is happily fulfilled, even though she lives in relative slavery. If, therefore, the problem of women today simply referred to their position in a patriarchal culture, the task would be much simpler. However, without considering the fact that the individual husband may be unsatisfactory and so produce discontent, other factors are also at work to create dissatisfaction. As Erich Fromm has said, "When a positive gain of a culture begins to fail, then restlessness comes until a new satisfaction is found." Our problem with women today is not simply that they are caught in a patriarchal culture, but that they are living in a culture in which the positive gains for them are failing.

Industry has been taken out of the home. The making of clothes has been entirely removed, and now it is necessary to know only the most rudimentary types of cooking. Factory-made clothes and canned goods have supplanted the industry in the home. Large families are no longer desired or economically possible. Also, other more emotionally tinged factors contribute to the housewife's dissatisfaction. The home is no longer the center of the husband's life. Once he ran a farm or a small business close to his home. In this his wife shared his problems, probably more than he realized. Today, a man's business is often far from his home and his wife's possible contribution to it may be nothing. If one adds to this the fact that the sexual life is often still dominated by puritanical ideas, the position of the present-day wife who tries to live in the traditional manner cannot but be one with a constant narrowing of interests and possibilities for development. Increasingly, the woman finds herself without an occupation and with an unsatisfactory emotional life.

On the other hand, the culture is beginning to offer her something positive in an opportunity to join in a life outside the home where she may compete with other women and even with men in business. In the sexual sphere, too, with the spread of birth-control knowledge and a more open attitude in general about sex, there is an increasing tendency in and out of marriage to have a sexual life approximating in its freedom that enjoyed by the male. However, these things do not yet run smoothly. In other words, we are not yet dealing with a stable situation, but one in transition; therefore, one in which the individual is confused and filled with conflict, one in which old attitudes and training struggle with new ideas.

Woman's restlessness began to make itself felt about the middle of the last century. Prior to that and even for some time afterward, the position of woman was fairly clear-cut and stable. Her training was directed toward marriage and motherhood. If she made a good marriage, she was a success. If she made a bad marriage, she must try to adjust to it because it was almost impossible to escape. If she made no marriage, she was doomed to a life of frustration. Not only was sexual satisfaction denied her but she felt herself branded a failure who must live on sufferance in the home of her parents, or of brother or sister, where she might have a meager emotional life from the love of other people's children. Not only must she suffer actual disappointment, but she had the additional burden of inferiority feelings. She had failed to achieve the goal demanded by the culture—and for women there was only one goal.

Even in those days there were a few exceptions. For instance, the Brontës, although leading very frustrated lives, at least were able to develop their gifts and to achieve success. But work and the professions were for the most part closed to women. If one's own family could not provide for an unmarried woman, she might find a home as governess or teacher in some other family. However, there were occasional daring women. As early as 1850 a woman had "crashed" the medical profession. She was considered a freak and accused of immorality. She had to face insults and gibes from her colleagues. Very slowly the number of woman physicians increased. Still later, they entered the other professions and business. On the whole, the number of women who in one way or another became independent of their families before 1900 was small. World War I speeded the process and gave the stamp of social approval to economic independence for woman. Since then, she has been able to enter almost every field of work for which she is physically capable, but even yet she is seldom accepted on equal terms with men.

Many interesting factors are revealed in this new situation of women. In the first place they are young in their present role. Comparatively few of them have the background of mothers or grandmothers who engaged in any work outside the home. They have to work out a new way of life with no precedent to follow and no adequate training from early childhood to help them take the work drive seriously or fit it into their lives. It is not strange that the outstanding successes are few and that the great majority of women effect some compromise between the old and the new. For instance, the majority still plan to work only until they marry. This is true not only of the relatively unskilled worker but often of the highly trained. This may mean that the young woman not only does not do her premarital job well and in a way to give her satisfaction, but also nothing in her premarriage activity is helpful in fitting her for the business of homemaker.

Second, even when the individual has the courage in herself to attempt the new road, she has to cope with emotional pressures not only from society as a whole but from the individuals most important to her. One of the most significant of these pressures is the attitude of a prospective husband who has his own traditions and wishes for his future wife and, since he is often confused in his attempt to adjust to the new ways of life, may interpret the woman's struggle to find a place for herself as evidence of lack of love or a slur on his manhood.

Even the attitude of parents is often far from constructive. They do not have as great an emotional stake in a daughter's business success as in that of a son, and they are less likely to make sacrifices for her career. Sometimes they actually oppose it. For example: a young woman announced her wish to study medicine. Both parents disapproved and persuaded her to seek her career in music. She acceded to their wishes and spent several years in study. At the end of that time, she remained dissatisfied and again expressed her wish to study medicine. This time the parents persuaded her to take up nursing. When she had completed this course, she again asked to be allowed to study medicine and finally obtained her wish. She proved to have outstanding ability.

Because so much of the child's ideals is modeled on attitudes of the parents, the girl may be further handicapped by incongruities built into her own ego. For example, a young woman brought up in a southern home, where nothing was expected of woman except to be charming, found herself in adult life in a profession where she must compete to hold her own. Both healthy and neurotic factors had driven her from her parents' adjustment. Her superior intelligence had stimulated her to go far in education, and lack of social ease—rising out of physical inferiority feelings—had reenforced this drive. Nevertheless, her ways of adjustment were definitely modeled on her past. Although she was in a position where she should be a leader with definite views and initiative to execute them, she was constantly deferring to men, seeking to flatter them by playing the yielding, clinging vine, accepting their advice even when she thought differently. Her conscious desire to be a modern woman led her to pretend to herself that she did not want to marry. To prove it she had several extramarital sexual affairs but in them she was frigid. She constantly felt humiliated because she had not achieved the traditional goal of marriage.

This example serves to show how the inconsistencies and conflicts—rising when a cultural situation is in a state of rapid transition—become a part of the neurotic conflict of the individual, even as they influence the form of the neurotic behavior.

Finally, social institutions put obstacles in the way of change of a woman's status. In the economic sphere she must usually accept a lower wage than men for the same type of work. She must usually be more capable than the man with whom she competes before she will be considered his equal.

Even with increased economic freedom, there is considerable variation in the social satisfactions available to independent women. In some groups any type of relationship with men or women is open to the woman who is emotionally able to accept it. In other groups a woman's social life may be even more restricted than it was in the days when she was overprotected in the home. In the latter groups, unless she shows great initiative in changing her situation, she may find herself forced to associate entirely with her own sex. While this is in itself a great cause for discontent, many individuals find a more or less satisfactory solution for its limitations, while others find neurotic security in the manless world. Thus it is possible for a woman teaching in a girls' school to reach the age of forty still living fairly happily on an adolescent "crush" level.

Whatever the problems created in the new life of woman, her status must continue to change for she is being driven out of the home by her restlessness due in part at least to her lack of occupation. The life of the married woman today who has no special work interest is not exciting. She has a small home, or in many cases only a small apartment. She may have no children; she may have at most three. Even if she does her own housework it is so simplified by modern inventions that it can fill only a few hours of her day. As has already been said, because of the nature of modern business life she often has very little share in her husband's interests. What can she do? She may make a cult of her child, or she may play bridge or have some other play life, or she may engage in some volunteer employment—in which she is apt to be no longer welcome since trained workers are increasingly preferred—or she may go to work seriously. The last solution is growing in popularity.[3]

Let us consider three frequently encountered types of reaction to the current situation: women who marry and try to live according to the old pattern but find themselves unemployed and often discontented; women who work and do not marry; and, women who marry and engage in serious work outside the home.

The first group, those who marry and have no other work interest, has already been discussed at some length. This is a very large group. It often happens that intelligent and capable women find themselves in this situa-

270

tion because they had not been aware of the reality before marriage and no preparation for any other type of life had been made. That is, these individuals had married with the fantasy that life after marriage could be lived somewhat in the old-fashioned way according to the pattern of the home life of their childhood. Many college women are in this group; especially college women who married immediately after graduation and did not fit themselves for any profession or work. Making a cult of the child is unfortunately a fairly frequent solution. By the term *cult* is here meant an anxious concern about the child's welfare where the mother goes to excessive lengths to apply all modern psychological and hygienic theories to the management of her child's development. This can be very destructive for the child.

Another type of woman finds in the marriage with no responsibility the fulfillment of her neurotic needs. This is the very infantile woman. For her marriage is a kind of sanitarium life. She often shirks childbearing and in her relationship to her husband she has the position of spoiled child. Many of these women could not survive outside the protected atmosphere of their marriages.

Of the second group, those who work and do not marry, there are two main subdivisions. First, there are those to whom work is everything; that is, there is no love life of significance. This woman differs from her predecessor, the old maid, in that she is economically independent. She may, however, be even more miserable because her life is often very isolated, whereas the old maid of the past generation usually lived in a family and had a kind of vicarious life. Many of these individuals do find some kind of sublimated satisfaction, for example, working for some cause even as their predecessors worked for religion. This group might be characterized as having found economic freedom without emotional freedom.

The second group are those who have a love life in addition to work. This love life may be homosexual or heterosexual, and the relationships may vary from the casual with frequent changes of partner to a fairly permanent relationship with one person, a relationship which may differ very little from marriage. In all of them, however, there is one important difference from a married partnership. The individual considers herself free although she actually may be very involved emotionally. She regards her work as the most important and permanent thing in her life.

In the group who marry and engage in work outside the home, several

271

possibilities of relationship exist. Husband and wife may continue to lead independent business lives. They may be interested in each other's work without being competitive in any way. There may be real enjoyment in the success of the other. This is the ideal situation. It is more likely to work when the two are engaged in different types of occupation.

The husband's resentment and competitive attitude may crush the wife's initiative, a situation which was more frequent a few years ago. The man feels that his virility is threatened. He fears that people will think he cannot support her or he fears that he will lose his power over her, and so forth. In such situations, if the marriage continues, the wife must give up her work—often without any adequate interest to take its place.

The wife who proves to be the better breadwinner may win out in the competition, especially since the depression. This is culturally a most revolutionary situation; it can make a great many difficulties. The woman needs extraordinary tact in handling it. If under the influence of her own cultural training she feels contempt for the husband or a desire to rub it in, matters can become very bad. In general, the man needs some face-saving explanation. He cannot say that he prefers to keep house, even when, occasionally, this is the case. He could not accept it himself, and most of his acquaintances would think less of him for it. So he has to be unable to get work and, therefore, keeps house to help his wife who is working, or he must be ill, or he must be getting an education, in all of which cases he is able to accept his wife's economic support without loss of self-respect. The following is a situation in which a man's neurosis provided a practical solution for this sort of marriage. A young woman who had been a schoolteacher was forced because of state law to give up her position when she married. The teaching had been a satisfactory means of expression for her, she found adjustment to the culturally usual feminine role in marriage difficult, and became more and more unhappy. After three years of marriage, during which two children were born, the husband developed a nervous breakdown and became unable to work. However, he had no serious difficulty in doing the housework and caring for the children. Because of the economic necessity, the woman again was able to get her teaching position and return to the life she enjoyed. By the complete reversal of the usual roles, this marriage was put on a firm basis. The neurosis saved face for the husband, and it is also likely that without it the wife could not have accepted the situation, although she certainly seemed to gain more by it than did he.

Thus far we have said almost nothing about childbearing. What has become of this important biologic function in our culture? In the present economic situation in the United States increase of population is not desired. The fact that small families are the rule is one of the factors driving women out of the home. Now that they are out of the home a kind of vicious circle is formed, for it is no longer convenient to be occupied in the home by one or two children. Much conflict centers here, for it is one of the problems of the culture which as yet has no generally satisfactory solution. Individual women have worked out ways of having both children and a career, but most women still do the one or the other; and in either case there are regrets and often neurotic discontent. The business or professional woman who had decided against children, consciously or unconsciously, does not want them; her difficulty arises from the fact that she often cannot admit this to herself. Perhaps some biologic yearning disturbs her, or some desire to have all of life's experiences, or perhaps there is merely the influence of the traditional cultural pattern which might be expressed thus: "A woman is expected to want a child." She may thus feel it her duty to prove her adequacy as a woman by having a child. She may resist, devote herself to her career, but it bothers her and makes her feel inferior. On the other hand, the problem is not solved by going to the other extreme and trying to prove one's adequacy as a woman by having a child or two. The women of past generations had no choice but to bear children. Since their lives were organized around this concept of duty, they seldom became aware of dislike of the situation, but there must have been many unwanted children then. Nowadays, when women have a choice, the illusion is to the effect that unwanted children are less common, but women still from neurotic compulsion bear children they cannot love. It seems likely that the woman who really desires a child will find herself able to give it the necessary love, whether she devotes her life to its care or entrusts it to another while she is working. Since solutions to the practical difficulties are being found by way of day nurseries and nursery schools, it is probable that any woman with a genuine desire for motherhood can find a way in this culture today.

While the change in woman's attitude toward sex has been implied in many of the foregoing remarks, it is a subject sufficiently important to merit separate consideration. Intimate records of the sexual life of women are not to be expected before the psychoanalytic era. They have been accumulating in the last fifty years, a period, however, in which great changes have been taking place.

Let us glance at the picture which Freud first described early in the 1890's. Young women of good family grew up apparently in sexual ignorance; they were allowed no legitimate opportunity to gratify their sexual curiosity in theory or in fact. At puberty they entered a life of severe restrictions by which an artificial form of behavior was fostered. Further general education was discouraged and, while on the one hand they were to show no interest in sex in any form, they at the same time must devote their lives to getting husbands. This situation must have led to profound confusion in the minds of many an adolescent girl. She knew she must marry, bear children, but never admit that she enjoyed sex. Certainly, adjustment was achieved by the women of that generation at great emotional cost. Freud's first insights about the importance of the sexual life and its significance in neurosis arose in such an atmosphere, at the very time women were beginning to be pushed out of the home. The fiction of purity, chastity, and innocence was becoming increasingly difficult to maintain. Reality pressures, in which Freud's discoveries had no small part, were making adequate sexual information more important. A greater frankness and sincerity about the sexual life was coming about. The problem could no longer be handled by overprotection and ignorance. As a result, the pendulum was swinging toward the revolt against all restraint which became manifest in the United States between 1920 and 1930. It then appeared not only that women were realizing their legitimate sexual stake in marriage, but even high-school girls felt a necessity for sexual episodes to herald in a rebellious way the coming of the new freedom. One of them, a patient, in comparing the old and the new, said, "Men used to think they had to pay a woman. Now they've discovered that the girls like it too." At any rate, escaping from chaperones, going into industry—in other words, leaving the protected convent-like atmosphere of the Victorian era—women found themselves overwhelmed with new emotional problems for which they had even less preparation than had they for the economic changes. Sexual freedom resulted, but in many cases the freedom was not without expense. The woman in trying to overthrow her early training was unable to get her own consent, as it were, and found herself frigid. The reverse swing of the pendulum appeared in the 1930's. While it may swing far back under

274

the influence of fascism, war may result in another forward thrust.

It is difficult to portray the sexual attitude of today's women. There are many different, often half-digested, attitudes. The culture still leans to the conservative side. The tendency is still to expect the woman to confine her sexual life to her marriage partner. Children born out of wedlock are still stigmatized in some groups, though certainly with nothing like the ferocity of fifty years ago. One still may encounter as a patient a woman who feels she can never get over the disgrace of having been pregnant two months before her marriage. While most of one's female patients accept sexual life out of marriage as a matter of course, many of them are unwilling to defy the culture to the extent of bearing children. Absence of virginity at the time of marriage is no longer a universal cause for dismay but it can still be disturbing to some people. In but few groups can the woman openly acknowledge that she has a lover. In general, she must be more secretive than is a man. In brief, in many situations today, a woman may have any kind of sexual life that she wishes if, and only if, she does not make herself conspicuous.

One result of these circumstances seems inevitable: marriage becomes much less important than it was. A woman once needed it as a means of economic support as well as a source of sexual satisfaction. Both factors have shrunk in importance. The companionship of marriage can conceivably be found in other situations; no satisfactory substitute has yet appeared to satisfy the economic and emotional needs of children.

The official attitude of the culture then is conservative but the practical attitude in certain groups is radical. The best examples of the latter are found in the group of women who work and have a sexual life outside of marriage, although the same types of behavior can also be seen in some married women. As suggested above, nominal freedom of behavior does not necessarily indicate inner freedom from conflict. Many women avail themselves of sexual opportunities, but cannot rid themselves of a sense of guilt arising from old ideas; or the sense of guilt may be repressed and in its place may come frigidity—a denying that the act is taking place—promiscuity as a kind of defiance of the inner prohibition, or other compromise behavior. Moreover, sexual freedom can be an excellent instrument for the expression of neurotic drives arising outside the strictly sexual sphere, especially drives expressive of hostility to men, or of the desire to be a man. Thus promiscuity may mean the collecting of scalps with the hope of hurting men, frustrating them, or taking away their importance, or in another case it may mean to the woman that she is herself a man. For example, a young woman whose business life threw her into sharp competition with men was proud of the fact that she acted like a man in her sexual life. She had a series of lovers to no one of whom she allowed herself to become attached. If she found herself becoming involved, she was upset until she had succeeded in discarding the man in such a way that he would conclude that she had no interest in him. This to her mind was acting like a man; permitting an emotional attachment to develop would have been acting like a woman.

It is then apparent that while the sexual emancipation of women may be a step forward in personality development for some, it may only offer a new means for neurotic expression to others.

Overt homosexuality among women is probably more frequent at the present time than formerly. The diminishing emphasis on marriage and children helps to bring it to the fore, and the social isolation from men that now characterizes some types of work must be an encouragement to any homosexual tendencies which exist. It seems that many women who would otherwise never give overt expression to these tendencies are driven together by loneliness, and in their living together all degrees of intimacy are found. The culture seems to be decidedly more tolerant of these relationships between women than of similar ones between men.

The question that is raised in any study of change, whether by evolution or revolution, takes the form: Can one say that people are more benefited or harmed? Have our women actually solved any of their problems in the last fifty years? When Freud analyzed his first cases, he described some of the basic conflicts which we still encounter, albeit the emphasis is different. Then, the young girl who might wish to be a boy could only give symbolic expression to this in the form of hysterical fantasies. Today, she may live out the fantasy, at least in part. In her business relations and in her sexual relations she may act in many ways like a man. Many a woman with severe personality difficulties uses the new opportunities provided by the culture for neurotic purposes without much benefit except that in so doing she is able to be a "going concern." On the other hand, many women use the present-day situation more constructively. As they acquire more freedom to express their capacities and emotional needs, they find less actual reason to envy the male. The handicap of being a woman is, culturally speaking, not as great now as it was fifty years ago.

NOTES

1 Sigmund Freud, *Studies in Hysteria* (New York: Basic Books, Inc., 1957).
2 For a period in the history of Soviet Russia some interesting improvements in the status of women came about.
3 We must not forget that there still are women in this culture who function successfully according to the old stable pattern of the last century and contentedly manage their homes. These women need not concern us.

The Role of Clara Thompson in the Psychoanalytic Study of Women*

Ruth Moulton

Clara Thompson was the first American woman to write a series of papers on the psychology of women. (There were six of these between 1941 and 1950.) A decade of controversy about Freud's views on the nature of women, beginning with Karen Horney's first paper in 1924, was followed by a relative dearth of papers on the topic in the turmoil connected with World War II.

During the war many analysts migrated to America. Some continued to write in the Freudian tradition, amplifying Freud's ideas without basic contradiction (Helene Deutsch, Ruth Mack Brunswick, Marie Bonaparte, Edith Jacobson, and Therese Benedek).

Others, however, began to evolve fresher approaches in America, where traditions were less binding and where the atmosphere was more conducive to the development of new ideas than it had been in Europe. The four most seminal psychoanalysts in this process were Harry Stack Sullivan, Clara Thompson, Erich Fromm, and Karen Horney.

Sullivan, born in upper New York State in 1892, began to study schizophrenia at St. Elizabeth's Hospital in Washington, D.C., under the guidance of William Alanson White. He was deeply influenced by sociological

*To be revised and published in a forthcoming book by Ruth Moulton, *Changing Concepts of Female Sexuality* (New York: Quadrangle Press).

field theory and the Sapir-Whorf communication theory, and applied them to his psychiatric work. He avoided Freudian terminology, for he had strong convictions about the nonsexual origin of neurosis, and he developed a unique theory about human development. Sullivan saw the development of a sense of oneself as an integrated, operating, aware individual as dependent on interpersonal relationships. He placed great emphasis on empathy between infant and mother (or mothering person); this empathy forms the basis of the child's sense of security in all subsequent relationships. The development of accurate communication—the use of words to express feelings about the nature of reality and (especially) about the important people in the child's world—is basic to the child's comprehension and ability to master the tasks that are appropriate to his age. Sullivan viewed sex as one of many important needs—one which can be a most pressing issue at times. The success with which sex is integrated into an individual's total life pattern depends, according to Sullivan, on the solidity of interpersonal relationships, traceable to early infancy. The impact of significant people on the malleable infant is more important, in his view, than the biological "givens," since these latter are easily influenced by social or cultural factors. Sullivan was primarily interested in looking at what goes on *between* people, whereas Freud had emphasized the instinctual, biological forces *inside* a person.

Sullivan greatly influenced the thinking of Clara Thompson, who worked with him for a time in Baltimore. He recommended that she go to Budapest to study with Sándor Ferenczi, one of the first European analysts to adopt a humanistic, interpersonal, flexible approach. She first went to Budapest in 1928, and continued to see Ferenczi during the summers until his death in 1933.

Clara Thompson expressed her ideas about women in simple, clear-cut language that is easy to understand. In fact, her contribution has in some ways been overlooked because it seemed like "common sense," like "something we always knew"—but, one could add, paid little attention to. A quiet, reserved person, she kept her distance from analytic power politics. She was a descendant of New England whalers, went to college in Providence, Rhode Island, and to Johns Hopkins Medical School. Her straightforward use of language stemmed not only from her Scandinavian background (she referred to herself as the "silent Swede"), but also from her contact with Sullivan, who tended to avoid analytic jargon and abstractions in the belief that simple language makes it easier for doctor and patient to arrive at "consensual" validation of what is meant by a given word or phrase.

In 1930 Thompson became the first president of the Baltimore-Washington Psychoanalytic Society. There she worked with Lucille Dooley, Frieda Fromm-Reichmann, and Mabel Blake Cohen. While each did her own thinking about women, there must have been significant cross-fertilization, for some overlapping and great compatibility is to be found in their ideas. When Clara Thompson moved to New York City in 1933, she trained and taught candidates at the classical New York Psychoanalytic Institute, but she also renewed friendships with Sullivan, Fromm, and Horney, who were all at that time in New York City. The four were sometimes referred to as the "cultural school."

Both Horney and Thompson, who shared many ideas between 1935 and 1941 while they were fellow dissidents at the New York Psychoanalytic Institute, left the Institute in 1941. They remained together for two years and then formed two separate institutes, both of which are still active training centers. (Karen Horney founded the American Institute for Psychoanalysis in 1941; Clara Thompson the William Alanson White Institute for Psychoanalysis in 1943). This bit of history, while incomplete and not essential to our topic, does suggest the interplay of various personalities and the influence of their backgrounds on the development of ideas about the psychology of women.

We may now turn to examine the contribution Clara Thompson made to psychoanalytic thinking about women. Her six most influential papers on women were written between 1941 and 1950 and are very pragmatic in tone, sticking close to clinical observation of women and the cultures in which they find themselves, with no effort to formulate new theories. Thompson recognized the limitations of her observations, which for economic reasons were largely restricted to the middle and upper classes and to a thinking, nonconformist, discontented group—a group that may have been more interested than were the majority of women in bringing about change. Since she was running an institute that was not in the mainstream of Freudian psychoanalysis, she attracted patients and students who were looking for a more liberal, progressive approach to personality problems, mental illness, and analytic training.

Most of the analytic patients she saw were quite different from those who originally came to Freud, not only because of the influence of

Freud's own work on sexual repression but also because women in America were in the 1940s "probably freer to live their own lives than in any other patriarchal country in the world. This does not mean that they have ceased to be an underprivileged group" (Thompson, 1941). The cultural attitude of discrimination, as Thompson saw it, is reinforced by family training and causes resentment toward men because of their privileged condition, as if men themselves were personally responsible for it. She makes no attempt in this paper (1941) to study early conditioning and individual traumatic factors, because she is interested in showing how women have dealt with an increasing awareness of their cultural inferiority. About the middle of the last century, when industry was taken out of the house, the home ceased to be the center of the husband's life, and large families were no longer desirable or economically feasible, woman's role and status changed, and her restlessness began to make itself felt. With the spread of birth control and more open attitudes toward sex, in and out of marriage, for women as well as for men, we were and still are confronted with a profound cultural transition. Women in 1941 were able to enter almost any field of work of which they were physically capable, but were seldom accepted on equal terms with men. The obstacles were both external, in the form of lower wages, and internal: parents frequently disapproved of their daughters' "new freedom," and "a prospective husband . . . has his own traditions and wishes for his future wife, and . . . may interpret the woman's struggle to find a place for herself as evidence of lack of love or a slur on his manhood." These remarks, made over thirty years ago, strike a singularly appropriate note even now.

Since working women were relatively young in their new roles, few of them having mothers or grandmothers who worked outside the home, they had to mold a new way of life with no precedents to follow. The majority planned to work only until they married and most of the rest effected some compromise between the old and the new. Thompson describes three types of reaction to what was in 1941 the "present situation." Women in the first group marry, with no other work interest, and find themselves unemployed and discontented, unprepared for any interesting occupation; they therefore make a "cult" of raising children, with anxious overconcern that has destructive effects on the child. Women in the second group work, do not marry, and too often find themselves forced to associate entirely with their own sex because social life is centered on marriage and family life. And those in the third group marry and work outside the home; husband and wife continue to lead independent business lives. There may be an ideal situation in which each enjoys the success of the other—but the man may feel his virility is threatened, especially if the wife happens at some point to earn more than he does. To avoid such a dilemma, wrote Thompson, some women compulsively (neurotically) underachieve or hide in being "mothers," bearing children they cannot love. Others, who welcome the freedom to have sex without children, find themselves feeling guilty, unable to overthrow early training, unable to get their own consent, as it were, and find themselves frigid. Promiscuity is another solution in which a woman acts "like a man" in her sexual life and collects male scalps in the hope of hurting men.

Thompson had a deep sense of sympathy and understanding for women who were frightened and confused by the cultural and personal conflicts that are inevitably connected with rapid social change. Yet she was so aware of how hard it is for people to free themselves from old stereotypes and role expectations that she accepted their failure to do so without contempt. She respected women who used analysis to do a better job with home and children, and encouraged those who were trying to break new paths.

Having stated her basic premises about the significant cultural factors in the psychology of women that were too often neglected by others who studied the "problem," Thompson goes on to comment on some of Freud's specific concepts. Many so-called feminine traits such as masochism, the neurotic need to be loved, and passivity are also found in men. Conversely the neurotic need for power and insatiable ambition are to be found not only in men but also in women (Thompson, 1942). The inhibition of natural aggression is often forced on a girl, especially at puberty, when she loses her relative freedom to enjoy many activities with boys, can no longer go about freely, and must not show overt interest in boys as this would be "unwomanly." She is trained to be insincere about her sexuality—ashamed of menstruation, self-conscious about her body—and yet expected to spend much time on her appearance in a way that encourages narcissism. The difficulties experienced by young girls at puberty are, claimed Thompson, at least partly the result of these new social pressures; they are not, she believed (contrary to Freud), due only to the difficulty of giving up the clitoris for the vagina—a renunciation that Thompson did not believe necessary. Thompson found a wide variety in women as to their paths of sexual development. Some of her women patients were not aware of the clitoris as a separate organ although they had explored its pleasurable sensations. Other women had early knowledge of the vagina and a long history of vaginal masturbation. Ignorance of the vagina, sometimes far into adolescence, was most frequently observed in hysterics.

As to penis envy, she found it in some patients and not in others, suggesting that other factors contribute to envy of the male (such as the parents' attitude toward the sex of their children). Penis envy could be seen as a symbolic expression of a wish for equality with men, as the penis represented male power and privilege. "There is not necessarily any evidence that the body situation is the cause of the thing it symbolizes" (Thompson, 1943). Sexual differences are obvious and thus become convenient marks of derogation in a competitive culture, where envy is a universal characteristic. The penis is the sign of the person in power, and can be seen as a sword for conquering and destruction. The woman feels cheated that she does not have a similar weapon. As long as she is expected to be dependent on a man, in danger of rejection if she is assertive or independent, and unable to get a clear sense of herself, she is apt to use this symbol as a rationalization for various feelings of inadequacy. Penis envy is most apt to occur in women who feel inadequate and unfulfilled in their feminine roles—which feelings may stem from an early unresolved dependency, from a domineering selfish mother, or from the undermining of self-esteem by a destructive mother or a disinterested or hostile father. (See "A Survey and Re-evaluation of the Concept of Penis Envy", by Ruth Moulton, *Contemporary Psychoanalysis,* Vol. 7-No. 1, Fall, 1970.) The girl may also suffer from a feeling of "uncleanness," a side effect of what Thompson (1950) calls "sphincter morality" where cleanliness is overemphasized by the mother; the boy's genitals are seen as cleaner, the girl's genitals as "messy" and odoriferous. This can cause a negative body image and low female self-esteem. Thus, penis envy may reflect many aspects of living and have little to do with the facts of biology except secondarily.

In discussing "the masculinity complex," Thompson wrote: "It is not useful to confuse the picture of the independent woman with that of an essentially pathological character structure, the masculinity complex" (Thompson, 1942). In the latter instance there is an exaggerated need for "freedom" and fear of losing identity in any intimacy. Women who fit this description fear dependency because it has been a serious threat to them early in life; the struggle for some form of superiority to men is thus an attempt to keep from being destroyed. Acceptance of the so-called feminine role may not be an affirmative attitude at all but an expression of submission and resignation. A woman may consent to be "used" for man's pleasure because she feels inadequate or unattractive and then feels resentment at her apparent lack of choice. Submission to get approval is not apt to lead to healthy, active participation on the woman's part; full participation results only from her playing her own unique role in love-making, exercising choices and preferences—and is apt to make her a less reluctant and much more exciting sexual partner.

The solution by way of neurosis may be a solution by evasion but it does reflect what is acceptable in our culture. With the passing of the old sheltered (female) life, our culture invites "masculinity" in women by seeming to encourage their more active participation in the outside world. But if women try to "ape" men they may become mere caricatures of themselves and lose sight of their own interests. The basic nature of woman—and of man—remains profoundly mysterious; and since it is so difficult for either sex to identify fully with the sexual feelings of the other, it is important for women to find their own ways to their own sexual identities. The basic "problem of a woman's sexual life is not in becoming reconciled to having no penis but in accepting her own sexuality in its own right" (Thompson, 1950). Her sexual drive may be less insistent, less consistent than that of a man; it may vary more in rhythm and quality, but it is not necessarily less. These aspects of Clara Thompson's thought seem very relevant today when we are still stressing that differences between the sexes need not imply inequality.

Some "culturalists" or their followers have gone too far, saying in effect that what determines human nature is the condition of the social relations in which the human animal evolves. They have attempted to disprove Freud's biological bias by denying the relevance of physiological differences—to reject his notion that neurosis was primarily feminine by rejecting psychological differentiation entirely. "The fact that both men and women possess common neurotic tendencies springing from common social soil, does not prove either the existence or desirability of a common psychological identity." (Dr. Bernard Robbins in a symposium on "Feminine Psychology" March 1950, Department of Psychiatry, New York Medical College.)The fact that both sexes fall prey to the same undifferentiated disease (neurosis) does *not* establish them as undifferentiated beings. Freud was wrong whenever he regarded as essentially feminine that which was essentially neurotic. But he was not wrong in clinging to the concept of an essential difference. Fromm stressed that to be equal in value as human beings does not imply sameness; that to deny difference is absurd. Freud's failure was not in the recognition of differences but in the conviction of their immutability.

During the 1950s Dr. Thompson turned her attention from the psychology of women to other topics such as transference and countertransference, and the emotional climate of psychoanalytic institutes. Her book *Psychoanalysis: Evolution and Development* (New York: Hermitage House, 1950) was the first to integrate the various theories of Freud and the early deviants—Adler, Jung, Rank, Ferenczi, Reich—and to compare them with later dissidents such as Sullivan, Fromm, and Horney. Thompson discusses differences in psychoanalytic thinking as part of an evolutionary process, reflecting the personalities of the various writers as well as their positions in time and social space. It is a clear and succinct text, excellent for teaching.

However, some of her later thoughts on the nature of women are to be found in a posthumous paper (1961) called "Femininity." She speaks there of the degree to which sexual activity is influenced by body structure, which cannot be overlooked as a factor although it need not imply weakness or inferiority. She found that women could have and enjoy many kinds of orgasm and should not constantly compare their responses to those of men. She notes that every culture has its own stereotype of femininity, and hopes that in ours the increasing cultural appreciation of women's strength will continue to add to individual women's self-respect and self-acceptance. And, finally, Clara Thompson contrasts women's helplessness in the age of chivalry with the rebellion against being a woman that was typical of the flapper in the 1920s; following this shift, she points out, came a strong trend toward emancipation and equality in the United States. Femininity is a changing concept in a changing culture.

The unconscious changes slowly, long after socio-cultural and legal changes have been effected. The notion of this "cultural lag" should give patience and courage to new feminists, who are understandably impatient some fifty years after the battle for suffrage. Present-day analysts, many of whom worked with Clara Thompson and her colleagues, are trying to help women use their new options—to break away from worn-out stereo-

285

types, to disregard the backward pull exerted by parents, peers, and husbands who may give lip service to a new freedom of choice for women but unwittingly add to the difficulties of achieving it. Women continue to be afraid of their own success, but we are all becoming more aware of this.

To summarize Clara Thompson's contributions to woman's increasing knowledge about herself, one can say that she called attention to the important cultural and personal conflicts that are the basis of contemporary feminist consciousness. She was an astute clinician and an inspired analyst who gave courage and self-confidence to many who worked with her. Her philosophy was a pragmatic humanism, and her freedom of spirit facilitated the growth of the new feminism in a quiet, forceful way. Erich Fromm has said of her that she was a

> thoroughly independent person, averse to rules and principles with which she did not agree; at the same time she did not endow her own theoretical principles with a halo that would make her fight all others. But while she was never a fanatic or one to intimidate others, it was one of her remarkable characteristics that she could not be intimidated. . . . This integrity within and loyalty to friends made it possible for others to trust her and rely on her. She was a person with fine appreciation of theory and, at the same time, with excellent common sense.*

BIBLIOGRAPHY

Gadpaille, Warren. "Research into the Physiology of Maleness and Femaleness," *Archives of General Psychiatry, 1972,* Vol. 26, pp. 193–207.

Green, Maurice (ed.). *Interpersonal Psychoanalysis: Selected Papers of Clara M. Thompson.* New York: Basic Books, 1964.

"Femininity," Albert Ellis and Albert Abarnel, eds. *The Encyclopedia of Sexual Behavior* (New York: Hawthorne Books,1961).

Moulton, Ruth. "A Survey and Re-evaluation of the Concept of Penis Envy," *Contemporary Psychoanalysis,* 7, 1970, pp. 84–104.

———. "Sexual Conflicts of Contemporary Women," *Interpersonal Explorations in Psychoanalysis.* Earl Witenberg, ed., New York: Basic Books, 1973.

Symonds, Alexandra. "Phobias after Marriage," *Journal of the American Psychoanalytic Association,* November 1971, p. 31.

Thompson, Clara M. "The Role of Women in This Culture," *Psychiatry,* Vol. 4, pp. 1–8, 1941.

*Foreword to Clara Thompson, *On Women,* ed. by Maurice R. Green (New York: New American Library, 1971).

_____. "Cultural Pressures in the Psychology of Women," *Psychiatry*, Vol. 5, pp. 331–339, 1942.

_____. "Penis Envy in Woman," *Psychiatry*, Vol. 6, pp. 123–125, 1943.

_____. "Some Effects of the Derogatory Attitude toward Female Sexuality," *Psychiatry*, Vol. 13, pp. 349–354, 1950.

_____. "Cultural Complications in the Sexual Life of Women," *Symposium on Feminine Psychology*, March 18–19, 1950, p. 54. Department of Psychiatry, Psychoanalytic Division, New York Medical College-Flower and Fifth Avenue Hospitals, 1950.

_____. *Psychoanalysis: Evolution and Development* (with Patrick Mullahy). New York: Hermitage House, 1950.

_____. *On Women.* New York: New American Library, Mentor Book, 1971.

Erikson on Erikson

Womanhood and the Inner Space (1968)

Erik H. Erikson

1.

There are a great number of economic and practical reasons for an intensified awareness of woman's position in the modern world. But there are also more elusive and darker reasons. The ubiquity of nuclear threat, the breakthrough into outer space, and increasing global communication are all bringing about a total change in the sense of geographic space and historical time, and thus they necessitate nothing less than a redefinition of the identity of the sexes within a new image of man. I cannot here go into the alliances and oppositions of the sexes in previous styles of war and peace. This is a history as yet to be written and, indeed, discovered. But it is clear that the danger of manmade poison dropping invisibly from outer space into the marrow of the unborn in the wombs of women has suddenly brought one major male preoccupation, namely, the "solution" of conflict by periodical and bigger and better wars, to its own limits. The question arises whether such a potential for annihilation as now exists in the world should continue to exist without the representation of the mothers of the species in the councils of image-making and decision.

The special dangers of the nuclear age clearly have brought male leadership close to the limit of its adaptive imagination. The dominant male identity is based on a fondness for "what works" and for what man can make, whether it helps to build or to destroy. For this very reason the

291

all too obvious necessity to sacrifice some of the possible climaxes of technological triumph and of political hegemony for the sake of the mere preservation of mankind is not itself an endeavor enhancing the male sense of identity. True, an American president felt impelled to say, and said with deep feeling: "A child is not a statistic"; yet the almost desperate urgency of his pleas made clear enough the need for a new kind of political and technological ethics. Maybe if women would only gain the determination to represent publicly what they have always stood for privately in evolution and in history (realism of householding, responsibility of upbringing, resourcefulness in peacekeeping, and devotion to healing), they might well add an ethically restraining, because truly supranational, power to politics in the widest sense.

This, I think, many men and women hope openly and many more, secretly. But their hope collides with dominant trends in our technological civilization and with deep inner resistances as well. Self-made man, in "granting" a relative emancipation to women, could offer only his self-made image as a model to be equaled, and much of the freedom thus won by women now seems to have been spent in gaining access to limited career competition, standardized consumership, and strenuous one-family homemaking. Thus woman, in many ways, has kept her place within the typologies and cosmologies which men have had the exclusive opportunity to cultivate and to idolize. In other words, even where equality is closer to realization it has not led to equivalence, and equal rights have by no means secured equal representation in the sense that the deepest concerns of women find expression in their public influence or, indeed, their actual role in the game of power. In view of the gigantic one-sidedness which is threatening to make man the slave of his triumphant technology, the now fashionable discussion, by women and by men, as to whether woman could and how she might become "fully human" is really a cosmic parody, and, for once, one is nostalgic for gods with a sense of humor. The very question as to what it is to be "fully human" and who has the right to grant it to whom indicates that a discussion of the male and female elements in the potentialities of human nature must include rather fundamental issues.

In approaching them, therefore, one cannot avoid exploring certain emotional reactions or resistances which hinder concerted discussion. We all have observed the fact that it seems almost impossible to discuss woman's nature or nurture without awaking the slogans for and against the all-too-recent emancipation. Moralistic fervor outlives changed conditions and feminist suspicion watches over any man's attempt to help define the uniqueness of womanhood, as though by uniqueness he could be expected to mean inborn inequality. Yet it still seems to be amazingly hard for many women to say clearly what they feel most deeply, and to find the right words for what to them is most acute and actual, without saying too much or too little and without saying it with defiance or apology. Some women who observe and think vividly and deeply do not seem to have the courage of their native intelligence, as if they were somehow afraid on some final confrontation to be found to have no "real" intelligence. Even successful academic competition has, in many, failed to correct this. Thus women are still tempted quickly to go back to "their place" whenever they feel out of place. A major problem also seems to exist in the relationship of leading women to each other and to their women followers. As far as I can judge, "leading" women are all too often inclined to lead in too volatile, moralistic, or sharp a manner (as if they agreed to the proposition that only exceptional and hard women can think) rather than to inform themselves of and give voice to what the mass of undecided women are groping to say and are willing to stand by, and thus what use they may wish to make of an equal voice in world affairs.

On the other hand, the hesitance of many men to respond responsibly to the new "feminist" alarm, and the agitated response of others, suggests explanations on many levels. No doubt there exists among men an honest sense of wishing to save, at whatever cost, a sexual polarity, a vital tension, and an essential difference which they fear may be lost in too much sameness, equality, and equivalence, or at any rate in too much self-conscious talk. Beyond this, the defensiveness of men (and here we must include the best educated) has many facets. Where men desire, they want to awake desire, not empathize or ask for empathy. Where they do not desire, they find it hard to empathize, especially where empathy makes it necessary to see the other in oneself and oneself in the other, and where therefore the horror of diffused delineations is apt to kill both joy in otherness and sympathy for sameness. It also stands to reason that where dominant identities depend on being dominant it is hard to grant real equality to the dominated. And, finally, where one feels exposed, threatened, or cornered, it is difficult to be judicious.

For all of this there are age-old psychological reasons. There appear to be themes of such strangeness that rational men will ignore them, preferring to take off on some tangent. Among these themes, the physiological changes and the emotional challenges of that everyday miracle, pregnancy and childbirth, have disquieted every man through childhood, youth, and beyond. In his accounts of cultures and historical periods, man acknowledges this merely as a probably necessary side show. He habitually ascribes man's survival to the proud coherence of the schemes of men, not remembering the fact that while each scheme was tested and many exploded, women met the challenge of keeping some essentials together, of rebuilding, and of bringing up rebuilders. A new balance of Male and Female, of Paternal and Maternal is obviously presaged not only in contemporary changes in the relation of the sexes to each other but also in the wider awareness which spreads wherever science, technology, and genuine self-scrutiny advance. Yet discussion in the present climate still calls for an acknowledgement from the onset that ambivalences and ambiguities of ancient standing are apt to be temporarily aggravated rather than alleviated by attempts to share partial insight in these matters.

2.

There is another general consideration which must precede the discussion of a subject which is so incompletely formulated and which always retains an intense actuality. Every worker will and must begin where he stands, that is, where he feels his own field and his own work have succeeded in clarifying, failed to do justice to, the issue as he has come to see it. But whenever he begins he is apt to be confronted with the remark which a Vermont farmer made to a driver who asked him for directions: "Well, now, if I wanted to go where you want to go, I wouldn't start from here."

Here is where I am, and where I must start from. In my preface to the book which grew out of the Youth issue of *Daedalus*,[1] I pointed out that that extraordinary symposium failed to develop fully—although Bruno Bettelheim made a determined start—the problem of the identity of female youth. This I felt was a severe theoretical handicap. For the student of development and practitioner of psychoanalysis knows that the stage of life crucial for the emergence of an integrated female identity is the step from youth to maturity, the state when the young woman, whatever her work career, relinquishes the care received from the parental

294

family in order to commit herself to the love of a stranger and to the care to be given to his and her offspring.

I have suggested that the mental and emotional ability to receive and give fidelity marks the conclusion of adolescence, while adulthood begins with the ability to receive and give love and care. For the strength of the generations (and by this I mean a basic disposition underlying all varieties of human value systems) depends on the process by which the youths of the two sexes find their individual identities, fuse them in intimacy, love, and marriage, revitalize their respective traditions, and together create and "bring up" the next generation. Here whatever sexual differences and dispositions have developed in earlier life become polarized with finality because they must become part of the whole process of production and procreation which marks adulthood. But how does the identity formation of women differ by dint of the fact that their somatic design harbors an "inner space" destined to bear the offspring of chosen men and, with it, a biological, psychological, and ethical commitment to take care of human infancy? Is not the disposition for this commitment (whether it be combined with a career, and even whether or not it be realized in actual motherhood) the core problem of female fidelity?

The psychoanalytic psychology of women, however, does not "start here." In line with its originological orientation, i.e., the endeavor to infer the meaning of an issue from its origins, it begins with the earliest experiences of differentiation, largely reconstructed from women patients necessarily at odds with their womanhood and with the permanent inequality to which it seemed to doom them. However, since the psychoanalytic method could be developed only in work with acutely suffering individuals, whether adults or children, it was necessary to accept clinical observation as the original starting point for investigating what the little girl, when becoming aware of sex differences, can know as observable fact, can investigate by sight or touch, can feel as intense pleasure or unpleasant tension, or may infer or intuit with the cognitive and imaginative means at her disposal. I think it is fair to say that the psychoanalytic view of womanhood has been strongly influenced by the fact that the first and basic observations were made by clinicians whose task it was to understand suffering and to offer a remedy, and that by necessity they had to understand the female psyche with male means of empathy and to offer what the ethos of enlightenment dictated, namely, the "acceptance of reality." It is in line with this historical position that they saw, in the reconstructed lives of little girls, primarily an attempt to observe what could be seen and grasped (namely, what was there in boys and hardly there in girls) and to base on this observation "infantile sexual theories" of vast consequence.

From this point of view, the most obvious fact, namely, that children of both sexes sooner or later "know" the penis to be missing in one sex, leaving in its place a woundlike aperture, has led to generalizations concerning women's nature and nurture. From an adaptive point of view, however, it does not seem reasonable to assume that observation and empathy, except in moments of acute or transitory disturbance, would so exclusively focus on what is not there. The female child under all but extreme urban conditions is disposed to observe evidence in older girls and women and in female animals of the fact that an inner-bodily space —with productive as well as dangerous potentials—does exist. Here one thinks not only of pregnancy and childbirth, but also of lactation and all the richly convex parts of the female anatomy which suggest fullness, warmth, and generosity. One wonders, for example, whether girls are quite as upset by observed symptoms of pregnancy or menstruation as are (certain) boys, or whether they absorb such observation in the rudiments of a female identity—unless, of course, they are "protected" from the opportunity of comprehending the ubiquity and the meaning of these natural phenomena. Now no doubt at various stages of childhood observed data will be interpreted with the cognitive means then available, will be perceived in analogy with the organs then most intensely experienced, and will be endowed with the impulses then prevailing. Dreams, myths, and cults attest to the fact that the vagina has and retains (for both sexes) connotations of a devouring mouth and an eliminating sphincter, in addition to being a bleeding wound. However, the cumulative experience of being and becoming a man or a woman cannot, I believe, be entirely dependent upon fearful analogies and fantasies. Sensory reality and logical conclusion are given form by kinesthetic experience and by series of memories which "make sense," and in this total setting the existence of a productive inner-bodily space safely set in the center of female form and carriage has, I would think, greater actuality than has the missing external organ.

If I, then, take my start from here, it is because I believe that a future formulation of sex differences must at least include post-Freudian insights in order not to succumb to the repressions and denials of pre-Freudian days.

3.

Let me present here an observation which makes my point wordlessly, through the observation of children at play. The children were California boys and girls, aged ten, eleven, and twelve years, who twice a year came to be measured, interviewed, and tested in the "Guidance Study" of the University of California. It speaks for the feminine genius of the director of the study, Jean Walker Macfarlane, that for more than two decades the children (and their parents) not only came with regularity, but confided their thoughts with little reservation and, in fact, with much "zest"—to use Jean Macfarlane's favorite word. That means they were confident of being appreciated as growing individuals and eager to reveal and demonstrate what (they had been convincingly told) was useful to know and might be helpful to others. Since before joining the California study I had made it my business to interpret play behavior—a nonverbal approach which had helped me to understand what my very small patients were not able to communicate in words—it was decided that I would secure a number of play constructions from each child and then compare their form and context with other available data. Over a span of two years, I saw 150 boys and 150 girls three times and presented them, one at a time, with the task of constructing a "scene" with toys on a table. The toys were rather ordinary—a family, some uniformed figures (policeman, aviator, Indian, monk, etc.), wild and domestic animals, furniture, automobiles—but I also provided a large number of blocks. The children were asked to imagine that the table was a moving-picture studio; the toys, actors and props; and they themselves, moving-picture directors. They were to arrange on the table "an exciting scene from an imaginary moving picture," and then tell the plot. This was recorded, the scene photographed, and the child complimented. It may be necessary to add that no "interpretation" was given.[2]

The observer then compared the individual constructions with about ten years of biographic data to see whether it provided some key to the major determinants of the child's inner development. On the whole this proved helpful, but that is not the point to be made here. The experiment also made possible a comparison of all play constructions with one another.

A few of the children went about the task with the somewhat contemptuous attitude of one doing something which was not exactly worth the effort of a young person already in his teens, but almost all of these bright and willing youngsters in somber jeans and gay dresses where drawn to the challenge by that eagerness to serve and please which characterized the whole population of the study. And once they were involved, certain properties of the task took over and guided them.

It soon became evident that among these properties the spatial one was dominant. Only half of the scenes were "exciting," and only a handful had anything to do with moving pictures. In fact, the stories told at the end were for the most part brief and in no way comparable to the thematic richness evidenced in verbal tests. But the care and (one is tempted to say) esthetic responsibility with which the children selected blocks and toys and then arranged them according to an apparently deeply held sense of spatial propriety was astounding. At the end, it seemed to be a sudden feeling of "now it's right" which made them come to a sense of completion and, as if awakening from a wordless experience, turn to me and say, "I am ready now"—meaning, I am ready to tell you what this is all about.

I myself was most interested in observing not only imaginative themes but also spatial configurations in relation to stages of the life cycle in general and to the forms of neurotic tension in prepuberty in particular. Sex differences thus were not the initial focus of my interest. I concentrated my attention on how the constructions-in-progress moved forward to the edge of the table or back to the wall behind it; how they rose to shaky heights or remained close to the table surface; how they were spread over the available space or constricted to a portion of that space. That all of this "says" something about the constructor is the open secret of all "projective techniques." This, too, cannot be discussed here. But soon I realized that in evaluating a child's play construction, I had to take into consideration the fact that girls and boys used space differently, and that certain configurations occurred strikingly often in the constructions of one sex and rarely in those of the other.

The differences themselves were so simple that at first they seemed a matter of course. History in the meantime has offered a slogan for it: the girls emphasized *inner* and the boys *outer* space.

298

This difference I was soon able to state in such simple configurational terms that other observers, when shown photographs of the constructions without knowing the sex of the constructor (nor, indeed, having any idea of my thoughts concerning the possible meaning of the differences), could sort the photographs according to the configurations most dominant in them, and this significantly in the statistical sense. These independent ratings showed that considerably more than two thirds of what I subsequently called the male configurations occurred in scenes constructed by boys, and more than two thirds of the "female" configurations in the constructions of girls. (I will here omit the finer points which still characterized the atypical scenes as clearly built by a boy or by a girl.) This, then, is typical: the girl's scene is a house *interior,* represented either as a configuration of furniture without any surrounding walls or by a simple *enclosure* built with blocks. In the girl's scene, people and animals are mostly *within* such an interior or enclosure, and they are primarily people or animals in a *static* (sitting or standing) position. Girls' enclosures consist of low walls, i.e., only one block high, except for an occasional *elaborate doorway.* These interiors of houses with or without walls were, for the most part, expressly *peaceful.* Often, a little girl was playing the piano. In a number of cases, however, the interior was *intruded* by animals or dangerous men. Yet the idea of an intruding creature did not necessarily lead to the defensive erection of walls or the closing of doors. Rather the majority of these intrusions have an element of humor and pleasurable excitement.

Boys' scenes are either houses with elaborate walls or façades with *protrusions* such as cones or cylinders representing ornaments or cannons. There are *high towers,* and there are entirely *exterior* scenes. In boys' constructions more people and animals are *outside* enclosures or buildings, and there are more *automotive* objects and animals *moving* along streets and intersections. There are elaborate automotive *accidents,* but there is also traffic channeled or arrested by the policeman. While *high structures* are prevalent in the configurations of the boys, there is also much play with the danger of *collapse* or downfall; *ruins* were exclusively boys' constructions.

The male and female spaces, then, were dominated, respectively, by height and downfall and by strong motion and its channeling or arrest; and by static interiors which were open or simply enclosed, and peaceful or intruded upon. It may come as a surprise to some and seem a matter

299

of course to others that here sexual differences in the organization of a play space seem to parallel the morphology of genital differentiation itself: in the male, an external organ, erectable and intrusive in character, serving the channelization of mobile sperm cells; in the female, internal organs, with vestibular access, leading to statically expectant ova. The question is: what is really surprising about this, and what only too obvious, and in either case, what does it tell us about the two sexes?

4.

Since I first presented these data a decade and a half ago to workers in different fields, some standard interpretations have not yielded an iota. There are, of course, derisive reactions which take it for granted that a psychoanalyst would want to read the bad old symbols into this kind of data. And indeed, Freud did note more than half a century ago that "a house is the only regularly occurring symbol of the (whole) human body in dreams." But there is quite a methodological step from the occurrence of a symbol in dreams and a configuration created in actual space. Nevertheless, the purely psychoanalytic or somatic explanation has been advanced that the scenes reflect the preadolescent's preoccupation with his own sexual organs.

The purely "social" interpretation, on the other hand, denies the necessity to see anything symbolic or, indeed, somatic in these configurations. It takes it for granted that boys love the outdoors and girls the indoors, or at any rate that they see their respective roles assigned to the indoors of houses and to the great outdoors of adventure, to tranquil feminine love for family and children and to high masculine aspiration.

One cannot help agreeing with both interpretations—up to a point. Of course, whatever social role is associated with one's physique will be expressed thematically in any playful or artistic representation. And, of course, under conditions of special tension or preoccupation with one part of the body, that part may be recognizable in play configurations: play therapy relies on that. The spokesmen for the anatomical and for the social interpretations are thus both right if they insist that neither possibility may be ignored. But this does not make either exclusively right.

A pure interpretation in terms of social role leaves many questions unanswered. If the boys thought primarily of their present or anticipated roles, why, for example, is the policeman their favorite toy, traffic stopped

300

dead a frequent scene? If vigorous activity outdoors is a determinant of the boys' scenes, why did they not arrange any sports fields on the play table? (One tomboyish girl did.) Why did the girls' love for home life not result in an increase in high walls and closed doors as guarantors of intimacy and security? And could the role of playing the piano in the bosom of their families really be considered representative of what these girls (some of them passionate horseback riders and all future automobile drivers) wanted to do most or, indeed, thought they should pretend they wanted to do most? Thus the boys' caution outdoors and the girls' goodness indoors in response to the explicit instruction to construct an exciting movie scene suggested dynamic dimensions and acute conflicts not explained by a theory of mere compliance with cultural and conscious roles.

I would suggest an altogether more inclusive interpretation, according to which a profound difference exists between the sexes in the experience of the ground plan of the human body. The emphasis here is on predisposition and predilection, rather than on exclusive ability, for both sexes (if otherwise matched in maturation and intelligence) learn readily to imitate the spatial mode of the other sex. Nothing in our interpretation, then, is meant to claim that either sex is doomed to one spatial mode or another; rather, it is suggested that in contexts which are not imitative or competitive these modes "come more naturally" for natural reasons which must claim our interest. The spatial phenomenon observed here would then express two principles of arranging space which correspond to the male and female principles in body construction. These may receive special emphasis in prepuberty, and maybe in some other stages of life as well, but they are relevant through life to the elaboration of sex roles in cultural space-times. Such an interpretation cannot be "proven," of course, by the one observation offered here. The question is whether it is in line with observations of spatial behavior in other media and at other ages; whether it can be made a plausible part of a developmental theory; and whether, indeed, it gives to other sex differences closely related to male and female structure and function a more convincing order. On the other hand, it would not be contradicted by the fact that other media of observation employed to test male and female performance might reveal few or no sexual differences in areas of the mind which have the function of securing verbal or cognitive agreement on matters dominated by the mathematical nature of the universe and the verbal agreement of cultural

301

traditions. Such agreement, in fact, may have as its very function the correction of what differentiates the experience of the sexes, even as it also corrects the intuitive judgments separating other classes of men.

The play-constructing children in Berkeley, California, will lead us into a number of spatial considerations, especially concerning feminine development and outlook. Here I will say little about men; their accomplishments in the conquest of geographic space and of scientific fields and in the dissemination of ideas speak loudly for themselves and confirm traditional values of masculinity. Yet the play-constructing boys in Berkeley may give us pause: on the world scene, do we not see a supremely gifted yet somewhat boyish mankind playing excitedly with history and technology, following a male pattern as embarrassingly simple (if technologically complex) as the play constructions of the preadolescent? Do we not see the themes of the toy microcosm dominating an expanding human space: height, penetration, and speed; collision, explosion—and cosmic superpolice? In the meantime, women have found their identities in the care suggested in their bodies and in the needs of their issue, and seem to have taken it for granted that the outer world space belongs to the men.

5.

Before going on from here, I must retrace my steps to my earlier statement that the observations reported "while not expected seemed to confirm something long awaited." They served to clarify many doubts mentioned earlier regarding psychoanalytic theories of femininity. Many of the original conclusions of psychoanalysis concerning womanhood hinge on the so-called genital trauma, i.e., the little girl's sudden comprehension of the fact that she does not and never will have a penis. The assumed prevalence of envy in women; the assumption that the future baby is a substitute for the penis; the assumption that the girl turns from the mother to the father because she finds that the mother not only cheated her out of a penis but has been cheated herself; and finally the woman's disposition to abandon (male) aggressiveness for the sake of a "passive-masochistic" orientation: all these depend on "the trauma," and all have been built into elaborate explanations of femininity. They all exist somewhere in all women and their existence has been shown over and over again in psychoanalyses. But it must always be suspected that a special method bares truths especially true under the circumstances created by the method, here the venting in free association of hidden resentments and repressed traumata. These same truths assume the character of very partial truths within a normative theory of feminine development in which they would appear to be subordinate to the early dominance of the productive interior. This would allow, then, for a shift of theoretical emphasis from the loss of an external organ to a sense of vital inner potential; from a hateful contempt for the mother to a solidarity with her and other women; from a "passive" renunciation of male activity to the purposeful and competent pursuit of activities consonant with the possession of ovaries, a uterus, and a vagina; and from a masochisic pleasure in pain to an ability to stand (and to understand) pain as a meaningful aspect of human experience in general and of the feminine role in particular. And so it is in the "fully feminine" woman, as such outstanding writers as Helene Deutsch have recognized, even though their nomenclature was tied to the psychopathological term "masochism"—a word significantly derived from the name of an Austrian man and novelist who described the perversion of being sexually aroused and satisfied by having pain inflicted on him (even as the tendency to inflict it has been named after the Marquis de Sade).

When this is seen, many now dispersed data fall into line. However, a clinician must ask himself in passing what kind of thinking may have permitted such a nomenclature and such a theory of development and their acceptance by outstanding women clinicians. This thinking is, I believe, to be traced not only to the psychiatric beginnings of psychoanalysis, but also to the original analytic-atomistic method employed by it. In science, our capacity to think atomistically corresponds to the nature of matter to a high degree and thus leads to the mastery over matter. But when we apply atomistic thinking to man, we break him down into isolated fragments rather than into constituent elements. In fact, when we look at man in the state of pathology, he is already fragmented, so that in psychiatry an atomizing mind may meet a phenomenon of fragmentation and mistake the fragments for atoms. In psychoanalysis we repeat for our own encouragement (and as an argument against others) that human nature can best be studied in a state of partial breakdown or, at any rate, of marked conflict because—so we say—a conflict delineates borderlines and clarifies the forces which collide on these borderlines. As Freud himself put it, we see a crystal's structure only when it cracks. But a crystal, on the one hand, and an organism or a personality, on the other, differ in the fact that one is inanimate and the other an organic whole which cannot be broken up without a withering of the parts. The ego, in the psychoanalytic sense of a guardian of inner continuity, insofar as it is in a pathological state is more or less inactivated; that is, it loses its capacity to organize personality and experience and to relate itself to other egos in mutual activation. To that extent its irrational defenses are "easier to study" in a state of conflict and isolation than is the ego of a person in vivid interaction with other persons. Yet I do not believe that we can entirely reconstruct the ego's normal functions from an understanding of its dysfunctions, nor that we can understand all vital conflict as neurotic conflict.

This, then, would characterize a post-Freudian position: the complexes and conflicts unearthed by psychoanalysis in its first breakthrough to human nature are recognized as existing; they do threaten to dominate the developmental and accidental crises of life. But the freshness and wholeness of experience and the opportunities arising with a resolved crisis can, in an ongoing life, transcend trauma and defense. To illustrate this, let me briefly remark on the often repeated statement that the little girl at a given stage "turns to" her father, whereas in all preceding stages she had been primarily attached to her mother. Actually, Freud insisted only that a theoretical "libido" was thus turning from one "object" to another, a theory which was, at one time, scientifically pleasing because it corresponded to a simple and (in principle) measurable transfer of energy. Developmentally seen, however, the girl turns to her father at a time when she is quite a different person from the one she was when primarily dependent on her mother. She has normally learned the nature of an "object relationship," once and for all, from her mother. The relationship to her father, then, is of a different kind, in that it becomes particularly significant when the girl has already learned to trust her mother and does not need to retest basic relationships. She now can develop a new form of love for a being who in turn is, or should be, ready to be responsive to the budding and teasing woman in her. The total process thus has many more aspects than can be condensed in the statement that the girl turns her libido from her mother to her father. Such transfer can, in fact, be reconstructed as an isolated "mechanism" only where the ego has been inactivated in some of its capacity to reorganize experience in line with emotional, physical, and cognitive maturation;

and only then can it be said that the girl turns to her father because she is disappointed in her mother over what her mother has seemingly refused to give her, namely, a penis. Now, no doubt, some old disappointments and new expectations play an eminent role in all changes of attachment from an old to a new person or activity, but in any healthy change the fresh opportunities of the new relationship will outweigh the repetitious insistence on old disappointments. No doubt, also, new attachments prepare new disappointments, for the inner-productive role which we assume exists early in rudimentary form will cause in the small woman such fantasies as must succumb to repression and frustration—for example, in the insight that no daughter may give birth to her father's children. No doubt also the very existence of the inner productive space exposes women early to a specific sense of loneliness, to a fear of being left empty or deprived of treasures, of remaining unfulfilled and of drying up. This, no less than the strivings and disappointments of the little "Electra," has fateful consequences for the human individual and for the whole race. For this very reason it seems decisive not to misinterpret these feelings as totally due to a resentment of not being a boy or of having been mutilated.

It will now be clear in what way the children's play constructions were unexpected and yet awaited. What was unexpected was the domination of the whole space by the sex differences—a "field" dominance going far beyond the power of any symbolic representation of the sex organs. The data were "awaited," above all, as nonclinical and nonverbal support of pervasive impressions concerning the importance of the "inner space" throughout the feminine life cycle. The life histories of the girls in the Guidance Study did not make sense without such an assumption, but neither did the case histories of women patients of all ages. For, as pointed out, clinical observation suggests that in female experience an "inner space" is at the center of despair even as it is the very center of potential fulfillment. Emptiness is the female form of perdition—known at times to men of the inner life (whom we will discuss later), but standard experience for all women. To be left, for her, means to be left empty, to be drained of the blood of the body, the warmth of the heart, the sap of life. How a woman thus can be hurt in depth is a wonder to many a man, and it can arouse both his empathic horror and his refusal to understand. Such hurt can be re-experienced in each menstruation; it is a crying to heaven in the mourning over a child; and it becomes a permanent scar

305

in the menopause. Clinically, this "void" is so obvious that generations of clinicians must have had a special reason for not focusing on it. Maybe, even as primitive men banned it with phobic avoidances and magic rituals of purification, the enlightened men of a civilization pervaded by technological pride could meet it only with the interpretation that suffering woman wanted above all what man had, namely, exterior equipment and traditional access to "outer" space. Again, such female envy exists in all women and is aggravated in some cultures; but the explanation of it in male terms or the suggestion that it be borne with fatalism and compensated for by a redoubled enjoyment of the feminine equipment (duly certified and accepted as second rate) has not helped women to find their places in the modern world, for it has made of womanhood an ubiquitous compensation neurosis marked by a bitter insistence on being "restored."

I will generalize, then, in two directions. I submit that in psychoanalysis we have not ascribed due importance to the procreative patterns intrinsic to sexual morphology, and I will try to formulate the assumption that procreative patterns, in varying intensity, pervade every state of excitement and inspiration and, *if integrated,* lend power to all experience and to its communication.

In assigning a central place to generative modalities I, too, seem to repeat the often obsessive emphasis on sexual symbols in psychoanalytic theory and to ignore the fact that women as well as men have all-human organisms fit for, and most of the time enjoyed in, activities far removed from the sexual. But while both sexual repression and sexual monomania *isolate* sexuality from the total design of human actuality, we must be interested in how sex differences, once taken for granted, are *integrated* in that design. Sexual differences, however, besides offering a polarization of life styles and the maximization of mutual enjoyment (which now more than ever can be separated from procreation) nevertheless retain the morphology of procreation. It would even seem that such unashamed explorations of the inner space as those now medically conducted into human sexual response in St. Louis reveal a vigorous involvement of the procreative organs in the excitement of every kind of sexual act.

306

6.

If the "inner space" is so pervasive a configuration, it should be found to have its place in the evolutionary beginnings of social organization. Here, too, we can call on visual data.

Recent motion pictures taken in Africa by Washburn and deVore[3] demonstrate vividly the morphology of basic baboon organization. The whole wandering troop in search of food over a certain territory is so organized as to keep within a safe inner space the females who bear future offspring within their bodies or carry their growing young. They are protectively surrounded by powerful males who, in turn, keep their eyes on the horizon, guiding the troop toward available food and guarding it from potential danger. In peacetime the strong males also protect the "inner circle" of pregnant and nursing females against the encroachments of the relatively weaker and definitely more importunate males. Once danger is spotted, the whole wandering configuration stops and consolidates into an inner space of safety and an outer space of combat. In the center sit the pregnant females and mothers with their newborns. At the periphery are the males best equipped to fight or scare off predators.

I was impressed with these movies not only for their beauty and ingenuity, but because here I could see in the bush configurations analogous to those in the Berkeley play constructions. The baboon pictures, however, can lead us one step further. Whatever the morphological differences between the female and the male baboons' bony structures, postures, and behaviors, they are adapted to their respective tasks of harboring and defending the concentric circles, from the procreative womb to the limits of the defensible territory. Thus morphological trends "fit" given necessities and are therefore elaborated by basic social organization. And it deserves emphasis that even among the baboons the greatest warriors display a chivalry which permits the female baboons, for example, to have weaker shoulders and lesser fighting equipment. In both prehuman and human existence, then, the formula holds that whether, when, and in what respects a female anywhere can be said to be "weaker" is a matter to be decided not on the basis of comparative tests of isolated muscles, capacities, or traits but on that of the functional fitness of each item for an organism which, in turn, fits into an ecology of divided function.

Human society and technology has, of course, transcended evolutionary arrangement, making room for cultural triumphs of adaptation as well as for physical and mental maladaptation on a large scale. But when we speak of biologically given strengths and weaknesses in the human female, we may yet have to accept as one measure of all difference the biological rock-bottom of sexual differentiation. In this, the woman's productive inner space may well remain an inescapable criterion, whether conditions permit her to build her life partially or wholly around it or not. At any rate, many of the testable items on the long list of "inborn" differences between human males and females can be shown to have a meaningful function within an ecology which is built, as any mammalian ecology must be, around the fact that the human fetus must be carried inside the womb for a given number of months, and that the infant must be suckled or, at any rate, raised within a maternal world best staffed at first by the mother (and this for the sake of her own awakened motherliness, as well) with a gradual addition of other women. Here years of specialized womanhours of work are involved. It makes sense, then, that the little girl, the future bearer of ova and of maternal powers, tends to survive her birth more surely and turns out to be a tougher creature, to be plagued, to be sure, by many small ailments, but more resistant to some man-killing diseases (for example, of the heart) and with a longer life expectancy. It also makes sense that she is able earlier than boys to concentrate on details immediate in time and space, and has throughout a finer discrimination for things seen, touched, and heard. To these she reacts more vividly, more personally, and with greater compassion. More easily touched and touchable, however, she is said also to recover faster, ready to react again and elsewhere. That all of this is essential to the "biological" task of reacting to the differential needs of others, especially weaker ones, is not an unreasonable interpretation; nor should it, in this context, seem a deplorable inequality that in the employment of larger muscles woman shows less vigor, speed, and co-ordination. The little girl also learns to be more easily content within a limited circle of activities and shows less resistance to control and less impulsiveness of the kind that later leads boys and men to "delinquency." All of these and more certified "differences" could be shown to have corollaries in our play constructions.

Now it is clear that much of the basic schema suggested here as female also exists in some form in all men and decisively so in men of special giftedness—or weakness. The inner life which characterizes some artistic and creative men certainly also compensates for their being biologically men by helping them to specialize in that inwardness and sensitive indwelling (the German *Innigkeit*) usually ascribed to women. They are prone to cyclic swings of mood while they carry conceived ideas to fruition and toward the act of disciplined creation. The point is that in women the basic schema exists within an over-all optimum configuration such as cultures have every reason to nurture in the *majority of women,* for the sake of collective survival as well as individual fulfillment. It makes little sense, then, when discussing basic sex differences to quote the deviations and accomplishments (or both) of exceptional men or women without an inclusive account of their many-sided personalities, their special conflicts, and their complex life histories. On the other hand, one should also emphasize (and especially so in a post-Puritan civilization which continues to decree predestination by mercilessly typing individuals) that successive stages of life offer growing and maturing individuals ample leeway for free variation in essential sameness.

For example, woman's life too contains an adolescent stage which I have come to call a psychosocial moratorium, a sanctioned period of delay of adult functioning. The maturing girl and the young woman, in contrast to the little girl and the mature woman, can thus be relatively freer from the tyranny of the inner space. In fact, she may venture into "outer space" with a bearing and a curiosity which often appears hermaphroditic if not outright "masculine." A special ambulatory dimension is thus added to the inventory of her spatial behavior, which many societies counteract with special rules of virginal restraint. Where the mores permit, however, the young girl tries out a variety of possible identifications with the phallic-ambulatory male even as she experiments with the experience of being his counterpart and principal attraction—a seeming contradiction which will eventually be transformed into a polarity and a sexual and personal style. In all this, the inner space remains central to subjective experience but is overtly manifested only in persistent and selective attractiveness, for whether the young woman draws others to herself with magnetic inwardness, with challenging outwardness, or with a dramatic alternation of both, she selectively invites what seeks her.

Young women often ask whether they can "have an identity" before they know whom they will marry and for whom they will make a home. Granted that something in the young woman's identity must keep itself open for the peculiarities of the man to be joined and of the children to be brought up, I think that much of a young woman's identity is already defined in her kind of attractiveness and in the selective nature of her search for the man (or men) by whom she wishes to be sought. This, of course, is only the psychosexual aspect of her identity, and she may go far in postponing its closure while training herself as a worker and a citizen and while developing as a person within the role possibilities of her time. The singular loveliness and brilliance which young women display in an array of activities obviously removed from the future function of childbearing is one of those esthetic phenomena which almost seem to transcend all goals and purposes and therefore come to symbolize the self-containment of pure being—wherefore young women, in the arts of the ages, have served as the visible representation of ideals and ideas and as the creative man's muse, anima, and enigma. One is somewhat reluctant, therefore, to assign an ulterior meaning to what seems so meaningful in itself, and to suggest that the inner space is tacitly present in it all. A true moratorium must have a term and a conclusion: womanhood arrives when attractiveness and experience have succeeded in selecting what is to be admitted to the welcome of the inner space "for keeps."

Thus only a total configurational approach—somatic, historical, individual—can help us to see the differences of functioning and experiencing in context, rather than in isolated and senseless comparison. Woman, then, is not "more passive" than man simply because her central biological function forces her or permits her to be active in a manner tuned to inner-bodily processes, or because she may be gifted with a certain intimacy and contained intensity of feeling, or because she may choose to dwell in the protected inner circle within which maternal care can flourish. Nor is she "more masochistic" because she must accept inner periodicities in addition to the pain of childbirth, which is explained in the Bible as the eternal penalty for Eve's delinquent behavior and interpreted by writers as recent as de Beauvoir as "a hostile element within her own body." Taken together with the phenomena of sexual life and motherhood, it is obvious that woman's knowledge of pain makes her a "dolorosa" in a deeper sense than one who is addicted to small pains. She is, rather, one who "takes pains" to understand and alleviate suffering and can train others in the forbearance necessary to stand unavoidable pain. She is a "masochist," then, only when she exploits pain perversely

310

or vindictively, which means that she steps out of, rather than deeper into, her female function. By the same token, a woman is pathologically passive only when she becomes too passive within a sphere of efficacy and personal integration which includes her disposition for female activity.

One argument, however, is hard to counter. Woman, through the ages (at any rate, the patriarchal ones), has lent herself to a variety of roles conducive to an exploitation of masochistic potentials: she has let herself be confined and immobilized, enslaved and infantilized, prostituted and exploited, deriving from it at best what in psychopathology we call "secondary gains" of devious dominance. This fact, however, could be satisfactorily explained only within a new kind of biocultural history which (and this is one of my main points) would first have to overcome the prejudiced opinion that woman must be, or will be, what she is or has been under particular historical conditions.

7.

Am I saying, then, that "anatomy is destiny"? Yes, it is destiny, insofar as it determines not only the range and configuration of physiological functioning and its limitation but also, to an extent, personality configurations. The basic modalities of woman's commitment and involvement naturally also reflect the ground plan of her body. I have in another context identified "inception" as a dominant modality already in the early lives and in the play of children.[4] We may mention in passing woman's capacity on many levels of existence to actively *include*, to accept, *"to have and to hold"*—but also to *hold on,* and *hold in.* She may be protective with high selectivity and overprotective without discrimination. That she must protect means that she must rely on protection—and she may demand overprotection. To be sure, she also has an organ of intrusion, the nipple which nurses, and her wish to succor can, indeed, become intrusive and oppressive. It is, in fact, of such exaggerations and deviations that many men—and also women—think when the unique potentials of womanhood are discussed.

As pointed out, however, it makes little sense to ask whether in any of these respects a woman is "more so" than a man, but how much she varies within womanhood and what she makes of it within the leeway of her stage of life and of her historical and economic opportunities. So far I have only reiterated the physiological rock-bottom which must neither be

311

denied nor given exclusive emphasis. For a human being, in addition to having a body, is *somebody,* which means an indivisible personality and a defined member of a group. In this sense, Napoleon's dictum that history is destiny, which Freud, I believe, meant to counterpoint with his dictum that destiny lies in anatomy (and one often must know what dicta a man tried to counterpoint with *his* most one-sided dicta), is equally valid. In other words: anatomy, history, and personality are our combined destiny.

Men, of course, have shared and taken care of some of the concerns for which women stand: each sex can transcend itself to feel and to represent the concerns of the other. For even as real women harbor a legitimate as well as a compensatory masculinity, so real men can partake of motherliness—if permitted to do so by powerful mores.

In search of an observation which bridges biology and history, an extreme historical example comes to mind in which women elevated their procreative function to a style of life when their men seemed totally defeated.

This story was highlighted for me on two occasions when I participated in conferences in the Caribbean and learned of family patterns prevailing throughout the islands. Churchmen have had reason to deplore, and anthropologists to explore, the pattern of Caribbean family life, alternately interpreted as African or as an outgrowth of the slavery days of plantation America, which extended from the northeast coast of Brazil through the Caribbean half circle into the southeastern part of the present United States. Plantations, of course, were agricultural factories owned and operated by gentlemen whose cultural and economic identity had its roots in a supraregional upper class. They were worked by slaves, that is, by men who, being mere equipment, were put to use when and where necessary and who often had to relinquish all chance of becoming the masters of their families and communities. Thus the women were left with the offspring of a variety of men who could give neither provision nor protection, nor provide any identity except that of a subordinate species. The family system which ensued is described in the literature in terms of circumscriptions: the rendering of "sexual services" between persons who cannot be called anything more definite than "lovers"; "maximum instability" in the sexual lives of young girls, who often "relinquish" the care of their offspring to their mothers; and mothers and grandmothers who determine the "standardized mode of coactivity" which is the minimum requirement for calling a group of individuals a family. These are, then, the "household groups"—single dwellings occupied by people sharing a common food supply and administered "matrifocally"—a word which understates the grandiose role of the all-powerful grandmother-figure, who will encourage her daughters to leave their infants with her, or at any rate to stay with her as long as they continue to bear children. Motherhood thus became community life, and where churchmen could find little or no morality, and casual observers little or no tradition at all, the mothers and grandmothers had to become fathers and grandfathers in the sense that they exerted the only continuous influence resulting in an ever newly improvised set of rules for the economic obligations of the men who had fathered the children. They upheld the rules of incestuous avoidance. Above all, it seems to me, they provided the only superidentity which was left open after the enslavement of the men, namely, that of the worth of a human infant irrespective of his parentage.

It is well known how many little white gentlemen benefited from the extended fervor of the nurturant Negro woman—southern mammies, Creole *das,* or Brazilian *babas.* This phenomenal caring is, of course, being played down by the racists as mere servitude, while it is decried by moralists as African sensualism or idolized as true femininity by white refugees from "continental" womanhood. One may, however, see at the roots of this maternalism a grandiose gesture of human adaptation which has given the area of the Caribbean (now searching for a political and economic pattern to do justice to its cultural unity) both the promise of a positive maternal identity and the threat of a negative male one, for the fact that identity relied on the mere worth of being born has undoubtedly weakened economic aspiration in many men.

That this has been an important historical issue can be seen in the life of Simón Bolívar. This "liberator of South America" was born in the coastal region of Venezuela, which is one anchor point of the great Caribbean half circle. When, in 1827, Bolívar liberated Caracas and entered it in triumph, he recognized the Negro Hipolita, his erstwhile wetnurse, in the crowd. He dismounted and "threw himself in the arms of the Negro woman who wept with joy." Two years earlier, he had written to his sister: "I enclose a letter to my mother Hipolita so that you give her all she wants and deal with her as if she were my mother; her milk fed my life, and I knew no other father than she" (translation not mine).

313

Whatever personal reasons there were for Bolívar's effusiveness toward Hipolita (he had lost his mother when he was nine, etc.), the biographic importance of this item is amply matched by the historical significance of the fact that he could play up this relationship as a propaganda item within that peculiar ideology of race and origin which contributed to his charisma throughout the continent he liberated—from his ancestors.

That continent does not concern us here. But as for the Caribbean area, the matrifocal theme explains much of a certain disbalance between extreme trustfulness and weakness of initiative which could be exploited by native dictators as well as by foreign capital and has now become the concern of the erstwhile colonial masters as well as of the emancipated leaders of various island groups. Knowing this, we should understand that the bearded group of men and boys who have taken over one of the islands represents a deliberately new type of man who insists on proving that the Caribbean male can earn his worth in production as well as in procreation without the imposition of "continental" leadership or ownership.

This transformation of a colorful island area into an inner space structured by woman is an almost clinical example to be applied with caution. And yet it is only one story out of that unofficial history which is as yet to be written for all areas and eras: the history of territories and domains, markets and empires; the history of women's quiet creativity in preserving and restoring what official history had torn apart. Some stirrings in contemporary historiography, such as attempts to describe closely the everyday atmosphere of a given locality in a given historical era, seem to bespeak a growing awareness of a need for, shall we say, an integrated history.

There is a real question then, whether any one field can deliver the data on which to base valid assumptions regarding the differences between the sexes. We speak of anatomical, historical, and psychological facts, and yet it must be clear that facts reliably ascertained by the methods of one of these fields by the same token lose a most vital interconnection. Man is, at one and the same time, part of a somatic order of things as well as of a personal and a social one. To avoid identifying these orders with established fields, let me call them Soma, Psyche, and Polis, for at least they can serve attempts to designate new fields of inquiry such as the psychosomatic field already existing and the psycho-political one sure to appear.

314

Each order guards a certain intactness and also offers a leeway of optional or at least workable choices, while man lives in all three and must work out their mutual complementation and their "eternal" contradictions.

Soma is the principle of the organism living its life cycle. But the female Soma is not only comprised of what is within a woman's skin and the variety of appearances suggested by modish changes in her clothes; it includes a mediatorship in evolution, genetic as well as sociogenetic, by which she creates in each child the somatic (sensual and sensory) basis for his physical, cultural, and individual identity. This mission, once a child is conceived, must be completed. It is woman's unique job. But no woman lives or needs to live only in this extended somatic sphere. The modern world offers her ever-greater leeway in choosing, planning, or renouncing her somatic tasks more knowingly and responsibly. So she can and must make, or else neglect, decisions as a citizen and worker and, of course, as an individual.

In the sphere of Psyche, we have discussed the organizing principle called ego. It is in the ego that individualized experience has its organizing center, for the ego is the guardian of the indivisibility of the person. Ego organization mediates between somatic and personal experience and political actuality in the widest sense. To do so it uses psychological mechanisms common to both sexes—a fact which makes intelligent communication, mutual understanding, and social organization possible. Militant individualism and equalitarianism have inflated this core of individuality to the point where it seems altogether free of somatic and social differences. But it stands to reason that the active strength of the ego, and especially the identity within the individuality, needs and employs the power of somatic development and of social organization. Here, then, the fact that a woman, whatever else she may also be, never is not-a-woman creates unique relations between her individuality, her somatic existence, and her social potentials and demands that the feminine identity be studied and defined in its own right.

I call the sphere of citizenship Polis because I want to emphasize that it reaches to the borders of what one has recognized as one's "city." Modern communication makes such a communality ever larger—if not global. In this sphere women can be shown to share with men a close sameness of intellectual orientation and capacity for work and leadership. But in this sphere, too, the influence of women will not be fully actualized until it reflects without apology the facts of the "inner space" and the

315

potentialities and needs of the feminine psyche. It is as yet unpredictable what the tasks and roles, opportunities and job specifications will be once women are not merely adapted to male jobs in economics and politics but learn to adapt jobs to themselves. Such a revolutionary reappraisal may even lead to the insight that jobs now called masculine force men, too, into inhuman adjustments.

It should be clear, then, that I am using my definitions concerning the central importance of woman's procreative endowment not in a renewed male attempt to "doom" every woman to perpetual motherhood and to deny her the equivalence of individuality and the equality of citizenship. But since a woman is never not-a-woman, she can see her long-range goals only in those modes of activity which include and integrate her natural dispositions. A truly emancipated woman, I should think, would refuse to accept comparisons with more "active" male proclivities as a measure of her equivalence, even when, or precisely when, it has become quite clear that she can match man's performance and competence in most spheres of achievement. True equality can only mean the right to be uniquely creative.

Most verifiable sex differences (beyond those intrinsic to sexuality and procreation) establish for each sex only a range of attitudes and attributes which to most of its members "come naturally," that is, are predispositions, predilections, and inclinations. Many of these can, of course, be unlearned or relearned with more or less effort and special talent. This is not to be denied; with ever-increasing choices given her by the grace of technology and enlightenment, the question is only how much and which parts of her inborn inclinations the woman of tomorrow will feel it most natural to preserve and to cultivate—"natural" meaning that which can be integrated and made continuous in the three basic aspects mentioned.

As a body, then, woman passes through stages of life that are interlinked with the lives of those whose bodily existence is (increasingly so by her own choice) interdependent with hers. But as a worker, say, in a field structured by mathematical laws, woman is as responsible as any man for criteria of evidence that are intersexual or, better, suprasexual. As an individual person, finally, she utilizes her (biologically given) inclinations and her (technologically and politically given) opportunities to make the decisions that would seem to render her life most continuous and meaningful without failing the tasks of motherhood and citizenship.

316

The question is how these three areas of life reach into each other—certainly never without conflict and tension and yet with some continuity of purpose.

To consider, in conclusion, one of the frontiers of women's work: the nature of engineering and science, for example, is well removed from the workers' sex differences, even as also scientific training is more or less peripheral to the intimate tasks of womanhood and motherhood. I am reasonably sure that computers built by women would not betray a "female logic" (although I do not know how reasonable this reasonableness is, since women did not care to invent them in the first place); the logic of the computers is, for better or for worse, of a suprasexual kind. But what to ask and what not to ask the monsters, and when to trust or not to trust them with vital decisions—there, I would think, well-trained women might well contribute to a new kind of vision in the differential application of scientific thinking to humanitarian tasks.

But I would go further. Do we and can we really know what will happen to science or any other field if and when women are truly represented on it—not by a few glorious exceptions, but in the rank and file of the scientific elite? Is scientific inspiration really so impersonal and method-bound that personality plays no role in scientific creativity? And if we grant that a woman is never not a woman, even if she has become an excellent scientist and co-worker, and especially when she has grown beyond all special apologies or claims, then why deny so strenuously that there may also be areas in science (on the scientific periphery of some tasks, and maybe in the very core of others) where women's vision and creativity may yet lead, not to new laws of verification, but to new areas of inquiry and to new applications? Such a possibility, I suggest, could be affirmed or denied only if and when women are sufficiently represented in the sciences so that they may relax about the task and the role and apply themselves to the unknown.

My main point is that where the confinements are broken, women may yet be expected to cultivate the implications of what is biologically and anatomically given. She may, in new areas of activity, balance man's indiscriminate endeavor to perfect his dominion over the outer spaces of national and technological expansion (at the cost of hazarding the annihilation of the species) with the determination to emphasize such varieties of caring and caretaking as would take responsibility for each individual child born in a planned humanity. There will be many difficulties in a new

317

joint adjustment of the sexes to changing conditions, but they do not justify prejudices which keep half of mankind from participating in planning and decision making, especially at a time when the other half, by its competitive escalation and acceleration of technological progress, has brought us and our children to the gigantic brink on which we live, with all our affluence.

New strength of adaptation always develops in historical eras in which there is a confluence of emancipated individual energy with the potentials of a new technical and social order. New generations gain the full measure of their vitality in the continuity of new freedoms with a developing technology and a historical vision. There, also, personal synthesis is strengthened and with it an increased sense of humanity, which the children will feel, too, even if new adjustments are demanded in the sphere of motherhood. Social inventiveness and new knowledge can help plan necessary adjustments in a society that is sure of its values. But without these values, behavioral science has little to offer.

We may well hope, therefore, that there is something in woman's specific creativity which has waited only for a clarification of her relationship to masculinity (including her own) in order to assume her share of leadership in those fateful human affairs which so far have been left entirely in the hands of gifted and driven men, and often of men whose genius of leadership eventually has yielded to ruthless self-aggrandizement. Mankind now obviously depends on new kinds of social inventions and on institutions which guard and cultivate that which nurses and nourishes, cares and tolerates, includes and preserves.

In my last conversation with him, Paul Tillich expressed uneasiness over the clinical preoccupation with an "adaptive ego" which, he felt, might support (these are my words) further attempts at manufacturing a mankind which feels so "adapted" that it would be unable to face "ultimate concerns." I agreed that psychoanalysis was in danger of becoming part of such vain streamlining of existence, but that in its origin and essence it intends to *free* man for "ultimate concerns." For such concerns can begin to be ultimate only in those rare moments and places where neurotic resentments end and where mere readjustment is transcended. I think he agreed. One may add that man's Ultimate has too often been visualized as an infinity which begins where the male conquest of outer spaces ends, and a domain where an "even more" omnipotent and om-

318

niscient Being must be submissively acknowledged. The Ultimate, however, may well be found also to reside in the Immediate, which has so largely been the domain of woman and of the inward mind.

NOTES

1 Preface, *Youth: Change and Challenge*, Erik H. Erikson (ed), New York: Basic Books, 1963.
2 For sketches of typical play constructions, see Erik H. Erikson, *Childhood and Society*, 2nd ed., New York: W.W. Norton, 1963, Chapter II.
3 Three films taken in Kenya, 1959: *Baboon Behavior*, *Baboon Social Organization*, and *Baboon Ecology*.
4 *Childhood and Society*, p. 88.

Once More the Inner Space:
Letter to a Former Student

Erik H. Erikson

1.

Dear Jean:

I find myself challenged by your commission to note down some retrospective thoughts on "Womanhood and the Inner Space." For you attended my course on "The Human Life Cycle" at Harvard and thus you know the intellectual context in which that essay was first presented: in an interdisciplinary discussion such as those cultivated in the American Academy of Arts and Sciences, where "interdisciplinary" means that each participant, in taking a stand on a given subject, communicates something of his place in the tradition of his field. And in such matters, context is all—as one quickly learns from the fate of such efforts in times when their subject matter becomes political in the wider sense. Then single passages are separated from the rest and isolated phrases assume a slogan-like life of their own. They are not merely "quoted out of context," but—with a vengeance—incorporated into a new one. This, at any rate, was impressed on me on revisiting the Harvard area, and hearing my views mentioned among those deemed inimical to womanhood.

So if you now ask me whether "the woman's movement has affected [my] thinking about women," I cannot bypass this development. In fact, I must take account of it in some detail not only as a personal experience but also as a phenomenon characteristic of the early stages of liberation movements. If we recognize in it a necessarily ruthless replowing of the whole ground of consciousness, we may also note that it is apt to plow under again some of the insights into unconscious motivation which now seem indispensable to the flowering of any modern liberation. But before I come to that let me confess the more recent and still growing impression that many young women do, indeed, seem to embody a new womanhood—at once vital and thoughtful, outspoken and loving. Here, as elsewhere, new and more universal identities are evolving. I must truthfully say, however, that this has confirmed rather than "affected" what, through a long life in a number of countries, I have learned to feel womanhood can be or could become wherever it frees itself from the mere obligatory and fashionable aspects of the then dominant roles, with all their built-in neuroticisms, and from mere reactive rebelliousness.

But if you should now insist on asking me to enlarge on what I mean by womanhood, I would not know how to answer. After all, I, too, am son and brother, husband and father to women: each a radiant and unique being, they are part of my existence and essence as I am part of theirs. Our joint experience at its best is an interplay of divergence appreciated and affinity confirmed. The special polarity of the erotic encounter, in turn, is so close to the secret of life that only poets would attempt to find the right words for it. At any rate, I could not write about women as a definable category of otherness—except in a clearly comparative subcontext such as the (admittedly slogan-like) emphasis on the "inner and the outer space." And this is true for women in other spheres—co-workers and students, just for example—where intellectual interplay transcends all differences. Come to think of it, wherever in human life a category of others turns into a bunch of "them," there is already something very wrong. And this, I think, I have come to understand: that many young women could face the suddenly highlighted awareness of their having been implicitly treated as "them" in such a variety of confining roles throughout history, only by vindictively lumping men together as "them," and by mistrusting totally where a little trust might prove treacherous. But vindication is not yet liberation.

Very well, then, I was to be mistrusted as a man—and as a Freudian. But I am glad (I think) that my essay in this book takes its place in a psychoanalytic anthology. You may remember the Vermont farmer whom I quote as saying to a motorist what critics often say less succinctly: "Well now, if I wanted to go where you want to go, I wouldn't start from here." With your anthology in hand like a map, it is clearer why I couldn't possibly be anywhere else and that, considering where I came from, I was doing all right being where I was.

Furthermore, in the Academy symposium on womanhood on which the article is based other essential viewpoints were so well taken care of by outstanding women and men that my job clearly was to start with a psychosexual theme. I had to explain where and why my own observations could not be fitted into those classical psychoanalytic formulations of womanhood which emphasized exclusively the organ that was *not* there on the outside. And I had to focus on what was very much there on the inside—visible and touchable only in its vestibular access, but certainly "known" early to all children except the most underprivileged urban elite.

But alas, in the minds of many feminists, I merely seem to have been granting—and with some condescension—a reasonable equivalent to maleness; and worse, I still seemed to believe in anatomy as well as in the unconscious. And let us face it right now: it is the idea of being unconsciously possessed by one's body, rather than owning it by choice and using it with deliberation, which causes much of the most pervasive anger. Here I had to learn that in women's liberation, as in other liberations spearheaded by the educated middle class, a corollary to the attempt to raise consciousness is the determination to repress the awareness of unconscious motivation, especially where it contributed to the adaptation to what suddenly appear to be the physical "stigmata" of sex, age, or race. Thus, in this post-Freudian era we face not only some of the standard repressions unearthed by Freud, but the re-repression of much that has been half understood and that, more fully understood in a new key, could help importantly in true liberation. To be sure, your anthology will reveal the glaring datedness of some of the theoretical paradigms of early psychoanalytic interpretation. But to continue a once truly revolutionary enlightenment, to redate systematically what belongs to the passage of time and to sift out what is lasting—that can mean to accept historical responsibility, and this is, I hope, what your commentators have done. As my own commentator, I can only offer a few thoughts as footnotes to what I have written and as indicators of what yet needs to be explored.

2.

So, to come to my paper and its (partial) fate. Let us see how some sentences, when used for political rhetoric, lost their theoretical halftones and, instead, took on one (inflammable) color. For example, you ask:

> One of the chief points which feminist writers take issue with, in your formulations about womanhood, has to do with the old controversy about nature vs. nurture. You write that, "The basic modalities of woman's commitment and involvement naturally also reflect the ground plan of her body; and that anatomy, history and personality are our combined destiny." Anatomy, feminists would argue, is only destiny insofar as it determines cultural conditioning. . . . "Erikson's whole theory," claims Kate Millett, "is built in psychoanalysis' persistent error of mistaking learned behavior for biology." What is your answer to this charge?

My answer is that if even staunch feminists concede that anatomy, to some extent, "determines cultural conditioning," then we really have no basic argument. We could start here as well as anywhere; the question is, only, where do we think we are going. To clarify *my* direction, I need only ask you (if in an uncomfortably professorial manner) to take another look at what you are quoting me as saying and to mark the little words "also" in the first part of my sentence and "and" in the second. "Also" means that the modalities of a woman's existence reflect the ground plan of her body *among other things*—as men's modalities reflect that of the male body. "And" says that history *and* personality *and* anatomy are our joint destiny. And if we should go all out, and italicize "combined" too, then an all-around relativity is implied: each of the three aspects of human fate must always be studied in its relation to the two others, for each codetermines the other. Such "systematic going around in circles" (as I have called it, so as not to overdo the word "relativity") takes some thought, which is indispensable to the study of human facts, but, I admit, inadvisable in pamphleteering.

Incidentally, I did not start this destiny business, and Freud did not either. Napoleon was the man of destiny to whom, naturally, history was all. Freud the doctor wanted to make things more concrete (and, no doubt, shake the great usurper's throne a bit) by reminding him of the power of motivations based on anatomy. And I, an heir of ego psychology, asked modestly whether we, ourselves, are not also part of our destiny? My "I" finds itself in a body that exists in a particular social place

323

and historical period, and attempts to make the most and best of it, while helping others to make the most and the best of themselves—and of me. A freer choice nobody can claim or grant to anybody, even if it would seem (and I will quote one such suggestion later) that they are implicitly guaranteed by the American Constitution.

You quote Kate Millett. It so happens that she was the first woman writer whose critique of my essay I read, while Elizabeth Janeway was the last. And since Janeway, in all her well-known clarity and responsibility, seems to repeat some of Millett's misreadings, I must assume that some stereotypes pervade much of what was written in between. So, while your readers have the whole paper before them, let me point out some critical examples.

The critique begins by referring to the play procedure described in my article as an "experiment" undertaken to provide scientific "evidence" for a particular "theory." Your readers are now familiar with the procedure. It was employed in the context of a long-range study of a large group of California boys and girls. For most of the first two decades of their lives, they were seen twice a year in the Guidance Study of the University of California, to be measured, interviewed, and tested. On the occasion of their visits during their eleventh, twelfth, and thirteenth years, I asked one child at a time to come into my study, to arrange with given toys on a given table "an exciting scene from an imaginary moving picture," and then to tell the "plot." The story was recorded and the scene photographed. An observational procedure, then, but no experiment.

How the *clinical* observation of free play has become an important tool in the recognition of a disturbed or anxious child's central problems is summarized in *Childhood and Society*. What I learned in Berkeley was that most older children would, outside of a clinical context, too, willingly, and some eagerly, invent a toy scene, projecting (unconsciously, one must assume) relevant life themes on the play construction. The wider implications of this phenomenon I have discussed more recently in my Godkin Lectures. (They will appear under the title—suggested by a line from William Blake—*The Child's Toys and the Old Man's Reasons*.) Thanks to the wealth of longitudinal data in the Berkeley Guidance Study's long-range "follow-up" I have, in fact, been able to review a few of those play constructions of the Berkeley children and show their relevance in the light of the course of their lives into the fifth decade.

324

At the time of the original procedure, I was fascinated by what I soon perceived as the "language" of *spatial representation*—that is, in the use of blocks: "How the constructions-in-progress moved forward to the outer edge of the table or back to the wall to which it was attached; how they rose to shaky heights or remained close to the table surface; how they were spread over the available space or constricted to a portion of that space." Now, the spatial aspect of the matter probably makes more immediate sense to persons who are visually inclined (and I was an artist before I became a psychoanalyst) and who have learned to "read" what children "say" in playing in space with things and forms. At any rate, it soon became apparent that girls and boys used space somewhat differently, and that certain configurations as well as themes occurred strikingly often in the constructions of one sex and rarely in those of the other.

Let me restate the main trends here, in order to emphasize that to build and to arrange are modes of spatial action. Where boys represent outdoor scenes without using any of the blocks, they emphasize the *free motion* of animals, cars, and people in the open spaces. If they build streets and crossroads, they *channel* traffic, which, in turn, may lead to *collisions* or be *stopped* by the traffic policeman. Where boys build structures, they are apt to build relatively *high* ones, to *erect* towers, and to add *protruding ornaments* in the form of cones and cylinders. On occasion, they accentuate such height by playing out the danger of collapse. And their structures *enclose* fewer people and animals than do the girls.

In comparison and contrast, girls, when arranging configurations of furniture without building any surrounding walls, emphasize the (safe) interior of houses. Where walls are built, the configuration is one of simple and low *enclosure*. And, indeed, these *contain* many more people and animals. When girls add a more *elaborate* structure, it is apt to be an ornate doorway *leading into* the enclosure; and there are scenes in which animals and (male) people *enter* or *intrude* into the interior.

Interestingly enough, some critical writers are teased into playing with the material even as they read about it. Janeway, in referring to my "famous experiment," summarized thus: "boys . . . use their toys and blocks to construct outdoor scenes of action where wild animals threaten and automobiles collide. Little girls prefer interiors where their dolls serve each other tea, or play the piano." (Elizabeth Janeway, *Man's World, Woman's Place* [New York: Morrow, 1971], p. 8) None of the children mentioned tea; nor did I. The significance of such reinterpretations seems to lie not only in the attraction of play, but also in the readers' inclination to embellish *role stereotypes* in the play content over the more mysterious *spatial configurations* on which my analysis of the use of outer and of inner space rests.

If I, then, abstract the configurations more often done by boys as dominated by height and downfall and by strong motion and its channeling arrest, and those done by girls as dominated by static interiors which were open or simply enclosed, peaceful or intruded upon, it is obvious that in the actual play constructions there is a rich interplay between form and content, between the spatial position and the narrative themes assigned to the dolls and toys. At the end, however, it would have taken a special effort to overlook the fact that the sex differences in the use of play space corresponded systematically to the morphology of genital differentiation: "in the male, an external organ, erectable and intrusive in character, serving the channelization of mobile sperm cells: in the female, internal organs, with vestibular access, leading to . . . expectant ova." But the matter certainly does not rest with this reduction to basic elements. It begins here. If I concluded that these differences may suggest a "difference in the experience of the ground plan of the human body," which, in turn, "influences the experience of existence in space," I proceeded, in the rest of the article, to apply this assumption to corresponding configurations observed under other conditions, such as in clinical experience, in the observation of animal behavior, and in historical accounts. A configurational exploration, then, but no "theory" as yet. But all these wider demonstrations are usually omitted in references to the essay, although they explain the Inner Space as a configuration denoting a series of concentric "surroundings" from the womb of origin and the maternal body and presence, to styles of dwellings, and from the quality of domestic or communal life to the "feel" of the universe.

To some critics it seems to follow immediately that, on the basis of my "proof," I declare men to *be this* and women to *be that*: as one publication (approvingly) had it, men, to me, are "penetrators" and women, "enclosers," men oriented outward, women inward. Likewise, where I claim that "male and female principles in body construction . . . remain relevant throughout life for the elaboration of sex roles in cultural space-times," Janeway concludes that, "according to this formula, men are active, women intuitive; men are interested in things and ideas, women in people and feelings." Worse, "there is a limit to learning . . . in Erikson's view, and that limit is involved with the ground plan of the body and is inescapable. . . ."

3.

Well, as you see, you have forced me to reread the paper and to clarify it for myself. You did not ask me what I would change if I could—which was wise, and fair to those who preceded me. But as one of your anthology's last living authors, let me say that I would have felt like changing very little except a few imprudent words and phrases as well as some ambivalently poetic ones. It was imprudent to say "the emphasis here is on predisposition and predilection, rather than on exclusive ability, for both sexes (if otherwise matched in maturation and intelligence) learn readily to *imitate* the spatial mode of the other sex." I should have said, instead, "to make use of, to share, and at times to imitate, the configurations most typical of the other sex." Play configurations can mean many things, and a variety of bodily and spatial experiences are shared, in principle, by both sexes. Both sexes, for example, grow up and stand upright, or may be living in high-rise apartments, and therefore have a variety of "reasons" to build tower-like structures—beyond the mere pleasure of putting block upon block. Likewise, both have a bodily interior and live in houses, and thus may wish to build enclosures. It is quite probable, therefore, that the playspace will at different ages be used variously for the expression of common and of different experiences, even as single children will demonstrate quite individual meanings. This, to me, makes it all the more convincing that our *pubertal children* demonstrated more clearly how differences in the experience of sexual maturation may appear in the playspace. But no matter how the interior and the exterior space are experienced, used, and represented at different ages, the sexual and procreative orientation becomes and remains—that much I must claim—a significant aspect of existence in space.

Now back to the department of clarification by italics. When Millett makes the (horrible) suggestion that I "define" the female as a "creature with a woundlike aperture," she refers to a sentence which claims that "children of both sexes sooner or later 'know' the penis to be missing in one sex, leaving in its place a woundlike aperture." ("Womanhood and the Inner Space," p. 296, above) The mere underscoring of the word *children* would emphasize that I am referring to infantile observations made at a stage of development when the inviolacy of the body is a matter of anxious concern leading to the well-known phobic "theories," which (as I insist throughout) are counteracted in the growing child's eventual awareness of a "protective inner-bodily space safely set in the center of female form and carriage."

That, in another passage, I did fail to italicize two even shorter words, seems to have invited an even weirder misunderstanding. On page 305, I speak as a clinician and note a particular *quality* in the transitory as well as the chronic depressions of women: "in female experience an 'inner space' is at the center of despair even as it is the very center of potential fulfillment. Emptiness is the female form of perdition." This, then, is a clinician's judgment. But I conceded that men can be peculiarly awed by the female sense of loss. Maybe for this reason, I use gratuitously poetic words in a further passage which ends with the words: "How a woman thus can be hurt in depth is a wonder to any man, and it can arouse both his empathetic horror and his refusal to understand. Such hurt," and I now italicize, "*can* be re-experienced in each menstruation; *it* is a crying to heaven in the mourning over a child; and it becomes a permanent scar in the menopause." "Can" means that such hurt may be but need not be experienced during menstruation; while "it" refers to "such hurt"—here taking on desperate depth in the mourning over the actual death of a child. Millett read it to mean mourning over each menstrual loss, wherefore she counted how many periods women average in a lifetime and how often, therefore, Erikson thinks, they are crying to heaven over a child not conceived. To older people like myself, the loss of a child by death was once a more expectable experience in family life, not to speak of past generations when all living children represented a triumph of survival.

Come to think of it, there must be some historical relativity in much that is written about such matters—and in much that is misunderstood. Janeway clarified for me one such issue mentioned in the paper, namely, the special historical dilemma of *American women.*

> To be told in Erik Erikson's words one is "never not a woman" comes as rather a shock. This is especially true for American women because of the way in which the American ethos has honored the ideas of liberty and individual choice. We can find, in fact, an excellent description of the psychological effect of these traditional American Attitudes in Professor Erikson's own classical study, *Childhood and Society.* "The process of American identity formation," he writes, "seems to support an

328

individual's ego identity as long as he can preserve a certain element of deliberate tentativeness of autonomous choice. The individual must be able to convince himself that the next step is up to him." Very well; but then what about the limiting restrictions of being "never-not-a-woman" . . . it is more than restricting, because it involves women in the kind of conflict with their surroundings that no decisions and no action open to them can be trusted to resolve. (Janeway, *Man's World, Woman's Place*, p. 99)

This challenging quotation makes plain the fact that I should not have written about American identity formation without specifying its meaning for American women—a theme I have approached in my recent Jefferson Lectures (*Dimensions of the New Identity*, in press). But it makes equally clear that such traditional oversight can not now be corrected by writing about women outside of the whole context of the *correspondences* in male and female experience at any given historical time. To make this systematic will be a gigantic job, since correspondences, in any instance under discussion, can counterpoint sameness and difference, mutual complementation and irreversible antagonism, compensations and irretrievable losses. In this letter, you will be glad to hear, I can touch on only a few of these correspondences. For example, if the reiteration (by a man) of such a verity as "never-not-a-woman" appears to be shocking, it must be considered that man is never-not-a-man, either. To this, some may respond, "but that is what he wants to be!" Yet, in developmental terms, a boy is not permitted even to *think* that he might ever *want* to be not-a-man with all the trimmings of manhood in his culture. In America this has meant to want to be or to make like being a *self-made man*, and one made in America, an ideal most invigorating and unifying under historical conditions which permitted and demanded a new national identity made out of a multiplicity of immigrant identifications, and this on a wide continent of expanding opportunities. That eventually a stance developed which maintained, at all cost, the semblance of self-chosen roles, sometimes to the point of caricature, all this only parallels other national stereotypes; and one could, no doubt, relate the unfreedom of women in any culture to the kind of freedom enjoyed by some men and barely lived up to by most. But in America, the emphasis on *choice* in all social roles has become an ideological faith which Janeway seems to feel is violated by any suggestion "that woman's role differs from man's because women are born differently." Her crescendo of complaint can make a man feel

329

quite guilty (somewhat like a mean older brother) for ever having brought up the subject; for such suggestion, Janeway says, "destroys any value that can be derived from the notion of roles . . . it knocks to the ground the idea of the role as a means of learning, of getting things done, and of communicating by means of behavior . . . it seems a sad waste to throw away such a valuable concept simply to put women back in their place." (Janeway, p. 93)

If here the self-made role is at stake, together with its time-honored method of convincing oneself that the next step is always up to the individual's choice, then, indeed, it must be said, that American women have not only not enjoyed equal political and economic rights, but have also been forced to assume (and learn to flourish in) roles which were meant, above all, to *complement* the male ideal of self-madeness and mobility in a "man's world" which thus by and large did dictate "woman's place."

Janeway, as you can see, alternately calls a role a notion, an idea, and a concept. And, indeed, it seems important to differentiate between the role concepts which emerge in a given country (such as Talcott Parsons' in this country) and the role ideology dominant in it. No true role *concept* would ignore the fact that functioning roles, if ever so flamboyant, are tied to certain conditions: a role can only provide leeway within the limits of what bodily constitution can sustain, social structure make workable, and personality formation integrate. A role *ideology*, however, would induce persons to convince themselves and each other at all cost, that their role choices can surmount all or some of these limitations. Women in America, having for so long lived in and with the ideology of the self-made man without fully partaking of it, may plausibly feel that in this very country of liberty and equality they have in some ways further to go than women in some other democracies, and this not only in the acquisition of the mere right and chance to participate equally in the men's game in economics and politics. For the very nature of that game, as is obvious in its procedural and verbal habits, excludes all but exceptionally adaptable and insistent women from being "one of the boys." And one may well ask whether women *should* play the game, even if they could, without changing its nature. Even where political and economic liberty provides the belated right to join men in self-made stances cultivated in American history, it will soon become obvious to liberated women that the American male, too, must learn to adjust to a limitation of *his* aspirations and dreams, namely, where they have led not only to the overexpansion of goals but also to the corruption of means, to the mechanization of motives, and to a restriction of personality potentials.

Equal opportunity for women, then, can only mean the right and the chance to give new meaning and a new kind of competence to (so far) "male" occupations. Only thus can women really influence future work conditions and marriage arrangements, life styles and forms of communal collaboration. At the end, only a renewal of social creativity can liberate both men and women from reciprocal roles which, in fact, have exploited both.

4.

Dear Jean, you inquire:

> In *Childhood and Society* (in the "Toys and Reasons" section on Black Identity) you have pointed out that the opposition of ideal and evil images is a fundamental fact of national or cultural identity: that the unconscious evil identity is the "composite of everything which arouses negative identification, i.e., the wish not to resemble it." Where the dominant identity is white Protestant male, the unconscious evil identity consists of images of the "violated (castrated) body, the ethnic outgroup, and the exploited minority." . . . In "Womanhood and the Inner Space," however, you do not talk about this aspect of female identity—the negative prototype which woman embodies for men. . . .

And you ask, more specifically:

> How does the small girl handle the inevitable observation that the qualities associated with having a penis (action, adventure, change, fighting, building, aggressing) are valued more highly in her world than those associated with having a vagina? If men unconsciously perceive women as castrated men (i.e. as their own worst fears), and if the dominant cultural identity is male, how can a little girl not absorb the view that her procreative morphology is somehow second-rate?

You are right: in my essay I concentrate on those aspects of the inner space which mark its importance—relatively neglected in psychoanalytic literature—for the woman's positive identity. Such positive aspects in the two sexes enhance each other, counterpointing differences as they share samenesses. If you then inquire about the fate of those *negative self-images* which the girl (you are right) inevitably absorbs as she grows up under the conditions emphasized in your quotations, we must learn to think of

331

them, too, in *correspondences*. This means, we must evaluate the negative as well as positive elements in the identity formation of *both* sexes, and this not only in terms of the "inner economy" of single persons (as we are so apt to do as clinicians) but rather in terms of the *emotional ecology* shared by all those whose identity formations are interdependent. Where one sex harbors negative images of the other, the resulting mutual defensiveness leads not only to acknowledged antagonisms but also to attempted resolutions in (more or less conscious) *social deals*. Incidentally, I have learned to like this word "deals" because it suggests a reciprocal bartering and bargaining, an apportioning and allocating of rights and duties, and this with varying outcomes, such as square deals, double and fast deals—and, of course, dirty ones. To speak of such deals helps me to relate (or to think we may learn to relate) the inner defences studied by psychoanalysis and the "political" machinations common in daily life. So let us play with a few correspondences between male and female existence, to see what happens to the negative identities in each.

Your readers, by now, will be fully informed, probably to the point of ennui, of all the proliferations of penis envy. It may provide just relief to remember that males must suffer a corresponding fear of losing or damaging a vulnerable and exposed organ of such magic prowess—and competitiveness. For there are, of course, real and imagined differences in male equipment, too, and a resulting inter-*male* penis envy. But if there is an element of what we call "overcompensation" in men's search for arenas of majestic accomplishment, men are not only making up for a fear of being immobilized and found to be wanting in stature and status, but probably also for a deep envy of the maternal capacity to produce what in all its newborn weakness, is and remains, after all, the most miraculous human creation in the universe: and it breathes!

Boys, of course, have mothers, too, and have internalized mother love with their (or some) milk. But only the girl, as we saw, has it (literally) in her to become a mother herself. Whether she learned to like or dislike her particular mother and what she stood for, she must transform her own early dependency into her own style of adult dependability. In whatever context she later chooses to be thus depended on, however, there are always deals permitting her to remain in some respects, dependent —and to make others overly so. The boy's and man's developmental job is apt to be quite different and yet reciprocal: namely, to doubly compensate for the pull to infantile dependence and to establish male autonomy while also finding ways of becoming clandestinely dependent on women and men in the adult scene. At any rate, to the boy and man, womanhood combines the highest as well as the lowest connotations, so that part of his own negative identity—the "effeminate" traits he must suppress in himself as he becomes a man—is in stark conflict with the maternal ideals he received from and continues to seek in motherly persons. Such conflicts, incidentally, creative men and women are able to resolve on a grand scale because they learn to feel and to depict the otherness usually suppressed; and although they suffer some (well publicized) agony on the way, they are sure of universal applause. For ordinary men and women love to witness, at least in the printed page or on stage and screen, the playing out of some bisexual freedom (and even the resulting tragedy) denied to them. Modern life may come to permit a much freer interidentification of the sexes in everyday life: we will return to this point.

But to come back to your question: if the little girl, then, feels inferior because of the boy's negative attitude to the woman in himself, she also knows that she is going to be assigned superior roles by a compensatory —if variably ambivalent—valuation given her traditionally in the roles of mother and sister, value-giver and teacher, lady-of-the-house, mistress, and playmate—all potentially confining roles and yet each endowed with a specific power which forces the man, in turn, to play his part. No wonder that, faced with some pained awareness of all this, some individuals of both sexes prefer trying out homosexual or otherwise interchangeable roles. However, without rare gifts or insights, they do not escape transparently analogous role complications.

Does all this express a clinician's habitual pessimism? The point is that these age-old conflicts call not only for liberty in socio-economic matters, but also for emotional liberation—whatever comes first. And a specifically psychoanalytic re-evaluation of sexual differences must ask not only what defensive deals individuals make with their own manifold identifications but also what deals men and women have made or are making with each other in order to complement each other's defenses and to come to some workable division of roles.

Beyond this, you may have noted (as others have, scornfully) that I always allow for the ideal case and seem to be making a case for the ideal in a given historical period; and, indeed, a strong *ego-ideal* provided by parents, elders, and leaders with consistent values is a prime psychological necessity and this especially as a counterforce against the (developmentally) more infantile and (collectively) more atavistic *super-ego* which mortgages all choices in life and in history. It is, therefore, important to watch, in the sudden shift of awareness brought about by an attempted liberation, the comparative fate of new ideals and of old super-ego pressures. The latter, after all, were the inner mainstay that helped to secure the traditional status quo and, it seems, can permit a liberation only at the price of turning guiltiness into consuming righteousness, and an erstwhile negative self-image into blind accusations against newly appointed enemies. Suddenly released from traditional bondage, repressed emotions upset much of the generational and sexual interplay. As youth in much of the world captured a great vision of peace (which *has* made a difference) it also vented a moralistic fury on the whole adult generation, and in the name of peace created new confrontations across the generational border. We are now aware of the moral exhaustion which can follow such forced realignment of images. In the women's movement, one can discern a corresponding moralistic projection of erstwhile negative self-images upon men as representing evil oppressors and exploiters. More difficult is that cold *self*-appraisal in historical terms which no true revolutionary movement can do without; and in our time, such historical terms must include what has been termed *psycho*-historical.

Do I mean (you probably suspect) that women should recognize their masochism in that inner collusion which I have postulated? Your readers will have read what I have to say about female masochism and the secret "enjoyment" of roles now characterized as oppressed. Here, too, I would again invoke the formula that "only a total configurational approach— somatic, historical, individual—can help us to see single traits in context rather than in isolated and senseless comparison." True, woman is prepared by physical constitution and tradition to bear some discomfort, pain, and special sensitivity associated with her procreative endowment; but this becomes a masochistic love of suffering only when she "exploits pain perversely or vindictively, which means that she steps out of rather than deeper into her female function." So I do not ascribe to a simple female masochism (or, indeed, to male sadism) the historical fact that woman through the ages has assented to an *accentuation* of the inner space as an over-all confinement and to an *exploitation* of masochistic potentials in roles in which she was "immobilized, infantilized, and prostituted, deriving from it at best what in pathology we call 'secondary gains' of devious dominance."

334

But so, we must now continue, have men accepted and inflicted on their own kind hardship and slavery, injury and death for the sake of the defense and conquest of those outer spaces which they needed for their victories. The corresponding exploitation of *their* masochistic as well as sadistic potentials has been hidden only by the imagery of heroism, of duty, and of work. So I should extend to men, also, my suggestion that only a new biocultural history (created by women and men articulately self-observing and communicative) could clarify the evolution of the masochistic potential in our man-made world, and of our overadjustment to it.

The inner psychological division necessary to maintain such a world of accentuated inner and outer spaces as I outlined in my paper, harbors, then, negative and positive identity elements in both men and women. It would take more than one letter to specify how all this *develops,* either ontogenetically or historically. But it is clear that where in girls a certain "inner-directedness," and, indeed, a certain self-contained strength and peace, was cultivated, they were also forced to abandon (and sometimes later to overdo) much of the early locomotor vigor and the social and intellectual initiative and intrusiveness which, potentially, girls share with boys; while most boys in pursuing the male role beyond what came naturally, had to dissimulate and to disavow what receptivity and intuitiveness they shared with girls. How each sex overdeveloped what was given; how each compensated for what it had to deny; how thus each managed to get special approbation for a divided self-image; and to what extent "oppressor" and "oppressed" (beyond the blatant arrangements for political and economic dominance) colluded with each other in enslaving each other and themselves—*that* is what I mean by the deals which men and women must learn to study and discuss. Here one would hope shared insight would transcend both self-blame and accusation and would not forget the grandeur of human endurance and competence in times of equally shared hardship in the country's history.

5.

You (finally) ask me what the effect of the relative accessibility of *abortion* and *birth-control* may have on the identity of women. These two words always strike me as being dangerously negative for an issue which makes mankind face the responsibility for its own life-giving power: "birth-

335

control" seems to associate the matter (choose one) with price-, pest-, or arms-control, and "abortion" with the elimination of waste. "Planned parenthood" is better; it emphasizes initiative and thoughtfulness, and assumes that the wish for parenthood exists. And, indeed, among many young adults, planned parenthood is becoming a voluntary joint experience of great meaning. For it attempts to give a few children their due, while it applies the energies saved from parental overcommitment to wider communal responsibilities. I have always called the dominant task of adulthood *generativity* rather than procreativity or productivity because I did want to allow for a variety of activities other than parenthood or the making of goods or money—activities which are, well, "generative" because they contribute to the life of the generations. Here, indeed, is a field of new leadership for young adults privileged enough to have choices and to recognize them.

The ideological leadership of young adulthood also seems all-important at this time just because it emphasizes the adventure of new ideals and plays down the grim moralism of old. True, we can see now —now that we can avoid it technologically—how motherhood was used to enslave women by the combined forces of instinctual drive, social tradition, and inner collusion. But, again, the mere attempt to right a wrong by turning it upside down and to claim that there is no instinctual need for parenthood and that parenthood is *nothing but* social convention and coercion will not liberate anybody's choices. A choice is free when it can be made with a minimum of denial and of guilt and with a maximum of insight and conviction.

Now, identity formation attempts to provide (and also to pretend) such choice at the conclusion of adolescence, when so many conflicting mental states are highlighted. For identity is a combination of self-images anticipating the future in the light of what was most coherent in the past; and it attempts to find use for or to contain what we have called the negative identity. An increased awareness of the problems of identity thus should give more power to young adulthood.

In view of all this, your questions regarding birth-control, when addressed to *me*, can only mean: if what we have subsumed in the image "inner space" is, indeed, so significant, both as the inner bodily ground of female procreation and as a dominant configuration in self-images and social roles—how can modern woman be aware of this *and* choose to be or not to be a mother if and when it suits her? And you are right, we are

336

facing the age-old question all over again, whether a person or a generation can simply choose to disregard as inconvenient or unnecessary any part of the instinctuality essential to man's bodily existence. In other words, on the way to liberate genitality but to restrict procreation, are we about to repress yet another "basic drive"? Or *is* it "yet another"?

Mankind, it is true, has learned to transform sexuality into a source of vital personal expression and into an art of intimate communication. Love has learned to borrow from necessity, and self-fulfillment from a natural mandate. All this—and sublimation—has helped to civilize mankind and has provided much of the fuel for its creativity. But it has also made us frightfully self-indulgent—and I mean indulgent of the single self, licensed by an individualistic ideology.

This is the time, then, to face a simple fact just because it was never more unpopular: not even psychoanalysis, while investigating the power of the libido, has sufficiently accounted for the procreative function of genital activity. In my article I point to modern investigations of the human sexual response which seem to reveal some involvement of the female procreative organs in the erotic excitement due to every kind of sexual act (p. 306). And, as I have insisted, even the great aim of psychosexual maturation (and of psychoanalytic cure)—namely the "primacy" of genitality over pregenitality—does not, in itself, assure adult maturity, unless genitality, in turn, becomes an intrinsic part of erotic intimacy, and intimacy, in turn, part of joint generative commitments. In reminding you of this, I realize why both pro- and anti-psychoanalytic liberationists may look at my contributions with mistrust: for how can one be totally liberated in one's genitality *and* be properly generative?

A theory of the life cycle rather suggests the opposite question: how can one maintain true genital liberation without coming to terms with generativity? In fact, we face here the question (and psychiatry will soon be up against it) whether the need for procreation can be simply ignored or repressed even for the sake of stringent economic considerations, not to speak of "free" sexuality or of fashionable role playing—even as genitality was once unsuccessfully repressed for the sake of, say, Victorian status seeking. I have already given, or implied, my answer: birth-control calls for new and combined insights both psychological and political. The hybris of planned progeny calls for a new religious context: a world order planned to provide for each child chosen to be born an equal opportunity

337

to develop fully within the sequence of generations.

You remind me that much is being written now by and about the new woman. I have not been able to read much in recent years, but my impression is that what is published is all too often written by writers, of writers, for writers. It represents a shared investment in a specific type of generativity. Good enough; but one would wish that, in matters so close to the core of human life, more writers would include in their awareness the less verbal, or, at any rate, less intellectual masses of women—whether workers or mothers or both—and ask what makes up the sense of existence in their days and nights, their years and stages of life, and their old age. To liberate *them* means to create new and convincing duties as well as rights, beyond the mere know-how of birth-control.

But to return once more to the men. Considering the brazen way in which, in the essay under discussion, I juxtaposed the inner and the outer space, you will not be too shocked if I now claim that, indeed, *birth-control* and *arms-control* are two corresponding technological developments which are stirring up both the male and the female self-images in order to combine them in a more all-human identity. As birth-control goes to the core of womanhood, the implications of arms-control go to the core of the male identity, as it has emerged through evolution and history. Atavistically speaking, armament originates in the extension of the man's strong right arm as the carrier of weapons and tools, and then in all those righteous wars which the human pseudospecies have waged against each other, wars such as no self-respecting species wages against itself in nature. Warfare, to be sure, has become a self-perpetuating institution, which justifies itself on political grounds as the logical outcome of former wars and of the treaties that ended them, forever incompletely. But warfare, as we surely have come to realize, also serves the periodical reaffirmation of uniformed masculinity with its simultaneous function of impressing itself, womankind, and the enemy—a "bird of fine plumage" both overly self-conscious and yet unconscious of its own drivenness. This, too, has served ideals, inventions, and deeds which mankind considers part of its proudest history. In these days, however, we are becoming aware of war's thoughtless exploitation and extermination of men, women, and children anywhere and the periodical and mandatory sacrifice of a generation of sons which our heroic history has entailed. We suddenly hear Homer in a new key; and the sight of the full grown men of the ages, deploying the age-old stance of militancy with righteousness, all the way from the jungles and the forests to the Wall Streets and Washingtons. But such new awareness, instead of exhausting itself in perpetual protest, must also lead to an assessment of the warrior's evolution from the man-to-man fighting spirit to the impersonal exercise of mechanical warfare and the cold engineering of annihilation. It is clear that arms-control comes first, and that the economic and motivational investment in super-weaponry must first be contained in an over-all attitude of mutual deterrence which will also deter the deterror. But this, no doubt, will make, and is already making specific demands on the male psyche, and must cause grave bewilderment in young men, whose adolescent mores still reflect the anticipation of periodic combat with some people of some other kind: and today, even when there is no war, the availability of small manageable weapons at home makes it possible for some peculiarly crazed young people impulsively to appoint any group and any person that "other kind" that must be exterminated. If birth-control, then, frees women for a choice of (alternating or simultaneous) roles other than motherhood or spinsterhood, arms-control, if understood in all its emotional implications, would permit men to become freer for roles not originally defined by a hunter's or a conqueror's imagery. Parenthetically, another question of yours concerns the widespread concern with inwardness on the part of many young men; this may well be pointing to a withdrawal of commitment from a variety of overextended fighting fronts and a new search for an inner anchor.

Which brings me to my conclusion—and I do mean also the conclusion of my previous paper. For (should I apologize?) I still believe what I said there in somewhat credal terms about the Ultimate residing in the Immediate. But I can apply this now to both sexes. To put a fuller existence above uncontrolled parenthood, and planned peace above unrestricted war, would call not only for new inventions but also for the redirection of human instinctuality. A more conscious and concerted sublimation of generativity from generation to generation cannot rely on the mere avoidance, prohibition, or inhibition of either careless procreation or thoughtless violence. Mankind needs a guiding vision. And fate usually makes it only too clear what the next vision *must* be: today, it must be a world order which would permit all children chosen-to-be-born anywhere on earth to develop to an adulthood that learns to humanize its own inventions—psychologically as well as technologically. This, I will

339

admit, may be an adulthood as yet to be invented or evolved. But I believe that, as women take their share in the over-all economic and political planning of affairs so far monopolized by men, they cannot fail to culti-vate a concerted attention to the whole earth as an inner space, no matter how far out any of the outer spaces may reach.

With all good wishes,

E.H.E.

Stoller

Facts and Fancies:
An Examination of Freud's Concept of Bisexuality (1973)

Robert J. Stoller

When he first began constructing the edifice of psychoanalytic theory, Freud placed the concept of bisexuality in the center,[1] and from those earliest days until the end, it remained there; few of Freud's ideas kept their original form as unmodified as "bisexuality." In fact, the central thesis—that bisexuality is at the heart of all psychopathology, from minimal to flagrant—never changed. In part it remained so fixed because no crucial new data arose from the laboratories in the fifty or sixty years of his theory building and in part because—a concept so fruitful for understanding normal and abnormal development and behavior—its very explanatory power must have corroborated for him its validity. We need not review his writings to demonstrate the above;[2] it may help, however, to recall generalizations within the grand concept.

He believed bisexuality was a natural law of biology (for instance: "Psycho-analysis has a common basis with biology, in that it presupposes an original bisexuality in human beings [as in animals]") (1, p. 171).* It was, at the least, a potential inherent in all cells and therefore in all tissues, organs, and organisms. Being a biological universal, he assumed it necessarily exerted its influence on the psychological, which, at bottom, is in itself a reflection of biology. "Bisexuality" was thus a referent for: overt homosexuality; pleasure in both homosexual and heterosexual in-

*Numbers in parenthesis refer to bibliography, pp. 362–364.

343

tercourse; identification with aspects of the opposite sex; cross-gender non-erotic behavior, such as effeminacy; friendship; the capacity of certain cells and tissues to shift appearance or function, or both, from that typical of one sex to the other; embryological undifferentiation; vestigial tissues of the opposite sex in the adult; an innate "force" that can influence behavior toward that of the opposite sex (2). The *anlagen* of bisexuality were the "bedrock" (3) of behavior, and its psychological manifestation—homosexuality—was the nidus from which psychopathology arose. He felt more than comfortable with such inclusive usage; he felt it was correct. To fail to see that these are all of one family was to throw away a concept of great power.

This paper has two purposes. The first—so very old-fashioned—is to maintain at this late date that bisexuality should still serve as a central theme in understanding human psychology, while the second is to suggest modifications and disagreements with aspects of Freud's beliefs on this subject. To do so, I shall break Freud's concept of "bisexuality" into its two implied parts, biological and psychological, and shall examine each from the viewpoint of recent data and concepts acquired from the study of intersexuals (patients with biological bisexuality) and from transsexuals (patients who, while biologically intact, believe they are members of the opposite sex). These "natural experiments" help us better discern to what extent the biological or the psychological (postnatal experience) contributes to psychic structure and development. Perhaps then we can see better why bisexuality, in its form Freud called "homosexuality," is a threat to psychic equilibrium. In addition, some flaws in Freud's use of the concept may become manifest.

I wish now to look more closely at Freud's use of "bisexuality" in a biological context to see if it cannot be sharpened by the findings of researchers in the last two decades.

Bisexuality and Intersexuality

Within the terms "bisexuality" and "intersexuality" lies the word "sex," which is defined by the nature of the chromosomes, gonads, external genitals, internal sexual apparatuses (e.g., prostate, uterus), hormonal state and secondary sex characteristics. Each of these[3] can show, in man, its potential for opposite-sexed qualities. Lower animals have even greater capacity to develop in the direction of the opposite sex; roughly, the lower in the evolutionary scale, the more this is so (for instance, there are adult fish and amphibia fertile in one sex and then the other).

At any rate, even human cells, tissues, and organs retain propensities toward shifting sex. Our view of the tissue *anlagen* has changed, however, since Freud's death. We now know mammalian, including human, tissue starts as female in fetal life, regardless of the chromosomal sex [reviewed in (2), (5)]. Then, after weeks of embryonic development, apparently as a result of a message communicated via the Y chromosome, certain cells in what will become the genital ridge start producing an androgen.[4] Once those first cells begin producing this masculinizing hormone, the contiguous cells are influenced by it, it is hypothesized, to begin also metabolizing this substance until the whole area has been organized by androgens into a male, masculinizing, proto-organ. Then, if not interrupted, the process of creating the maleness goes at its predestined pace, the end result being the biologically normal male. But we recall that without the androgens at the start, the masculinization does not occur.[5] Contrary to what Freud found psychologically and then extrapolated as if it were a biological fact, a clitoris is not a little penis; rather, anatomically, a penis is an androgenized clitoris [see (7) for illustration]. *In both sexes*, enough androgen at the right time produces an anatomically and physiologically normal penis; *in both sexes* the absence of androgen at the right time produces an anatomically and physiologically normal clitoris. So it is with other tissues (which, except for the brain, need not concern us here). In the case of the brain, evidence, clear-cut in animals and more modest in humans (2, 5) reveals that this organ also responds as above; the brain is female in that *in both sexes* feminine behavior results if male hormones are not added. Without proper amounts of androgen at the critical perinatal period, the organizing of brain physiology necessary for masculine behavior does not occur, while androgens at the critical period result in masculine behavior in the adult—*regardless of the sex of the animal.* (What makes this general rule less clear in humans is that humans are much more susceptible, in the origins of their behavior, to nonbiological forces than are lower animals.)

It is likely, then, that Freud was wrong in thinking the "natural" sex is the male, a belief that became the biological "proof" of his thesis that women are inferior (8). But the idea that each sex carries in its biology aspects of or potentials for the opposite sex has not been refuted; instead, that finding is invariably confirmed[6] (2, 5).

"Intersexuality" is the term used at present for a significant shift of one or more of the criteria for determining sex in the direction of the opposite sex. For instance, there may be too many sex chromosomes (e.g., XXY: Klinefelter's Syndrome) or too few (e.g., XO: Turner's Syndrome); and there are innumerable anatomical and physiological forms of intersexuality: gonadal dysfunctions; hermaphroditic appearance of external genitals; poorly formed or absent internal sexual apparatuses; disruption of normal sex hormone production or consequences. We need not be concerned with the details. But we do want to know—just as did Freud—what effect these somatic disorders have on psychological function. Freud felt intersexuality (biological bisexuality) was a necessary part of overt homosexuality (psychological bisexuality) and also of the "latent homosexuality" of heterosexuals, manifested in both sexes as "masculine protest" (3).

The evidence today does not confirm Freud's belief that intersexuality significantly alters behavior. On the contrary, it confirms one of his greatest discoveries: psychological forces are crucial in forming human gender behavior. In fact, I would add, such forces can almost always overpower the biological.[7]

The following vignettes exemplify this:

1. *The proper diagnosis of sex is missed at birth and not made until latency:* Two siblings, both chromosomally male, with normal male internal sexual apparatuses and normal testes, were born with the testes cryptorchid, the penis the size of a clitoris, the urethral meatus opening in a female position, and the scrotum bifid so that it seemed to be labia. With the external genitals appearing normally female, both children were assigned to the female sex and raised as girls. At the time the diagnosis of maleness was made on each (suspicion having been raised by the "inguinal tumors"—in fact, the cryptorchid testes), both were unquestioning of their femaleness or femininity. The parents were told the diagnosis, the decision made to have the children remain as girls, and the necessary surgical and hormonal treatment to create female anatomy embarked upon. No psychological problems have been encountered in the six years since the diagnosis was made.

2. *The diagnosis of sex is properly made at birth, but, despite the impossibility of making a functional penis, the child is raised as a boy:* This infant, with approximately the same hermaphroditism as in the first example, was, however, accurately diagnosed as a male at birth. The parents were so informed, the child assigned to the male sex, and subsequently raised unequivocally as a male. As an adult, he has no gender identity problem, though

346

he has never-ending realistic problems with his totally inadequate penis.

3. *Because of an enlarged phallus, the diagnosis at birth is "this is neither a boy nor a girl, but it looks more like a girl; so raise it as if it were a girl":* This infant suffered in fetal life from hyperadrenalism, with excessive adrenal androgens produced so that the external genitals were masculinized; in all other regards, the infant was a normal female: chromosomes, ovaries, uterus, vagina, etc. As an adult, the patient, chronically psychotic, with a never-ending rumination about genitals and symbols of genitals, tries to live as a woman but instead believes she is a freak, different from all other human beings (12).

4. *The diagnosis of maleness is made at birth and the child raised unequivocally as a boy despite being an otherwise biologically normal female with hyperadrenalism:* This infant's genitals were not just masculinized in a hermaphroditic direction as in case 3, but the clitoris was a normal penis, with penile urethra, with external lips fused as in a male's scrotum, indurated so that the lips have the appearance of scrotum with enclosed testes. So the infant was thought to be male. Unfortunately, at age 6, precocious puberty (typical in such cases) caused menstruation to start. Since the vaginal outlet was blocked by the penis and scrotum, an acute abdominal crisis (peritonitis) occurred, caused by menstrual blood in the abdominal cavity; at that time, the proper diagnosis of sex was made. The pediatrician recommended to the parents that the child's sex and gender be changed and instructed the family to buy girls' clothes and get the child a girl's hairdo. Follow-up in later years reveals a child unable to progress in school, with severe speech defect, no friends, clumsy, and grotesque-appearing in girls' clothes.

5. *Biologically normal female identical twins:* One of these twins was raised by her parents so that all feminine behavior was encouraged; her twin was raised with strong encouragement of masculine behavior. The twin raised in a masculine manner is, as an adult, a female transsexual; the feminine twin is engaged to be married (13).

In other words, the clinical evidence scarcely supports Freud's belief in the power of the biological to create psychological bisexuality. Such "bisexual" conditions as transvestism (fetishistic cross-dressing) and homosexuality are not, even in part, as Freud contended, the result of constitutional bisexuality. (It must be emphasized, however, that he felt these clinical conditions took their form from postnatal experiences.)

But perhaps the most telling example of the rule that in humans the environment overpowers the biological is the male transsexual, in whom a rather complete reversal of masculinity and femininity occurs as a result of an aberrant mother-infant relationship: excessively close, nonfrustrating, prolonged symbiosis, in the absence of a demonstrable biological defect.

Bisexuality and Transsexualism

Freud, we know, conceptualized (though without so labeling) a biological and a psychological bisexuality, the first the "bedrock" of the second. Both, he felt, were present in varying degree in all humans depending on constitutional variations and life experiences. He said that in some cases the biological was the heaviest contributor, in some the psychological, but most were an inextricable mix of the two. Although he did not have a separate term for biological bisexuality,[8] he did for psychological bisexuality; he called it homosexuality. Here again we run into trouble with vocabulary and definition because of Freud's propensity for all-inclusive concepts. While exercising this skill may reveal formerly hidden commonality, it risks our losing discrimination; the word—the concept and its adhering theory—overpowers reality-observation. In addition to shared features, there really are essential differences between the perversion homosexuality and affection for a friend; between gentleness in a man who loves women's bodies and the absurdly soft behavior of an effeminate homosexual; between cross-dressing that raises up an erection and cross-dressing in a transsexual who, never excited by women's clothes, wishes always to wear such clothes because no others feel appropriate. To me the gain bought by calling all these "homosexuality" is not worth the loss in discriminating differences in the clinical pictures, the psychodynamics, the etiologies, and the treatments.

Knight (14) once noted, in regard to using "homosexuality" to explain psychosis:

> Many analysts have long been aware that Freud's theory leaves something to be desired in the way of completeness. It begins with the fully developed homosexual wish, the first step in the formula, "I love him," and proceeds with the various ways in which this repressed wish is denied and projected. It does not explain why the paranoiac developed such an intense homosexual wish phantasy, nor why he must deny it so desperately. Other men also develop strong homosexual wishes which are repressed in other, non-psychotic ways or are acted out in overt homosexuality, perhaps even with a minimum of psychic conflict. Why does the developing paranoiac react so frantically to the dimly perceived

348

homosexual drive in himself? Is the homosexual wish so much more intense in him than it is in other men who successfully repress it without forsaking reality testing, or is it that the need to deny the homosexuality is so much greater? And if the latter is true, why is this need to deny so terrifically strong? Why is the thought of homosexual contact with another man so completely intolerable? . . . It is often presumed by the therapist, for example, that if he can by reassurance, re-education and interpretation make the paranoid patient's homosexual wishes more acceptable to him, he could give up the delusions which represent a denial of these wishes. And so the therapist tries cautiously and tactfully to bring the homosexual conflict nearer the surface, supporting the patient's ego with reassurance that after all homosexuality is not so terrible, that every man is bisexual at first, and that every man has a certain amount of latent homosexuality. But somehow this sort of therapeutic approach not only does not relieve the patient but often makes him more paranoid than ever. . . .

Let us now re-examine aspects of what Freud meant by "homosexuality." If we do so, we can extend our understanding of its meaning and of its potential pathogenicity.

Again, I shall agree with a major part of Freud's thesis but disagree with lesser ones. The major agreement is that qualities to which he pointed still can be found inherent in psychic development and function: masculinity and femininity are both present in men and both in women; children experience an inverted oedipal love and carry its memory and effects through life; men usually fear being feminine and erect a masculine protest, and women suffer penis envy; fear of being homosexual is common in heterosexuals. I disagree on two less global issues. First, Freud discovered that object choice, zone of libidinal fixation, and oedipal conflict are not perspectives that adequately account for the pathogenic factor—dread of homosexuality—without adding his *deus ex machina*, ruminations on biology. Rather than having to speculate on biological forces that must be invented to fill in gaps in the explanation, the study of transsexualism suggests data that more satisfactorily aid our study of the pathogenic influence of bisexuality (homosexuality). Second, this influence may be more fateful in men than women.

THE FIRST: DREAD OF HOMOSEXUALITY

Thinking in terms of a transsexual mechanism—the desire to be a member of the opposite sex—shifts the emphasis, in a search to explain homosexuality's danger, from the object chosen to the more fundamental issue of maintenance of one's sense of existing, of identity. I believe that those who fear homosexual impulses do so in part because they fear that these desires indicate a weakness (weakening) of their sense of being fully anchored in their own sex. (Perhaps a greater contribution to that fear are the omnipotent-impotent storms of rage created and unmodulated in some infants by their mothers. Because of this paper's focus, the role of trauma, frustration, oral and anal hostility, and resultant restitution in homosexuality [e.g., 15, 16] or even more so in psychosis [e.g., 17] will not be considered herein.) In addition, a crucial factor I take as a given shall only be briefly noted here. It is that dread of homosexuality is culturally induced. In other times or places, in contrast to Western society today, a homosexual act *can* be a momentous affirmation of one's masculine identity, weighted with a sense of lofty maleness. Vanggaard (5, see also Karlen [6]) reviews data wherein the homosexual act was used formally, publicly, religiously to convey manliness from a man to a boy and to bind adult lovers to an honorable manliness. These findings again confirm that it is not homosexuality *per se* that threatens but weakening of sense of identity. In cultures like the above, where the ideal is to be a manly male, an erect penis is not only an organ of pleasure but much more, a symbol—phallus—of power and honor. To touch it or receive its semen is to be granted its *mana*. What is unworthy in such cultures is to be unable to love a woman well, for that, not the anatomical homosexual act, demonstrates lack of manliness.

Let me elaborate. Transsexualism is, by definition, the most profound distortion there is of masculinity and femininity. We shall only consider, however, male transsexualism,[9] which to me is *a keystone for understanding the development of masculinity and femininity in all people.* Freud did also, though this is not obvious (there was no such term available or clinical state made explicit then). He hinted at its presence in describing castration anxiety, that crucial element in oedipal development (19–21). I would make the transsexual quality suggested in Freud's findings manifest by adding that to lose one's penis is not the whole of the threat of castration; the penis is only the insignia, the repository of that fundamental of identity, one's sense of maleness. The danger in castration is not organ loss but the far more profound loss of one's sense of existing.[10] He moved toward this conclusion, in more graceful terms, when he modified the concept of anxiety (23) to give it its existential cast, e.g., separation anxiety, weaning, or the prototypical birth experience.

On looking at one of Freud's great clinical tests for his theory that homosexuality (bisexuality) is at the heart of human behavior—the Schreber case (24)—we find that the homosexuality of which he speaks is not really concerned with what we commonly recognize as genital, erotic homosexuality but with something more primitive—change of sex.[11]

When, in analytic theory, it is said that one fears homosexuality, the implication is that one fears succumbing to impulses for sexual relations with a person of the same sex. These are fearful because, allegedly, they imply flight from the more desired heterosexual impulses, fixation upon forbidden but desired body parts (e.g. anus), and incest with the parent of the same sex; this is how Freud sees Schreber's homosexuality. But at the center of the clinical picture is the transsexual desire: Schreber's sex is changing. He gradually comes to feel, at first with paranoid fright and later with megalomanic voluptuous pleasure, that he is being supernaturally influenced so that his body is changing to female and that he shall procreate a new race. These fantasies are not just a matter of object choice, libidinal zone, or oedipal conflict.

Commentators since Freud have felt his homosexual explanation is incomplete. We have noted Knight (above). Klein (25) and Rosenfeld (26) see choosing a same-sexed object as a defense rather than a fundamental source of pathology; in view of the frequent finding (27) of a dangerous, overpowering mother in effeminate homosexuals, one is not surprised if such men fear female bodies, defensively turn to homosexuality, and call upon their remaining masculinity to mock femininity (28).

In time the view of Schreber's psychosis shifted from father to the mother hidden behind. Fairbairn (29) argues that Schreber has a horror of the primal scene because it provokes rage at mother's infidelity. MacAlpine and Hunter (30) carry the involvement with mother deeper, believing he wished to be a female, because, like his mother, he wanted to procreate. They make the following comments, with which my present ideas agree:

> Schreber's behaviour cannot be understood in phallic and genital terms, nor in terms of libidinal drives directed towards other persons. It is very different from homosexuality in which a man *qua* man desires sexual relations with another of the same sex. Clearly passive homosexual urges, whether conscious or unconscious, should be sharply distinguished from the confusion about their own sex invariably found in

351

schizophrenics. That in the primary fantasy of change of sex or belonging to the opposite sex, homosexuality is likely sooner or later to play a part secondarily, is undisputed. However great the importance ascribed to homosexual libidinal drives in Schreber's illness, fundamentally they remain a secondary issue. Homosexual behaviour, or homosexual wishes, as also anxiety about them, may be entirely due to primary uncertainty and confusion in sex identity and need never appear in the disease picture. One might say that the more overt homosexual behaviour or transvestitism, the less frankly psychotic the patient, a view supported by the course of Schreber's illness.

The primary delusion of a change of sex may appear in patients in various guises, often as the only symptom: complaint of excessive hairiness in women, lack of hairiness in men, symptoms associated with "change of life" in women and even men, following hysterectomy, complaints about voice being too high or too low, the breasts being too small or too flat, differences between the right and left halves of the body, etc. Examples could be multiplied *ad infinitum.* Not uncommonly female patients complain of having a male mind in a female body, and male patients that they have a female mind: and request their body be altered accordingly, by surgery and hormones. When supported by physicians, especially endocrinologists, and surgeons, it accounts for the cases of change of sex reported in the newspapers. These two entirely different types of homosexuality have been consistently confused in psychoanalytic theory, in fact have never been distinguished, because of adherence to the doctrine of libidinal wish-fulfilment as the basis of psychiatric symptom formation. (pp. 404–405)

Searles (31) stressed the threat from Schreber's mother's cannibalistic strivings, deflected onto his brutal father.

White (17) has, I believe, the most correct thesis: "Primitive, destructive-dependent, oral-impulses towards the mother were of crucial importance in the case" of Schreber (p. 57). In line with my desire not to discuss the unconscious destructive impulses in homosexuality, and especially the more violent ones in paranoia, I wish to use White's ideas further only to note his emphasis on Schreber's fight against profound identification with mother:

> Being forced to relinquish the mother—being in a sense deserted and forsaken by her—Schreber defended himself against this loss and the unresolved, infantile, oral tensions within him by an early, primitive identification with the mother which was, in turn, defended against by an all-out identification with father (p. 62). . . . Beneath this compulsive masculine identification Schreber remained secretly an infant who wished to be the sole possessor of the mother—possession made possi-

ble only by magical, primitive identification with her—a symbolic, magical merging with her (p. 63).

Freud, and I think almost everyone else so far, equates the idea of believing oneself a member of the opposite sex with the psychic dangers of losing penis and testes: " . . . the idea of being transformed into a woman (that is, of being emasculated) . . ." (23, p. 18). The word "emasculated," illuminated by data, may help us. The crucial feature is that an emasculated man is not a woman; he is a desperate man.

I would agree that with practically no exception, all the males we shall ever see, in our practices or anywhere else, fear castration. This fear, with its underlying threat to one's identity as a male, creates a lot of what we judge in males to be masculinity, and when severe it contributes to that detour on the road to masculinity we call perversion (32). But how many analysts have seen the exception: a male who has had no observed period of masculinity in his life, from infancy on, who, from the start, never prized maleness or masculinity? Yet that is the history of the true transsexual, not to be confused with the homosexual, transvestite, paranoid psychotic, and others who also request "sex transformation," with all of whom analysts have always been familiar.

One can argue that the transsexual has hidden, valued masculinity; how can that claim ever be fully countered? I can only reply that even if it is true, there still is no other[12] condition in which no overt masculinity has been observed at any time in life, from infancy on.

I have tried to dissect clear the clinical picture of the transsexual from the more complicated states—the normal and the perverse—in which ideas of sex change appear as regressive phenomena (28). If we do not separate out the purer form of femininity seen in the transsexual, we miss comprehending in all males—as Freud did—the full significance of the symbiosis with mother and its tidal pull, not just to regression to "the good breast" but to *being the same as mother*, which would be the destruction of masculinity.

I agree with Fairbairn, MacAlpine, and Hunter, and especially Searles and White, who, in that order, get closer to what I think is the essence of that regression toward merging with a primitive mother. But I would take the process of identifying with her to a still more primitive level. For all these authors, identification with mother was a device invented for defense;[13] I too believe it is that but additionally think the state of oneness with her in everyone, psychotic or not, is even more primitive, that it occurs before there is enough ego structure to go about the sophisticated work we call identification. This state of oneness, I believe, is not produced only out of an infant's memory of intense, oral gratification but also in nonmental primordial processes (instigated by the outside world or by inner, physiological activity) such as imprinting and classical, visceral, and operant conditioning, acting directly on the brain, before there is any mental apparatus, or in later months of infancy, bypassing the nascent ego.

I am struggling here with a speculation, that in regressing toward merging with mother, one moves toward two different forms in which she has primordial representation. The first is a vague memory of a blissful state (summarized incompletely in the expression "the good breast") and becomes part of what we call the mind. The second (for which there is as yet almost no theory or terminology) is whatever form—it is not identification—imprinted or conditioned data take, silent and not of the mind, though influencing it as would, say, adrenal or thyroid activity. The words "incorporation," "introjection," and "identification" connote motivated activity directed toward an object sensed to be not oneself. This means there must be a psyche (mind) advanced enough to comprehend the object (part object) and wish to take it in, with the corollary that the object's representation can be extruded (projection). But our theory must also make room for other, nonmental mechanisms (i.e., not motivated by the individual) by which the outside reality also is emplaced within.

Freud has taught us what we now find clinically, that transsexual fantasies (one of the meanings of what he called homosexuality) are ubiquitous, minimal in normals, more pervasive in the effeminate male or masculine female, marked in those with gender disorders, and most extreme in transsexualism. Whence do they arise? Why are they too dangerous for most people to face, and why, for the transsexual, is there no fear at all of changing sex? Let me review my thesis of the earliest stage in the development of masculinity and femininity, core gender identity: the sense of belonging to the male or the female sex. In taking this detour, we may then see that change of sex is a threat for any male who has achieved masculinity but no threat for the transsexual. (Males are emphasized here because, as noted below, I believe these issues are less disturbing to most females.)

354

Whatever biological attributes the infant brings into the world that can contribute to masculinity and femininity, these do not play the major role in even the earliest stages of gender identity[14] formation; parental effects do. When the influence of parents, mother by far the more important in the first months, encourages in a male behavior the mother considers masculine, then biological attributes will potentiate the effects of rearing. But the mother who will create a feminine boy can do so despite his biologically normal maleness. Given these biological factors, such as the priming of the male's brain with androgens or varying levels of physiological aggressivity, what influences the earliest stage of gender identity development?

The appearance of the infant's genitals at birth starts the process; the assignment to a sex begins the process of creating gender identity. If the infant appears an anatomically normal male, the mother is so informed at the moment of birth, setting off within her and the father a complicated process, idiosyncratic for each parent but carrying common features for that society. That is, the child is named, clothed, held, and dealt with in innumerable exchanges subtle and gross, all of which express, via mother's body impinging upon her infant's perceptions, her attitudes and wishes in regard to *this* male or *this* female. Then the infinite, nonconflictual repetition of the acceptance of that assignment by parents and later by the rest of the world reinforces in the infant-child his growing sense of belonging to that sex. This sense, which is nothing more or less than "I am a male" or "I am a female," is powerfully augmented by the appearance and sensations of the external genitals as the prime insignia of sex assignment. In time, as we know especially from Freud's work on oedipal development, this certainty of belonging to a sex becomes complicated, for the belonging brings privileges and responsibilities, identifications and dangers, defensive mechanisms for protection of the sense of one's sex, and forms of behavior and fantasies demonstrating how complicated and ambiguous this process of developing masculinity and femininity can become. These newer psychic structures and processes overlay the core gender identity and make masculinity and femininity far more complex.

But for all these later developments, that first sense is fixed and unalterable in the first few years of life (22). That it is not due to one's *sex* but rather to one's *appearance*—or, more precisely, to how parents respond to that appearance—as a member of that sex (i.e., the more crucial factor is psychological, not biological), is seen in studies of hermaphrodites (33, 22). In these people, the general rule holds, as the vignettes earlier indicated, that parental attitudes and behavior determine what the child believes.[15]

In brief, core gender identity results in the normal from a combination of hidden (and as yet unmeasured), only modestly effective and easily overturned, biological factors and more powerful, measurable, parental attitudes and influences playing upon the child. While the firmness of one's masculinity or femininity may shift with circumstances, this sense of being a male or being a female, if once established, does not alter throughout life. It withstands the effects later in life of brain damage, psychosis, character disorder, and all other internal and external influences, if firmly established from the start.

Our psychoanalytic theory has not yet taken these findings into account. The study of disorders in the development and maintenance of masculinity and femininity has, I believe, mostly considered the effects of frustration, trauma, conflict, and attempted resolution of conflict in various stages of the oedipal situation. Psychoanalytic practice reveals anxiety as the primary force in creating and modifying normal masculinity and femininity or the perversions; it is not a technique that permits the adult patient to discover much about primary autonomous ego sectors of infancy. The analyst has perforce spent his time more immersed in theory and findings of "instinct vicissitude" than in observing or theorizing on nonconflictual forces in infancy.[16] These forces, which can be observed by watching mother-infant interactions, not by analyzing the transference of adults, are such processes as imprinting; visceral, classical, and operant conditioning; and other forms of behavioral modification.

This review of the development of core gender identity serves what purpose? To establish that the sense of belonging to one's sex is firmly set by powerful, silent,[17] nonconflictual forces at work from birth. These ideas form the basis for a theory of the development of masculinity and femininity in some ways at odds with Freud's. He picks up the story of gender development not at the beginning of life but only after core gender identity is formed and fixed and after the infant's relationship with its mother has markedly advanced over the amorphous, at most part-object, state of the first months. While in time Freud came to credit the pre-oedipal period and the crucial importance of mother in personality development, he never questioned that the male's relationship with his mother was fundamentally heterosexual. Freud therefore makes what I consider two errors. The first was that he assumed as a biological given that maleness was the firmer, more natural state (which as we have noted, present-day research contradicts). The second was that he said the male is off to a healthier start because his relationship with his mother is by definition heterosexual. On the other hand, he said, the little girl bears the double burden of inadequate biology (femaleness) and homosexuality in the mother-infant relationship.

But his argument is awry; one ought not define heterosexuality and homosexuality anatomically but rather according to identity. Anatomy is not really destiny; destiny comes from what people make of anatomy. For the little boy is only anatomically, not psychologically, heterosexual in the first period of his life; that heterosexuality comes only after a massive piece of work, performed with some difficulty and pain. We know of that struggle—separation and individuation—especially from Mahler. In order to advance to *the heterosexual state which then is the origin of the oedipal conflict* the little boy must break from the original, primal symbiosis in which he and his mother are at first merged. He must, as Greenson puts it (34), "disidentify" from his mother. If he and his mother do not set up a reaction in which both willingly (even if at times reluctantly) decide that they will relieve each other's bodies and psyches from the oneness of the womb and the early months of life, then the boy will be enfolded in his mother. This will occur not only in a manner that will cripple the development of the usual ego functions, but also the two will be bound in a linking of gender identity: the boy will feel himself to be a part of his mother's femaleness and femininity.

Fanciful? Here again is where the study of the transsexual becomes a central contribution to understanding fundaments of personality development. In the extreme situation which the transsexual "experiment" establishes, one sees what happens if the loving, maternal preoccupation (35), the symbiosis, is too complete, too gratifying, too lengthy through the hours of the day and night and too extended as the months and then years pass. We know this symbiosis is not the same as that seen in other little boys, and you may be familiar with my conviction that this excessive symbiosis leads to the extreme femininity (36, 28).[18]

The transsexual "experiment" demonstrates that when the mother-infant symbiosis is too gratifying, neither mother nor infant will want to separate from each other—*and the principal effect is extreme femininity in the*

357

little boy. To the extent a mother prolongs this symbiosis, normal enough in the first weeks or months, and to the extent that she must at every moment gratify the infant, to that extent will femininity creep into the core gender identity; at the extreme of such a continuum is transsexualism. But milder degrees of this process are present in almost all mothering, and therein, I believe, is the origin of Schreber's transsexual fantasies, the fears of "homosexuality" so much more marked in men than in women, and the roots even of much of what is called masculinity—preoccupation with being strong, independent, untender, cruel, polygamous, misogynous, perverse. Only if the boy, assisted especially by his mother and perhaps even in the early months to a lesser extent by his father, can comfortably separate himself from his mother's femaleness and femininity, can he then begin to develop that later, non-core gender identity we call masculinity. Only then will he see his mother as a separate and heterosexual object whom he will desire. Only then, on desiring her, can he enter into the oedipal conflict, expose his now developing masculinity to risk, fight for preservation of that masculinity and for the desired heterosexuality, and in time surmount this conflict in the manner so familiar to analysts. While it is true the boy's first love object is heterosexual, he must perform a great deed to make this so: he must first separate his identity from hers. Thus the whole process of becoming masculine is at risk in the little boy from the day of birth on; his still-to-be-created masculinity is endangered by the primary, profound, primeval oneness with mother, a blissful experience that serves, buried but active in the core of one's identity, as a focus which, throughout life, can attract one to regress back to that primitive oneness. That is the threat lying latent in masculinity, and I suggest that the need to fight it off is what energizes some of what we are familiar with when we call a piece of behavior "masculine." So—something I never quite articulated before—in one sense, the process of the development of core gender identity is not the same in males as in females. There is a conflict built into the sense of maleness that females are spared; core gender identity in males is not, as I have mistakenly said (37), quite so immutable. It always carries in it the urge to regress to an original oneness with mother.

Perhaps now we can see better why sex change does not make the transsexual anxious. Rather than some convoluted explanation whose purpose is to preserve theory (e.g., the transsexual eagerly seeks castration in order to avoid castration anxiety), we can say that the transsexual, of the male sex but feminine gender, acts as does everyone else: preservation of one's sense of self, not one's anatomical appearance, determines behavior. The male transsexual does not try to change gender, only sex, so that his body will conform to his psyche.

THE SECOND DISAGREEMENT: THE INFLUENCE OF HOMOSEXUAL IMPULSES ON MEN AS COMPARED TO WOMEN

And females? Not only are they probably the stronger, not to say the primary sex, but their very "homosexuality" may give them an advantage. Once again we recall that the anatomical "homosexuality," looked at from the mother-infant relationship in the first months, need not threaten the girl. Developing indissoluble links with mother's femaleness and femininity in the normal mother-infant symbiosis can only augment a girl's identity. If a mother can lay down *that* foundation in her daughter, then a strength—a permanence, a part of identity—is well situated and can serve the child even in the face of later gender adversities, as in the oedipal situation.

Of course, when mother does in time become a distinct, separate, whole object for the growing girl, the latter has, as Freud said, a homosexual relationship with her primary love object. How this can contribute to pathology later in life if poorly handled by the child's parents has been the subject of many studies and need not be reviewed again here. Certainly, when the early symbiosis is grossly defective (e.g., a frozen mother), a girl is especially vulnerable to searching forever for a good mother in overtly homosexual affairs (38).

That femininity has a more stable base in "primary identification" with mother than does masculinity—penis envy notwithstanding—may be shown in our experience that "homosexual" accusations are less frequent in women than in men, both in the psychotic and nonpsychotic (39–42, and no reports to contest this finding); psychotic women usually suffer heterosexual hallucinated experiences and accusations. In addition, it has been my experience in analyzing women not being seen for primary gender disorders that they were much more casual about trying out a homosexual experience than my male patients and that those heterosexual women who did so expressed little guilt, raised up few defenses subsequently, and found their way toward emotional growth in analysis unimpeded by the homosexual affair.[19] Khan reports similarly (43), suggesting that in his patient the homosexual relationship was a necessary piece of acting out on the way toward maturity.

Conclusions

In summary then, homosexuality—bisexuality—which Freud felt threatened everyone and which he found so fundamental that he had to ascribe its origin to biology, may be seen more precisely as a nonbiological threat to one's sense of core gender identity, of existence, of being. I am suggesting that the sense of maleness and the later development, masculinity, are a bit less firmly established in males than the sense of femaleness and femininity in females. This is so because males have such an intimate relationship at first—when, without much ego structure, they are so permeable—with someone of the opposite sex and so must overcome what actualizes in the transsexual: excess merging with mother. Within even the fortunate little boy's sense of maleness is buried more primitive merging with mother's identity. The same merging in the little girl only strengthens her sense of femaleness. This first bisexuality[20] may make the little boy a bit more vulnerable from the start, leaves him with less fixed and dependable identity, puts him in greater jeopardy in oedipal development, and as a result makes him more prone to the development of perversion.[21]

I think we know now better why "homosexuality" is such a threat to males. Deep within, unless well protected by good parental care, the pull toward merging again into mother's femaleness terrifies and enthralls men; it is the Siren's Song. We read Schreber to see that, and we recall Freud's insistence on the fundamental power of "bisexuality" in order to confirm this modification of his theories of sexuality.

That is why I agree with Freud about the importance of bisexuality. That is why I study transsexualism: rather than being taken only as a bizarre oddity, it is the key test, in fact, the paradigm for Freud's theories of sexual development in both males and females.

N O T E S

1 "Since I have become acquainted with the notion of bisexuality I have regarded it as the decisive factor, and without taking bisexuality into account I think it would scarcely be possible to arrive at an understanding of the sexual manifestations that are actually to be observed in men and women" (1, p. 220). (Numbers in parenthesis refer to bibliography, pp. 362–364)

2 This was done elsewhere (2).

3 This is not yet demonstrable in the chromosomes (XX in females and XY in males), but when the myriad of genes making up the chromosomes are available to study in the near future, bisexual propensities will probably be demonstrated. At present, there is an interesting theory that the Y—male—chromosome is the product of an ancestral X chromosome damaged eons ago, with the happy result (evolutionarily speaking) that sexual relations—the mixing of chromosomes—was invented (4).

4 The difference between male and female hormones can be very small biochemically; for instance, one step in the normal metabolism of testosterone in the male is progestin, a female hormone (6).

5 This description is incomplete, necessarily leaving out qualifying details.

6 In scientific circles these days, it is out of style to talk of bisexuality; other words replace it, such as sexual biopotentiality, sexual neutrality, sexual dimorphism (9–11). While each connotes a wrinkle of disagreement based on laboratory findings, they do not end the usefulness of "bisexuality." None of these modern terms denies that aspects of both sexes are present in all animals, including man.

7 The very rare possible exceptions to this rule are reviewed in (2, 5).

8 He spoke of "bisexual disposition," "bisexual constitution," "bisexual organization," "cross inheritance," or "the organic factor in homosexuality."

9 Female transsexualism is quite different from male in its origins; I believe it is a form of homosexuality and the product of a forever unresolved, unconscious chronic trauma (18).

10 Those born without a penis or who lose it traumatically may suffer anguish but not such catastrophes as, for instance, loss of ego boundaries, i.e. loss of sense of self as in confusional states and psychosis, if the underlying identity is already stable (22).

11 This discussion of Schreber does not imply belief that dread of homosexuality is the *cause* of Schreber's schizophrenia (called "paranoia" by Freud). I think, rather, the dread is only a *manifestation* in the psychosis.

12 See note 7.

13 White, for instance, says (17, p. 65): "One of the most important delusional results of the influx of female nerves into Schreber's body was that he developed womanly breasts. He thus became the sole possessor of that which he had so reluctantly renounced so many years earlier. This feminization could also be considered as a re-emergence of the very early identification with the mother which occurred when she forsook little Daniel and withdrew from him as she taught him the 'art of renouncing.' "

14 Gender identity: the mix of one's masculinity and femininity, the first stage of which is core gender identity.

15 See note 7.

16 Hartmann, in constructing theory and, more richly, Winnicott, with theory and observations, have pointed the way to our understanding non-conflictual development in the infant; no one like Winnicott, for instance, has turned us, by his studies of mother-infant dynamics, toward the study of the infant's capacity to love. Such work has not, however, focused on masculinity and femininity.

17 That is, there may be no visible response to them in the infant and they are silent in the adult's psychoanalysis.

18 One can argue all day from theory that the infant must have severe conflict in this relationship and that he must suffer from such experiences as are provoked by his good breast–bad breast fantasies. But this cannot be demonstrated to be present or to be effecting anxiety. However one wishes to conceptualize what goes on inside the infant,

the fact is that this is an infant whose mother spends all her moments protecting from the ordinary frustrations and traumas of infancy so necessary for normal development. There is no other condition—normal or abnormal—in which such a symbiosis has been reported. To discard it as a part of the explanation for the production of transsexualism is unwarranted in the absence of adequate data.

19 Those women who were fearful or guilt-laden about homosexuality were either overt homosexuals or women living a primarily heterosexual life but with a sharp homosexual edge to them (which guilt restricted to a rare homosexual impulse, glance, or caress, with the other side of the coin being generalized dislike, distrust, and envy of men).

20 If I stooped to neologizing, I would reserve "bisexuality" for the biological state of having aspects of both maleness and femaleness present (e.g., genital hermaphroditism) and talk of the psychological quality of having aspects of both masculinity and femininity as "bigenderality."

21 We do know that the perversions are much more common in males than in females.

BIBLIOGRAPHY

1 Freud, S. (1920). "The Psychogenesis of a Case of Homosexuality in a Woman." *Standard Edition* 18. London: Hogarth Press, 1955.

2 Stoller, R. J. "The 'Bedrock' of Masculinity and Femininity: Bisexuality." *Archives of General Psychiatry* 26:207–212, 1972.

3 Freud, S. (1937). "Analysis Terminable and Interminable." *Standard Edition* 23, p. 252. London: Hogarth Press, 1964.

4 Ohno, S. "Evolution of Sex Chromosomes in Mammals." *Ann. Rev. Genet.* 3:495–524, 1969.

5 Gadpaille, W. J. "Research into the Physiology of Maleness and Femaleness." *Archives of General Psychiatry* 26:193–206, 1972.

6 Whalen, R. E. Personal communication.

7 Overzier, C. *Intersexuality.* London and New York: Academic Press, 1963, p. 349.

8 Freud, S. (1932). "Femininity." *Standard Edition* 22. London: Hogarth Press, 1964.

9 Rado, S. "A Critical Examination of the Concept of Bisexuality." *Psychosomatic Medicine* 2:459–467, 1940.

10 Marmor, J. Introduction, in *Sexual Inversion.* New York: Basic Books, 1965.

11 Money, J. "Sexual Dimorphism and Dissociation in the Psychology of Male Transsexuals," in *Transsexualism and Sex Reassignment,* eds. R. Green and J. Money. Baltimore: The Johns Hopkins Press, 1969.

12 Newman, L. E., and Stoller, R. J. "Spider Symbolism and Bisexuality." *Journal of the American Psychoanalytic Association* 17:862–872, 1969.

13 Green, R., and Stoller, R. J. "Two Monozygotic (Identical) Twin Pairs Discordant for Gender Identity." *Archives of Sexual Behavior* 1:321–327, 1971.

14 Knight, R. P. "The Relationship of Latent Homosexuality to the Mechanism of Paranoid Delusions." *Bulletin Menninger Clinic* 4:149–159, 1940.

15 Socarides, C. W. *The Overt Homosexual.* New York: Grune and Stratton, 1968.

16   Khan, M. M. R. "Foreskin Fetishism and its Relation to Ego Pathology in a Male Homosexual." *International Journal of Psycho-Analysis* 46:64–80, 1965.

17   White, R. B. "The Mother-Conflict in Schreber's Psychosis." *International Journal of Psycho-Analysis* 42:55–73, 1961.

18   Stoller, R. J. "Etiological Factors in Female Transsexualism: A First Approximation." *Archives of General Psychiatry*. 2:47–64, 1972.

19   Freud, S. (1905). *Three Essays on the Theory of Sexuality. Standard Edition* 7. London: Hogarth Press, 1953.

20   —— (1907). "Analysis of a Phobia in a Five-Year-Old Boy." *Standard Edition* 10. London: Hogarth Press, 1955.

21   —— (1925). "Some Psychical Consequences of the Anatomical Distinction Between the Sexes." *Standard Edition* 19. London: Hogarth Press, 1961.

22   Stoller, R. J. *Sex and Gender*. New York: Science House, 1968.

23   Freud, S. (1925). "Inhibitions, Symptoms and Anxiety." *Standard Edition* 20. London: Hogarth Press, 1959.

24   —— (1911). "Psycho-analytic Notes on an Autobiographical Account of a Case of Paranoia (Dementia Paranoides)." *Standard Edition* 12. London: Hogarth Press, 1958.

25   Klein, M. *The Psychoanalysis of Children*. London: Hogarth Press, 1932.

26   Rosenfeld, H. "Remarks on the Relation of Male Homosexuality to Paranoia, Paranoid Anxiety and Narcissism." *International Journal of Psycho-Analysis* 30:36–47, 1949.

27   Bieber, I., et al. *Homosexuality*. New York: Basic Books, 1962.

28   Stoller, R. J. "The Male Transsexual as 'Experiment.' " *International Journal of Psycho-Analysis*. To be published.

29   Fairbairn, W. R. D. "The Schreber Case." *British Journal of Medical Psychology* 29:113–127, 1956.

30   MacAlpine, I., and Hunter, R. A.: *Daniel Paul Schreber. Memoirs of My Nervous Illness*. London: Dawson, 1955.

31   Searles, H. F. "Sexual Processes in Schizophrenia." *Psychiatry* 24:87–95, 1961.

32   Stoller, R. J. "The Term 'Perversion.' " Read at the 28th Psycho-analytical Congress. Paris, July 1973.

33   Money, J.; Hampson, J. G.; and Hampson, J. L. "Imprinting and the Establishment of Gender Role." *Archives of Neurology and Psychiatry* 77:333–336, 1957.

34   Greenson, R. R. "Disidentifying from Mother." *International Journal of Psycho-Analysis* 49: 370–374, 1968.

35   Winnicott, D. W. "Primary Maternal Preoccupation," in *Collected Papers*. London: Tavistock, 1958.

36   Stoller, R. J. "Création d'une Illusion: L'extreme Femininité chez les Garçons." *Nouvelle Revue de Psychanalyse* 4:54–72, 1971.

37   ——. "The Sense of Maleness." *Psychoanalytic Quarterly* 34:207–218, 1965.

38   ——. *Splitting*. New York: Quadrangle, 1973.

39   Klein, H. R., and Horwitz, W. A. "Psychosexual Factors in the Paranoid Phenomena." *American Journal of Psychiatry* 105:697–701, 1949.

40   Greenspan, J., and Myers, J. M., Jr. "A Review of the Theoretical Concepts of Paranoid Delusions with Special Reference to Women." *Pennsylvania Psychiatric Quarterly* 1:11–28, 1961.

363

41   Klaf, F. S. "Female Homosexuality and Paranoid Schizophrenia." *Archives of General Psychiatry* 1:84–86, 1961.

42   Modlin, H. C. "Psychodynamics and Management of Paranoid States in Women." *Archives of General Psychiatry* 8:263–268, 1963.

43   Khan, M. M. R. "The Role of Infantile Sexuality and Early Object Relations in Female Homosexuality," in *The Pathology and Treatment of Sexual Deviation,* ed. I. Rosen. London: Oxford Univ. Press, 1964.

Notes on Contributors

Karl Abraham (1877–1925), born in Bremen, Germany, was called the first German psychoanalyst. He met Sigmund Freud for the first time in 1907, after Abraham had completed his medical studies and several years of intensive psychiatric training in mental hospitals: he held a psychiatric appointment at Bleuler's clinic in Zurich and worked for three years with C. G. Jung. Abraham and Freud became friends almost immediately upon their meeting, and Abraham was to become a member of the trusted inner circle, "the Committee of the Seven Rings" which consisted of Freud, Abraham, Sándor Ferenczi, Ernest Jones, Hanns Sachs, Otto Rank, and Max Eitingon. In December, 1907, Abraham moved to Berlin, where he became the first German physician with a private psychoanalytic practice. He founded the Berlin Psychoanalytic Society and Institute early in 1910.

Although Abraham wrote relatively little in comparison with some of his colleagues, many of his clinical studies have become classics and are studied in psychoanalytic institutes and teaching programs. His most important contributions were in the study of orality, character development, and the psychodynamics of psychosis.

Princess Marie Bonaparte (1882–1962) was born near Paris, daughter of a Monte Carlo Casino heiress named Françoise Blane and Prince Roland Bonaparte, grandson of Lucien Bonaparte, brother to Napoleon. Her mother died a month after Marie was born. When her father died, in 1924, Marie found among his papers five little black notebooks she had written between the ages of seven and ten. She had no memory of the books or their content, even when she studied them closely at the age of forty-two. Having read Freud's *Introduction to Psychoanalysis* at her father's deathbed, she determined to learn more about the copy books and her childhood through psychoanalysis, and to find a new "father" as well. "All my life," she wrote, "I was to care about the opinions, approval and love of only a few 'fathers,' selected ever higher and of whom the last was to be my grand master Freud."

After her analysis with Freud, she trained to become a lay analyst and eventually, under Freud's guidance as a friend and teacher, turned her attention to the study of female sexuality.

Marie Bonaparte founded the Paris Psychoanalytic Society in 1926 and was extremely influential in the psychoanalytic movement in Europe. She saved Verlag, the publishing house of Freud, from bankruptcy in 1929, and personally saved Freud's letters to Fliess from destruction. She helped hundreds of Jews escape Nazi persecution, and served as a European way station for refugee analysts en route to the United States. During the war she moved from France to Greece to the Cape. On returning to France in 1945 she again began work as a teacher, writer, and psychoanalyst at the new Institute in the rue Saint-Jacques.

Marcia Cavell teaches philosophy at the State University of New York at Purchase and is a Special Candidate at the Columbia Psychoanalytic Institute for Training and Research. She is the author of numerous articles in philosophy and psychoanalysis.

Robert Coles, M.D., is a child psychiatrist on the staff of the Harvard University Health Services. He is currently living in Albuquerque, New Mexico, where he works with Indian and Chicano families. Dr. Coles is the author of several books, including *Children of Crisis* (in three volumes: he won the Pulitzer Prize in 1973 for volumes two and three), a study of Erik Erikson's work, and most recently, *Farewell to the South*. Dr. Coles is a regular contributor to several periodicals, including *The New Yorker* and *The New York Review of Books*.

Helene Deutsch, M.D., was born in Przemysl, Poland, in 1884. She graduated from the University of Vienna Medical School in 1912 and was analyzed for a year by Freud in Vienna in 1918. During that year she became the second woman admitted as a full member of the Vienna Psychoanalytic Society. She was supervised by Freud and continued to work closely with him for almost twenty years. In 1925 she helped found the Vienna Psychoanalytic Training Institute and was its first director. Franz Alexander invited her to the United States in 1934, and in 1935 she emigrated with her husband, Dr. Felix Deutsch, and their son to Boston. There she lectured at the Boston Psychoanalytic Institute, taught psychiatry at Boston University, and was an associate psychiatrist at Massachusetts General Hospital. She is now retired and lives in Cambridge, Massachusetts.

Helene Deutsch has written a great deal about women. Her two-volume *Psychology of Women*, published in 1944 and 1945, was the culmination of a number of papers and articles written over a period of twenty years. The first of these papers, "The Psychology of Woman in Relation to the Functions of Reproduction," is reprinted here. Other books by Dr. Deutsch are: *Neuroses and Character Types* (1965), *Selected Problems of Adolescence* (1967), and, most recently, *Confrontations with Myself* (1973).

Erik Homburger Erikson was born to Danish parents in Frankfurt, Germany, in 1902. He was a selectively interested student with artistic talent in a "humanistic" high school and skipped college to wander about Europe working, drawing, and reading. In 1927, at the invitation of his friend, Peter Blos, he moved to Vienna to join him in a small experimental school set up for children, some themselves undergoing treatment, of parents interested in psychoanalysis. The Freudian circle found Erikson sympathetic to their ideas and ways of thinking and admitted him to training at the Vienna Psychoanalytic Institute, where he specialized in child analysis. His training analysis was conducted by Anna Freud, and he became a full member of the Vienna Institute and of the International Psychoanalytic Association upon graduation in 1933.

Soon, with Hitler rising to power in Germany, Erikson emigrated to the United States, settling in Boston to become that city's first child analyst. With an appointment at the Harvard Medical School, he worked for a time at Massachusetts General Hospital and Harvard's Psychological Clinic. In 1936 he accepted a full-time research position at Yale's Institute of Human Relations. In 1939 he moved to Berkeley, where he participated in a long-term study of normal child development. He resumed his private practice in San Francisco and conducted training analyses for the San Francisco Psychoanalytic Institute. In a variety of studies, Erikson was relating Freud's stages of psychosexual development to the child's social capacities and needs in specific cultural milieus, to make what he called "a restatement of the theory of infantile sexuality." His first book, *Childhood and Society* (1950), asserts his view of the developing ego in the psychosocial stages of the human life cycle.

In 1950 Erikson left his first professorship in the University of California rather than sign a special loyalty oath which was later declared unconstitutional. He served as a senior staff member at the Austen Riggs Center in Stockbridge, Massachusetts, from 1950 to 1960, wrote a great deal during this period on the subject of youth and identity, and turned to the psychoanalytic study of history. In 1960 he returned to Harvard as a professor of human development and a lecturer in psychiatry. He is now officially retired and living in California, but he continues to write and to teach in the San Francisco area.

In addition to *Childhood and Society*, Erikson has published numerous books and articles, including *Young Man Luther* (1958), *Insight and Responsibility* (1964), *Identity: Youth and Crisis* (1968), *Gandhi's Truth* (1969), and *In Search of Common Ground: Conversations with Erik H. Erikson and Huey P. Newton* (1973).

Sigmund Freud was born in 1856 in Freiberg, a small Moravian town which was then in the Austro-Hungarian Empire, although it is now part of Czechoslovakia. In 1860 his family moved to Vienna, where Freud was to live for more than seventy years. He entered the University in 1873 and eventually decided to become a doctor—not out of a special love for science but from a curiosity about human relations and nature: he made the decision to enter medical school upon reading Goethe's *Du Natur.*

After graduation from medical school Freud worked at Vienna's general hospital in psychiatry and was especially interested in the anatomy of the brain. In 1885 he went to Paris to study with the famous neurologist, Jean-Martin Charcot, who was using hypnotism in the treatment and study of hysteria and other nervous diseases. In 1886 Freud returned to Vienna to set up a medical practice specializing in the nervous diseases, while continuing as an instructor at the university.

Over the next several years he worked with a number of hysterical patients, using what he had learned from Charcot and relying for the most part on hypnotism. He found, however, that not every patient could be hypnotized, and that of those who could be, not all were permanently cured. Gradually he began to abandon the directive techniques of hypnosis and to employ a new method later to be called "free association." In 1895 he published with Josef Breuer their *Studies on Hysteria,* and in 1896 first used the term "psychoanalysis."

He began to analyze himself in 1897, and wrote *The Interpretation of Dreams*, based on what he learned in self-analysis, in 1898 and 1899. The book was published in 1900. *Three Essay on the Theory of Sexuality,* published in 1905, traced the development of the sexual instinct from its origins in infancy and childhood; it was one of the most important and shocking books Freud wrote, and he continued to amend and expand it during the next twenty years. The first International Psychoanalytic Congress was

370

held at Salzburg in 1908, and in 1909 Freud visited Clark University in Worcester, Mass., where he delivered his *Five Lectures on Psycho-Analysis.* The *Introductory Lectures on Psycho-Analysis* were delivered at the University of Vienna between 1915 and 1917. In 1919 and 1920 Freud was formulating his ideas about the death instinct in *Beyond the Pleasure Principle.*

The Ego and the Id was published in 1923, and in 1925 Freud wrote his first paper specifically about female sexuality, "Some Psychical Consequences of the Anatomical Distinction Between the Sexes." This paper, read on Freud's behalf by Anna Freud at the Hamburg International Psycho-Analytical Congress (September 3, 1925), is a complete reassessment of Freud's earlier views on the psychological development of women. The new ideas formulated in the 1925 paper (reprinted here on p. 17) are further developed in two later papers: "Female Sexuality" (1931) (p. 39), and Lecture XXXIII of the *New Introductory Lectures,* "Femininity" (1933) (p. 73).

Freud was forced to leave Vienna to escape the Nazis in 1938, and moved to London, where he died in 1939.

(I cannot in this brief space begin to suggest the development of Freud's ideas or their significance, and so have simply outlined the major biographical details of his life. For further information about Freud's life, thought, and work, see: *The Life and Work of Sigmund Freud,* by Ernest Jones [New York: Basic Books, 1961], *Sigmund Freud,* by Richard Wollheim [New York: The Viking Press, 1971], and A. A. Brill's Introduction to *The Basic Writings of Sigmund Freud* [New York: Random House, 1938].)

Barbara Charlesworth Gelpi, born in 1933, received an A.B. and an A.M. degree in English literature at the University of Miami in Coral Gables, Florida. In 1962 she was granted a Ph.D. from Radcliffe College. She has since taught English at the University of California at Santa Barbara, at Brandeis, and at Stanford. In 1965 she published *Dark Passages: The Decadent Consciousness in Victorian Literature.* She is now teaching in the English Department at California State University, San Jose.

Karen Horney (1885–1952) was born in Hamburg, Germany, and received her M.D. from the University of Berlin in 1913. She was trained in psychiatry at Berlin-Lankwitz, Germany, from 1914 to 1918, and was analyzed during World War I by Karl Abraham and Hanns Sachs. In 1919 she entered private practice as a psychoanalyst and became a member of the faculty at the Berlin Psychoanalytic Institute, where she continued to teach until 1932. There were essentially three phases to her career as a psychoanalyst: the Berlin years, from 1919 to 1932; a second phase beginning with her emigration to America in 1932 to be Associate Director of the Psychoanalytic Institute in Chicago, and ending with her resignation from the New York Psychoanalytic Institute in 1941; and a final phase extending from 1941, and including her work as a dissident, to her death in 1952.

Horney's earliest papers suggest her disagreements with orthodox psychoanalytic theory and indicate her intense concern with the social and cultural determinants of human behavior. Many of her papers discuss problems of feminine psychology and challenge widely held psychoanalytic views of femininity. Feminine masochism, she wrote, is not an inevitable consequence of female anatomy, but "must be considered as importantly conditioned by the culture-complex or social organization in which the particular masochistic woman has developed" ("The Problem of Feminine Masochism," *Psychoanalytic Review*, 1935, 22, 241–257). Her ideas came increasingly into conflict with the established analytic community in America, and that conflict led to her departure from the American Psychoanalytic Association in 1941. After the split, Karen Horney helped found a new institute (the American Institute for Psychoanalysis) and the Association for the Advancement of Psychoanalysis.

Her books include *Feminine Psychology, The Neurotic Personality of Our Time, New Ways in Psychoanalysis,* and *Self-Analysis, Neurosis and Human Growth.*

Elizabeth Janeway is the author of several novels and a major work of nonfiction, *Man's World, Woman's Place.* Mrs. Janeway is past president of the Author's Guild, a member of the Board of Trustees of Barnard College, a Berkeley Fellow at Yale, a director of the MacDowell Colony, and a member of the executive board of P.E.N. She is currently working on a sequel to her study of social mythology, and on a new novel.

Emma Rauschenbach Jung, was born in 1882. Her family came from the town of Schaffhausen in Switzerland. In 1903 she married Carl Gustav Jung; she had four daughters and a son (and, eventually, nineteen grandchildren). Her chief scholarly interest was the Grail legend, and she worked for many years on it, adding Provençal to her knowledge of Latin and Greek in order to study the legend. When she died in 1955 her work on the significance of the Grail was still unfinished. It was finally published in 1960, having been edited and completed by Marie-Louise von Franz. She lectured at the C. G. Jung Institute, was a member of its Curatorium, and was president of the Analytical Psychology Club in Zurich. Two of her lectures have been published together under the title *Animus and Anima.*

Joel Kovel, M.D., was born in 1936 and educated at Yale College and Columbia Medical School. He is currently with the Albert Einstein Medical School and the Psychoanalytic Institute of the Downstate Medical Center, both in New York City. His writings, which include *White Racism: A Psychohistory* (New York: Pantheon, 1970), are mainly concerned with the cultural applications of psychoanalysis.

Margaret Mead is currently Curator Emeritus of Ethnology at The American Museum of Natural History in New York, and Visiting Professor of Anthropology for the Department of Psychiatry at the University of Cincinnati's College of Medicine. She was born in Philadelphia in 1901, received her undergraduate degree from Barnard in 1923 and her Ph.D. in anthropology from Columbia in 1929. Dr. Mead holds numerous awards and honorary degrees and has taught and lectured in many parts of the world in anthropology, education, psychology, contemporary culture, and related fields. She is past president of the American Anthropological Association. In the course of her work in the South Seas, she had to learn to use seven primitive languages. She is the author of many books and articles, including *Coming of Age in Samoa* (New York: Morrow, 1928), *Male and Female* (New York: Morrow, 1949), *New Lives for Old* (New York: Morrow, 1956), *Culture and Commitment* (Garden City, N.Y.: Doubleday, 1970), and most recently *Blackberry Winter: My Earlier Years* (New York: Morrow, 1972).

Juliet Mitchell was born in New Zealand in 1940. In 1944 she moved to England and was educated at King Alfred School, London. She read English at St. Anne's College, Oxford, and from 1962 until 1970 lectured in English literature at Leeds University and then at Reading University. She is one of the editors of the *New Left Review* and has written and lectured throughout England, Europe, and the United States on women and women's liberation. She is the author of *Woman's Estate* (New York: Pantheon, 1972) and of a new book, *Psychoanalysis and Feminism*, to be published by Pantheon in 1974.

Ruth Moulton, M.D., is a psychoanalyst who lives and practices in New York City. She is a graduate of the University of Chicago and received her M.D. from that institution in 1939. During her psychiatric residency at New York State Psychiatric Institute she entered analytic training, working with Dr. Clara Thompson, Harry Stack Sullivan, Erich Fromm, and Frieda Fromm-Reichmann. She was graduated in 1946 from the New York Branch of the Washington School of Psychiatry which later was incorporated as the William Alanson White Institute of Psychiatry, Psychoanalysis and Psychology. She has been on the faculty there ever since, as a training and supervising analyst. She was Director of Training from 1960 to 1970 and is currently Chairman of the Council of Fellows. She is Assistant Clinical Professor of Psychiatry at Columbia University. She has been a member of the American Psychoanalytic Association since 1947, and is a charter member of the American Academy of Psychoanalysis. She has published several articles on the psychology of women and is now working on a book on changing concepts of femininity.

Ethel Spector Person, M.D., is a psychoanalyst who lives and practices in New York. Born in 1934, she graduated from the University of Chicago in 1956 and from New York University's College of Medicine in 1960. Dr. Person is an Associate in Psychiatry at Columbia University's Department of Psychiatry, and a Lecturer in Human Development at Columbia College. She is also on the faculty of Columbia University's Psychoanalytic Clinic for Training and Research. For the past three years she has been conducting research in the area of cross-dressing and gender identity.

Robert J. Stoller, M.D., is a psychoanalyst and Professor of Psychiatry at the University of California at Los Angeles School of Medicine, where he teaches medical students and psychiatric residents. He is a member of the American Psychoanalytic Association, and received his psychoanalytic training at the Los Angeles Psychoanalytic Institute. Dr. Stoller is the author of numerous papers on the development of gender identity. He has also published two books on the subject, *Sex and Gender: On the Development of Masculinity and Femininity* (New York: Science House, 1968) and

374

Splitting (New York: Quadrangle, 1973). A third volume in that study, *The Choice of Sex*, is soon to be published in England by the Hogarth Press. In addition to his research in gender identity, Dr. Stoller has a continuing interest and involvement in research in medical education.

Clara Thompson, M.D. (1893–1958) was born and raised in Providence, Rhode Island. In 1912 she began premedical studies at the Women's College of Brown University in Providence, and she entered Johns Hopkins medical school in 1916. During a summer of work at St. Elizabeth's Hospital in Washington, D.C., she met William Alanson White, then superintendent of the hospital. She became friends with Harry Stack Sullivan, one of the major influences of her career, during her psychiatric residency at Johns Hopkins. After her residency Thompson began private practice in Baltimore, and spent the summers of 1928 and 1929, and then two years beginning in 1931, studying in Budapest with Sándor Ferenczi. In 1930 she was elected the first president of the Washington-Baltimore Psychoanalytic Society.

On her return from Budapest, Thompson moved to New York and became involved with the group of dissidents at the New York Psychoanalytic Institute led by Karen Horney. When Horney was forced to resign from the Institute in 1941, Thompson and three other faculty members resigned with her in protest. In 1943 a group of analysts including Thompson, Sullivan, Erich Fromm, and Frieda Fromm-Reichmann set up a New York branch of the William Alanson White Foundation's Washington School of Psychiatry. The curriculum, as in Washington, attempted to integrate psychoanalysis with anthropology, political science, and social psychology; and Clara Thompson was named executive director.

Thompson remained with the William Alanson White Institute in New York and continued to lecture, write, teach, and conduct a private practice until her death in 1958. Her books include *Interpersonal Psychoanalysis: The Selected Papers of Clara M. Thompson* (New York: Basic Books, 1964), *Psychoanalysis: Evolution and Development*, A Review of Theory and Therapy (with the collaboration of Patrick Mullahy), (New York: Hermitage House, Inc., 1950), and a paperback edition of her papers about women, *On Women*, edited by Maurice Green (New York: Mentor, 1971).

This book was composed in Baskerville on ComCom's computer driven composition device, at Haddon Craftsmen in Allentown, Pa.
It has been printed on Sebago Antique paper supplied by Lindenmeyr Paper Corp., New York.
The printing and binding has been done by Haddon Craftsmen, Scranton, Pa.
Designed by Jacqueline Schuman.